DOWN

DOWN WEAVERS LANE

Also by Anna Jacobs

SALEM STREET

HIGH STREET

RIDGE HILL

HALLAM SQUARE

SPINNERS LAKE

JESSIE

OUR LIZZIE

LIKE NO OTHER

LANCASHIRE LASS

OUR POLLY

LANCASHIRE LEGACY

DOWN WEAVERS LANE

Anna Jacobs

Hodder & Stoughton

Copyright © 2002 by Anna Jacobs

First published in Great Britain in 2002
by Hodder & Stoughton
A division of Hodder Headline

The right of Anna Jacobs to be identified as the Author
of the Work has been asserted by her in accordance with the
Copyright, Designs and Patents Act 1988.

2 4 6 8 10 9 7 5 3 1

A CIP catalogue record for this book
is available from the British Library.

ISBN 0 340 75058 8

Typeset in Bembo by Hewer Text Ltd, Edinburgh
Printed and bound in Great Britain by
Mackays of Chatham plc, Chatham, Kent

Hodder & Stoughton
A division of Hodder Headline
338 Euston Road
London NW1 3BH

To Teena Raffa Mulligan,
another of my lovely writer friends

Part One

Chapter One

Emmy Carter sat on the low wall near the corner of their alley, alone as usual but enjoying the mild sunshine and hugging her knees as she watched the bustle of the busy Manchester street. Her contentment turned to anxiety as she saw her mother come out of their house and say a loving goodbye to George Duckworth, heedless of who was watching them kissing. Why could she not be more careful with her men-friends in public? Even in Little Ireland, where only poor people lived, none of the respectable women would speak to 'that Carter woman' or let their children play with her daughter.

Scowling now, Emmy drummed the heels of her broken-down shoes against the wall and shoved back the hair that was hanging in a matted tangle over her shoulders. It wouldn't last with this man, any more than it had lasted with the others. Her mother never seemed to pick men who would be faithful or even treat her kindly, and when they went off with other women – as they invariably did – Madge would weep and wail for days, before searching desperately for another protector.

George Duckworth might be good-looking in a beefy sort of way, though he had a bit of a belly on him, but Emmy never felt comfortable with him. Something about the way he looked at her made her shiver and want to cross her arms protectively in front of her chest. She was glad she had not yet grown a

3

woman's body and wished she need never do so if it made men look at her like they did her mother.

She sighed. Why was her mother so besotted with George? Certainly, since he'd been coming to visit, they'd eaten far better than usual because he was generous enough with his money, but Emmy would much rather have gone hungry. She was used to that. It didn't frighten her. George did.

He strode off down the street, arms swinging, shapeless felt hat pulled down over his forehead, and Madge twirled round a couple of times as she did when happy about something, then sauntered back into their house with a dreamy smile on her face. Sticking her tongue out at the boy across the road Emmy followed her mother inside, listening to the footsteps echoing up the three flights of rickety stairs above her and trying not to make any noise herself as she followed. It was a game she played with herself sometimes, turning into a shadow. It was useful when she was out after dark.

'There you are! Guess what? We're moving.' Madge danced her daughter round the room. 'Moving, moving, moving – away from this hovel! What do you think of that, eh?'

Emmy pulled away. 'But you said we'd be staying here. And these are the best rooms we've ever had.' The attic was large, with room for Madge to sleep in one corner behind a ragged curtain. There was even a tiny room on the other side with a proper door to it. This was the first time Emmy had ever had somewhere of her own to sleep, and even if it was under the slope of the roof and you could only stand up in the middle of it, she loved having somewhere to take refuge when men came to visit her mother. In their last lodgings she'd had to go and sit outside on the stairs whenever her mother had a visitor and it had been cold in winter as well as uncomfortable, with men going up and down the stairs at all hours.

Madge made a scornful noise in her throat. 'Well, they're not the best rooms *I've* ever had. I was born to a decent family with a whole house of our own, a big one. And when I was with your father we lived in style, with four bedrooms and a maid to do the rough work. Why, Emerick would have given me anything I

4

wanted – *anything at all!* – and after he died I was so upset they feared for my life and . . .'

Even though she'd heard this story so many times she could have recited it by heart, Emmy didn't interrupt but lost herself in her own thoughts and let her mother run on. What did it matter if they'd once lived well? *She* couldn't remember it. *If* it was true! All she could remember was going to bed hungry many a time, and wearing old clothes that had holes in until a kind neighbour mended them and taught her to sew when she was five. Which had annoyed her mother so much she had provided Emmy with better clothes from then on. Well, most of the time, anyway.

Madge's voice droned on and on, talking about George now. Emmy knew that if she said anything disapproving about him her mother would grow angry and lose that happy expression – and it would not change a thing. When her mother decided on something she never listened to anyone else, let alone considered what might go wrong. No, she just rushed in and did whatever took her fancy. At thirteen going on fourteen, Emmy knew she had far more common sense. She often thought her mother was like a butterfly, fluttering around aimlessly most of the time and never settling for long anywhere.

Until George appeared in their lives it had been a while since the last regular protector and Emmy had hoped there wouldn't be another, that her mother would stay in this job which involved singing as well as serving booze. Madge might even – it was the girl's dearest wish – stop having visitors at night. Emmy hated the men coming to their room, absolutely hated it, especially now they had started looking at her as well.

What a stupid thing to wish for! Even if they didn't need the money, her mother didn't consider life complete without a man and kept fooling herself that one of them would marry her so that she'd be *safe*. Her mother used that word with such longing it sometimes brought tears into Emmy's eyes. As far as the girl could see there was no safety anywhere in the world and it was a stupid thing to hope for.

The ladies at the Mission said this world was a vale of tears and only a preparation for the next life. Emmy had met the ladies three moves ago. They ran a Bible School every Sunday for poor

5

children and she still went there sometimes, even though it was a long walk from here. The ladies gave you bread and cheese if you listened to their stories and learned to sing their hymns. Some of the tunes were nice, but the words were long and Emmy often had no idea what she was singing about. But it was always warm in the Mission and they told you stories from the Bible as well as singing hymns.

They'd even started teaching Emmy to read and she could now spell out the simpler words and write her name quite clearly. Her mother had laughed at that and for a while it had amused her to practise reading with her daughter, something Madge was really good at. They would spell out words together on a cracked slate she'd brought home one day. Then she'd grown tired of that game, in spite of Emmy's pleas for more lessons, and the slate had vanished one night in a sudden move.

'Where are we going to live this time, then?' Emmy asked when at last her mother stopped speaking and sat staring into space.

'Northby, where I grew up. But we won't be going there for a week or two yet.'

'But you always say you'll never go back. And we won't know anyone in Northby. You said your mother and father were dead.'

'Well, I've changed my mind about going back, haven't I? And we'll know George. He has an alehouse there and it must bring in good money, for he's never short of a shilling or two. So we'll be *safer* there.'

'Are you going to work for him?'

'Maybe.' Madge sighed and added, 'You do what you have to in this world, my girl, or else you starve – as you should understand by now.' She looked at Emmy and added thought-fully, 'We'll have to see if we can get a regular job for you as well. George said he'd help me find one. You're more than old enough, for all you're so short and skinny. I was a woman grown at your age, though I've always wished I were taller.' She frowned as she studied Emmy. 'You're getting far too pretty for your own good, or you would be if you'd do something with all that hair. We'll wash it before I go to work and comb out those tangles. But I'm not having you messing around with men, so we'll keep your skirts short and your tops loose then you'll still look like a child. It'll be safer.'

As if Emmy would mess around with men. She hated them! And if they went to Northby they'd be in George Duckworth's power, which made her shiver to think of it. Here at least she always felt that if anything happened to her mother she could ask the ladies at the Mission to help her find a place in service. They'd offered to do that already, but she couldn't leave Madge, who wouldn't be able to cope on her own. Besides, the two of them had fun together some-times. No one could make you feel happy like her mother did when she was in a good mood. That was one of the reasons why men liked her.

When Madge went out to work that night Emmy went to bed and bolted the door of her room from inside. She was not tired and as she lay there staring up at the night sky through the tiny skylight, she kept seeing again the gloating expression on her mother's face and hearing the boasts about what George had promised to do for them. A whole house of their own, good furniture, nice clothes, plenty to eat . . .

Why should he do all this? It didn't make sense. He wasn't a kind man, whatever her mother said. Even Emmy could tell that.

When she got back from work late that night, Madge Carter checked her daughter's bedroom door and smiled to find it locked. Lighting a candle, she used it to stare at herself in the specked mirror on the mantelpiece, grimacing at what she saw. One of the younger women had called her a 'silly old bugger' tonight. She wasn't old, not really, but she wasn't young, either. She'd been pretty once and it upset her to see the wrinkles round her eyes, the faded colour of her hair and the sagging skin under her chin. Emmy looked very like the way her mother had in her youth and the contrast made Madge feel worse about herself. Her daughter had the same light brown hair falling in waves about her shoulders, though her eyes were hazel with gold flecks like her father's had been, not blue like her mother's. Emerick had had such pretty eyes for a man.

Madge sighed as she moved away from the mirror. In the daytime men no longer looked at her as she walked by, though she could still pass for pretty in night's kinder shadows. But once your looks faded you had no chance of bettering yourself. George was her last chance, she was quite sure of that. If she didn't keep him happy it might be hard to find another man to love her. If only . . . but it was no use lingering on what might have been. When Emerick had died suddenly and agonisingly of a pain in the belly, she and her daughter had been sent away by his family and the money they'd given Madge hadn't lasted. She had not dared ask them for more and had soon found out then how useless the words *if only* were when you and your child needed something to eat.

She sighed and went to stare out of the dormer window at the rain, which was now pelting down and turning the cobbled street and rows of grey slate roofs to shiny black in the moonlight. Feeling a bit down, she picked up the bottle of gin she'd brought home with her, unable to resist the warmth it gave – not to mention the feeling that everything would turn out well this time. She was glad Emmy had gone to bed because her daughter looked so disapproving when she drank. As if a woman who'd been as badly treated as Madge had didn't deserve all the comfort she could get! Finding a glass, she poured out a measure and took a good swallow, sighing in relief as warmth began to spread through her body.

As memories of her husband flooded through her she sipped daintily from the glass – only sluts drank out of the bottle. Emerick had been kind as well as good-looking and fun. George couldn't hold a candle to him. He could be ruthless, cruel even. She knew that. But with him looking after her she felt safe again – well, more or less.

Cradling the glass in her hands she sat on, her feet aching from all the running to and fro tonight. She wished George were with her now. He'd have driven away these miseries with his strong, warm body and his exciting plans for getting rich.

When she grew tired she rested her head on her arms and

woke up later, shivering, to a dark room, rain still beating against the windows and a fire that had gone out. As she stumbled across to her bed she admitted to herself that she was dreading going back to Northby, something she'd sworn never to do. Her father and mother had been a pair of old miseries and she'd been glad to get away from them and their suffocating respectability. They might be dead but her brother Isaac was still living in the town with his ugly old hag of a wife. He had married for money but it hadn't brought him much joy when he was younger and she doubted that things would have changed since.

It was a long time before Madge could get to sleep, thinking of the price she might have to pay for being with George. Would have to pay. And in Northby, of all places. She was not so stupid she didn't realise what he wanted her for. But she also knew she could make him laugh, surprising amusement out of him as no other woman could. She prayed it would be enough to hold him.

Hands stuffed into his pockets, Jack Staley watched his father Jem and brother Tom black their faces with soot from the chimney and listened to them joking with one another. He felt so furious at the way they were risking their lives that the words he'd been holding back burst out. 'They'll be waiting for you!'

Big Jem Staley grinned at his second son. 'They won't, you know. We've planned it all out careful-like. They've only got one watchman at Rishmore's tonight because th'other 'un fell ill.' He winked. 'Suffering from a severe case of knock on the head. Old Phil won't give us no trouble. We s'll smash up them damned new weaving machines afore they can bring in the military.' He cocked his head on one side. 'Sure tha doesn't want to come wi' us, lad?'

'Aye, very sure, Dad. I don't agree with what you're doing.' Big Jem's expression darkened. 'I should *make* thi come. I'm 'shamed to see a son o' mine holding back when there's summat important to be done.'

'You couldn't force me,' Jack said simply, folding his arms and staring challengingly at him. 'I'm near as big as you two now an' I'd kick up a right old fuss. You couldn't keep what you're doing secret with me yelling an' struggling all down the street.'

Tom broke the tension, as he usually did. 'An' you're twice as stubborn as we are, too.' He laughed, cuffing Jack affectionately about the ear. 'Leave him be, Dad. He allus was an old sobersides.'

But a sob from his mother made Jack grab his father's arm and beg once again, 'Don't do it, Dad! Look how you're upsetting our Mam.'

Jem glanced towards his weeping wife, a guilty yet stubborn look, then shook his head. 'She's allus gettin' upset about summat. Any road, I can't let th'other lads down. Not now. Nor I don't want to.'

Jack kicked the toe of his shoe against the table leg in a rhythm that emphasised his words. 'You're wrong about all this, Dad. *Wrong!* Violence won't get you anywhere an' it won't stop the Rishmores from using them power looms, neither. *It won't!*' To his mind you had to be stupid as well as dishonest to steal or damage the property of other people, especially ones as rich and powerful as the Rishmores who had just taken delivery of some new power looms at the mill. The handloom weavers like his dad were up in arms about it, but you couldn't stop progress or prevent the rich from doing as they pleased. Look how old Mr Rishmore ordered folk around at work, even his own son, and dismissed them on the spot if they didn't do exactly as he said.

Jem shrugged and wrapped a muffler round his neck to hide the lower half of his face. 'Suit thysen, lad. But don't come crying to me when they throw thi out of work because a damned metal monster has taken thy place in t'mill. All I can get now is damned checked cloth to weave, an' me a skilled weaver an' all. Things'll get worse if we don't do summat, mark my words. If women can work them new machines, why should they take men on at all when it costs 'em twice as much in wages? Who'll be the breadwinners then? Women, that's who. It's unnatural, that's what it is, an' we won't stand for it!'

He went across to give his wife a quick, bracing hug. 'Don't wait up for me, Netta love.'

He said that quite often, Jack thought, though it was usually because he was going out to the alehouse for a wet with the lads.

She flung her arms round her husband's waist, begging, 'Don't go, Jem! Think of the childer, if you won't think of me.'

He pushed her roughly away. 'I *am* thinking of them childer. Six on 'em we've raised, Netta Staley, an' what for? To see 'em go hungry, that's what. To see our Jack take a job in that damned mill like a slavey, 'stead of getting his own loom upstairs here. We have to show Rishmore we shan't put up with it an' *force* him to stop buying them damned machines.'

His anger made Netta sink down on her chair and close her eyes, but tears still trickled down her cheeks. 'They'll call out the soldiers on you,' she said in a dull voice. 'Mr Rishmore threatened it an' he'll do it too. You'll be shot and killed like my uncle was at Peterloo. It's not ten year since that happened an' it'll happen again. An' I'll never forgive you for dragging our Tom into it. Never.'

'He didn't have to drag me, Mam,' Tom said gently. 'I happen to agree with him.'

She looked at him, all her love for her handsome first-born showing in her face. 'Then you're as daft as he is, lad. What shall me and the kids do if owt happens to you two?'

'Ah, nowt's going to happen to us. We can allus run away if there's trouble, can't we?'

'Right, then, are thi ready, Tom lad?' Jem crammed his old felt hat down over his eyes and turned to leave, stopping briefly to call to Jack, 'Keep that door latch on, son. I don't want anyone comin' in an' seein' we're not home.'

When the sound of his father's footsteps had died away and all that was left was the patter of rain beating against the windows, Jack went across to put his arm round his mother's shaking shoulders. 'Don't take on, Mam. They'll likely be all right.'

But she continued to weep and made no effort to go to bed. 'Four on 'em there are upstairs, four childer younger than you. Your dad doesn't care about me, but he ought to think about them.'

Jack didn't say anything. Maybe his father would care about

her more if she didn't nag him all the time and make his life a misery. He felt sorry for them both. They should never have got wed, they were so unsuited. And his father drank too much, which had left the rest of them hungry more than once. It wasn't so bad now because though handloom weaving paid less and less, for all his father and Tom's hard work, Jack and Meg were bringing in money as well. But he would never forget going to bed with an empty belly when he was younger and seeing his mother go without to give the little 'uns a bite or two more. His dad had never gone without, though.

Meg, who was only eighteen months younger than he was, crept down to join them.

'You should have gone with 'em, our Jack.' She scowled at him. 'I'd be with Dad if I were a man.'

'Then it's a good job you're a girl, isn't it?' he threw back at her.

An hour later they heard hoofbeats, then shouting and shots in the distance. Netta moaned and began to sob again, but when Jack went towards the door, she screamed and flung herself in front of him. 'You're not going out!'

'Just to see what's happening, Mam.'

'No. You're not leaving this house!'

She fell into such a passion of weeping he couldn't leave her. He and Meg had to half-carry her back to her chair.

They were still sitting in front of the fire half an hour later when the door burst open, sending the clumsy wooden latch clattering to the ground. As the parish constable came striding in, Netta moaned and clutched Jack's hand.

'Mrs Staley?'

Jack was puzzled. Eli Makepeace knew perfectly well who she was because Northby was a small town.

His mother nodded, her eyes huge with fear in her thin face.

Eli took a deep breath and said it badly, because there was no way to soften such news. 'I'm afraid your husband's dead. He was shot while attacking the property of Mr Rishmore. And your son Thomas has been arrested and taken to prison.'

She let out one piercing scream then fainted.

Jack tried to get to her, but the constable stepped between

them and when Jack would have shoved him out of the way, the soldier who had accompanied him stepped forward, raising his rifle threateningly.

'We need to have a word with you first, lad,' Eli said. 'You see to her, lass!'

Jack hardly heard him. He was watching Meg kneel beside their mother, tears running down her cheeks. She had been their father's favourite. Although Jem Staley was big and rough, he had loved his children and Jack had a hundred memories of him cuddling or teasing the younger ones, calling Meg his little pet lamb . . . He couldn't believe his father would never do so again.

He stood still, not daring to give way to his own grief. He wanted to, though, wanted to weep like a great babby because the last thing he'd done was quarrel with his father – and now they could never make it up.

Eli looked severely at him. 'Where have you been tonight?'

He pulled his thoughts together hurriedly. 'At home with my mother.'

The constable ran a hand across Jack's shoulders and squinted at his face, touching his hair briefly.

The soldier still had his rifle at the ready, so Jack stood still and let them do as they chose. At other times he liked and respected Eli Makepeace for they were both in the church choir. Tonight, however, Eli was on *their* side.

'His hair's dry an' so are his clothes,' Eli said in a formal voice. 'Will you bear witness to that for me?'

The soldier stepped forward and made sure of this for himself before nodding. 'Aye. This one's definitely not been outside.'

Eli turned back to Jack, his voice a little less harsh. 'Why didn't you go with your father, Jack lad?'

'Because I'm not stupid.' But now he almost wished he had, because he was at home safe and Tom had been clapped in jail. He realised Eli was speaking again and forced himself to attend.

'Well, you've done the right thing. Mr Rishmore wants a list of them as stopped at home. I'll see your name goes on it. It'll likely keep you your job.'

Jack would have liked to tell him to mind his own business,

13

but he'd been working in the mill for long enough to know you didn't get on the bad side of old Mr Rishmore. Gesturing towards his mother he said, 'Thanks. She'll need my wages now.'

Eli nodded and stepped back. 'Aye. She's lucky to have a sensible son like you.'

As he and the soldier turned to leave, Jack followed them to the door and asked in a low voice, 'Where have they taken Dad's body?'

'To the church hall. He'll go into a pauper's grave unless you've money put by for a proper burial?' Eli looked questioningly at the lad, who shook his head.

'And our Tom?'

'He'll likely wind up in Lancaster County Gaol till the next Assizes. It's a serious matter, machine breaking is.'

Jack had to ask it, though the words nearly choked him, 'Will they – hang him?'

Eli shrugged. 'That or transport him. He was a damned fool. The whole town's full of fools, it seems, my own cousin among them.' He clapped Jack on the shoulder, the only sympathy he dared offer, then moved towards the door, signalling to the soldier to follow him.

When the two men had left, Jack leaned his head against the wall near the door and tried to hold back the sobs that were choking his throat, but they wouldn't be held in. He couldn't believe his dad was dead. Jem Staley had always dominated this house, been so full of life and vigour. And Tom – further sobs came out, strangled, harsh noises – Tom had been Jack's best friend as well as his brother. He could not imagine life without him.

It was a minute or two before he could control himself enough to turn and then he saw Meg still kneeling by their unconscious mother, chafing her hands and weeping quietly.

She looked up as he came across the room and offered in a small, tight voice, 'I'm sorry for what I said to you, Jack. You were right not to go out tonight. Do you think Sam Repley was with them?'

'Aye, I should think so. He's another damned hothead like our Tom.'

She sobbed aloud at that, a rare thing for a lass who usually kept her feelings to herself.

He put his arm round her, saying, 'Meg, Meg.' But what comfort could he offer when he still felt raw with his own grief?

She stared down at her lap. 'I've allus liked Sam. Even when I were a little 'un.' Her voice was dull, her whole body drooping.

Jack gave her another hug. She wasn't quite fifteen, but she seemed older suddenly. 'Eh, love, you allus did choose a hard road. Could you not have settled your fancy on a lad as wasn't so wild?'

'Sam's allus been special. An' he cares about me, too. He said so.'

'You should be thinking of our Dad an' Tom now, not an outsider.'

'I am thinking of them. But I'm thinking of all as were out machine breaking tonight as well. I heard you ask if they'd hang our Tom. They might hang them all.' She began sobbing.

He could not think of anything to say that was worth saying, so he watched his mother. She was conscious now, he could tell from the way her eyes were moving behind her closed lids. 'Mam?' he said gently.

She groaned and kept her eyes closed as if she didn't want to face reality.

'Mam,' he said more urgently, and at last she opened her eyes.

'Tell me it isn't true?' she begged, clutching his arm.

'You know it is.' He expected her to weep hysterically or even faint again, but she didn't.

Swallowing hard, she sat up and asked, 'What are we going to do, Jack? How can I feed them childer now?' Her voice rose. 'I'll kill myself, aye an' them too, afore I let anyone put us in the poorhouse.'

'It won't come to that.' But he couldn't be certain. He looked round, feeling bitter. Recently they'd been living more comfortably than ever before, but now, despite his brave words, he couldn't think how they would possibly manage – always supposing Mr Rishmore let him stay on at the mill. He wasn't earning a man's wages yet. Old Rishmore didn't pay you full wages till you were eighteen. Said he wasn't encouraging early marriage. His mother's voice, low but still throbbing with suppressed hysteria, made him look round.

She clutched his arm. 'Promise me you won't leave me, Jack. Promise me you'll always be there to look after us. Promise you won't desert us like your father did.'

'No one can always be there,' he protested.

She screamed and shook him, then began to weep hysterically, saying, 'Promise me, promise me!' over and over.

So wild was her appearance that he feared for her reason and could not refuse what she asked. 'I promise I'll do my best, Mam.'

It was some time before she stopped weeping then she fixed her eyes on his face and demanded, 'You won't go getting married and leaving us with nothing?'

'Mam, that's not fair,' Meg put in.

Netta rounded on her. 'You shut up, you young slut! We s'll be lucky if you've not getten a bairn in your belly, the way you've been carrying on with that Sam.'

Jack saw his sister flinch as if their mother had struck her and stepped between them as he often did. 'Mam, if I do get married it'll not be till the little 'uns are grown an' able to look after theirsen. An' I'll allus make a home for you.' There was nothing he could do to help his father now and his brother's fate was in the hands of the judge, but somehow he would find a way to look after his mother and the others, that he vowed most solemnly. And as Joey was only two, it would be a good many years before he would be free of that promise. He knew it and did not flinch from it, not when he saw the anguish on his mother's face, not when he thought of Shad, Joey and young Ginny going hungry.

On that thought, he called up the stairs, knowing the children could not help but be awake after all the noise, for the walls were thin, 'Come on down, you lot.'

They stood huddled by the foot of the stairs, pressed close together. His mother made no move towards them so Jack did, gathering them to him and saying in a voice which broke on the dreadful words, 'You heard it all, didn't you? Our Dad's been killed and our Tom's in prison.'

The two youngest looked up at him only half understanding the significance of this and Shad gulped audibly as he nodded. He was old enough at eleven to know how hard it was to set bread on the table every day.

'Us Staleys cannot do owt now but stick together,' Jack went on. 'We mun help one another as best we can. An' help our Mam, too.' He'd hoped his mother would come over to them to reinforce what he was saying, but she didn't. She stayed where she was, on her own, sobbing and rocking to and fro, still perilously close to hysterics. He knew then that the main reason he must stay with her was the children. Someone had to care for them properly and his mother grew more selfish as she grew older. He looked across at Meg, also standing by herself, and jerked his head in a silent invitation to join them.

She stepped across and put one hand hesitantly on Ginny's shoulder, then all of the children were hugging one another, weeping together for their father and brother.

Jack didn't need the knocker-up rapping at his bedroom window in the morning to wake him because he'd hardly slept. Tom usually shared this bed with him, while Shad and Joey slept on a mattress in the corner. It felt wrong to have the whole bed to himself, lonely too. And in his mind's eye he kept seeing Tom, manacled and perhaps bleeding, because the soldiers weren't gentle when they were dealing with a riot.

His mother stared at him when he went downstairs at his usual time to go to the mill and said, 'Eh, you look different, older!'

Jack certainly felt different. He knew himself to be a man grown now, one with heavy responsibilities – and all this just two weeks past his sixteenth birthday. It wasn't fair, but then life rarely was. He must just get on with it. And the first thing to do was see if he still had a job.

★   ★   ★

It was all for nothing, Jack kept thinking as he joined the other people making their way towards the big brick building that dominated the town. The new machines were still there and now many families were deprived of their breadwinners, his dad was dead, Tom in jail – and all for nothing. Folk nodded to one another but there were no cheery greetings and banter. Not this morning. And more than one face showed eyes swollen by tears.

The big mill gates were closed, with only the little side gate open, so they had to queue to get in. Constable Makepeace was standing outside with a soldier, both of them very watchful, so no one said anything as they stood there in the rain.

Inside Isaac Butterfield stood in the little boxed-in shelter, with his wages book on its wooden stand, checking them in one by one. He was as much part of the mill as the Rishmores were.

As his turn came Jack held his breath, praying they would not turn him away.

Mr Butterfield looked at him, then said his name as usual and ticked the big book.

Jack let out his breath and passed through the gate. Maybe there was hope still. He shuddered as he looked round the rain-slicked mill yard. There were signs of damage everywhere: stones and pieces of broken glass swept into piles, the windows of the weaving shed gaping to the weather.

Mr Graslow was standing outside his little office in the weaving shed. He nodded to Jack and muttered in a low voice, 'Sorry about your father, lad.'

'Thanks.' Jack went to fetch the broom and started his first job, sweeping out Mr Graslow's little office with even more care than usual. He then went to fill the oil cans. One or two people muttered words of sympathy as he passed and he wished they wouldn't because they made him want to sob like a little lass.

Some faces were missing. No one commented or asked where they were.

There were people coming and going in the yard and office all morning, and men mending the broken windows, but no one in the weaving shed with its rows of noisy, clanking machines looked up, just kept their heads down and worked steadily.

18

There was one woman in between each pair of machines tending them, the odd child fetching and carrying for the women, while the few men left in the mill now mainly worked in the engine house or drove the drays that fetched the yarn or took the bolts of cloth to be finished or dyed.

Jack had been kept on when other lads were turned off, either because they'd grown older or because the machines had been changed. Mr Graslow, the overlooker, said he was a smart young fellow and was training him up to act as assistant overlooker when he was older and the mill grew bigger, as Mr Rishmore said it would. Jack had been proud of being singled out for that, though if there were any other sort of work available he'd not have chosen to work in such a noisy, stifling place as the mill, with its rows of machines thumping away day in, day out. Now, as main bread-winner, he was terrified of being turned off and for all his grief he worked harder than any of the others.

The hours passed and Mr Graslow didn't say a word about the machine breaking. What did this mean? Only – if they were going to turn Jack off, why had they let him start work? When Mr Rishmore dismissed anyone, they usually had to get out of the mill straight away, often with him beating them about the shoulders with his walking stick.

After the half-hour dinner break, during which people ate their snap in near silence, the overlooker laid a hand on Jack's shoulder as he was about to go back to his work.

'Mr Samuel wants to see you in the office.'

Feeling a hundred years old Jack nodded and crossed the yard to stand in front of the polished wooden counter in the outer office.

The elderly clerk in the corner had his head down and was scratching busily with his quill, while Mr Butterfield, the head clerk, was standing behind the counter, grim-faced. He greeted the lad with, 'Wait over there, Staley.'

There were no seats, so Jack stood by the wall for a good half hour until the worry had built up inside him like a ton of lead. He felt sure now that he was going to lose his job, then they'd all be turned out of their house and have to go on the tramp to beg for a living. Or be sent to the poorhouse.

At last he heard a bell ring and Mr Butterfield came out from behind the counter to show him into the master's room.

Mr Samuel, the master's son, who was the same age as Mr Butterfield, was sitting behind his father's big polished desk today, looking very stern. He said nothing, staring at Jack as if sizing him up. The lad stood quietly. He had never been inside this room before but it was just as luxurious as folk said, with a thick carpet on the floor, velvet curtains at the window and solid pieces of well-polished mahogany furniture everywhere you looked. He felt so nervous he wondered if he'd even be able to frame a word.

Mr Samuel was not as severe in his dealings with the operatives as his father, but he was still strict enough. He fined those who came late to work or who disobeyed the rules by leaving the places where they toiled without permission. There were rules for everything, it seemed sometimes. You had to sweep the floor where you worked four times a day, oil the machinery at regular intervals, not speak to anyone while you were working except about the work itself. Folk joked that you had to piss carefully, too, or they'd fine you for doing that wrongly. No one was joking today, though.

Jack usually managed to escape without a fine and he'd have to be doubly careful now because they would need every farthing he could earn. Every single one.

If he still had a job.

'Go and stand in front of the desk,' Mr Butterfield whispered, giving him a poke to make him move forward.

Mr Samuel picked up a piece of paper and studied it.

Feeling resentful as well as afraid Jack stood where the clerk pointed, clasped his hands tightly in front of him and waited. What did the paper say? Surely there was nothing they could accuse him of?

Mr Samuel finished reading, set the paper down and stared at Jack again. 'You didn't go machine breaking with your father and brother last night, Staley. Why not?'

'I didn't think it was right, sir.'

'Why not?'

'Because you can't stop progress, even when it hurts you and yours. And because the machines are your family's property, not ours.'

Mr Samuel consulted another piece of paper. 'I'm told you go to church regularly and are a member of the choir.'

'Yes, sir.' The main reason he went to church was for the school Parson ran after the Sunday services, where you could learn to read and write. Jack didn't particularly enjoy the services or hold any strong religious beliefs, but Parson had coaxed him to join the choir when they found his voice had developed into a good baritone. He enjoyed the singing.

'Parson Bradley speaks well of you, says you're an apt pupil, rarely miss a reading class. And he says your voice would be missed from the choir.'

'Yes, sir.' He would thank Mr Bradley later for those kind words.

'I've decided not to dismiss you, but I'll be watching you carefully from now on. As long as you continue to attend church regularly and sing in the choir and –'

Jack debated whether to agree, then realised he could not build his new life on lies. 'I'm sorry, sir, but I don't think I'll be able to do that, though I'll be sorry to miss my Sunday classes, I shall indeed.'

Mr Samuel's expression grew chill. 'Explain yourself, if you please.'

'I'm the main wage earner now, with Dad dead and our Tom – gone. I've got a mother, a younger sister and two younger brothers, one only two years old, to support. I'll have to see if there's any extra work to be had on Sundays and –'

'On the Sabbath day!'

'Sir, I don't *want* to break the Sabbath,' Jack said hastily, knowing the Rishmores made a fuss about Sabbath observance, 'but I can't let the little 'uns go hungry and we can't live on my wages, let alone there's the rent to find.'

Mr Samuel glared at him. 'I'm minded to dismiss you for that impertinence!'

'I wasn't meaning to be impertinent, sir, truly I wasn't.' Jack heard his voice cracking with anguish as he got the words out. 'But I don't make promises I can't keep.'

After a short silence, Mr Rishmore asked, 'What sort of work are you likely to find on the Lord's Day?'

'Anything I can, sir. I don't rightly know what. Maybe helping out at the livery stables or working on a farm. Whatever turns up. I can't afford to be choosy, can I? It'll be life and death for us.'

Mr Samuel was drumming his fingers on the desk now, frowning down at the piece of paper. 'You're living in one of our houses, are you not?'

'Yes, sir. In Upper Bank Street.'

Silence, then Mr Samuel said, 'We must find you another house. You won't need the third floor now. And I will reduce the rent to sixpence a week on condition that you attend church *every single Sunday*.'

Jack gaped at him. 'Sir?'

'They say charity begins at home, do they not? I am a firm believer in Sabbath observance, but I can see that your money will not be enough to feed your brothers and sisters until you're earning a man's wages. You would not earn as much on a Sunday as the rent I remit.'

'No, sir. I – don't know what to say, sir. I'm that grateful!'

'You showed principle, lad, both in refusing to join your father in his criminal attack on our property and in refusing to promise what you could not carry out. See that you continue to live an honest Christian life.'

Jack felt dazed as he made his way back to the weaving shed. Mr Graslow smiled, clapped him on the shoulder and said he was glad not to have to train someone else. But as well as the burden of his sorrow, Jack now had the added burden that for the first time he and his family needed to accept charity. He hated the feeling being beholden gave him, as if someone had put shackles on his feet. Until now he had been able to get away occasionally on fine weekends, going for a tramp across the moors and clambering up the crags. He loved rock climbing, though his mother would have a fit if she knew about that. But now he wouldn't dare take a single Sunday off.

He looked round as he started to sweep his corner of the floor for the third time that day, and it came to him even more forcibly than before that if he ever had a chance to get away from all this, he would. His father had protested about him not getting his own loom at home, but any fool could see that the days of handloom weaving were nearly past so Jack had got a job at the mill instead.

The noise of the machines seemed twice as deafening that afternoon and he felt as if the walls were closing in on him. That made him feel angry at his father, who was to be buried in a pauper's grave the next day; angry at Tom, too, for they'd spoiled his life as well as their own.

But he and Tom had shared a bed all their lives, knocked around together, protected one another. He would miss his brother so very much. Tears welled in his eyes at the thought and he brushed them quickly away with his sleeve, hoping no one had noticed.

At the end of the day he put his things away and filed out quietly with the others, saying, 'Good night, Mr Butterfield,' to the clerk who was counting them out, as he or the other clerk counted them all in every morning.

The following morning Mr Butterfield beckoned to Jack when he arrived at the mill and the lad's heart began to thump in panic. Had Mr Rishmore changed his mind? Was he going to be dismissed after all?

'There's a house in Feather Lane. Mr Samuel says you're to move there at the weekend. And the rent will be sixpence a week only.' When Jack said nothing, the clerk added quietly, 'He's being very generous. You should be grateful.'

'Yes, sir. I am.'

'And I mentioned your father's funeral. Mr Samuel says you can have an hour off to attend and he won't dock your wages.'

'Thank you, sir.' Jack would rather not have gone. It horrified him how his grief for his father was all mixed up with anger. But he would go for his mother's sake. During the night he had heard muffled sobs from the front room downstairs, where she had slept with his father.

Yesterday evening she had looked like an old woman, her

hair straggling and unkempt, her eyes red and swollen. And she'd shrieked at little Joey for laughing softly over some game or other. As if a child of two could understand what was happening!

It had galled Jack to see how touchingly grateful she was to the Rishmores for their charity. *Grateful!* To the very people who had called in the soldiers and caused his father's death!

He had no older brother to laugh with now, nothing to laugh at, either, and the anger seemed to have settled inside him in a hard, hot lump.

Chapter Two

It was four weeks before George turned up in Manchester again, and though he sent a couple of messages through his cousin Gus, who was a carter, Madge's spirits sank lower and lower as the days turned into weeks.

When there were heavy footsteps on the stairs one afternoon she looked up eagerly. That sounded like . . . There was a double rap on the door and she called, 'Come in, George!'

He peered round the door, grinning at her. 'Not interrupting anything, am I?'

She squealed in delight and flung herself into his arms, laughing as he swung her round and kissed her soundly.

'Where's the girl?' he asked, breathing deeply.

Madge smiled knowingly. 'Out buying a loaf. She'll not interrupt us if I tell Ma Hurley to stop her coming up.'

'I don't think your daughter likes me.'

'Oh, she'll come round. Give her time. She doesn't trust men, that's all, and she's not old enough to find them interesting, thank goodness.'

'She's going to be pretty, though, when she grows up. Very pretty.'

Madge forced a laugh. 'When she learns to wash her face properly and comb her hair. Anyway, I'll just nip down and tell Ma I'm busy.'

When she got back he was sitting at the table. He opened his arms and pulled her down on his lap. 'It's all fixed, love, an' I've found you an' the lass a place to live. Took me longer than I'd expected because there's been some trouble in town – a group of fools trying to smash Rishmore's new looms. They brought in the military and one fellow was shot dead. Serve the stupid bugger right. There are others waiting for trial. They'll be hung or deported.'

'Poor things.'

'You're too soft-hearted. I keep telling you that.'

She shrugged and changed the subject to the one nearest her heart. 'Where's our new house, then?' When he said nothing, she pretended to punch him. 'Where? Tell me about it.'

'It's in Weavers Lane.'

She stilled. 'Where exactly in the lane?' It was the main street of the long narrow town and there were good parts and bad.

'Just past Grandma Hickley's shop.'

Her face fell. 'Oh, George, no! Those old weavers' cottages were falling down when I lived in Northby. They must be in a dreadful state now. Which one have you rented for me?'

'Not a whole cottage, just a room. You can't get a whole cottage for love or money at the moment unless you work for Rishmore's. All the cottages not belonging to them are crowded out. But Jen Miggs has a spare room and she'll see you're all right. It's the biggest room in the place, the front bedroom.'

'One room? *Only one room?* We've got two here. What am I going to do with Emmy while I'm working, pray? She's old enough to notice things, you know.' Madge tried to get off his lap, bitterly disappointed that he had broken his promise, but he wouldn't let her go. So she pushed his shoulders away with her hands, stared him right in the eyes and said firmly, 'I'm not going back to live in those conditions. I'd rather stay here.'

'And how will you manage without me? I can't spare the time to keep coming over to Manchester to see you once I've got my new alehouse up and running. It's bigger than the old one and it's going to make my fortune.' He chuckled. 'That and the girls upstairs!'

Still she held him off. 'I'll have to find someone else to look after me, then, won't I?' But her heart sank at the thought.

'You won't find anyone else as generous as me and you

know it, Madge Carter. You were desperate when I met you, selling your body to feed yourself.'

'It was only a couple of times.'

He threw his head back and laughed. 'We both know that's not true. You've been doing it for years. And who got you the job in the boozer anyway? I've only to say the word and you'll lose it again.' As she stared at him in shock, he changed tactics and said persuasively, 'Ah, Madge love, give it a chance with me. The room is just a start. When I'm making more money, I'll move you somewhere decent, I promise. And I'll make sure your customers pay well, pick and choose them myself – not like now. If it wasn't for the girl you could live over the alehouse with my other lasses, but you said you didn't want her there and I can see why.'

There! He'd said it openly. *Her customers.* Tears came into Madge's eyes and she stared down at the folds of her skirt. 'I wanted to – stop having customers. Just be with you, George.'

His voice grew sharper. 'Madge lass, I'd far rather keep you for myself, you know I would, but how can we get any money together if you don't help out? You do want us to have money, don't you?'

She was weeping now, tears sparkling on lashes that were still long, brimming in eyes that were still pretty. 'Promise me you'll move me out of that house as soon as you can, George. Promise me you'll let me stop doing *that* as soon as we can afford it.' She took a deep breath. 'You said once you'd marry me.' She felt him stiffen against her and it was a moment before he spoke.

'Well, I can't marry you or anyone because I've got a wife already. When she took bad I thought I'd be free and I would have wed you, but she up and got better, the bitch. She can't compare with you, Madge, an' I pay her to stay away from me – her and her sharp tongue.' His wife had died the year before, but he kept up the pretence that she was still alive because there had been a few women after him. He kissed Madge's lips and wiped away her tears with one callused fingertip. 'I will move you somewhere better, though, just as soon as I can. I promise.'

She sagged against him. 'Oh, George, I did want us to be married properly. I love you so much.'

He rolled his eyes at the ceiling. Stupid bitch! Did she think he'd marry someone as old as her? He enjoyed her company because she was not only good in bed but fun to be with. Best of all, though, he knew he could make money from her. She might be old, but she knew her trade.

He kept soft-talking her, choosing his words carefully. 'Mmm, I know, love. I wanted us to get wed, too. But it wasn't to be.' He let her snuggle up to him for a minute or two more, stroking her hair, which he knew she liked, then said more briskly, 'So are you coming to Northby or must I find myself someone else?'

'I'll come.' But she sighed even as she spoke.

'Right then, my cousin Gus will come and pick you up tomorrow morning about ten o'clock. He'll drop off a couple of crates and some straw tonight for you to pack your things.' He looked round and said pointedly, 'You've not got much stuff to move, have you? Stick with me and I'll buy you some much prettier things. You and Emmy will be settled in Northby by teatime tomorrow.'

Madge tried to look happy, but the idea of living in the town where she'd grown up – though it had been a large village then, without the new rows of mill houses George talked about – still worried her. 'I wish it were somewhere else,' she muttered, 'anywhere but Northby. I don't want to see my family again.'

'Ah, there's only your brother left. He might not even recognise you – or you him.'

She could see that George's patience was running out, so summoned up a smile. 'He'll probably ignore me completely, knowing him. I don't know what I'm worrying about, really.'

'Nor do I, lass. Things are only going to get better for us. Now, how about saying thank you properly?'

It didn't occur to him to ask who her brother was, any more than it occurred to her to tell him. As far as she was concerned, her brother was nothing to her now and she'd taken another surname because she didn't want to disgrace the memory of Emerick.

★　　★　　★

28

When Emmy came home carrying a new loaf, the landlady peered out of her room near the front door. 'Your ma's got a visitor.'

'Who is it?'

'That big fellow she's been seeing. He must have plenty o' money. She's right up to date with the rent.'

Emmy hesitated then went outside again to perch on her favourite bit of wall, casually side-stepping two urchins bent on tripping her up and giving the nearest one a shove. 'I'll scratch your eyes out if you try to take my bread,' she threatened.

They hooted with laughter but turned away. Emmy Carter could defend herself better than most and had a piercing voice that brought folk running. Besides, she'd chosen her vantage point on the wall carefully. If they openly attacked her, the man in the small shop opposite would come out with his cudgel. He'd done it before to make sure his customers felt safe.

It was nearly two hours before the front door banged open and George went striding away down the street without even noticing Emmy. By that time she had eaten the crust from one end of the loaf, picking it off piece by piece with her fingers.

When she went up to their room she expected to find her mother still in bed, but to her astonishment Madge was piling the few dishes from the crockery shelf and the three cooking implements, kettle, stew-pan and long-handled frying pan, all rarely used, on to the table and frowning at them. 'Oh, hello, love. Put the loaf down and help me decide. We're leaving tomorrow morning. Should we take all these things with us? This plate's cracked, for a start.'

'We're leaving tomorrow!'

'Yes. Isn't it exciting? I'm sure you'll like living in Northby.'

Emmy was sure she wouldn't. 'Couldn't we wait a day or two so we can say goodbye to people?'

Madge avoided her eyes. 'Who's there to say goodbye to?'

'Well, the ladies at the Mission.'

'Them! They've given you some silly ideas, them nose-in-the-air ladies have. You're better off without them. They don't understand what life is really like for poor folk.'

'But they've been teaching me to read and they gave me this dress.'

'I'll buy you plenty of dresses from now on. You won't need anyone's charity.'

But Emmy knew she would. Whenever her mother had money it went on gin or clothes for herself, not on her daughter unless the need was urgent.

George's cousin Gus turned up an hour later and dumped a couple of battered boxes, one full of straw, in their room. Grumbling about the steepness of the stairs, he went on his way after a caution to them to be ready on time the next morning.

Within an hour they had packed everything except for their bedding, which they could bundle up in the sheets when they got up. There had been no need to start packing so early, but Emmy knew her mother and did not protest.

When there was nothing else to do Emmy sat on the stool and Madge on their one chair, a rickety wooden thing with a spoke missing from the back.

'Not much to show for all my hard work, is there?'

Emmy tried to cheer her mother up, worried she'd start drinking again. 'If I can find work in Northby, we'll be able to buy some much nicer things.' She dreamed sometimes of a little cottage with curtains and tablecloths, sheets and soft blankets. And a polished brass fender which she'd keep nice and shiny. The ladies had one in the Mission and she loved its bright gleam.

She wished she looked older or was taller – and wasn't Madge Carter's daughter. She earned a few pence here and there when she could, helping out in the kitchen of the inn at the end of the street, running errands or minding people's babies. The only thing that would resign her to moving to Northby would be finding a proper job and having her own money coming in regularly. When she'd first started earning she'd given all the hard-earned pennies to her mother, proud of bringing something in. But after seeing them spent on gin, she had started keeping the odd coin for herself sewn into her only petticoat which she never, ever left lying around. Those pennies were needed when you were hungry and there was nothing at home to eat.

She did wish she could have said goodbye to the kind ladies at the Mission, though. She was going to miss them. How would she improve her reading and writing now? You had to be able to read and write to get a job in service, they'd told her, and becoming a maid in a respectable household was her greatest ambition.

As they drove north out of Manchester the next day in Gus's slow, lumbering cart, Emmy breathed in deeply. She hadn't realised how much fresher the air was outside the city. It had stopped raining now, so everything looked clean, with drops of water sparkling on leaves and blossoms. She stared round in amazement at fields and meadows, dry-stone walls, trees covered in new leaves of a tender green and the odd whitewashed farm house. Would Northby be like this? She did hope so.

It wasn't. Of course it wasn't. Northby was a big disappointment, hardly large enough to be called a town, and when you looked down on it the rows of red brick houses lay like scars along the sides of the narrow Pennine valley. At the upper end there were a few bigger stone houses, with a church in the middle and a mill on the lower ground to one side. It had a big square pond next to it. The moors were still green, but below them smoke lay like a haze over everything in the valley. It poured out in thick charcoal-coloured clouds from the tall mill chimney and rose in smaller trails of transparent grey from the chimney pots of houses.

'It's grown a lot bigger!' Madge exclaimed, staring around. 'Look at all those new houses they've built!'

'Ah, well, it's the mills,' Gus said. 'Brought a lot of work into Northby, they have, especially Rishmore's, the big 'un. T'others are only little places, but still, they provide a few jobs for folk. Old Rishmore owns most of the town now. He's the one as built most of them new houses over there. Had to have somewhere for his new workers to live, didn't he? Eh, folk have moved here from all over the place, from as far away as Ireland even – though them Papist buggers could go back again to their bogs and I shouldn't miss 'em a bit.'

At the outskirts of the town he reined in his two horses, which were now looking tired. 'Here we are, then.'

On one side of the road was a dry-stone wall, beyond which stretched a ploughed field, while on the other was a row of tumble-down stone houses, three storeys high with big windows on the top floor. Some of the panes were cracked and broken, stuffed with rags to keep the weather out, and the houses were leaning against one another as if they might otherwise fall down. The roofs were sagging and even the chimneys looked crooked.

Emmy looked at her mother, pleading wordlessly for this not to be their new home.

'This is the lower end of Weavers Lane,' her mother announced in a tight voice that said she was not happy, either. 'George has got us a room here.'

'Mum, are you sure we can't find somewhere better?' Emmy whispered.

'We're not paying for it, are we, love?' She forced a smile. 'Ah, it's just temporary, to give us a start. I dare say George will find us somewhere else quite soon.'

Gus sniggered. 'If you think he'll find you a whole house, you're far and out. He'll not spend a penny more than he has to, old George won't. Terrible fond of keeping his money to hissen, my little cousin is.' George was a big man, but Gus was even bigger and picked up one of the tea chests as if it weighed nothing. Shoving the front door open with his shoulder, he carried his load inside without bothering to knock and disappeared up the stairs.

Madge hesitated just inside the front door and Emmy stayed close to her mother.

A voice from the back shouted, 'Who's there?'

Gus came clumping downstairs again. 'It's only me, love. I've brought you your new lodgers.' He went out for more of their things.

An old woman appeared from the rear, wiping her hands on a grubby pinafore. 'You'll be Madge Carter. I'm Jen Miggs an' I don't allow no fighting in my house.'

Emmy took an instant dislike to her, hating the way she eyed them up and down. And what did the old woman mean, fighting? Her mother didn't behave like that. It was men who got into fights usually, or the lowest sort of street walker. Her mother talked nicely and she made people laugh, not get angry.

'Are you the best he could find?' Jen asked Madge scornfully, then grasped Emmy's arm with one bony hand and held her at arm's length to study her carefully. 'How old is she?'

'Only ten.'

Emmy cast a startled glance sideways. Her mother knew very well she was thirteen.

'Ten last month,' Madge said airily.

'She's well growed for ten. Pretty, too. A year, two at most, an' she'll be ready to join you.'

'She's not going into it,' Madge declared. 'My daughter's going to have a better life than me.'

Jen laughed, a wheezing choking sound that went on and on until she hacked up a gob of phlegm and spat it into a ragged handkerchief. 'Don't allow no spitting on the floor, neither,' she commented as she stuffed the handkerchief back into her apron pocket. 'I get gentlemen visiting here sometimes an' they like things kep' nice.'

Emmy felt a shiver run down her spine as she realised what sort of house this was. It was bad enough that her mother let men visit her and use her body, but Emmy wasn't going to do that. Never, ever.

'They all say their kids aren't going into it,' Jen said once she'd stopped laughing. 'It never happens, though. Young flesh brings in more money than old an' they can't resist that.' She cast a scornful look in Madge's direction. 'Well, aren't you going to bring the rest of your things in? George said to send you down to the alehouse as soon as you arrived. Your lass can unpack the stuff an' get the room ready. She's plenty old enough for that.'

The house was bigger inside than it looked, running backwards for three or four rooms. But they were shown only one room at the front on the first floor.

Emmy stared round it in dismay, hating the thought of having no privacy.

'It's nice and clean,' Madge said, with a bright, false smile

33

fixed in place. 'And I'm glad there's a table and proper bed. Four chairs, with mine. That's really nice.'

'George sent 'em round. See you keep everything clean.' Jen started to leave, then turned back again. 'Come and get directions from me when you're ready to go into town. George wants to see you soon as you arrive.'

'I know Northby,' Madge said, losing her smile. 'I grew up here.'

Jen peered at her. 'I don't recognise you. What was you called then?'

'Never you mind. I'm Madge Carter now and that's all anyone needs to know.'

As Jen stared her mouth fell open in sudden recognition. 'I thought you looked familiar. Madge Butterfield! That's who you are.'

'Shh! Not any more. I don't want to – you know, embarrass my family.'

Jen cackled. 'Call yoursen what you like. It don't worry me.'

When she had left Madge fumbled in the side slit in her skirt to find the purse hanging on its string beneath. She pressed a florin into Emmy's hand. 'I'd better go and see what George wants. If you walk into town with me, lovie, I'll show you round a bit. There used to be a bakery behind the church. We'll get a nice new loaf and some cheese. Growing girls need good food.'

'Why did you tell her I was only ten?' Emmy whispered, pushing the florin carefully into a little pocket she had sewn into her skirt waistband.

'Because it'll keep you *safe* for a year or two, that's why. It's a good thing you're so small or we'd never get away with it. If your breasts start to grow we'll have to bind them flat.' Madge fished out their small mirror from one of the bundles, studied her face in it and searched for her rouge pot, leaving things lying all over the table as she did so. She slapped the colour on with a liberal hand. 'There, that's better.' She pinched Emmy's cheek affectionately. 'Now we're both nice and rosy.' Picking up her shawl, she draped it round herself before turning towards the door, fluffing up her hair absent-mindedly with one hand.

'Aren't you going to wear your bonnet, Mum?'

'No, I'm not. It's a small town. By the end of the evening, everyone's going to know what I am.' Taking a deep breath, she led the way out, tossing her hair back and fixing another of those bright, glassy smiles on her face.

It was a week before Isaac Butterfield found out that his sister had returned to Northby. He was writing out invoices in his small private office when the overlooker poked his head round the door. 'Good. You're alone.'

It was not unusual for Martin Graslow to call in for a chat, because the two men were old friends, but when he glanced furtively over his shoulder before slipping into the office and pulling the door to behind him – a door that was never normally closed during working hours – Isaac put down his quill pen with a sense of foreboding. He sat bolt upright with his hands resting on either side of the ledger while he waited to find out what was wrong. Wasn't it enough that they'd lost some of their workers in the recent troubles, that the town was still uneasy, that folk scowled at him as he passed, that someone had thrown mud at his wife?

Martin swallowed and seemed to be having difficulty speaking, so Isaac said brusquely, 'Spit it out, man!'

'I thought I'd better come and warn you, lad. Your Madge is back in Northby.'

Isaac could not move for a moment or two, so shocked was he. 'Are you – sure it's her?'

'Aye. My sister thought she saw her in town, so I asked round, quiet-like. When I heard there was a new barmaid at the Horse and Rider, I went to see for myself. And there's no doubt about it. It is your Madge.' He'd been shocked at how raddled she looked, though, she who had once been the most beautiful girl in Northby.

Isaac didn't doubt his friend because in his youth Martin had come courting Madge for a time. 'What was she doing there? Serving?'

'Serving, singing and – eh, lad, I'm sorry to have to tell you, but she's whoring too.'

Isaac spoke in a tight voice. 'She turned into a whore a long time ago, after that fellow she was living with died. His family paid her off, but you know Madge. She never could manage her money. She wrote to Father for help, but he wouldn't have anything to do with her.'

Martin gaped at his friend. 'You never said!'

'Is it likely I'd tell folk? Especially you, lad. I thought at least she'd have the sense to stay away from Northby. I . . . he stared down at his clenched fists for a moment, remembering, ' . . . I went to see her after Father died, when I heard she was in need. She had a child, a bonny little lass. I gave her some money on condition she never came back to Northby and she promised faithfully she wouldn't. But our Madge never could keep a promise – as you know better than most.'

Martin's voice softened for a moment. 'I was sorry to lose her, she was such a pretty little thing. But Emerick Reynolds was besotted with her and his family had money, so I thought she was set for life.' He sighed. 'She looks old now, Isaac, old and worn.'

'Shop-soiled, you mean!' Isaac snapped, and it was a minute or two before he could rein in his anger and pull himself together. 'Thank you for letting me know, lad. I'll have to warn Lena tonight and hope the girls don't find out. Maybe I can persuade Madge to leave.' Though Lena would go mad if he gave his sister any money. She was going through a funny time of life, his wife was, and could fly off the handle for nothing. Well, she'd always had a nasty temper and it'd only got worse as the years passed.

'I doubt your Madge could leave town, even if she wanted to. She's one of George Duckworth's girls now. And she still has the daughter with her. I saw them on the street together one evening. The lass looks very like Madge used to.' Martin sighed. 'It put me in mind of when we were all young. They're staying down the end of Weavers Lane, at Old Jen Miggs' place.'

'They would be. And the lass is probably working *with* her mother!' Isaac said bitterly.

Martin frowned and pictured the little girl. 'Nay, I don't think so, lad. She looked nobbut a child an' – well, fresh and unspoiled.'

'So did Madge, even after she ran away.' Isaac felt bitterness flood through him. George Duckworth was making a name for himself in town as a bully and procurer. If *he* was Madge's protector and was benefiting from her immorality, they'd have little chance of persuading her to leave quietly.

When Martin had left, Isaac buried his head in his hands, humiliation scalding through him. Then he straightened his shoulders and picked up his quill again. He mustn't let this get him down. People might not find out, and even if they did, Mr Samuel would never blame him for his sister's sins.

But it was a while before he started writing and then he found he'd broken the quill by jabbing it into the inkwell too hard, so had to get out a new one. Adjusting the quill cutter and making sure he had a good point calmed him down, so when his employer poked his head into the office and said, 'I'm going out for a bit, Isaac lad,' he was able to nod calmly.

There's got to be something I can do about this, he thought when he was alone again, then gave his head an angry little shake and forced himself to concentrate on his work. His elderly assistant would be back soon with the reply to an important message because old Mr Rishmore didn't trust the mails. And Isaac wasn't paid to sit here and worry about family matters.

But he'd keep his wife and daughters well away from his sister and niece, he definitely would.

A few weeks after her arrival in Northby Emmy walked slowly up Weavers Lane. She loved the part near the town centre, where the nicer houses began, and especially the area beyond the church where the rich people's houses were. Here lived the lawyer, the owner of the bank and some of the owners of various businesses, though the shopkeepers, of course, lived over their shops. The largest house of all, Mr Rishmore's Mill House, was set a little beyond the others where the road sloped upwards, commanding an excellent view of the long narrow valley that sloped down from east to west.

She liked to linger outside the houses to watch what was happening: gardeners tending flowers and lawns, maids coming out of side doors to shake rugs, boys delivering things. Didn't rich people have to go to the shops? she wondered. She had never lived so close to them before and envied the little girls from one house who wore pretty clothes and went out walking on fine afternoons accompanied by a lady dressed all in dark colours with a severe expression on her face. Imagine having clothes so nice, and dainty shoes that were all glossy with polish!

She was bored and wished she had more to do. For all his promises George hadn't found her a job yet – well, not one that her mother approved of – and Emmy was finding time hanging heavy on her hands. In Manchester she had known their neighbours, done little errands for them, earning a penny or two most days, been able to walk for miles watching the world. Here, you could walk from one end of the town to the other in ten minutes and people regarded her with suspicion. Some women drew their skirts aside as she passed, so they must know who her mother was already.

She was feeling weary today because it was like the bad times when she was younger. Now she had to sit outside their room on the stairs at night while her mother had men in to visit her. Sometimes it was George himself, but other times it was strangers, some of them quite well dressed and very furtive, hiding their faces behind their hats as they passed her. Others were drunk, falling over their own feet and making a lot of noise.

Her mother said nothing about these men, but she looked unhappy most of the time now. Emmy had tried to persuade her to go back to Manchester, but all she would say was, 'There's no going back, lovie. There never is.'

As she walked home Emmy saw an older lady come out of one of the cottages, a funny little place that had been crammed in between two others and always looked slightly crooked. The lady looked pale, as if she had been ill, but she smiled at Emmy so the child slowed down and offered her a tentative smile in return.

'It's a lovely day, isn't it?' The lady turned her face up to the warmth of the sun.

Emmy stopped walking. 'It is. An' your garden's lovely, too, missus.' It was a tiny patch of ground, but it was crammed with flowers and Emmy often stopped to admire it. She had thought the lady old, but now realised she was only a bit older than her mother, but very frail-looking.

The lady nodded, her eyes lingering on the flowers, then she sighed. 'It's getting too much for me. I can't bend down properly any more.'

'I could help you with it if you'd show me how,' Emmy offered. 'I've got nothing else to do an' I like flowers.'

'Do you know anything about gardening?'

'No, missus, but you could sit on the step and tell me what to do, couldn't you?'

After a pause the lady nodded. 'Why not? But you must let me pay you for your toil, child.' She could see that the girl was poor, with much-mended clothes, so even the few pence she could spare would help, she was sure.

The woman next door looked over the low stone wall dividing the gardens from one another and clicked her tongue in annoyance at the sight of Emmy. 'Get away from here, you!' she shouted, flapping one hand.

Tears filled Emmy's eyes and the little bubble of hope burst, but she turned away obediently.

'No, wait a minute, child!' the lady called.

The woman next door began to whisper to her, gesturing towards Emmy with many frowns and shakes of the head.

When she had finished speaking she scowled at the child while the kind lady stood thinking. Emmy waited, hardly daring to breathe. Would she be allowed to stay? To work in this pretty garden? To learn how to grow flowers?

'I think I'll make my own judgement, Hessie, thank you. The child isn't to blame for what her mother does.' Again the lady beckoned to Emmy. 'Come in and tell me about yourself, dear.'

Hope began to bloom again as Emmy followed her inside. The door led straight into a little sitting room that was just like her best dreams. It had a wooden floor, shiny with polish, and a neat rug in front of the fireplace, though there was no fire lit on this warm spring day. There were curtains at the window and

39

ornaments on the mantelpiece, with a rocking chair and a sofa set temptingly to either side.

'Eeh, it's lovely in here!' Emmy exclaimed.

The lady looked round as if she'd never seen it before. 'I suppose so. I'm used to bigger places, but this will have to do me now. Come into the kitchen and we'll have a cup of tea together, shall we?'

So Emmy sat down at the table while the lady fussed to and fro, brewing the tea in a pretty china teapot and serving it in china cups with matching saucers. She brought out some scones, too, and set butter and jam in front of Emmy with a simple, 'You look hungry, child.'

Daintily, remembering the fancy table manners her mother sometimes insisted on and at other times forgot, Emmy ate a scone and drank some tea. When the lady crumbled her own scone and didn't eat much, Emmy said earnestly, 'You should eat it all up, missus. You look like you've been ill.'

'I have, but I don't have any appetite.' She sighed and stared into the distance for a minute or two then looked back at her young visitor. 'So, tell me about yourself, child. What's your name?'

'Emmy Carter.' She took a deep breath, because it was better to be sent away now than to get used to coming to this lovely place and then have that treat suddenly taken away from her. 'And your neighbour's right, missus. My mother isn't – she isn't respectable. She works in the alehouse and – and men come to visit her.' Emmy stared down at her plate, waiting for the harsh words that would send her out of this little paradise.

'You poor child.'

Emmy raised her eyes, saw only kindness and burst into tears. She found herself gathered into her kind hostess's arms, shushed and rocked as she wept out her frustration and unhappiness with her life in Northby. When the tears stopped flowing, she was presented with a white handkerchief, neatly folded.

'I'll dirty it.'

'It doesn't matter. It'll wash.'

Emmy applied it to her eyes and cheeks, enjoyed the soft

smooth feel of the fine cotton against her skin, then blew her nose on it. 'I don't usually cry. It doesn't do no good.'

'No. I don't usually cry, either.'

'What have you to cry about, missus?'

'My name is Tibby Oswald. My family used to call me Matilda – you may call me Mrs Tibby. My husband lost most of our money and when he died I had to leave my pretty house near the church and come to live here. I miss James very much and I miss my big garden and house, too. I had servants then, but there's just me now.'

Emmy stared at her. 'Well, I think this house is lovely an' if I lived somewhere like this I'd be happy as anything. Me and my mother only have one room and when the men come, I have to sit outside on the stairs till they've finished.'

'Lord, I thank you for bringing me this child, to show me how lucky I am,' Tibby murmured. She closed her eyes for a moment then looked at Emmy. 'I'm in need of some help around the house as well as the garden. You're right, I have been ill. Are you in need of regular work? I'll pay you for it, though I can't give you much, I'm afraid. How old are you?'

Emmy wriggled and looked over her shoulder before whispering, 'I'm thirteen going on fourteen, but my mother says it's better to tell people I'm only ten.'

Tibby considered this for a moment, eyes half-closed, then decided that if the mother was trying to protect the child, she could not be all bad. She smiled at Emmy, who was watching her anxiously. 'So – would you like to come and work for me?'

'Oh, I'd love to, Mrs Tibby. I'm a good worker. Everyone says so. But I'll have to ask my mother.'

'Ask her to come and see me, will you? Though she'd better use the back door or my neighbours will be scandalised.'

Emmy nodded and gave her a beaming smile. 'I'd really like to work for you, Mrs Tibby.'

When her mother came home, George was with her, so Emmy grabbed her blanket and went to sit on the stairs. But her mother and George were quarrelling not going to bed together, so she crept closer to the door to listen to what they were saying.

'I'm not having Emmy working at the alehouse, George, and that's flat. I'd rather go back to Manchester.'

There was the dull sound of a thump and a cry of pain from Madge.

'You'll do as I tell you,' he shouted.

Emmy bit her forefinger hard. She knew better than to interrupt. It'd do no good. But she hated it when anyone hurt her mother.

'I'll do as you say about everything else, but not about Emmy. *I mean it.*' The last words were shrieked and there was the sound of a chair falling over.

A thud and a yelp showed that George had hit her mother again. The girl put both hands in front of her mouth to hold back her sobs. George was a big man. But if he got his way about Emmy working for him in the alehouse, she'd run away, much as she'd hate to leave her mother. She was sure she could find her way back to Manchester and ask the ladies at the Mission to help her, but she didn't really want to leave now that she'd had such a wonderful opportunity offered her. She set her ear to the door again.

'You haven't the money to get back to Manchester,' George sneered. 'Think I don't know how much you spend on gin?'

'I've only to go to my brother and he'll pay me to leave Northby.'

There was the sound of footsteps dodging around the floor and then more furniture being knocked over and her mother's voice, shrill with fear, 'I won't change my mind about this, George, not if you beat me to death I won't.'

There was dead silence for a minute or two, then he said more quietly, 'Look, you know she could make us a fortune later if we handle her right. I want her somewhere I can keep an eye on her. Men are looking at her already. I don't want anyone spoiling her for my better customers.'

'I'm *not* having her going into this sort of work, George. Never.'

More silence. Emmy sat with her shoulders hunched and her

arms tightly clasped around her knees, fear shivering through her.

'Look,' Madge said in a soft, persuasive voice, 'let me find her a job somewhere she'll be safe. I'm sure I'll be able to come up with something.' Her laughter was suddenly very harsh. 'Believe me, no one is going to take more care that my daughter stays away from the lads than I am.'

'You'd better, you daft bitch. You've got something worth good money in that child.'

'Leave it till later, George. She's too young yet.'

'Ah, have it your own way. But make sure you keep her safe. I'm not having her giving it away for nothing.'

'I knew you'd see it my way. Ah, don't frown at me like that, my lovie. Come to bed. I haven't been with anyone else tonight. Let's enjoy one another a bit. There's no one gives me pleasure in bed like you do . . .'

Emmy sat hunched in a tight ball, listening to the familiar sounds of a man's pleasure, hating this life.

When the noises showed that George was getting ready to leave the girl went along the landing towards the rear, playing shadows again. She waited in the darkness till he'd clumped down the stairs. Only after the front door had banged shut and his footsteps faded away into the distance did she go back into their room, where she found her mother lying on the bed staring out at the moon.

Madge didn't even turn her head. 'Is that you, Emmy?'

'Yes, Mother.'

'Lock the door, lovie. We don't want anyone else disturbing us tonight.' She sat up and reached for her wrapper. 'We need to talk, you and I.'

Emmy went to pick up one of the fallen chairs and sit on it. 'I heard what you were saying to George. I won't work for him, not in that way. I won't do that sort of thing for anyone, not even if *you* ask me, Mother.'

Madge's eyes filled with tears. 'I wouldn't ask you to. That's why I said you were only ten. Things are different for those who have a rich man to look after them, but I never found anyone who wanted me for a regular mistress.' She sighed.

'But saying I'm ten will only put George off for a while. He hasn't given up, you know. And you said "later",' Emmy finished accusingly.

'That was just to buy us some time. If we can find you a job somewhere safe, we've got a year or two before we need worry and by then I'll have thought of something else. It's a good thing you're not a big strapping girl.' Madge began to pace up and down the room, her voice low, her expression distraught. Several times she paused to take a sip of gin, pouring it carefully into the glass she always insisted on.

Once she stopped to say in anguished tones, 'I didn't mean to bring you to this, lovie. Oh, if only your father had lived!'

She wept a little, then in one of her lightning changes of mood, dashed away the tears. 'No use getting maudlin, is it?' She went to pour herself another gin, saying coaxingly, 'Just to warm my bones, lovie. Then we'll think about finding you a job somewhere safe.'

When Emmy went to sit beside her on the bed, her mother put an arm round her, so they were cuddling close. Emmy loved these rare moments when her mother showed her love. 'I've already got an offer of a job,' she said.

'What?' Madge grasped her daughter's arm tightly. 'What have you been doing? Who is this with?'

'It's the lady who lives in that crooked cottage just before the bend. Mrs Oswald her name is, only she says I'm to call her Mrs Tibby. She's been ill and needs help in the house and garden.'

'A maid's job? Mmm, that might do for a while. Is she a lady or a rough sort?'

'A lady. Her husband died. He lost most of their money, she said.'

Madge nodded slowly and thoughtfully. 'Yes, that might do it. They like to keep their maids respectable, ladies do. How much is she offering?'

'She didn't say, wants you to go and see her. And she says to use the back gate.'

Madge grinned. 'She's definitely respectable, then. Ah, don't look like that. I don't mind using the back entrance. I'll go and see her tomorrow morning. Wake me early. We'll wash our hair. We want to make a good impression, don't we?' She yawned. 'You'd better get to sleep now, lovie.'

'Aren't you coming to bed?'

'No, I'll just sit and have a think. I'm not tired.'

Which meant, Emmy knew, that her mother intended to drink the rest of the bottle. And it was no use trying to stop her because that only made her worse. So Emmy took off her top clothes and lay down on the bed in her shift, sure she'd have trouble falling asleep, but waking to find that it was light and that her mother was snoring on the pillow next to her.

Chapter Three

June–July 1826

Lena Butterfield was furious when she found out that Isaac's sister had returned to Northby to shame them. She was so furious she forgot to guard her tongue and as a result their two daughters heard every word of their parents' quarrel. Well, there had been rather a lot quarrels in the past year or two, and they'd learned to tread carefully around their mother's chancy temper.

Lal, who was thirteen and considered herself almost a woman, listened shamelessly at the door, even though Dinah, who at eleven was definitely still a child, tugged at her arm and tried to persuade her to come away. In the end Lal cracked her sister about the ears, Dinah set up a loud squalling and their parents came rushing to see what was wrong.

'We couldn't help overhearing what you were saying,' Lal said when Dinah had been calmed down. 'I thought your sister was dead, Father.'

'I wish she *was!*' Lena declared. 'The woman's come back to ruin us.' She went to put an arm round each of her daughters and stare accusingly at her husband. 'And how I'm ever going to hold my head up again in this town, I don't know. No one will speak to me when they find out what she's turned into. No one!' She burst into loud, angry sobbing.

Dinah at once began crying again but Lal turned to her father. 'What are you going to do about it?' she demanded, hands on hips and square chin jutting out.

47

It was his wife he spoke to. 'I'll go and see Madge, offer her money to go away.'

Lena's tears stopped instantly. 'You'll not give that harlot a penny of our money. My dowry money wasn't meant for such as her. I wouldn't give her a farthing, even if she were starving!'

'But, my dear, how else can I persuade her to leave?'

'You must go and see old Mr Rishmore. He's a magistrate. Tell him to have her arrested and put in the house of correction. She's a woman of low morals, isn't she? She'd feel at home there.'

Isaac looked at her in horror. 'I hope Mr Rishmore will never find out about my sister and he certainly won't hear about her from me. It would seriously lower me in his esteem.'

Lena laughed as harshly as a cawing crow. 'Of course he'll find out. Everyone will find out in a tiny place like Northby – if they don't know already. *Beg* him to help you. Show him you don't care about her.'

Isaac shook his head. He knew he couldn't have Madge put into a house of correction. It would kill her. She'd once been the pretty little sister he loved very much indeed and he'd been dreadfully upset when she ran away. 'I shall do no such thing. It'll be best if we simply ignore her existence.'

'What about the daughter? Shall you ignore her too?' his wife demanded. 'How old is she now?'

'She must be about the same age as Lal, if I remember rightly.'

'She's old enough to work with her mother, then,' Lena said bitterly. 'They start young in that business.'

He hated to think of that, for he was fond of children and shuddered when he saw so many of them selling their bodies in the streets of Manchester. 'Martin said the daughter looked to be only a child still, slight and not very tall, unlike our dear Lal who is so well-grown for her age.'

'That's worse, then.' Lena clutched her bosom dramatically. 'She'll be knocking on our door and asking to play with her cousins next.'

'If that girl comes anywhere near me, I'll throw stones at her or scratch her eyes out,' Lal said viciously, for she was old enough to understand the problems of having disreputable relatives and was already dreading what other children might call out after her in the streets.

'No, no, my dear! We shall not even speak to them and I'm sure they won't bother us,' Isaac said soothingly, casting a pleading glance towards Lena. 'My sister was never a vindictive woman and I'm quite sure she won't try to harm us. Madge was just a – a bit careless in her ways. Now, let us talk of pleasanter things, if you please.'

But when the girls went to bed that night Lal lay awake for some time thinking about the situation. She was determined to get a look at her cousin. Perhaps if she made the girl's life miserable, her aunt would leave Northby. If her father wouldn't do anything about these unsavoury relatives, then Lal would.

But first she had to find out who her enemy was.

Early on Saturday morning Jack Staley was walking back to the mill after delivering a message to a supplier for Mr Butterfield. It had rained overnight but was sunny now and that had tempted him to linger for a moment or two outside the town to enjoy the birdsong and spring flowers. He ached sometimes to get out into the fresh air, especially up there on the tops where the wind blew clean.

After a while he sighed and continued on his way. There was work waiting for him at the mill, though at least Saturday was a shorter day and they finished at four o'clock. But his mother wanted some things doing about the house, then they would be going to the market to see if they could pick up any bargains in left-over food. Since his father's death it sometimes seemed as if he never had a minute to himself, and when his brother's trial came up, he was sure it would bring them more misery at home as well as the stigma of having a convicted felon in the family.

His mother was now talking of finding ways to go and visit Tom in Lancaster County Gaol. Jack would also have liked to visit his brother, whom he was still missing dreadfully, but could see no way of finding the money, let alone getting time off work. They'd sold the two looms his father and Tom had used but got very little for them, and what was left after moving house to Feather Lane, one of the original streets of cottages in Northby, had been put aside for a rainy day.

He sighed. Mr Bradley said they took folk who'd been sentenced to transportation out to Australia and had shown him on the big globe where it was, right at the other side of the world. Months it took to get there, seemingly. Jack couldn't understand distances like that, for he'd never even left Northby, except to go for walks on the tops. Neither had Tom.

He heard the shrieks and yells from a distance and at first smiled because it sounded like a group of little lasses playing. But as he got to the end of the narrow ginnel between two cottages and stepped into Weavers Lane, he realised the sound was not a happy one and hurried round the bend to see what was wrong. He stopped in shock as he recognised Mr Butterfield's daughters pelting a third girl with dirt and stones.

The stranger was picking up the stones and throwing them back with considerable accuracy, but they had her trapped in an angle between two houses and with two against one were beginning to wear her down. It was obvious the attack was premeditated, for the Butterfield girls had gathered a pile of stones. Their backs were towards him but every line of Lal's body spoke of anger and determination. She was throwing the stones as hard as she could as well as scooping up mud from a puddle and hurling that, heedless of whether she splattered herself.

Their victim had a cut on her cheek already and was trying to protect her face against the furious onslaught as well as throw back some of the stones. Even as he watched, Lal rushed forward and bowled the stranger over, beginning to pummel her as hard as she could and calling on her sister to come and kick their victim.

Horrified, Jack ran forward. 'Hoy! Stop that at once, Lal Butterfield!'

The older girl paused briefly to see who it was. 'You mind your own business, Jack Staley!' Turning back, she slapped her victim across the face.

The lass underneath her had managed to pick up a small

stone and she immediately clouted her attacker on the head with it, but she was too small to throw the bigger girl off.

With a howl of fury as well as pain, Lal tried to scratch the other girl's eyes out.

Jack hauled her off, then ranged himself in front of the victim, who scrambled to her feet. 'Stay there a minute and I'll see you home,' he tossed over his shoulder, then gave Lal a shake and said, 'Stop that screeching, you!'

'She hit me!'

'Well, you hit her first.' Cautiously he let go of her.

For a moment everyone stood still, the only sounds being the faint noise of other people in the distance. Lal was panting from her exertions as she glared first at him then at her victim.

Dinah tugged at her sister's arm and whispered, 'Come away now, do.'

Lal tossed her head. 'I'll get her next time,' she promised. 'You won't always be around to save her, Jack Staley.'

He grabbed Lal's arm as she turned to walk away. 'Why are you doing this? Whatever would your father say to such behaviour?' Everyone in town was well aware that Dinah always did as her elder sister said, so he ignored the younger girl.

'*She's* got into me!' Lal gestured scornfully towards the stranger, who was trying to wipe the dirt off her face.

'Why? What's she done to you?'

'Come to live in Northby, that's what. Our mother's furious about it and so am I.'

'She's our cousin,' Dinah explained in her quiet, whispery voice, earning herself an immediate punch in the ribs from her older sister.

'What did you have to say that for?' Lal demanded. 'Now he'll tell everyone and they'll all scorn us for being related to someone like *her*.'

Jack looked down in puzzlement at the girl he was protecting. He could see nothing terrible about her. Indeed, she was a pretty little thing, or would have been had she not been splattered with muck. 'You'd better tell me the whole tale now,' he ordered Lal. 'I won't pass it on to anyone else, I promise.'

She glared at him, her broad face screwed up into ugliness and her coarse, curly hair bouncing with the vehemence of her words. 'You'd better not. We don't want anyone to know she's our cousin. Her mother's a harlot,' she didn't know exactly what that meant but it was clearly bad, 'and *my* mother says people won't speak to us any more because of her. So we don't want them staying in this town, either of them. My mother says *she* is probably just as bad as her mother.'

He studied the stranger again. She had a very sweet face and he didn't believe this pretty child could possibly be a whore. Faces and eyes didn't lie as tongues often did. 'You're making it all up.'

'I am not! She lives in that house,' Lal pointed dramatically, 'and calls herself Emmy Carter.'

Jack tried to deflect future trouble, something he was becoming adept at with his own brothers and sisters now that he was the man of the house. 'Well, if you attack the girl every time you see her, you'll draw attention to yourselves and people will start to wonder why. You'd be better ignoring her and pretending you've never even heard of her.'

Lal considered this, scowling. '*She* might tell people.'

Jack looked at the girl. 'You wouldn't, would you?'

Emmy looked up at him, such a strong young man and yet with a kind face and gentle eyes. Other people had hurried past while she was being attacked, making no attempt to help her, but he had stopped to protect her. 'Why should I say anything? I don't want people to know I'm related to someone as nasty as *her*.'

Lal glared at her.

'There you are,' said Jack. 'You didn't need to worry at all, let alone attack this poor lass. There's usually a better way to sort out problems. If people fought all the time, they'd get nowt done.' Or get themselves killed like his father.

Lal stuck her tongue out at Emmy and walked away, pausing to shout over her shoulder, 'You'd better not tell or I'll come back and kill you next time!'

Dinah hurried after her.

When they'd vanished from sight, Emmy let out a shuddering sigh. Jack smiled down at her and she gave him a wobbly smile before trying to straighten her clothes.

'You'll not get it off till it's dried, love. You'd better go home and put something else on.' He saw she was trying to hold back tears and asked, 'What's up?'

'I haven't *got* anything else decent to wear and I'm supposed to be starting work for Mrs Oswald this morning at nine o'clock. What will she say when I turn up like this?' She indicated herself with a despairing sweep of the hand.

'If you tell her what happened, she'll understand, I'm sure.'

'But I wanted to make a good impression!' Emmy tried to brush the mud off, but it only made smears on the worn cloth of her bodice.

He enjoyed watching the play of sunlight on her hair, the sweep of her long lashes, the gentle curve of her lips. No wonder Lal Butterfield was angry at her. Lal was as plain as they came and her bad temper and bullying ways were legendary among the children of the town. It'd do her good to go and work in the mill, where the high-spirited lasses and hard work would soon knock the rough corners off her, only she wouldn't need to do that. Her father might not be rich like the Rishmores, but he earned good wages and lived in a big, comfortable house.

Realising suddenly how time was passing Jack said hastily, 'I have to get back to work now. Will you be all right?'

'Yes. And thank you for your help.' Emmy stood watching him as he hurried off towards the town centre. *Jack Staley*. That's what the horrid Lal girl had called him. She repeated his name so she wouldn't forget it, then with a sigh she walked on, opened the gate of Mrs Oswald's little cottage and knocked on the front door. She had no choice but to go to work as she was.

When Tibby saw the state Emmy was in, she exclaimed in shock, 'Whatever's happened to you, child?'

Emmy tried to control herself but couldn't and burst into tears, sure she was going to be turned away before she even started her lovely new job.

Tibby could not bear to see the child weeping so despairingly and took her in her arms, drawing her inside the house. Cuddling her close, she murmured meaningless comforting phrases and waited for the storm of tears to pass.

Emmy soon calmed down. 'I sh-shouldn't be doing this, ma'am.' She tried to pull away. Her mother had told her to call her new mistress 'ma'am' and had given her advice about how to behave. Emmy still couldn't believe that Madge had really had a maid once, because she always did embroider the truth, but perhaps she had been one herself because the advice made sense for once.

Tibby debated for a moment then lost the battle with propriety. When had she ever been one to stand on her dignity? 'Ah, child, it's been a year since I've had anyone to cuddle. Don't push me away.' She led the girl towards the sofa and made her sit down on it, dirty dress and all. Putting her arm round the thin shoulders, she said gently, 'Tell me what happened.'

With some prompting Emmy told the story of her encounter with the two girls who had pelted her with mud and stones.

'Did you know you had relatives in town?' Tibby asked when the tale came to an end.

'Yes, ma'am, but not who they were. The young man who helped me called one of them Lal Butterfield.'

Tibby knew that name and was surprised by it. 'Was she a big, strapping girl with light brown hair a similar colour to yours?'

'Yes, she was.'

'Then her father is Isaac Butterfield, head clerk at Rishmore's. Did your mother say how you're related to them?'

'You won't tell?'

'No, of course not.'

'I think Mr Butterfield is my mother's brother.'

Tibby tried to remember what she knew about the Butterfields, but her family had lived ten miles away and she had not known Northby and its inhabitants very well before she and her husband moved to the town, by which time there had been no sign of Isaac Butterfield having a sister. 'Well, you don't have much choice about your relatives, I'm afraid. My family didn't want me to marry my dear James, said he wasn't good

54

enough for me, but we were happy together right until the day he died.'

Her voice became husky as she added, 'The only sadness was when we lost our beloved daughter to a putrid sore throat, and then we were sad together, which helped a little.' She sat for a moment lost in her own memories, then stood up and pulled the child with her. 'Come through into the back and we'll have a nice cup of tea. We'll have to wash those clothes of yours to get the mud off and you've bled all over your bodice.' She smoothed back the soft hair and clicked her tongue at the bruise already showing blue against Emmy's forehead and the trickle of dried blood coming from it.

'I'm sorry to cause you such trouble, Mrs Tibby. I'd have gone home for clean clothes, but I've been growing lately and – and I haven't got any others, not really.' She had asked her mother to buy her some more, but Madge never seemed to have any money left lately. Still, perhaps Emmy could save her own money now.

'Then it's lucky that I've got some old clothes you can use.' Until now Tibby hadn't been able to bear the thought of giving her daughter's clothes away, but somehow she didn't mind Emmy having them. There were a couple of simple dresses, high-necked and plain, which would suit the child, though the hems would have to be taken up because Charlotte had been tall for her age, taking after her father's family, not Tibby's, for the Armisteads were usually quite small in stature.

It had been a long time since a morning had passed so quickly. Tibby found herself humming as she hemmed one of the dresses, then sent Emmy upstairs with a jug of warm water to wash and change. Afterwards she showed her helper what needed doing, but by noon she was tired, so easily did she run out of energy nowadays, and had to rest quietly on the sofa while the child bustled around the house, working steadily and only needing to be told once how to do a task.

As the afternoon wore on and the shadows lengthened across the street, Tibby said reluctantly, 'I think you'd better go home now, dear. You can keep the dress. I'll finish shortening the hem of the other one for you tomorrow.'

Emmy hesitated, looking down at herself. She had never owned clothing that was not stained and torn before and was tempted. But she knew what would happen if she took the dress home, so she shook her head. 'I can change into it when I come in the mornings, ma'am. I'd rather not take anything home.' She saw her new mistress looking puzzled and confessed, 'I'm afraid my mother might pawn it if she needed money. She just takes the first thing that comes into her mind when she's short.' With a blush she added, because she knew already that this kind lady would not scorn her for it, 'She drinks gin sometimes, you see, and then she can behave very foolishly.'

'That must be hard for you, dear.'

Emmy nodded. She hated even the smell of gin.

'Very well. We'll keep your things in the little bedroom at the back of the house and you can change into them every morning.'

At the door Emmy hesitated then said in a rush, 'I did enjoy myself today, Mrs Tibby. I hope I've given satisfaction.'

'You have given me great satisfaction with your work and I've enjoyed your company, too.'

In fact, the place felt quite empty when the door closed behind Emmy. And far too quiet. Tibby didn't know who was doing the other the bigger favour, she or Emmy, just that she had felt happy and useful today for the first time since her husband's death.

Two weeks later, George came round to see Madge late one night. He hammered on the door of their room and when Madge recognised his voice, she staggered across to open the door to him, still fuddled by the gin she'd drunk after her last visitor had left.

Emmy rolled out of bed at the first sound of his voice and slipped on her dress, grabbing a shawl and blanket ready to go and sit on the stairs, It had been a cold wet day, for all it was June, and she could not help shivering. She tried to slip past George, but he laughed and caught her, pawing at her.

'She's young and firm, Madge, and her titties are starting to grow,' he taunted, and found himself suddenly attacked by feet, fists, nails, anything Madge could hit him with.

For a moment he stood there in shock, then his expression turned nasty. But as Madge swung even more wildly, missed and sat down on the floor with a thump, his mood changed again and he threw back his head to roar with laughter. He went on for so long that someone in the room next door banged on the wall and yelled at them to shut up.

'You look after your own, at least,' he said, hauling Madge to her feet and pulling her into his arms. 'I like that in a woman. No need to defend your cub against me, though. I have better things planned for her when she's old enough, as I've told you.'

Outside on the landing Emmy heard what he had said and shuddered, wrapping the blanket more closely around herself and leaning her head against the wall. She wished the stairs were not so draughty. And she'd rather tramp the roads than do *that*, especially now she'd experienced another sort of life.

It seemed a very long time until he came out again, his clothing in some disarray now. He stared at her, frowning. 'Have you nowhere better to go when your mother's working?'

Emmy shook her head, holding the blanket more tightly around herself.

'What about that old woman you work for?' he asked, swaying on his feet, his face on a level with hers, since he was lower down the stairs.

'What do you mean?'

'Has that Mrs Oswald got a spare bedroom?'

Emmy nodded.

'Ask her if you can live in. Tell her you'll work for less money.'

'There'll be no one to look after my mother if I do that. She needs me. She can't bear to be alone.'

He was silent for a long time, then said in tones of mild surprise, 'Another one as is loyal.' After that he walked off without another word.

She heard him fumble with the front door then go clumping off towards town. With a weary sigh she went back into the bedroom to find her mother sprawled across the bed, snoring.

Emmy could not bear the thought of sleeping in a bed still warm from *him*, so went and lay down on the rag rug on the floor in front of the embers of the fire, as she did sometimes.

The next day George came tramping back down the lane just after noon, a scratch decorating his face where Madge's nails had raked it. He seemed in the best of humours and was whistling tunefully. Emmy saw him through the front bedroom window, for she and Mrs Tibby were putting clean sheets on the bed, sheets which smelled of fresh air and soap, unlike those on her own bed. She sighed and stopped work for a moment to watch him.

'What's wrong, dear?'

Emmy beckoned her across and pointed. 'That's George Duckworth. My mother works for him. He doesn't usually come to see her so early in the day, so I can't help wondering what he wants. I don't like the way he looks at me sometimes.'

An hour later there was a knock on the back door and when Emmy went to open it she found her mother there, looking as tidy as she ever got nowadays.

'Can I speak to Mrs Oswald, lovie? I won't come in. Just ask her if I can have a minute or two of her time.'

Tibby hurried to the door, afraid Emmy's mother might be here to take her away.

The child lingered nearby, eavesdropping in case this un-expected visit meant trouble.

'I've been thinking, Mrs Oswald,' Madge began. 'You're being very kind, taking Emmy as your maid, given the circum-stances. But people won't like it, her coming back to me every night. I wonder – if she took less wages, could she maybe live in?'

Silence, then Tibby said briskly, 'That sounds like a good idea to me, but I'd have to hire her by the year if we did that, which I'm quite willing to do. It's the usual arrangement, you know.'

Madge nodded. 'Yes, I do know. I had a maid of my own once.' She saw the surprise and disbelief on the other woman's face and spread her arms wide, looking down at herself in sudden disgust. 'You don't think I was always like this, do you? You don't think I *wanted* to turn to this sort of life?'

'Can you not – find some other way to earn your bread?' Tibby watched Emmy's mother stare for a moment into the distance as if she saw something dreadful there, then shake herself and focus on her present task again.

'No, Mrs Oswald, I can't. It's too late for me now. But I want better for my daughter. She'll learn a lot working for you and I thank you for it.'

'Then we shall make an agreement. I'll take Emmy for a year. She may come and see you occasionally because I wouldn't keep a mother and daughter apart, whatever people say.'

'If it's all right with you, I'd rather come and see her. I'll come to the back door, be discreet. You see, I'm moving into the alehouse and I don't want her coming to that place.'

Inside the house Emmy gasped and clapped one hand over her mouth. She had no doubt this was all being done at George's prompting. Why? And the answer was obvious, of course. He hadn't changed his mind about her, but he wanted her kept somewhere safe till she grew up and in the meantime would make do with her mother. She moved forward, not even trying to pretend she hadn't overheard. 'Do you have to go and live with him, Mum?'

Madge laughed, a short bitter bark of sound. 'It's the best thing for me, lovie. I'll be *safe* with George. No walks home through the dark streets. No worries about anyone breaking into my room. Well, as safe as I'll ever get anyway.'

Emmy doubted that. She felt anything but safe when that man was around.

However, as a result of his interference she found herself living in what was, to her, paradise, and was grateful for that at least. And she had a whole year before she need worry about things, as well as a clean house which she loved to polish and where they could keep everything nice. She even had a room of her own and decent clothes to wear. What more could you want in life?

Sometimes in the town she passed Lal and Dinah, and the

older girl made scornful remarks if no one else was around about 'harlot's daughter' and 'I haven't forgotten you'. But Emmy found it easy to ignore them and always walked past as if she hadn't heard.

Sometimes she saw Jack Staley in the distance, in a hurry usually. She didn't go up to him, thinking he might not want to speak to her. But when she met him one day in the lane that led from the end of Weavers Lane into the countryside that still touched the town at this end, he stopped at once, smiling at her.

'Hello, lass. How are you going on?'

She smiled at him, feeling shy but delighted that he wanted to speak to her. 'I'm fine, thank you, Mr Staley. I'm still working for Mrs Oswald and I live in now. She's really nice.'

'My friends call me Jack,' he said, returning her smile. He could see she was happy. She had filled out a little, her hair was shining and her clothes were clean. She would be lovely when she grew up, he realised, beautiful even. Her cousin Lal was like a caricature of this delicate creature, same colour hair but crinkled instead of softly waving beneath the bow that tied it back. And Lal was shaped like an overstuffed bolster where Emmy was slender.

'You work at the mill, don't you?' she asked and saw his face cloud over. 'Don't you like it there?'

Somehow he found himself able to talk to her. 'No, I hate it. But I've got no choice. My father's dead and there's only me to look after Mam and the others.'

'They're lucky to have you, then. My mother didn't have anyone to help her. That's why she – um – got into trouble.'

He could not hold back his bitterness. 'I'm not so lucky to have my family hanging like millstones round my neck.'

'You should be glad you've got someone to love. I'd give anything to have a brother or sister and not always be on my own.'

His large hand curled round hers for a moment and the anger he'd been bottling up eased just a little. 'I suppose so. I never thought of it like that. Do you get lonely, then?'

She nodded. 'Mmm. Well, I used to. Not since I've been with Mrs Tibby, though.'

The church clock struck the hour and he sighed. 'I have to get back to the mill. It's been nice talking to you, Emmy.'

She stood and watched him go, then went back inside. She didn't tell Mrs Tibby about the encounter but kept it to herself, a small secret that gave her immense pleasure. Jack Staley wasn't exactly a friend but he didn't scorn her and perhaps they might chat now and then if they met.

He probably didn't need a friend, but she would love to have one.

On one of her mother's visits, while they were walking along a country lane nearby, Emmy told her about the two girls who had thrown stones at her and asked if they really were her cousins.

'Yes, lovie, I'm afraid so. Though they're a miserable lot, the Butterfields, always praying and nagging people to be tidy. I was glad when my Emerick took me away from them.'

'Haven't you tried to see your brother since you came back?'

'What, Isaac? No, not me. He's as bad as our father, so respectable he daren't smile for fear his face would crack in half. And he married Lena Simmleby, who wouldn't have taken him if she could have got anyone else, only she couldn't because she's a nasty, ugly, spiteful creature. He only married her for her money, I'm sure. My father put him up to it.'

That made Emmy very thoughtful. How foolish of her mother to have left a respectable family for the sort of life she was leading now – even if they were strict. But it didn't take much thought to work out why. Her mother had met her father and gone away with him because he was handsome and loved her. And in doing so she'd taken a lot from her daughter: family, respectability, hope. No decent man would want to marry someone with a mother like hers. And Emmy wasn't going to marry someone who wasn't decent, let alone give herself to men for money, so she'd have to stay unmarried. She'd worked that out already.

She didn't for a moment believe her father had married her mother, whatever Madge claimed. Everyone knew men didn't marry women like her. But it was at least a relief to know she came from respectable stock. That sort of knowledge gave you a bit more confidence in yourself, somehow.

As Tibby Oswald grew a little stronger, partly thanks to her young handmaiden's cosseting and partly because she now had something to live for, she began to talk of them attending church regularly. 'Just because I've come down in the world is no reason to neglect my duties to my Maker,' she said one fine, sunny day in July. 'In fact, we'll go to church tomorrow and every Sunday morning from now on. It'll make a nice little outing and I've hardly been through its doors since I moved to Weavers Lane.'

She had shown Emmy her old home, a larger house set higher up the hill overlooking the church. She had had to sell it to pay for poor James's funeral and headstone, and to pay off his debts. After she had moved she hadn't gone about much, for it was easier to live in poverty when you didn't bump into former acquaintances every day. But gradually she had learned to hold her head up again, to nod to ladies she knew – though she didn't accept any invitations to take tea with them, partly because she could not return their hospitality and partly because she didn't want anyone patronising her. Going to church would show everyone how worn and old-fashioned her best clothes had become, but they were clean and well-mended, weren't they? That must suffice for her pride.

'Are you sure you're strong enough to walk up the hill?' Emmy worried.

'Definitely. I haven't felt this well for a long time. Now, what shall we wear?'

'I don't think I'd better go with you, Mrs Tibby. People won't like it.' And anyway, Emmy had never been inside a proper church. The Mission was one thing, where the ladies knew you weren't from a respectable home and didn't mind if your clothes were ragged, but she'd seen well-dressed people coming out of Northby parish church on Sundays and she knew such people would look down their noses at her.

'You're coming to church with me,' Tibby said firmly. 'And

62

if anyone tries to stop you, they'll be stopping me too. I do so love a stained glass window on a sunny day, and I've heard they have a good choir, too, since the new choirmaster took over. I shall enjoy the singing. I had a little piano once, did I tell you?' She sighed, then put her regrets firmly aside and went on making plans.

Sunday saw Emmy following her mistress hesitantly inside the church, which was a stone edifice far older than most of the bustling little town it now served. As she had expected there were whispers at the sight of her, but she tried not to show her embarrassment.

Then she saw Jack sitting to one side with a group of other young men and his presence made her feel better, for no reason she could fathom. When he turned his head and smiled, she gave him a quick smile back. One person wasn't ashamed to know her, at least.

However, when Lal Butterfield followed her parents into church and stopped with a squeak of shock at the end of the rear pew where Mrs Oswald had left her maid sitting with some other servants and poorer people, Emmy began to worry, so vicious was the glance Lal threw at her.

As the Butterfield family took their places in one of the pews halfway down she saw her cousin tug at her mother's arm and whisper something, then a look of outrage come over the mother's face. Mrs Butterfield nudged her husband and leaned across to whisper in his ear, and Emmy saw him turn round and rake the rear pews with his eyes until he saw her. She also noticed and was surprised by the sadness that came into his face. It was as if he had recognised her. Which didn't make sense because she had never seen him before, since he worked long hours in the mill every day and certainly did not spend any time down at her end of Weavers Lane. Unless she reminded him of her mother? Yes, that'd be it.

Emmy didn't understand most of the ceremony and couldn't read the long words in the hymnbook, so just imitated the actions of those around her and pretended to sing with them.

When Parson asked the choir to sing, Jack went forward to stand with the others at the front, there being no choir stalls in this small, plain church. Their singing was so lovely it brought tears to Emmy's eyes. She had never heard music like that. Organ grinders made scratchy sounds compared to this, and although she'd enjoyed watching the little monkey that collected the coins for one man, the music hadn't affected her as this did.

After the service was over the Rishmore family led the way out into the churchyard and then the better class of people filed out behind them, so that pew after pew emptied into the river of rustling silk skirts and dark superfine coats that flowed towards the sunshine. The Rishmore ladies, a mother and daughter whom Mrs Tibby had pointed out in town, were today wearing very large hats so loaded with ribbons and trimming that it amazed Emmy how they kept these monstrous creations balanced on their heads. The two gentlemen from the front pews carried top hats and put them on as they went outside.

Emmy watched it all wide-eyed, utterly fascinated by life among respectable folk.

As the church continued to empty the rustling silks were followed by the plainer garments of the less affluent families, whose menfolk had a variety of headgear and whose womenfolk wore mainly bonnets, though also with a great many ribbons and trimmings fluttering on them. The Butterfields were among these and the three females of the family looked the other way as they passed Emmy's pew, but Mr Butterfield slowed down for a moment to stare right at her and look sad again.

Someone poked Emmy in the back and she realised it was time for the occupants of the final pew to leave the church. Even the poorer men around her were carrying caps or hats of some sort, and the women had on simple bonnets. No wonder Mrs Oswald had fussed about finding Emmy a straw bonnet to wear. She reached up to stroke the lovely silky ribbons tied under her chin. Such a pretty shade of blue and hardly showing any wear at all. It was one of Mrs Tibby's own.

When she got outside Emmy saw her mistress in conversation with another lady so went to stand in the shadow of one of the stone buttresses to wait for her, knowing Mrs Tibby walked better if she had someone's arm to hold. A sharp jab in the ribs made her spin round in shock.

'What are *you* doing here among decent folk?' Lal hissed.

'I'm attending church with my mistress. I'm maid to Mrs Oswald now.'

'You won't be once she finds out about your mother.'

'She knows already. I told her myself.'

'I don't believe you.'

A shrill voice called, 'Lal! Where have you got to?' and a woman came round the corner of the church, stopping in shock. 'Come away from that creature at once!' she said in a low voice. 'Whatever are you thinking of, Lal Butterfield?'

'I'll make you sorry, coming to church with decent people!' Lal hissed at Emmy then flounced off.

Mrs Butterfield's voice floated back to Emmy. 'Don't you dare speak to her again! Don't even look in her direction. What if someone saw you?'

The voices faded away and with a sigh Emmy turned back to see if Mrs Oswald was still talking.

'Don't listen to Lal, lass, You're doing the right thing, coming to church.'

She spun round to find Jack Staley standing a few feet away, smiling down at her.

He moved forward, thinking how lonely and unsure of herself she looked. 'How are you, Emmy? Lal hasn't been attacking you again, has she?'

'No, just – you know, saying things.'

'Well, a few words won't kill you. How are things going on with your new mistress?' As Emmy told him all her news, he watched her eyes sparkling with happiness and thought how jealous Lal must be of her far prettier cousin, however much superiority she pretended.

'Who is your friend, Emmy dear?'

Emmy flushed with embarrassment for not having seen that Mrs Tibby was ready to leave. 'Oh, I'm sorry to keep you waiting, ma'am. This is Jack Staley, the one who rescued me when those girls were throwing stones at me.'

Tibby Oswald studied him and liked what she saw. 'It was kind of you to intervene, young man.'

'I can't abide cruelty,' he said simply. Then he glanced round and realised the rest of Parson's class had filed into the little church hall next door. 'I'm sorry, I have to go to the Reading Class now. Pleased to have met you, Mrs Oswald.'

As she watched him leave Tibby thought what a good-looking young man he was and yet how gentle his smile was. It wouldn't do for him to get too friendly with her maid, however, for the girl's sake.

Emmy watched Jack go. 'I didn't think he'd speak to me in front of everyone.'

'He seems a very nice young fellow. Clean and decent, though he could do with a new jacket. He's growing out of that one. What did you say his name was?'

'Jack Staley.'

'Now where do I know that name from . . . Oh, my! It was a man called Staley who was killed in those dreadful riots in April. You don't suppose that was his father, do you?'

'I don't know, ma'am.'

Tibby abandoned her speculations, looking round with a weary sigh. 'Well, my dear, shall we make our way home now? I've enjoyed the service, but I'm feeling rather tired. I've been talking to our new Parson's wife. I thought I recognised her face. Mrs Bradley is the cousin of a lady I used to know when I was a girl and . . .' Talking gently, she led the way home.

She didn't say that Prudence Bradley had tactfully raised the matter of Emmy's parentage and that Tibby had told her firmly that she was a good girl, not to be blamed for her mother's behaviour, and was the best maid Tibby had ever had, so cheerful and hard-working.

She sighed. She had felt a bit out of place among the congregation in the churchyard until Mrs Bradley had come over to speak to her. She had seen some ladies she used to know glancing scornfully at her shabby clothes and making no attempt to renew their acquaintance. Well, the Lord didn't care whether you were rich or poor, only whether you were a good person or not, and Tibby didn't intend to stop coming to church now that she had plucked up the courage to start again. It would be something to look forward to, because the choir was indeed a good one and so was the new organ old Mr Rishmore had donated in memory of his wife. As for the sermon, dear Mr Bradley had chosen an interesting topic which would give her something to think about during the following week.

If only her poor, dear James hadn't been so trusting with his savings. If only some dreadful person hadn't robbed him in the street, hitting him over the head so viciously he had died there before anyone found him. And James had had hardly had any money on him, only his old silver watch and chain. She still wept at night sometimes thinking of that, and still missed her old home and comfortable life.

Then she looked down at the clear-eyed child walking beside her. Well, at least she wasn't lonely any more. You had to count your blessings, indeed you did. The two of them could help one another because from what the child had let fall, she had led a very lonely life.

Chapter Four

1826-8

In September Jack came home from the mill one day to find his sister cooking the evening meal, banging the dishes about and looking furiously angry. 'Where's Mam?'

'Gone to see our Tom.'

He couldn't take it in for a minute, just stood there holding out his chilled hands to the fire and frowning at her. He was bone weary after a particularly frustrating day and soaked to the skin because it was pelting down outside. 'What do you mean?'

'I mean, she's sold her wedding ring and gone off to see our Tom in Lancaster.'

'Sold her wedding ring?'

'Can you do nothing but repeat what I say, Jack Staley?' Meg yelled. 'She said to tell you she had to see him again or it would kill her. She left our Joey an' Ginny with Mrs Farron next door an' just up and went.'

He closed his eyes and sagged down into his mother's rocking chair. 'She must have been desperate to sell that ring. She's always stroking it and saying it's all she has left of Dad. Why didn't she tell me?'

'Because she knew you'd persuade her out of doing it. I only found out this morning after you'd left, and when I told her not to waste her money, she clouted me round the ears. He's allus been her favourite, Tom has. An' I've allus been the one she doesn't like.'

He ignored her last remark because it was true, though he could never understand why. Meg was a bit sharp-tongued, but she was a good, hard-working lass. 'I should go after Mam.'

'What with? She's taken all the housekeeping money, too, 'cept for what she paid Mrs Farron to look after the little 'uns, so I hope you've got something tucked away or we'll all go hungry.'

He looked at her in shock. 'She took *all* the food money?'

His sister nodded.

'The savings too?'

Another nod.

'But how did she think we'd manage?'

Meg shrugged. 'I asked her that. She said she'd be sleeping in cheap lodging houses an' at least we'd be warm an' comfortable.'

'Eh, I hope she'll be all right.' He looked out of the window. 'She'll be soaking wet and cold.'

'It's her own fault.' Meg looked at him and her mouth trembled for a moment. 'I hope our Tom's not – suffering.'

He nodded, wishing desperately that he could have gone to see his brother, too.

They could do nothing but wait for three long days, coming home each night hoping to see their mother but finding the house empty. Jack borrowed some money from Mr Bradley for food and Meg grudgingly prepared the evening meals. Shad, who was eleven, had a job at the dye works now, fetching and carrying for one of the men there. It didn't pay much, only two shillings a week, but everything helped and the man he worked for gave him something to eat at midday as well as teaching him about dyeing. Ginny, who was eight, kept wondering aloud where their mother was, but Joey was very quiet, sucking his thumb and cuddling up to his big brother when offered the chance.

Remembering his own childhood and the boisterous caresses and play from his father, Jack always tried to show his little brother as much affection as possible. Their mother had changed a lot since their father's death and didn't like anyone to touch her any more, and Meg went out whenever she could to get away from the constant nagging and slaps.

Worry over how his mother was managing was eating away at Jack and he wondered whether to ask Mr Bradley's help and advice. Maybe he should go and look for her? Only how was he to manage that? They had no money and nothing of value to sell. Besides, he didn't dare put his job at risk by taking time off. Old Mr Rishmore had been very short-tempered since the loom-breaking.

However, just as Jack felt he could bear the worry no longer, he came home from the mill one night to find his mother sitting slumped in the rocking chair, looking grey and exhausted, her clothes crumpled and dirty. She smelled sour. Normally she would have washed herself as soon as she got in, but today she hardly seemed to be aware of what was happening around her. He went to kneel beside her and chafe her hands. 'Eh, Mam, why didn't you tell me what you were planning?'

She stared at him as if she didn't recognise him, then blinked and reached out to touch his hair fleetingly. 'He wept when he saw me, Jack. Our Tom. Stood there skriking like a babby.'

He swallowed hard. He couldn't imagine his confident older brother weeping.

'Don't be angry at me, son. I had to go. I just had to see him again!'

She suddenly began to cry, keening in a shrill tone, rocking to and fro, so consumed with anguish that he didn't know how to help her, could only hold her in his arms and make shushing noises.

When her passion was spent she slumped back in the chair with her eyes closed. 'I'm that thirsty. Do we have any tea in the house?'

'Aye.' He went and brewed her some from the dust and leaves at the bottom of the tea caddy, making it extra strong and hang the extravagance. He watched her slurp it down thirstily, then poured more hot water on to the same leaves to make a weaker second brew. 'How does Tom look?' he asked at last.

'Thinner – and dirty. They don't keep them clean in those places, you know.' Netta pressed her hands against her chest, her head bowed for a minute, then went on, 'His eyes are that sad, Jack. You'd think he was forty year old, not nineteen. An' he sent you his special love, said he was sorry you'd been left with everything on your shoulders.' She looked at him, her eyes brimming still. 'What if they hang him, Jack? I think it'd kill me.'

'Mr Bradley's going to write and ask for clemency, ask them just to transport him. He said Tom would have got off more lightly if he hadn't thumped a soldier when they tried to capture him.'

His mother began to sob again. 'I shall never see him again, I know I shan't.'

They sat together for a little longer, with her holding his hand tightly, then Meg came in and peace was at an end.

'So you've come back, have you, Mam? You should remember you have other children as well as Tom! How did you think we were going to eat when you took all the money?'

'Meg, don't!' Jack begged.

His sister ignored him. 'How could you do it? Every week you take nearly every penny I earn, and I'm dressed in rags, and then you go an' spend all that on seeing our Tom.' She stared defiantly across the room. 'Well, from now onwards I'm keeping some of what I earn for mysen.'

'Meg, that's not fair!' Jack rebuked.

'Life's not fair. Haven't you realised that yet? And *she* isn't fair to us, neither.'

'Don't talk to Mam like that.'

'I'll talk any way I want. I'm one of the breadwinners here an' I have a right to my say. You may want to spend your life looking after her an' the other kids, but I don't.'

Jack took a hasty step towards her, furious that she would behave like this when their mother was so upset.

'Don't!' Netta grabbed his jacket to hold him back. 'Let our Meg keep some of her own money. You're only young once and it doesn't last. Soon as the childer start coming it's a struggle just to put bread in their mouths. I could maybe do a bit of scrubbing or get a day's washing every now an' then at one of the big houses. I'm not going to be such a burden on you from now on – as long as you'll keep your promise an' stay with us.' She looked at him with haunted eyes. 'I couldn't do it on my own, Jack, I just couldn't. Some women manage all right when they lose their husband, but I'm not one of them.'

'You might find yoursen another fellow,' Meg tossed at her. 'That'd be a big help to the rest of us.'

Netta shook her head and for a moment her eyes were blind with memories. 'Nay, I want no other after your dad. I couldn't love another fellow like I loved my Jem. Eh, he was that good-looking when he was younger, I thought I was set for life when he wanted to wed me.' She sighed. 'No, I just couldn't bear anyone else to touch me.'

Jack could not gainsay her. 'I'll keep my promise, Mam.' Though he knew well enough that her memories of her husband were flawed. Well, let her think that way if it gave her comfort.

'Funny way you two had of showing your love, then. You did nothing but quarrel. An' as for you, our Jack, you're a soft fool to give in to her,' Meg snapped and whisked out of the house, banging the door behind her.

It was weeks before the final trial would take place. Mr Bradley had explained to Jack about the others being just committal hearings and having to wait for the Assizes before a judge could make a final decision on such a serious case.

Watching his mother fret and worry, Jack wondered if these rich folk realised how hard it was on the families of the accused who had to wait such a long time to find out what would happen to their loved ones. His mother looked years older since his father's death and his sister's tongue had never been so sharp, while he felt weighed down with sadness and responsibility — and terror that they would hang his brother.

Even if they only sentenced Tom to transportation, he would be lost to them and that was a hard thing to face.

Near the time for the trial, the Parson came round to tell his mother that Mr Samuel was to attend it and put in a plea for clemency. He would take Constable Makepeace with him to give evidence. Since it was his family's property the men had attacked and he who had been bashed, there was hope that this would sway the judge to be lenient. But apparently old Mr Rishmore was angry about what his son was doing and had washed his hands of the whole business.

'Will it really make a difference if Mr Samuel does that?' Jack asked quietly as he showed Mr Bradley out. 'I want the truth, please.' He was the one who would have to deal with his mother.

'He thinks so. It'll still be transportation for your Tom, his lawyer thinks, and the Rishmores will be satisfied with that as punishment.' He patted his young companion's shoulder. 'If you ever need someone to talk to, lad, my door is always open.'

Jack nodded but knew he wouldn't take advantage of this offer. What good would talking do now? No one could help Tom's family face their loss, and Jack missed his brother's cheerful presence and his father's solid warmth every single day. But the Parson was a kind man and it had been a good thing for the town when he took up the living. His wife was exactly the same, always helping folk in trouble.

When Mr Samuel came back from the trial he called Jack and the others who had family members involved into the mill yard and told them gravely what sentences their sons, husbands and brothers had been given. Only Tom had been sentenced to transportation, because he had used violence against a soldier, and he would be sent to the hulks in London. He would stay in one of these rotting old ships, which were used as extra jails, until he left for New South Wales, never to return.

All Jack could do was write a letter to Tom, find out from Mr Bradley where to send it – and lie awake at night wondering how his brother was and where he was now. He did a lot of that.

His sister's friend Sam Repley had been let off with only a fine and some uncle had come forward to pay it. His sister was missing Sam greatly, he knew, more than Jack had expected her to, since he agreed with his mother that at fifteen she was too young to get wed. But Sam had gone to live with the uncle, not returning to Northby when released from jail. Well, there wouldn't have been a job here for him any more, would there?

The uncle had a farm, it seemed, with work for his nephew. But if he'd really cared about her, Sam should have come and said goodbye to Meg, or at least sent her a farewell note. She had wept over him several times, Jack had heard her in the night.

He sighed as he went about his work. He seemed to be beset by worries on all sides since his father's death.

As the months passed Jack continued to act as head of the household and to work at the mill, doing all sorts of odd jobs in the evenings and on Saturday afternoons as well to earn extra pennies. Mr Samuel occasionally stopped to speak to him in the mill yard and would then walk off looking smug, as if it pleased him to see Jack bobbing his head and saying, 'Yes, sir. We're all grateful for your help, sir.'

Charity was a heavy burden to bear, though, and if Jack ever could he'd leave Northby and find a job where you didn't have to kow-tow to anyone, a job where there wasn't all that noise beating at your ears from dawn till dusk from those metal monsters which wove the cloth better and faster than men ever could.

He thought it must be wonderful to have a little shop and that became the dream into which he escaped sometimes. Life would never get boring, there'd be so many different things to do, and you'd be in charge of how you worked, which must be wonderful. They had shopped in the town centre before his father's death, but things were cheaper down at the far end of Weavers Lane, so they walked the extra distance now. He would watch Grandma Hickley serving the customers in her little shop when he bought things for his mother. The old woman was slow and clumsy, and didn't keep things as clean as he'd have done. Eh, he could have done everything so much better.

He mocked himself. Fine dreams these were! He was stuck in that bloody weaving shed for life, he reckoned. And that was if he was one of the lucky fellows who were kept on.

The only good thing about going to Grandma Hickley's shop was that he sometimes saw Emmy Carter on his way back. She'd be working in the garden of the cottage or helping her

75

mistress take a short stroll in the evening. The sight of her always brightened his day. She was so pretty and her smile was warm and friendly.

He didn't attend the Bible reading classes any more, because he had grown too skilled to need them, but he was still in the church choir and that was his only real escape from his mother and her never-ending complaints. It was hard going out to rehearsals after work, because he didn't finish till eight o'clock at night and had to be in the mill at six o'clock sharp the next morning. But he looked forward to the singing, which seemed to lift his heart.

One Sunday Mr Bradley took him aside after church.

'Do you think you could help out at the Sunday reading classes, Jack? We're to have several classes now and we need another teacher for the beginners. Mr Samuel himself suggested you for the boys. He's very keen for the young people of the town to learn their letters and wants my wife to start a girls' class now as well.'

Jack sighed. This would eat further into his precious spare time. He had been thinking maybe on fine Sundays he could get out on the moors after church. That surely wouldn't be considered breaking the Sabbath?

'We can pay you two shillings a week if you do, Mr Rishmore says.'

Jack looked down at his wrists, caught by a sudden fancy. They wore shackles in prison, but he had shackles, too, invisible ones that kept him dancing to a rich man's wishes. That made him wonder whether Tom had arrived in Australia yet. He didn't even know how long it took to get there. 'Yes, I'll do it, sir. It'll mean I'll be able to pay you back more quickly.' For he had borrowed the money from Parson to redeem his mother's wedding ring and then had a big argument with Mr Roper the pawnbroker about the price he should pay for it. Only his threat to ask the Parson to intervene had made Mr Roper stop trying to ask twice what he had given Jack's mother for it and be content with a smaller profit.

And since his mother's visit to Lancaster Jack had another worry. Meg was growing wilder all the time, knocking around the streets after she finished work with a group of young people whose main aim in life seemed to be making loud nuisances of themselves. He spoke to her about it, forbidding her to go out at night, but she laughed in his face.

'If you try to stop me, I'll leave home. If you want my wages, you'll have to let me have fun in my own way. We aren't all solemn and stuffy like you, Jack Staley. The other lads laugh at you, did you know? It's like living with a parson, living with you.'

That hurt. It really did. When did he have time to enjoy himself? He would look up at the moors sometimes and long to be there, striding along with the wind blowing in his face.

By the end of 1827 Jack was earning a man's wage. He went to the office when they raised his pay and told Mr Butterfield he didn't need help with the rent any more.

'I respect you for that, Jack,' he'd quietly replied, 'and so will Mr Samuel. I'll tell the rent collector.'

Meg said he was stupid because now he would be little better off, but he had his pride and that meant more than money to him.

Most of his friends were walking out with lasses now and talking of marriage. Some got wed as the months passed and were proud of their little houses and the rickety furniture they'd scraped together. One became a father and talked with a gentle smile about his infant son who was the light of his life now, it seemed.

Jack wished them well, of course he did, but it only gave rise to another dream he couldn't see himself achieving: to have a quiet little cottage of his own and a wife to share it. And though she wasn't old enough yet to wed anyone, he even knew the lass he fancied. Emmy Carter, of course. Her pretty face invaded his dreams regularly and he admired her as well as fancied her. Look how well she cared for that nice old lady she worked for, how trim and neat she kept herself, and how she'd risen above her mother's immorality. As he'd tried to rise above the disgrace his father and brother had brought to the family.

But Emmy told him one day she was never going to marry. 'I'd never bring my mother's shame to any man.'

'It's her shame, not yours,' he insisted. She just smiled sadly and said that made no difference to most folk.

'Well, we Staleys have been shamed, too,' he offered.

She gave a sad attempt at a smile. 'It's not the same. They think I'm like my mother, and if a woman isn't considered respectable they treat her whole family badly.'

'You don't deserve that.'

She shrugged. 'Well, I've got no choice, so I'm determined not to marry.' Then she brightened. 'But Mrs Tibby has hired me for another year. Isn't that wonderful? I love working for her.'

His mother found out he'd been talking to Emmy and reminded him shrilly of his promise to look after her and the others.

'I've no plans to go courting, Mam. Emmy's just a friend.'

Netta laughed harshly. 'There's no such thing as a lass who's "just a friend". Especially one with a mother like yon. She's after you, that one is.'

'She's not like her mother!' he shouted back, furious to hear Emmy maligned. The accusation made him so angry he walked out of the house, ignoring his mother's shrieks at him to come back.

He didn't need her reminders. However hard he thought about it – and he'd racked his brains many a time – he could only come to one conclusion: he could not afford to marry until he was much older, if then. Imagine bringing other mouths into the world to feed when he still had his mother, brothers and little sister Ginny dependent on him.

One day Meg came home and announced defiantly that she was walking out with a fellow and intended to get married soon. As his mother burst into one of her storms of weeping, Jack sent the younger kids outside, then begged Meg not to rush into anything.

She stood by the door, arms folded, with a defiant look on

her face. 'You won't change my mind whatever you say, Jack. I want a home of my own, away from *her*.'

'Have you thought about what your leaving will do to the rest of us? How shall we manage without your wages?'

'That's your business. You've had most of them ever since Dad died, so I reckon I've done my share now.'

'Who is he?' Jack tried to think who he'd seen her with.

'Ben Pearson.'

'What? You can't mean that! He's a drunkard.'

'Not now he isn't. I've told him if he wants to marry me, he has to drink less and he is doing.'

'But he's years older than you!'

Meg smiled and her voice softened as she said quietly, 'He's mad for me and I like him better than the younger lads. An' it'll be a relief to get away.'

Their mother emerged from her handkerchief to say, 'He's just soft-talking you. It'll not last once you're married. He'll booze all your money away.'

'It will last! Ben loves me and I love him.'

Jack looked at his sister. She was, after all, barely seventeen. 'Well, there's no reason for you to rush into marriage yet, is there?'

'Yes, there is.' Meg looked around scornfully. 'Ben's looking for a job in a place where there's more going on than in this stupid town. An' if you get short of money, our Ginny can allus leave school and find hersen a job. You're spoiling her, Jack, with all that education. What good will fancy sewing and reading do her?' Her voice softened. 'It's you as should be getting the schooling, not us. You're the clever one in this family.'

'I have my books. I haven't stopped learning.' For Mr Bradley lent him books and newspapers regularly and he even owned four books of his own now, as well as a Bible. But it was very difficult to read quietly in the crowded little house, with his mother wanting to talk about how the day had gone, and his brothers and sisters quarrelling, laughing or just being exuberant and full of youthful energy.

'You should be finding yoursen a lass an' getting wed, our

Jack,' said Meg, unrepentant. She turned to her mother. 'You're not being fair to him. *You* could be walking out with Phil Gritten if you wanted. Now his wife's dead he's looking for another. And since he's not got any childer, he'd be a father to yours. He's a really nice fellow, Phil is, but no, you wouldn't even see him when he came to call.'

'Meg!' Jack said warningly.

She scowled at him. 'Why do you let her do this to you?'

'Because it's my duty and anyway I promised her.' And because the children would have an unhappy time of it without him.

Netta emerged from her handkerchief again to hurl at her daughter, 'I'm not wedding anyone else because I'm loyal to the memory of your father. An' I don't need to *force* Jack to stay with us, he wants to.'

'Well, more fool him. An' Dad wasn't loyal to *us*, was he, when he went and got hissen killed doing something like that?'

Which frank talking soured the atmosphere in the little house for days.

In the end Meg arranged to get married one Saturday after work. Her mother refused to attend the wedding, but Jack took the children along to watch his sister make her vows. Meg's expression was softer than usual and she looked almost pretty, while Ben had a fond look on his face.

Afterwards Meg came home for her few possessions and went to live in one room with her new husband. Within a few weeks Ben had found another job and they'd moved away to Rochdale.

'You can come and see us any time,' Meg told Jack before she left. 'It'd do you good to get away from here. But don't bring Mam. She hasn't a civil word for Ben an' she'll drive him back to the drink if she goes on at him like she did last time she saw him.'

'You'll let us know your address?'

' 'Course I will.'

But although a carter brought a badly spelled note from Meg

saying she and Ben were fine and giving their address, that was all they heard for some time.

Jack missed her greatly. She was the closest to him in age now and in spite of her sharp tongue he loved her and knew her worth. He kept his feelings to himself, though, because his mother still hadn't a good word to say for her elder daughter.

On Christmas Day Jack could bear it no longer and went for a walk on the moors in all the glory of a bright frosty day, in spite of his mother's shrill protests that she needed a bit of company. The beauty out there moved him so much he found himself sobbing for no reason, unable to stop until some of the grief and frustration had poured out of him.

But he didn't tell anyone about that, of course. Not even Emmy Carter, the only one now to whom he could talk about his problems.

Chapter Five

1828–9

In May 1828 old Ebenezer Rishmore dropped dead in the mill he'd created from a few handlooms and which was far more important to him than his family. One minute he was standing in the weaving shed berating a young woman who had dared leave her loom to answer a call of nature, the next he was clutching his chest. With a long groan he sank to his knees and fell sprawling at her feet.

She let out a piercing scream that could be heard even above the noise of the machinery and edged away from him, calling for help.

People rushed towards her, but Martin Graslow got there first and gave her a good shake. 'Be quiet, you fool, and tell me what happened!' He knelt beside the still figure, but could find no sign of life. After a moment he sat back on his heels and looked up in shock. 'He's dead. Go and fetch Mr Samuel, quick! Don't say the old man was shouting at you, just that he'd stopped to talk to you. No use stirring up trouble if you don't need to.'

She nodded and rushed off across the mill yard to fling open the door of the office and yell dramatically, 'Come quickly. Mr Rishmore's just dropped dead.'

Isaac and Samuel went pounding across the yard, with her panting along behind them because now she had got over the initial shock, she didn't wish to miss any of the excitement.

When Samuel looked down at his father he could see at once that the old man really had passed away. Strange how quickly a body lost its humanity. He bent his head for a moment in prayer for his father's soul, then turned to the overlooker, his voice rough with emotion. 'Have his body carried through to the office, please, Martin.'

Isaac, who had known Samuel Rishmore since they were both lads, laid one hand on the new master's shoulder and gave it a squeeze.

Samuel gave him a flicker of a smile, appreciating the gesture which no other worker in the mill would have dared make, then walked slowly back to the office, trying to come to terms with what had just happened with such brutal finality.

As the day passed half of him continued to do what was expected, expressing sorrow, sending word home to his wife who had kept house for them all since his mother's death. But behind the solemn façade of grieving only son, the other half of him relished the position in which he now found himself. He and his father had been disagreeing about the future of the mill for some time and suddenly it had been given over into his hands. He did not intend to 'mollycoddle the operatives' as his father had contemptuously said about some of his suggestions, but he did believe it was his duty as a Christian gentleman to treat them humanely – those who behaved themselves, that was. There were certain employees whose private lives were a scandal and who would be given one warning now, especially those living openly in sin, to remedy matters or lose their jobs.

Kneeling by his bed that night, he prayed long and hard that he would always know his duty, but as he climbed into bed, his elevated mood slipped and his thoughts turned to his daughter's marriage. They would have to put that off for a year at least. He had been seriously considering young Marcus Armistead, the son of his closest business colleague. However, Jane could not marry while in mourning for her grandfather.

Anyway, he and Claude Armistead had not yet got down to the hard bargaining – or informed the young people of what was planned – so it could wait. For the moment the mill would take priority over everything else as Samuel reorganised things to his own liking.

He fell asleep with a smile on his face.

Rishmore's mill was closed on the afternoon of the funeral and all the operatives were provided with a black armband and ordered to walk to the churchyard behind the coffin as a sign of respect. And if they enjoyed the rare chance of an outing during the daytime, they were not stupid enough to let that show in their faces. After the funeral service they were to walk back to the mill, where food and mugs of strong tea would be provided for them.

'Th'owd man would have a fit if he knew about all this fuss,' Martin Graslow said to his friend Isaac Butterfield, who had been invited to ride to the funeral in one of the carriages and then partake of more stylish refreshments at the big house. 'He didn't believe in pampering his operatives or letting owt stop them machines from running till knocking-off time, old Rishmore didn't.'

Only with Martin could Isaac be frank. 'Mr Samuel – no, we must learn to call him Mr Rishmore now that he's the master, must we not? – takes a certain pride in being a compassionate employer.'

Martin grinned. 'Well, good luck to him, I say. Why should poor folk be ill treated by them as they toil for? It'll be nice to have an easy afternoon, won't it, and they've not stinted on the food.' Almost as an afterthought he added, 'How's your Lena taking the invitation to the big house?'

Isaac rolled his eyes. 'Hasn't stopped fussing since she heard. Driving us all mad about what she should wear. But I'm not going to buy her a new outfit just for the funeral, let alone there isn't time to get one made up, so she's had to be content with wearing her grey and trimming her bonnet with new black ribbons.' And the fashionable mass of ribbon loops was not at all flattering to his wife's broad features, though he hadn't said anything about that, since she was mightily pleased with her efforts and in a good humour for once.

*   *   *

85

The funeral passed without incident, a dignified occasion with the coffin carried to the church on a dray from the mill. This had been covered in black cloth, with flowers and greenery piled around it, and black ribbons tied in the manes and harness of the horses. Professional mutes had been hired from Manchester to show that an important man had passed away, and caused a great buzz of comment when they appeared carrying their banners and wearing wide black sashes over their overcoats, with 'weepers' of black cloth trailing from their top hats. All agreed that it was the grandest funeral anyone had ever seen.

After the interment the guests were driven to Mill House where they were provided with lavish refreshments, which they consumed as avidly as the mill operatives were consuming their bread and ham and plum cake a few hundred yards down the hill.

Before Isaac left, Samuel introduced him to a young man who had been standing by the window looking bored. 'This is my cousin's youngest: Alfred Rishmore. I'm bringing him into the mill since I've only a daughter to follow in my footsteps. I'll be putting him in the office first, where he can learn how things are run. I rely on you to show him the ropes, Isaac lad.'

He slapped the young man on the shoulder and Alfred produced a sickly grin, nodding to Isaac in a condescending way.

Samuel nodded dismissal then turned to say in a low voice to his head clerk, 'Only last week my father asked for Alfred to be given a chance so I feel I have to heed his last wishes, especially since old Walker needs pensioning off with his eyesight so bad. But if the lad doesn't do his work properly, then he's out, relative or not. I'll employ no drones in my mill.' He smiled suddenly. 'I remember how you helped me learn about the office work. I think you must have been born sensible, while I was a bit restless in those days. That's why my father made me marry early. He thought it'd settle me down. I've never forgotten how you used to make up errands to rid me of some of my energy. Nor do I forget how loyally you've served our family all these years.'

Isaac escorted his wife home feeling a glow of intense

satisfaction. Samuel Rishmore did not offer gratuitous compliments. His father had never offered any.

Isaac found it hard going with Alfred Rishmore. Apart from the fact that the young man looked down his nose at the head clerk, he wrote a poor hand, did not take nearly enough care with transcribing figures into the account books and ledgers, and worked very slowly indeed. No matter how many times he was rebuked, he showed no signs of improvement, heaving sighs as he worked, fiddling with his quill or just sitting staring into space. He was, quite clearly, reluctant to be there at all.

When the paperwork began to fall behind, something which had never happened before, Isaac tried to decide what to do. Should he tell Samuel or not? No, he'd give Alfred a little more time to settle down. After all, it was hard for a young man to be shut up in an office all day.

Then one day he realised that his new assistant clerk had been drinking beer during the hour he had taken for luncheon instead of the half-hour he was officially permitted. Shocked to the core, Isaac went in to see his employer at the end of the day. 'Sir, I'm afraid that young man will not do.'

Samuel listened in silence to the recital, asked one or two questions then nodded agreement. 'I feared as much. His father was a ne'er-do-well and I've noticed the lad wool-gathering several times myself. Send him in to see me as soon as he arrives tomorrow morning and I'll deal with the matter.' He frowned and stared into the flames of the cosy coal fire that warmed his office, then said abruptly, 'We'll have to find someone else to help you.'

'Sir—' Isaac hesitated.

'Spit it out, man. You need never fear to speak openly to me.'

'Well, if you're going to involve me in expanding the business as you've indicated, I shall need two people to help me: a clerk and someone able to undertake a variety of tasks. I have a clerk in mind, actually, a man I've met once or twice who would like to move back to Northby to be near his elderly parents. But for the other position, I feel we need someone who knows the work of the mill and is not too finicky to dirty his hands.' He hesitated again.

'You have someone in mind for that as well?'

'Yes, sir. Jack Staley.'

Samuel raised his eyebrows. 'Big Jem's son? Are you sure?'

'Yes, sir. The lad's always been sensible and since his father's death he has been the support of his mother who is a weak reed, I'm afraid.' To Isaac there was nothing more important than work, family and church, in that order.

Samuel nodded thoughtfully. 'Bradley speaks very highly of the lad, too, and now employs him to help out with the young men's Sunday reading class. We need a literate workforce in this new era, Isaac.'

'Yes, sir. I am well aware of that.'

'Jack Staley doesn't look like a clerk, though. He's a muscular young fellow, big built like his father. And he certainly doesn't dress like a clerk.'

'No, sir. But there are going to be confidential messages to be sent to your new colleagues in Manchester, as you know because we can't always wait for the mail to come and go. Also messages need to be taken quickly sometimes to Mr Armistead at Moor Grange or payments to our suppliers. I'm sure we could entrust those to Jack and perhaps have him taught to ride a horse or drive a trap. But if we did decide to give him a trial, I fear we'd have to help him acquire some more suitable garments, given the circumstances of the family. I thought we might also offer him a small rise in wages?'

'Hire your clerk, then, and we'll give Jack Staley a month's trial on the same wages as now – if it doesn't work out, he can keep the new clothes. If it does, he can have his rise as well. But if you have any doubts, any doubts at all . . .'

'I shall send him back to the weaving shed, sir.'

Jack was summoned to the mill office the following afternoon and found only Mr Butterfield there, with no sign of the languid young gentleman whose airs and graces had been amusing the operatives for the past few weeks.

'Ah, Staley.' Isaac Butterfield stared at him over the top of his pince-nez. 'Come into my office and close the door behind you.' He waved Jack to a seat, then explained, 'Young Mr Alfred has had to leave us and we need two more people for the office. We are considering you for one position.'

'Me? But I'm not a clerk, sir!'

'You can read and write a legible hand, I gather. Indeed Mr Bradley and Mr Graslow both speak very highly of your intelligence.'

Jack thought of the big office with its shelves of ledgers, its mahogany pigeon holes full of papers and the high sloping desks, each with its tall wooden stool. The thought of being shut up in it every day did not please him, though at least it would be quieter than the weaving shed. 'I – don't know what to say, sir.'

Mr Butterfield gave him an understanding smile. 'If you're thinking that you don't wish to be penned up in here day after day, I should tell you that there will be important messages to be taken to various persons in the town, *highly confidential* messages which we would not entrust to just anyone. And as you grow more used to the work, you will be sent on similar errands into Manchester. You would need to learn to drive a trap to reach some places, but the stage coaches are very reliable nowadays for going into Manchester.' He saw Jack's face brighten a little and added, 'Mr Rishmore is having dealings with some Manchester merchants, you see, though you will not discuss that fact with anyone else.'

Jack stared at him in amazement. 'How did you know I felt like that about being shut up indoors?'

'I've noticed you sometimes at the end of the day staring up longingly at the sun as you leave the mill. It would be surprising if someone of your age – what are you, eighteen, nineteen? – wanted to spend every day crouched over a desk. You will have other duties in the mill as well. For instance, you can take over the task of checking the operatives in and out every morning, and ordering supplies according to the needs of the various sections. But I will not disguise the fact that there will necessarily

89

be many hours devoted to doing the accounts and copying correspondence, and I shall expect that work to be done meticulously.'

When Jack still didn't speak, Isaac prompted, 'Mr Rishmore is prepared to give you a month's trial. If you prove satisfactory it will also mean a rise in your wages. I know your family will welcome the extra money. Have you heard from your sister lately?'

Was there nothing Mr Butterfield did not know about him? 'No, sir. I'm worried about her.' But maybe with the extra money he'd be able to hire a trap and go across to Rochdale to look for her. She had promised to keep in touch. Something must be wrong.

'Then you will accept the position? Good.'

'I'll do my best to give satisfaction. Only –' Jack looked down at himself and then at his superior '– I don't think I have the right sort of clothes to work in here.'

'No. We shall sort that out later in the morning. I believe Mr Roper deals in second-hand clothing and I'm sure we'll find you something suitable in his stock. And, since there is no time like the present, perhaps you would go and tell Mr Graslow that you will be working for me from now on? He knew I was to make this offer to you.'

As Isaac watched the young fellow stride across the mill yard, he could not help thinking that if he had had a son he would have wanted one like this: sturdy, loyal and with an innate honesty that shone out of his face. That made him wonder if Jack might not be a good match for Lal – if he did well in this new job, that was. It wasn't going to be easy to find his elder daughter a husband, but money could be a wonderful inducement and she would have a generous dowry. But first he would see how Jack dealt with this opportunity for advancement.

Thinking of family reminded him of his sister. He'd caught occasional glimpses of her and poor Madge had aged more than he'd have expected. Martin said she rarely left the inn during daylight now. Her daughter was apparently working as a maid and sounded to be a decent young lass, which was one mercy. Ignoring his sister's presence in town had been the right thing to do, even though his wife still worried that someone might find out about the relationship and shun them because of it. He sighed at the thought of his wife. Lena's temper was growing increasingly uncertain, making life at home difficult.

He realised he had been sitting staring into space and shook his head in annoyance at himself. He was being paid to manage Mr Rishmore's office not sit and worry about his own affairs.

To his surprise Jack found his new work in the office far more congenial than the noisy weaving shed. There was more variety in his days than he had expected and he enjoyed learning to drive a trap, taught by Mr Rishmore's coachman. But there was a lot of writing to do and that was not nearly as enjoyable. The ink soon stained his fingertips blue, however much he scrubbed them.

And although he went across to Rochdale twice, hiring a trap from the livery stables to do so after work on Saturdays, he could get no word of his sister which added another anxiety to his life.

His mother said Meg had made her bed and now must lie on it, but Jack could not help feeling that something must be wrong for her not even to send them a message.

Emmy had never been so happy. Mrs Tibby was more like a favourite aunt or grandmother than a mistress dealing with her maid, and the girl could not help realising how lonely the poor old lady had been and how much she still missed her beloved husband. They rarely saw Emmy's mother nowadays, and when they did Emmy noticed that she had grown very thin, with a bitter twist to her mouth that had not been there before.

Mrs Tibby herself remained frail, often taking to her couch by mid-afternoon. As soon as she had learned enough about housekeeping, Emmy did nearly all the physical work. She might be small, but she had felt strong and healthy ever since coming to work for her dear mistress who saw that she ate well and regularly.

However, with the good food and happy life, Emmy began to grow. She did not become much taller, but there was no hiding the fact that she now had a woman's shape. That worried her a lot because sometimes she saw George Duckworth in the street and, although he never approached her, he would stop and study her thoughtfully. Those encounters made her shiver.

When Mrs Tibby found out how poorly her new maid could read and write, she began teaching her. They would spend time on this together most afternoons and gradually Emmy grew skilled enough to read her mistress's favourite novels aloud, because the latter's eyes were not good, even when she used her late husband's spectacles to magnify the print.

Tibby also tried to teach the girl as much as she could about arithmetic because dear James had been a firm believer in universal literacy. 'The Three Rs, my girl,' he used to say, 'they're what lift folk out of poverty. Not just reading, but being able to manage the pennies.' She was not gifted at arithmetic herself and, although she made heroic efforts to keep her household accounts, rarely got her columns of figures to balance and agonised over them in secret.

As the first months of 1829 passed, Emmy could tell that her mistress was worrying about something and in the end insisted on an explanation. It must be to do with money because it was several weeks since she'd been paid any wages and she had even used some of her own small savings during the past week or two when there was not enough money to meet their simple needs.

After weeping softly into her handkerchief Mrs Tibby at last explained what the trouble was. 'My family, the Armisteads, are quite well off but when I insisted on marrying my dear James, who was an employee of my father's, they disowned me. Not that I ever regretted marrying him, but it's hard to lose your family. I've never heard from my brother Claude since. Only my younger brother William ever spoke to me again and when he died, he left me a small income.' She stopped to mop her eyes again. 'That two guineas a month is all I have now, for my dear James was cheated out of his money by a man we had thought our friend. I – I have managed for a while, but my savings are quite used up now.'

She stared down at her damp handkerchief then looked at Emmy with brimming eyes. 'Two guineas is not enough to live on, not with the rent to pay, though I try hard to manage. Lately I've had to sell a few things. It's very embarrassing to visit the pawnbroker and – and I do miss my things, but one has to eat.'

'You shouldn't have taken me on!' Emmy was horrified. 'It's my wages that do it.'

'Dear child, employing you was the best thing I could have done. I think I should be dead by now without your help and company.' Another tear rolled down Tibby's wrinkled cheek as she added, 'Today I feel rather poorly so I'd welcome your arm up the lane. We must have some more money and I can't collect my allowance from the bank for two more weeks, you see.'

'Where are we going?'

With a blush Tibby replied, 'Mr Roper's pawnshop. And – will you put this in the shopping basket, if you please?'

Emmy did not comment as she put the small bundle wrapped in a piece of linen into the basket. But they made slow progress up Weavers Lane because her mistress kept stopping to sigh and rest for 'just a minute'. Northby's shops and one small bank were clustered together where the street widened before it divided to pass on either side of the church. The area was big enough to hold the weekly market but not grand enough to be called a square, so folk just called it Market Place. At this hour on a Tuesday the street was almost deserted, which was what Mrs Tibby had hoped for.

Roper's pawnshop was located just before Market Place in a little alley which ran off Weavers Lane to the left. As they were about to turn into it they saw a lady coming towards them whom Mrs Tibby knew from church. She clutched Emmy's arm tightly and hissed, 'Walk on past! She mustn't know.'

After she had exchanged greetings with the lady Mrs Tibby said faintly, 'We'll go and look in the window of the draper's, shall we?' Only when Mrs Renford was out of sight did she give a shuddering sigh. 'I think we may return now.'

They retraced their footsteps and, after another quick glance round to make sure no one else was approaching, slipped along the alley and into the shop.

In Manchester her mother had sometimes sent her to pawn-shops, but Emmy had never been inside this one before. It smelled the same as the others, of sweaty old clothes, dust and mouse droppings, and she wrinkled her nose in disgust.

Mr Roper appeared through the curtain-hung doorway behind the counter and stood waiting for them, arms folded.

He might have offered her mistress a civil greeting, Emmy thought indignantly. It was as if he was showing scorn by this rudeness and the poor lady didn't deserve that.

After much fumbling in the basket with hands that shook visibly Mrs Tibby produced her pretty silver salt cellar and asked in a wobbly voice, 'How much can you give me for this, Mr Roper?'

'Ten shillings,' he said after a cursory glance. 'There's not much call for such things in Northby. And it isn't very good quality silver, either.'

Mrs Tibby picked it up again, giving it a loving caress with her fingertips as she did so. 'Oh, dear, I had hoped for more than that. I know it cost my dear husband a great deal.' When Mr Roper did not move or speak, she sighed and said, 'Very well, then,' in a breathless voice before pushing it towards him.

Emmy had seen the prices given on many such objects in pawnshops and felt sure the man was trying to cheat her mistress. Somehow she could not bear that to happen to her gentle, kindly lady and anger gave her the courage to intervene. 'That's not a fair price, Mrs Tibby.' She picked up the salt cellar from the counter.

Her mistress looked at her in dismay. 'Is it not?'

'No. This is solid silver and it's very pretty. I'm sure it's worth far more than ten shillings so I think we should take it else-where.'

Mr Roper gave a sneering, braying laugh. 'There's nowhere else in Northby *to* take it, young woman, and this is between your mistress and me, so keep your nose out.' He turned to scowl at the older woman. 'See here, missus, if you go away and then come back wasting my time when I've made my offer, it'll be only nine shillings you'll get for it.'

Mrs Tibby could not hold back a squeak of dismay but

Emmy was made of stronger stuff. 'Then I shall have to ride into Rochdale on the carrier's cart to see what I can get there, shan't I?' she said, eyes challenging his. 'Come along, ma'am. You're looking tired. Let's go home now.' She had never been to Rochdale, didn't even knew whether there was a pawnshop there, but her bluff worked.

'You cheeky young madam! How can you know what's fair or not?' Mr Roper reached out to try and snatch the salt cellar back. When Emmy lifted it out of reach he snapped, 'Twelve shillings then, out of the goodness of my heart.'

That made Emmy certain she had been right about the object's value, so she repeated firmly, 'Come along, Mrs Tibby dear!' and guided the old lady outside.

'Fifteen shillings and that's my final offer!' he shouted after them from the shop doorway.

'Don't you think we should accept?' Mrs Tibby whispered.

'No, I don't! I'm sure it's worth much more than that.'

There were tears in Mrs Tibby's eyes as she whispered, 'But how are we to buy food? I – I don't have any money left, Emmy.'

'I'll go into Rochdale if necessary from now on and pawn your things for you there. The carter will give me a ride for sixpence. And I still have some housekeeping money left for us to be going on with.'

They walked in silence for a while and Mrs Tibby sighed in relief as they reached the cottage. When they got inside she looked at Emmy and asked in a low voice, 'Do you really think he's been cheating me? I was going to take him two of my silver apostle spoons next.'

'Spoons?' Emmy couldn't remember seeing any apostle spoons.

'I have a whole set of them hidden in the attic and a few other things too,' Tibby whispered, fanning herself with her hand. 'Oh, dear. This is all so distressing.'

She subsided on the sofa and began fiddling with her cuff, so Emmy knew she still wanted to talk and waited patiently with her mistress's cloak over her arm.

'I usually take the first price Mr Roper offers because I'm so ashamed of having to visit a place like that.' Mrs Tibby sobbed suddenly and put a hand up to her mouth, as if to hold more tears back.

Emmy went across to pat her mistress's arm and crouch beside her, still trying to work out the logic of this other plan. 'But surely your spoons would be worth more as a whole set?' she asked gently.

'I was trying to keep one or two, just to remind me of my dear James, who bought them for me in better times. They have such dainty little figures on the ends. Oh, my goodness. I'm feeling quite poorly and now my heart is fluttering.' She pressed one hand to her breast.

'We shouldn't have gone out today, Mrs Tibby. You sit there and rest while I make you a pot of tea.'

'Only if you'll share it with me.' She looked at Emmy, shame still showing on her face. 'I'm sorry, dear. So stupid. I do hate dealing with that man. But what else am I to do? I couldn't possibly manage without you now. And besides,' she smiled and squeezed the girl's hand, 'I've grown very fond of you.'

'And I you,' Emmy said, delighted to see her mistress's face looking happy again. 'Now, let me bring you some tea and I'll think what to do. You leave it all to me.'

That night Emmy lay awake for a long time worrying about how she could help Mrs Tibby. In the end she could only think of Garrett's Bank. They visited it every month to collect the allowance and Mr Garrett dealt with Mrs Tibby personally because he had apparently been slightly acquainted with her husband. He had a kind face and was always polite. Surely he would advise Emmy how best to sell the silver for her mistress? She would go and see him the very next day.

The following day she duly took the silver salt cellar into town. Outside the bank she paused for a moment, feeling nervous. She decided to wait for a gentleman who was inside to come out, but as she stood there she felt as though the bank itself was keeping watch on her through the bull's eye glass in its many-paned bow window.

When at last the customer left, Emmy took a deep breath,

pushed open the door and walked inside, trying to behave as if she had every right to be there. As she had expected, the teller stared down his nose at her but she walked to the counter with her head held high. 'I have a message from my mistress for Mr Garrett. She's not well, you see.' She waved a folded piece of paper at him.

'I can take that for you, young woman. You may wait over there for the reply.'

'I'm sorry, sir, but she made me promise to give the letter into his hands personally.' Emmy held on to the paper tightly until he muttered something, pulled his pince-nez off his nose and vanished through a door at the rear.

John Garrett was in a good mood that day because his conservative approach to banking was paying off and he was not experiencing the same problems as some of the other small banks in the neighbourhood, so he agreed to see Mrs Oswald's maid. When she came in he did not ask her to sit. 'I believe you have a letter for me from your mistress?'

Emmy swallowed hard. 'I'm afraid there is no letter, sir. I wanted to speak to you – to ask you to help my mistress – and this was the only way I could think of to do it. I'm very sorry for having lied to your teller, but please don't send me away without hearing what I have to say!'

When he frowned, she rushed into her prepared speech. 'Mrs Oswald has fallen on hard times and I don't know where to turn for help for her. *Please*, sir!'

He waved a hand, which she took to mean she should continue. 'Mrs Oswald has some pieces of silver which she's been selling because she's short of money. They're lying in her attic and I'm terrified someone will steal them and then how will she manage? Mr Roper the pawnbroker has been cheating her, giving her far less than her things are worth. I don't want her to deal with him again.'

Mr Garrett stared at the young maid in amazement. Mrs Oswald was not an important client, though every customer deserved the bank's best attention, of course, but he didn't like to think of such a frail lady being cheated. 'Are you sure of that?'

'Oh, yes, sir. I was with her yesterday when Mr Roper

offered her ten shillings for this.' Emmy produced the salt cellar from the bottom of her shopping basket and set it on the desk. 'I persuaded her to refuse.'

John examined the piece which was very pretty. 'You were right. This is worth a great deal more than he offered.' He frowned. His bank was not a charity and he was not a man of fortune with a rich family behind him but the younger son of a farmer who had done well for himself. His father had started lending money to people in the neighbourhood, and under John's guidance they had set up a small bank. However he had to be careful what he did because if you helped too many people who were in difficulties you could go under yourself if they defaulted on payments. 'What exactly is it you want me to do for her, young woman?'

'Let her keep the silver here at the bank, sir. I didn't know it was in the house – we live at the bottom end of Weavers Lane and it isn't *safe* to keep it there. Mr Roper must wonder what else she has and – well, it would be very easy to rob a poor old lady, wouldn't it?'

John Garrett inclined his head, relieved by the reasonableness of this request. 'We'd be happy to look after it for her.' He saw the girl still hesitating and with a wry smile asked, 'There's something else, isn't there?'

'Yes, sir. Could you please advise my mistress on how best to sell her things? Two guineas a month isn't enough to live on, you see, even though I don't take any wages now I know how short of money she is.'

His fancy was tickled by the courage and loyalty of this young lass who by her speech came from a humble background. Mrs Oswald's silver would probably turn out to be mostly worthless, but it would not hurt to look at it and he could certainly help her sell it to best advantage. In fact, he would also waive his commission on the sales. That much he could do to help. He smiled at the eager young face. 'Mrs Oswald is fortunate in her maid, I think. Ask her to come and see me at four o'clock tomorrow afternoon and we'll take tea together while I advise her. Oh, and bring the silver. All of it.'

★   ★   ★

Mrs Tibby was so surprised by what Emmy had done she could not speak for a minute or two, then grew very agitated. 'Oh, dear! James was always the one who dealt with banks. I shan't know what to say if we're to discuss my finances. And I'm sure Mr Garrett will not want to look after my little bits and pieces.'

'I've already explained to him how matters stand. Please, *dearest* Mrs Tibby, come and see him. We can take all your good silver with us to put in his vault. It really isn't safe to keep it here.'

'Well – you won't leave me alone with him?'

'Not if you don't want me to.'

After much brow-wrinkling and sighing, Mrs Tibby decided that dear James would want her to do this and Emmy breathed a sigh of relief.

The following afternoon Mrs Tibby dressed in her Sunday best, a gown that was worn and old-fashioned but not yet patched. Emmy fetched the silver down from the attic and wrapped it all up in old rags so that it would not chink and betray what it was. The now-unused best cutlery service was heavy and had its own wooden box, and it surprised Emmy how many other bits and pieces there were. She had already arranged with the neighbour's lad, who made coppers here and there by offering his services pushing a small handbarrow, to trundle the things into town for them for sixpence.

'And how about a kiss as well?' he asked Emmy.

She drew herself up. 'Certainly not! Who do you think I am, you cheeky thing?'

'You're the prettiest girl in Weavers Lane, that's who.'

'Well, I don't kiss anyone, so tell me if you want the job or not, and don't you ever talk to me like that again.'

When they arrived at the bank, the teller came out to help Emmy carry the silver inside, while Mrs Tibby gave the lad his sixpence, her last coin and one which Emmy had 'found' on the mantelpiece.

'If you would care to take a seat, ma'am, I'll inform Mr Garrett that you're here,' the teller said, his manner quite different from yesterday. 'He is expecting you.'

Emmy went to stand behind her mistress, whispering, 'See. I told you.'

When the teller came back to ask Mrs Oswald to follow him, she took Emmy's arm and insisted her maid come too. She was faint and quivery, seeming overwhelmed by the situation, and Emmy just hoped Mr Garrett would understand what a timid lady she was outside her own home.

He did. There was no mistaking it when someone's face was white with nervousness or their hand shook in yours. He looked at the maid, saw how she was standing behind her mistress with one hand unobtrusively on a trembling old shoulder, and thought again how lucky Mrs Oswald was to have her.

He had intended to conduct their business, such as it was, rapidly but politely. Instead he found himself saying, 'Perhaps you'd like your maid to stay?' When he received a nod, he went on, 'Now, my dear Mrs Oswald, let us see how best to help you. That's what banks are for, you know, to look after our customers' financial interests. Indeed, you should have come to me for help sooner.'

She shed some tears and thanked him with a voice so muffled by her handkerchief that only a few words escaped, among them, 'So kind . . . no wish to be troublesome . . . dear husband always . . .'

But John Garrett became his usual shrewd self when he examined the pieces of silver. 'These are very fine. Not large, but well-crafted pieces. Your husband had excellent taste.'

Mrs Oswald cast a quick relieved glance over her shoulder at Emmy then nodded. 'Dear James was very fond of a fine piece of silver. He said they were pleasures as well as investments.'

In the end it was decided that Mr Garrett would lend her some money, using the silver as surety while he sold some or all of it. 'You must take your time to decide what you wish to keep and what you wish to sell, my dear lady. Afterwards, we'll deposit the rest of your money in a savings account for you. That way you will gain interest on your principal, so it will last you longer.'

She nodded, but Emmy could see that her mistress did not really understand what he was talking about beyond knowing she would have some money again. Well, Emmy didn't under-stand either. She asked him to explain about interest: '—so that my dear mistress can be sure she's understood you correctly.'

Their eyes met and he smiled in a way that said he realised who needed to understand everything. As he explained how banks paid interest on deposits, his attention was mainly on the girl. When she'd nodded to show she understood, he turned back to her mistress. 'I'll send you a letter once I know how much your possessions are worth, Mrs Oswald, but in the meantime,' he pressed an envelope into her hand, 'this is an advance payment on account.'

Emmy heard it chink and guessed it contained coins. She could not help beaming at him for his tact and understanding, and was surprised when he winked at her.

After they'd left, John Garrett sat pondering Mrs Oswald's problems. He knew she was related to the Armisteads and after some thought decided to write to the family to ask if they were aware of the extreme hardship their elderly relative was experi-encing.

However, when he went home that night he found his wife seriously ill of an inflammation of the lungs. For weeks her life was feared for and he completely forgot about Mrs Oswald's problems.

In November of that year the Staleys were settling down to their evening meal, the children whispering to one another as their mother dished up the food. Jack watched them fondly, plea-santly tired after a day spent mostly out of the office. Thinking he heard a faint sound he looked round. No, he must have been mistaken.

Then it came again, someone at the door. It'd be a neigh-bour wanting to borrow something. A lot of that went on in the middle of the week.

When he opened the door he found a woman there, clutching a baby, a big bundle at her feet. He didn't recognise her at first. Then she lifted up her eyes and said, 'Jack!' in a faint, wheezing voice and crumpled at his feet.

He managed to prevent the baby from falling, but didn't manage to catch the woman as well.

'Mam, come here!' he roared at the top of his voice.

There was dead silence behind him, then a clatter of footsteps as the whole family came running out to see what was making their Jack yell like that, something he rarely did.

He shoved the baby into the arms of the first one to arrive. 'Look after it!' Then he bent to pick up his sister. 'Bring her things in, Shad!' As he carried Meg into the house, he could not believe how light she was. She was as pale as a corpse, even her lips seeming colourless. He laid her down on the rug in front of the fire, tears coming into his eyes to see what a terrible state she was in. Her clothes were ragged and dun-coloured, her legs bare of stockings and so blue-white she must be chilled through. The leather soles of her ill-fitting shoes had worn through in places and were soaked, while the tops were held together by frayed string. She had left Northby properly clad and shod, married to a man able to earn a decent living if he stayed off the ale. What had happened to her? Had Ben Pearson caused this by going back on the drink? Because if so, he'd have Jack to answer to.

He reached out to smooth a lock of damp hair from Meg's clammy forehead. She did not stir and her breathing was so shallow it barely lifted her chest. 'Eh, she's in a bad way. Someone fetch me a blanket, quick!' He heard the faint gasping cry of a sickly baby from behind him. 'Can you tend to the babby, Mam? It sounds hungry.'

She nodded. 'It's nobbut a few months old, but I can try it with some warm milk. I doubt she'll have any, the state she's in.'

Jack wrapped his sister up in the blanket, then sat with her on the rug, holding her in his arms as if he could transfer his own warmth and energy into her. He watched with relief as her cheeks took on a faint pinkish tinge from the heat of the fire and at last her eyelids fluttered open. She looked up at him, whispered his name then closed her eyes again. Tears trickled out of them.

'Man's getting the babby some milk, Meg,' he said gently. 'What's it called?'

'Nelly.'

'How long is it since you've eaten?'

'Can't – remember.'

'Well, you just lie here in the warm and we'll get you some of Mam's good broth. You can tell us what's happened later, when you're feeling better.'

His mother beckoned Ginny across. 'You hold the baby while I'll get the milk and broth ready.'

Meg nestled her head against Jack's chest and began to speak in a faint voice. 'I thought I'd never get here. I walked over the tops from Rochdale. No one would stop to give me a ride.' She sobbed suddenly. 'He's dead, you know. My Ben's dead. Fell off a cart and hit his head. When they brought his body home, I thought I was going to die too. The baby was only two weeks old then. I tried to find work, but no one would take me on for more than an odd job here and there, and it was hard to look after Nelly properly. The Relief gave me some money at first to tide me over, then the man said I had to go in the poorhouse but I wouldn't. Not till I'd seen you, asked you to help me. They take your babies away from you in that place and she's all I've got now.'

'Nay, why should you go into the poorhouse when you've allus got a home with us?'

She looked up at him and gave a long, shuddering sigh. 'What would we do without you, Jack? You're the best brother in the whole world.'

He had to swallow hard or he'd have been weeping with her.

His mother knelt beside him with a bowl of broth containing small pieces of bread. 'You hold her up, Jack, an' I'll spoon some food in.' As her daughter's eyes closed again, she shook the thin shoulder. 'Stay awake, Meg. You'll not get better if we don't get summat down you.' After a few spoonfuls she looked across at Ginny, who was feeding the child, and said, 'Your babby's supping its milk. Were you still feeding it yoursen?'

'No. My milk dried up.'

As Netta glanced back towards the baby, she frowned. Nelly was not taking her food with any great enthusiasm and she had a frail air to her. 'How old is she, then?'

'Five months.'

Netta didn't say it, but Nelly was so small she was amazed to hear she was that old.

It wasn't for a few days, until his sister's fever had subsided and the baby had picked up a bit, that Jack realised he had yet another burden to carry now. But he could never have turned Meg away.

Chapter Six

One day in December John Garrett was looking out of the window of the bank, feeling pleased that his wife was now well again, when he caught sight of Mrs Oswald in the street. She was leaning heavily on her young maid's arm and walking slowly and awkwardly, as if her hip pained her. Guilt flooded through him. He had not written to the Armisteads about their elderly relative and had done nothing about the rest of the silver, either. He must have it valued. Though maybe that would not matter so much if the Armisteads could be persuaded to do their duty.

He went straight back to his office and composed a suitable letter, sending it off within the hour by messenger since the Armisteads lived only an hour's drive away. Then he settled to work with all the satisfaction of a man who had done his best to help someone weaker than himself.

The Armistead family usually took luncheon together at Moor Grange when they were all home, as they were today. Claude was not in the best of humours, having just spent some time talking seriously with his son. He looked across at Marcus with a frown as they sat down. He found his only child both an exasperation and a disappointment, for although the family was rich enough that Marcus need not work for a living, Claude did not like to see a young man living in idleness or – which was more likely with his son – getting into mischief with women, since he seemed hell-bent on proving that his small stature did not imply a lack of virility.

But Marcus had not settled well into the family business, wanting to take wild gambles by sending dubious merchandise to the colonies – something Claude did not approve of. He had built his own reputation as a prosperous Manchester merchant on sound goods and practices, enjoying the challenge of finding markets for Lancashire goods around the world and making his profit by acting as a middleman.

The maid brought in a note just as they were finishing the meal and he stared at it in surprise, for his correspondence usually went to his business chambers in Manchester. Who would be having notes hand delivered to a house in such an isolated situation on the edge of the moors? He used his butter knife to open it, read it once, then a second time more slowly.

'Did you realise my sister Matilda's husband had lost all his money before he got himself murdered?' he demanded of his wife, though there was no reason why Eleanor should know that, any more than he had. They had simply assumed when they heard of James Oswald's death that he would have provided properly for his widow. She certainly hadn't tried to contact them since. He tapped the letter sharply. 'It appears that all she has to live on is a tiny annuity which William set up before he died. This letter is from the bank owner who pays her the money, suggesting we help her. She's penniless, selling her possessions to put bread on the table apparently!'

His son and wife were both staring at him in amazement.

'Why did she not ask us for help?' Eleanor frowned as she licked butter delicately off one plump fingertip. 'Marcus, pray pass me the gooseberry conserve.'

'Perhaps she thought I would follow my father's example and refuse to acknowledge her.'

'And shall you?'

'How can I do that? Think how would it look – an Armistead reduced to paupery! But of all the inconveniences . . . She's still living in Northby – *Northby of all places!* – in some hovel. What are the Rishmores going to think?'

'We've plenty of time to remedy matters before the marriage. They'll be in mourning for the next year.' Eleanor took another large bite of toast.

Marcus grimaced. Jane Rishmore had a face like a horse and was taller than he was. 'I'm only twenty-three. There's surely no hurry for me to marry and . . .' His voice tailed away as his father turned on him a basilisk stare that reminded him suddenly of the last time he'd had to confess to having debts he could not settle.

'Given your behaviour over the past year or two, I would prefer to have you settled,' Claude told him. 'Besides, Rishmore and I have certain joint ventures in mind and there is no way to guarantee loyalty that is half as reliable as a judicious marriage.' He glared at his son, who spent far too much time and energy chasing women – any woman, it seemed, even a reluctant one. No, the sooner Marcus was wed the better. Claude needed a grandson whom he could mould into a strong man capable of running the family concerns efficiently and honestly, something he doubted his son capable of.

Marcus scowled down at his plate, biting back a protest. His parents had definitely decided on Jane Rishmore, then. There was no bearing it! But his father had made it plain he was prepared to behave generously in financial matters only for as long as his son and heir did exactly as he wished in other matters.

Eleanor broke the silence. 'What exactly do you wish to do for your sister, Claude?'

He shrugged. 'We've plenty of room here. She can live in the east wing and need only eat with us when we don't have guests or when the Rishmores come to call.'

'She'll need her own maid.'

He waved one hand dismissively. 'That won't cost much. We'll drive over to Northby tomorrow and bring her back with us. You can both come with me to show the Rishmores how this family cares for its own.'

Emmy woke early and shivered her way quickly into some clothes. She crept downstairs in the dark to get the embers of the kitchen fire burning again with judiciously placed pieces of wood and coal, then swung the kettle over it. Like her mistress she wished they had a proper cooking range so that they could bake and stew food more easily, but they managed.

Mrs Tibby was too frail to lift heavy pans and kettles now, though, and how would she ever manage on her own? But George Duckworth had taken to staring at Emmy with such a gloating air lately that she knew the day was coming when she'd have to leave Northby. She'd been wondering for a while how to tell Mrs Tibby of her fears.

She took a cup of tea to her mistress then went to get the hot brick she'd buried under the ashes the previous night, wrapping it in rags and a piece of old blanket before carrying it upstairs. Its warmth helped take the night's stiffness out of Mrs Tibby's painful joints.

When Emmy went down to drink a cup of tea herself it was to a cosy kitchen, the rain outside beating against the window panes. Thanks to Mr Garrett's help, they now had a coalhouse full of best brights and a little money in the bank. If they continued to be careful, there was enough to cover their modest needs for several years.

If George allowed her to go unmolested that long.

The day passed in domestic pursuits and in the early afternoon Emmy began to read one of Miss Austen's tales to her mistress, a book whose characters firmly believed it necessary for a man to have thousands of pounds a year before it was worth marrying him. Mrs Tibby had tried to explain to Emmy how the rich lived, but it was beyond the girl's comprehension and she derived more pleasure from her mistress's enjoyment of this book than from the tale itself.

Neither of the women thought anything of it when they heard the sound of wheels and horses' hooves as a vehicle stopped outside. Emmy didn't even bother to go and look out of the window, so when footsteps approached their door and someone banged on it loudly they were both startled.

'Who can that be?' whispered Mrs Tibby.

Emmy peered out of the window. 'It's a private carriage and there's a gentleman at the door.'

They stared at one another in shock as the knocker sounded again, then Emmy straightened her pinafore. 'I'd best answer it.'

The gentleman was not very tall and was rather portly, dressed in best broadcloth with a heavy greatcoat to keep him warm and a top hat protecting his head from the rain. He stared down his nose at Emmy and asked, 'Does Mrs Oswald live here?'

'Yes, sir.'

'I'm your mistress's brother. Well? Don't stand there barring the way, girl! Show me in!'

There was a gasp from behind Emmy and she turned to see her mistress push herself to her feet, her face chalky-white. Without thinking she rushed across to support Mrs Tibby.

The gentleman followed her inside, removing his rain-sprinkled top hat and giving it a quick shake, then unbuttoning his greatcoat. He didn't look best pleased and Emmy began to worry about what he was doing here.

Claude watched with a frown as the maid gently coaxed her mistress into sitting down. His sister looked very frail and old, and it galled him to see an Armistead living in such a hovel.

The girl turned to him, saying with a familiarity of which he disapproved, 'She's not well, sir, and I'm afraid you've startled her. Please close the door and take a seat.'

That young woman would have to go, he thought, doing as she bade him while scowling at her. She was far too pretty for a maid – especially with young Marcus around – and too forward in her ways. 'Why did you not tell us you were in need, my dear Matilda?' asked Claude, keeping his voice gentle.

Standing behind her mistress's chair Emmy saw the look of shame on Mrs Tibby's face and felt angry on her behalf, but knew better than to speak. Her mistress might treat her more like a young relative than a servant, but this man was staring at her as if she were a worm and for two pins he'd tread on her.

'My father said never to call myself an Armistead again – and I knew dear William was dead,' Tibby faltered, then began to weep softly into her handkerchief. 'I didn't think you'd want to help me, Claude.'

'Go and ask my wife and son to join me!' he ordered Emmy, then he turned back to his sister, speaking in a soothing manner though Eleanor was much better at dealing with weeping females than he was. 'You were wrong, Matilda. Of course we'll help you. We would have done so sooner had we known you were in trouble.'

Mrs Armistead swept into the tiny cottage and studied her surroundings with a mouth twisted briefly by disapproval, then bent over the old woman, calling her 'Matilda, my dear'.

It annoyed Emmy that both visitors spoke to her mistress as if they were dealing with a stupid child. She waited by the front door, wanting to close it and keep the chill, damp air out. But the young man who had helped his mother from the carriage was standing in the way, not even looking at the old lady just staring at Emmy herself with a hot, devouring gaze. He was short and plump with a soft, full mouth and very pale eyes.

'What's your name, girl?' he demanded in a low voice.

To Emmy's relief his mother interrupted. 'Marcus, come and say hello to your aunt. And you, girl, close the door and wait in the kitchen until you're needed! Set a kettle on the range. Your mistress clearly needs a cup of tea and I would appreciate some refreshment myself.'

But the young man moved only a half-step backwards and Emmy had to press against him to get past. To her horror he squeezed her breast as she did so. His father noticed and smiled. What sort of people were these? But though Emmy felt outraged she did not say anything to embarrass her mistress. Closing the kitchen door firmly behind her, she leaned against it for a moment, shuddering. There was something about that young man that revolted her.

And what did this visit mean?

In the parlour Claude did not waste any time. 'We've come to rescue you from this dreadful hovel, my dear sister.'

She stared at him in shock. 'What do you mean?'

'I mean, we're here to take you back to live with us.'

'But I'm very comfortable here,' she protested, not at all sure she wanted to be rescued if her brother was going to look at her so scornfully. 'Dear Emmy looks after me very well, I do assure you, Claude. If you could just see your way to . . . if we just had a little more money, only a very little, I could manage perfectly well here.'

Eleanor, who had been studying the furniture and her sister=

in-law's shabby, old-fashioned gown, gave a scornful sniff. 'I can see that your girl keeps everything clean – I do not fault her there – but, my dear sister, you should be living in a manner befitting your station. There's plenty of room for you at the Grange, and living with us, you need never lift a finger again as long as you live.'

'At the Grange?' Tibby asked faintly.

'Well, where else should we take you but to your old home?' Claude forced another smile, wondering if his sister had lost her wits. 'Now, where is that girl with the tea? Eleanor, my dear, perhaps you'd go and see what she's doing?'

'Emmy can't prepare the tea any more quickly,' Tibby said, quick in defence of her maid. 'There's isn't a range, only the kitchen fire.'

'I'll go and see what she's doing,' Marcus offered.

'You will *not!*' his mother snapped.

He scowled, then fell into a reverie as his father chatted to his old aunt. That maid was a dashed pretty girl – and not too tall. He didn't know when he'd ever seen a more angelic face, though what he'd like to do with her was far from that. She had an untouched air to her and he'd bet she was a virgin. A thrill shot through him at the thought. If there was one thing he loved it was breaking in a virgin to be obedient and responsive to his special needs.

In the kitchen Eleanor made no pretence that she was doing anything but checking the place. She ran a finger over various surfaces, nodding in approval as she found them dust-free.

Emmy watched in amazement. 'I dust every day and keep things clean, just as Mrs Oswald showed me,' she said as the inspection went on.

'Don't be pert, girl! The house *is* clean, I will admit, but you are in need of a lesson in knowing your place.'

For her mistress's sake, Emmy pressed her lips together and said nothing more.

Eleanor watched, hawk-eyed, as the girl made the tea. The impudent creature knew how to set a tray, at least. She would offer her a reference after they'd taken Tibby away from here but she could not employ someone so pretty at Moor Grange, not with Marcus even worse than his father about young women.

When the tray was ready, she preceded Emmy into the miserable excuse for a parlour, not attempting to hold the door open for the girl.

Emmy had to catch the door with her foot or it would have knocked the heavy tray out of her hand, which annoyed her. It seemed to her that rich people had no manners. She waited until Mrs Armistead was comfortably seated before she moved into the room, which felt very crowded. And that horrible young man was staring at her again. She'd like to black his eye for him!

'Put the tray here then leave,' Eleanor ordered. 'I shall serve tea for your poor mistress.'

Emmy did as ordered, but the way the young man continued to stare at her made her shiver and instinctively keep as far away from him as she could.

'Why do we not take you home with us today, Matilda?' Claude asked as he sipped his tea.

In the kitchen with her ear pressed against the door Emmy stiffened in horror at this suggestion. Not today! Not till they'd had time to say a proper goodbye. It had only taken her a few minutes to realise that whether they wanted her to continue as Mrs Tibby's maid or not, it would not be safe for her to be in the same house as that young man, but at least her worries about her mistress would be dealt with, so she would have only herself to think about.

Her main problem had just been solved for her, really. Now she could leave Northby and get away from George. Why, then, did she not feel happy about it all? Why did she want to weep?

In the tiny sitting room, Tibby Oswald was trying to hide her bewilderment from her relatives. She couldn't believe they had suddenly started to care what happened to her. She knew she wasn't clever but James had been and she remembered him saying once, 'Never trust your family, love. You don't know the half of the things they got up to when they wanted to make money. They'd swear black was white, the Armisteads would.'

Her father had refused permission for her to marry James and had tried to match her with someone more 'suitable'. But she had refused and when James had suddenly inherited a small legacy, she had not hesitated to marry him. She was twenty-one by that time, so they could not stop her. Of course her father had washed his hands of her but she'd not minded because she was so happy with her beloved husband.

If Mr Portley hadn't cheated them out of their money they might have been happy still, but only a few days after James had discovered it someone had waylaid him one evening on his way to provide Constable Makepeace with evidence. His poor dear body had been savagely battered and the murderer never caught. Constable Makepeace said it was probably Mr Portley but the man had vanished, never to be seen again in Northby. The thought that he had escaped justice still hurt.

And now the family wanted her to move back to the Grange, leaving the town where she had so many happy memories.

She realised suddenly they were all looking at her as if expecting an answer. 'I'm so sorry – this has all been such a shock, I simply can't make a decision so quickly.'

'You don't have to decide anything. We shall look after you now.' Claude was somewhat offended that she had not accepted his offer at once.

Because her whole life was at stake Tibby found the courage to ask bluntly, 'Why?'

And when they all looked at her as if they didn't understand her question, she said, 'Why are you doing this? The family has ignored me for years. There must be a reason.'

The Armisteads all began soothing and cajoling her again so she waited till they'd finished and said simply, 'You still haven't explained why.' James had taught her that, too. *Stick to the point, Tibby. Don't let people distract you. If you want to know something, keep asking.*

Eleanor suddenly burst out laughing and said, 'Tell her. She deserves the truth.'

Claude looked at his wife as if questioning her judgement, but when she made an encouraging gesture with one hand, shrugged and said, 'We are negotiating a marriage with Rish-more's daughter. He would not think well of us if we left my sister living in need. We didn't know about your difficulties until this week or we'd have acted before.'

Suddenly it all made sense. Tibby looked at Eleanor and said simply, 'I should prefer a place of my own. A cottage would be enough, somewhere a little larger than this, perhaps. But I admit I should like to have my family nearby, and – and I should like a promise that I will be buried in Northby churchyard next to my dearest James.' She closed her eyes and sighed. 'Could you not give me that?'

'My sister live in a cottage? Certainly not! And since we have the carriage outside it would make sense to take you home with us now,' her brother pressed.

She shook her head. 'Oh, no. I must say goodbye to the people who have been kind to me, and Emmy and I must decide what to take with us. No, no! I can't possibly go now. And Emmy must come too of course.' She looked across at Eleanor. 'Take them away, please, my dear. It's all too much for me today.'

With a nod Eleanor stood up. 'You cannot force her to come with us,' she told her husband. 'I shall return alone in two days' time and make plans with your sister. Will that suit, Matilda?'

'Yes, dear. It'll suit me very well. Thank you.' She raised her voice. 'Emmy!'

So Emmy went to open the door for them – as if they couldn't do it for themselves! Last to leave was the son, who paused next to her to grasp her arm with one hand and tilt her chin upwards forcibly with the other before saying, 'If I ride over to Northby, can you get some time off?'

'No.' She tried to step backwards, but his hand tightened on her arm till it hurt and she could see that he was enjoying hurting her, so she kicked him hard in the shins.

He yelped and his grasp slipped for a minute, so that she could step quickly back towards Mrs Tibby who had seen what was going on and was looking horrified. Emmy waited there for him to leave.

'I'll be back,' he said savagely, and left without a word to his aunt.

Emmy rushed across to slam the door and slide the bolt across it to make sure he couldn't sneak back inside. 'I'll just watch them go,' she said to her mistress.

The son got inside the carriage, a groom slammed the door on him and climbed up behind, then they drove off through the rain which had not let up all day.

When Emmy turned round she saw Mrs Tibby weeping and went to comfort her.

'So silly, Emmy. Why am I upset when this means I shall be looked after even if my money does run out?'

'Because it means things must change.'

'Not between us, my dear.'

Emmy could not lie to her, so she sat down on the sofa, took her mistress's hand with its papery skin in hers and said quietly, 'I'm afraid so. You saw how your nephew looked at me. And – I've been meaning to tell you for a while – now that I'm grown up, my mother's protector wants to use me as he uses her. I'd have had to leave you soon anyway because he'd force me, I know he would. At least this way I can be sure you'll be safe. And I can be safe, too.'

Mrs Tibby looked at her for a long time, then took her maid's hand and held it against her cheek, saying in a quiet, sad voice, 'Nothing ever stays right, does it?'

'No, it doesn't.' Emmy could feel tears welling up, then they escaped and both of them were sobbing in each other's arms.

Eleanor Armistead returned to find that Tibby was prepared to be sensible. Fortunately the maid had 'made other arrangements' because the girl wasn't the sort to work in a gentleman's residence, really, for all she knew how to keep a house clean. Even if they hadn't had Marcus to consider.

So five days after the Armisteads' first visit Emmy said a tearful goodbye to her mistress as they cleared up the house together for the last time and waited for the Armistead carriage to arrive.

'You will be here this afternoon when the farm cart comes to take my furniture?' Mrs Tibby asked for the tenth time.

'Yes, of course,' Emmy said gently.

'And you will come to me if you're ever in trouble? Promise!'

'I promise.'

'And you'll write to me?'

'If I can.' She had promised all this several times, but her mistress was in a fluttery mood and seemed to need a lot of reassurance.

When they heard the carriage arrive, the two women looked at one another and embraced, saying nothing because everything had been said now.

Emmy went to open the front door, relieved to see only Mrs Armistead. She had been afraid Mrs Tibby's nephew might have accompanied his mother and had lain awake worrying about what a rich man like him might do to get his way with her. How stupid of her! As if he'd care that much about a simple maidservant like her! He'd probably forgotten she even existed by now.

Eleanor Armistead made short work of the farewells. 'Please show the men what you want to take with you today, Tibby. The farm cart will be here later for the rest of your things.'

Turning to Emmy she said in a cooler tone, 'I shall be happy to furnish prospective employers with references about you, if you need them. Here is my address.'

She did not bother to enquire what exactly the girl was going to do now, which was a good thing because Emmy had decided to sleep on the floor of the empty house that night. The rent was paid until the end of the week, after all, and she still had to say goodbye to her mother. She would get a ride into Manchester with the carrier and go to the ladies at the Mission to ask their help in gaining a new position. If they could not help her, she'd go to a domestic employment agency. Mrs Tibby had told her about these places and had written out a reference for her which had brought tears to Emmy's eyes, it said such lovely things about her. Well, it was easy to be loyal to a mistress as kind as hers.

After she had waved goodbye to Mrs Tibby, Emmy did not let herself weep any more. No use looking back, she told herself with a sniff. She had to make a new life for herself, but not, she was determined, a life like her mother's. Never, ever that, even as a rich man's mistress – something her mother seemed to think was desirable.

An image of Jack Staley swam before Emmy, but she banished it. She'd always known he could not marry her, for he had even heavier responsibilities than before since his sister and her child had come back to live with them. She'd seen Meg in the street carrying the baby, which was a pale, thin little thing, but pretty. Meg was thin, too, and looked sharp and bitter, though she might have been pretty once.

Emmy sighed. She would have liked to have a husband and family, too. She loved little children and often watched them as she walked in the town.

And she would miss her dear mistress sorely. The tears overflowed again, try as she might to hold them back, and the empty house echoed with her sobs.

Chapter Seven

The big farm cart arrived at eleven o'clock and it did not take long for the two men to carry all Mrs Tibby's furniture and possessions out, wedge them in place and lace up the canvas hood. Then the man driving it told the horses to 'Walk on!' and they left without a backward glance.

Feeling unsettled and with tears still threatening, Emmy walked aimlessly round the empty house, hating the emptiness of the rooms and the way her footsteps echoed on the bare boards. The roof timbers were creaking and groaning as if someone was moving about upstairs. Had those noises always been there? Why had she not noticed them before? It was quite chilly, but although there was some coal left, she had let the fire die down in case someone came to investigate the smoke when the house was supposed to be empty.

She decided to go and say goodbye to her mother. A brisk walk would warm her up. She wasn't looking forward to the meeting because Madge always smelled of gin lately and her conversation was vague and disjointed. But Emmy had fond memories of the woman her mother had once been – feckless perhaps, but loving and able to make you laugh and enjoy life so much in the good times. It would not feel right to leave without a proper farewell.

She waited in an alley opposite the alehouse, which was just behind Market Place, wondering how to find out whether George was in or not. The last thing she wanted to do was bump into him in case he tried to stop her leaving. When a woman she had met while out walking with her mother came out of the alehouse, Emmy followed her to ask if Madge was in.

'Yes, but she's still a-bed. Eh, you don't usually come visiting here, lass. Is summat wrong?'

'No. Is George around?'

'Nay, you've just missed him.'

'That's all right. It's my mother I want to see, really. It's just — easier without him around.'

The woman smiled. 'I know what you mean. He always has to know everything, doesn't he? But at least he looks after us girls. There are worse than him, far worse.'

Emmy went in by the kitchen door. One of the maids was yawning and complaining about a busy night, but stopped to ask who she was.

'Oh, Madge's girl. You're older than I'd expected. Your mam isn't awake yet. She was working late last night.' She and the other kitchen maid exchanged glances and tittered.

'You should tell her to keep off the gin,' the older one said. 'It rots your insides, gin does. Your mother's in the first room on the right at the top of the stairs, love. Just go on up.'

Emmy went through the door at the back of the kitchen, hating the smell of stale beer, unwashed bodies and pipe smoke that came from the big public room. She did not feel at all comfortable here and resolved to keep her visit short. No one answered her knock, so after a moment's hesitation she opened the door and peeped in.

Her mother was lying staring at the ceiling. When she saw Emmy she brightened and pushed herself into a sitting position. 'George told you, then? You've agreed to do it?' she asked eagerly.

'I haven't seen him. Agreed to what?'

Madge's face fell. 'He heard your mistress was leaving so he went to see you, to tell you about his plans. You must have just missed him. He's had an offer of good money if he sets you up with this rich gent who's seen you and wants you. And you'll get money from the gent, too. That's not like what I do. You'll be *safe*, lovie, even when he tires of you, because George will look after you.'

'I wouldn't agree to do something like that. You know I wouldn't.'

Madge's face crumpled and she got out of bed, coming across to take hold of Emmy's arm and give it little shakes to emphasise what she was saying. 'Oh, lovie, *no!* It won't be like what *I* do. You'll be set up *proper* in your own house. You'll have a maid, want for nothing. You *can't* be stupid enough to turn down an offer like that.'

Emmy realised it wouldn't take George long to walk down to Weavers Lane and back. 'I just came to say goodbye to you, Mam. Mrs Tibby's family have taken her to live with them, so I'm leaving Northby.' She kissed her mother's cheek, removed the hand that was still grasping her forearm and turned to leave.

'Noooo!' Madge wailed. 'No, you can't! He'll throw me out if you leave. He was so pleased about it this morning. Emmy, no!' She flung herself after her daughter and grabbed her, pulling her back. 'Just stay and listen to what's proposed. *Please!* If you love me, you'll do it. You have to.'

Emmy tried to push her mother away, but Madge suddenly turned nasty and pulled her back by the hair, taking her by surprise. She knocked her daughter over and the two of them rolled to and fro on the floor with Emmy desperately trying to get away.

Suddenly someone hauled her mother off her and a voice said, 'What the hell's going on here? You know I don't allow fighting.'

Emmy stared up at George, who had moved Madge roughly aside. Her heart sank at the gloating look in his eyes.

'She was trying to leave,' Madge explained. 'So I stopped her.'

'Well done, dear,' he said, as if he were talking to a child. 'I won't forget that. You did right to keep her here.'

'She wouldn't even listen to what you were offering.'

'She will now.'

Emmy scrambled to her feet and straightened her clothing. 'I have to go. I've got someone waiting for me and –'

'You've got no one waiting for you,' he interrupted. 'The cottage is empty, just like Mr Armistead said it would be.'

Emmy stilled. *Mr Armistead?*

'He's taken quite a fancy to you, that young gent has. I don't blame him. You've grown into a lovely young woman and I'd bet my life you're a virgin still.'

Emmy could not help blushing.

George chuckled, a nasty little sound. 'If you weren't I'd give you some training myself in pleasuring a man, but it's worth too much, your maidenhead is. Armistead is willing to pay well for his pleasures, but this has to be kept quiet, him being about to wed Rishmore's beanpole of a daughter. It wouldn't do for them to find out he's got a fancy piece on the side.'

Emmy spoke loudly before he could say anything else. 'I hate Marcus Armistead and I'll kill myself before I let him touch me!'

'How can you hate him when you don't even know him? He may be a short arse, but he's a gentleman. Coming over this very evening, he is. Knows his aunt's moving out and trusts me to make sure you're available.' He looked at her assessingly and shook his head at her stubborn expression, making a tutting sound under his breath. 'I never thought you were stupid, girl. Here's a big chance for all of us to make some good money – and afterwards, if you'll put yourself in my hands, I'll make sure you're well paid for your favours. Not street corner stuff like your poor ma, but good linen sheets and silk clothes and gentlemen visitors only. You'll be able to retire in comfort one day. I treat my girls decently. Ask any of 'em.'

Emmy looked him straight in the eye and said loudly, 'I won't do it.' She had always hated what her mother did, couldn't bear the thought of strange men pawing at her, doing *that* to her.

George laughed indulgently. 'You will, you know. You can do it the easy way or you can fight me and get hurt, but you'll still do it.' He was holding her by the arm as easily as he would a naughty child. Grinning, he ran his other hand down her body.

Emmy tried to kick him, but it was like kicking a stone wall. Her mother stood to one side doing nothing. 'Mother, help me!' she begged. 'Don't let him do this to me!'

But Madge shook her head. 'It's for the best, lovie. You'll see. The world's a hard place if you don't have someone to look after you.'

Emmy sobbed. She could not believe her own mother would do this to her. As she felt the hand around her arm slacken, she jerked away. She managed only two steps, but fought and kicked and scratched, when he restrained her again.

'Ouch! Bloody hellion! Don't just stand there, get some strips of cloth to tie her up,' George shouted at Madge. 'She'll change her mind when she sees it's nothing to be frightened of and how much money she'll earn for one night's work.' They always did.

Emmy began to scream, making as much noise as she could, struggling so wildly she knocked over a chair and made George curse when she bit his hand.

He put one hand over her mouth. 'Shut up, you fool!' He gave her a shake. 'Or I'll have to gag you.'

She shut up but only because she wanted to be free to shout for help again when an opportunity arose.

He pressed her face down on the bed while he bound her hands and feet, then rolled her over and scowled down at her, hands on hips. 'We'll talk again when Mr Armistead's finished with you. And don't think you'll get away from me.'

Emmy stared up at him, feeling helpless and terrified.

His voice became less harsh. 'Ah, you're making a fuss about nowt, Emmy lass. It might hurt a bit the first time, but it'll soon be over an' you'll wonder why you got so het up.' He stepped back from the bed and looked at Madge. 'You're not going to be silly about her, are you?'

'No, George. You know I love you and I'll always do what you want. Besides, it's for her own good. It'll set her up for life. But you will remember your promise, won't you – only the best for my Emmy, only *gentlemen* visitors?'

'Of course I will. Now, you keep an eye on the stupid bitch for me while I go and make the other arrangements.' He cast a mocking glance towards Emmy as he added, 'Gag her if she tries to scream. And do your best to talk some sense into her, Madge. Armistead will be here as soon as it's dark.

'Your ma's right,' he told Emmy. 'Women need a man to protect 'em. If you have any sense at all in that pretty head of yours, you'll think about pleasing him tonight, not angering him, then afterwards you'll let me look after you properly.' Trouble though she was he had rarely seen a lass as pretty as her.

Emmy waited till his footsteps had died away then looked at her mother. 'How could you help him tie me up?' she demanded, her voice breaking on the words.

Madge bowed her head for a minute, then looked at her and repeated, 'I'm thinking of your future, lovie.'

'But I don't want a future like that.'

'You'll soon get used to it. It's nothing really.'

'Will you really gag me if I scream for help?'

Madge nodded. 'I have to do as George says or I'll lose everything.'

'That man Marcus Armistead . . . he's horrible, Mother. Cruel. You can see it in his eyes. He makes my flesh crawl. I can't bear the thought of him even touching me.'

Madge laughed scornfully. 'Do you think I like *any* of 'em touching me? Well, I don't. I hate it. But men need it, can't do without it – and if I'd had someone like George looking after my interests when I was young and pretty like you are, I'd be safe now.' She sighed at the thought. 'Well, it's too late for me, but it's not too late for you. And if *you* have money, you'll not let me starve, I know, because you're a kind girl.' Madge had been worrying for a while about what would happen when she was too old to attract a customer. Going across to a shelf she got down a bottle, pouring herself a glass of gin but never taking her eyes off her daughter.

Emmy said nothing more. Closing her eyes, she tried to think what to do. There was no one to know she was missing, even, so she had to escape on her own. Even if she didn't – her thoughts faltered for a moment as she contemplated the horror of that – she would not stop struggling against these men who wanted to use her, no, not as long as there was breath in her body.

She wriggled carefully, testing her bonds, but the pieces of cloth were tied too tightly for her to get away. And her mother was still watching her, sipping the gin delicately as if it was the only thing that really mattered to her. Its faint almost perfumed smell sickened Emmy.

She glanced towards the window. It was getting dark quickly now. He would be on his way.

Jack heard that Mrs Oswald had moved away and gone back to her family. It caused much discussion in the town to think that the old lady could be so closely connected to the Armisteads and no one know. As dusk settled gently on the narrow streets, he told his mother he needed a breath of fresh air and strolled down the Lane to look at the house where Emmy had lived.

No lights in the windows, no smoke coming from the chimney – and no Emmy inside.

He went to peer through one of the windows and saw only an empty room, so wandered off again, kicking at pebbles and feeling angry with both himself and his father. With nothing to offer her he had no right to care that she'd gone, but he did.

Meg seemed to be permanently angry since her return. She'd said little about her life with Ben, especially when their mother was around, but her eyes grew wistful on the rare occasions she did mention him. Only with the baby did she relax, cuddling little Nelly whenever she could, utterly devoted to her.

Their mother looked after the baby during the day so that Meg could bring in some money, but she wasn't best pleased by the situation, especially as Nelly was sickly and needed a lot of attention. Meg complained about how Mam treated the child and Jack often had to play peacemaker and intercede in their quarrels, for the sake of the other children.

Meg had got herself a job with Mr Roper of all people, acting partly as housekeeper and partly assistant in the pawnshop. With her new hard attitude to the world, she had no trouble dealing with the folk who came in to raise money. And when Jack worried that Roper would try to seduce her, she laughed harshly. 'Just let him try! Just let anyone try!'

Jack couldn't bear to go back home to more quarrels yet, so called in for a glass of ale, drank half of it then wandered out again, unable to settle. Cold as it was, with frost crackling on the edges of the puddles and his breath clouding the air, he still did not go home. At one point he found himself standing outside the mill and frowned at its dark bulk. This was his daytime prison, though Mr Butterfield sent him out regularly on errands and those outings kept him from going mad.

His home was his night-time prison, but who else was there to look after his brothers and sisters except him? Why, Joey was still only six. Imagine that gentle little lad shut up in the grim workhouse Northby shared with three other parishes! It didn't bear thinking of. And his sister Ginny was still at school. Now that they weren't scratching for every penny, Jack had insisted she stay on for another year or so. Let her be a little lass, play and make friends. She was only nine, after all. And, please God, let her never have to face whatever had turned Meg into such a harsh, unhappy creature. He smiled as his thoughts moved to Shad who was still at the dye works. He was a bright, cheerful lad, growing up fast and promising to be as large as his father and brothers.

Jack should be thankful, really, that things had turned out so well, considering what Jem had done. Count his blessings. Not feel so angry.

But it had cheered him up to look at Emmy sometimes and dream a little. Or even to stop and speak to her. Just occasionally. And now she was gone.

He sighed. A young man could not help dreaming, even if he knew those dreams could never come true.

Once it was fully dark George returned to the alehouse. This time he did gag Emmy, laughing at her struggles to spit out the wad of material as he tied it in place. Then he wrapped her in a blanket, picked her up and carried her out as easily as a bundle of firewood.

Looking back she saw her mother sitting staring into a glass of gin, not even glancing up. *Mother, look at me!* Emmy pleaded inside her head, but Madge didn't stir.

George had a small handcart waiting outside. He laid Emmy

down carefully in it on a featherbed, whispering, 'We don't want you covered in bruises, do we? Or catching cold?' He covered her with sacking and she lay in stifling darkness, bumping helplessly around as the cart rattled over the cobble stones. The noise stopped abruptly as they began travelling over softer ground. Emmy wondered where they were going, but her head was covered up and she could gain no idea of their direction.

Where was George taking her? Would Marcus Armistead be waiting for them? Would he really force himself on her? Her forehead felt clammy, her stomach queasy, as if she was going to vomit, and she could not help shuddering and moaning softly in her throat.

All she could hold on to was the determination that whatever happened tonight, she would never willingly follow her mother's path. Never. And even George would not be able to watch her every minute of the day and night. There would be an opportunity to get away later even if she didn't succeed now. There had to be.

But what then? She could not flee to Mrs Tibby, because her former mistress was an Armistead and lived in the same house as *that man*. The ladies in Manchester, then. She'd flee to them. They'd help her, she was sure. That thought steadied her, but only a little.

The cart stopped and she stiffened in apprehension. As the sacking was removed she saw a sky full of stars. They looked so clean and bright above her they brought her a sudden feeling of comfort. They would still be there tomorrow – and so would she. She would survive whatever this night brought.

And she would not be a willing participant. Never that.

In the big house next to the mill at the very top of Weavers Lane Jane Rishmore heard her father come home early and go with her mother into the room they all called the library, though it had but one bookcase in it and only she ever read the books that contained. Or she had done until her father found out what she was doing and forbade her to touch 'his books' again, because they were unsuitable for a woman and why was she pretending to understand them? She had understood them, though. She was not stupid.

When her parents shut the door behind them, she knew they must be discussing something important because there were no servants in that part of the house at this hour. Thanks to some judicious eavesdropping, she guessed it was her future. Her mother had been talking about marriage lately, saying it was a woman's duty to marry well and the parents' to choose a suitable husband.

Jane closed her eyes for a moment to control her frustration, then went to sit on the window seat and stare out across the moors as dusk stained the lower land with shadows. Each patch of darkness crept outwards to join the next, gently laying a veil over the countryside. In the other direction she could see the lights of the town, street lamps and the bright glow from windows, so that every evening Northby seemed to be defying nature and holding back the darkness for a few hours.

Not for the first time she wished she could go out and stride across the moors, stride until she could walk no further – and never come back to Northby again. Her father had picked out her husband without consulting her, a little pudding of a man with shifty eyes and faded beige-brown hair that was already thinning. He'd been chosen because of his family connections, not for himself – as had she. She was inches taller than Marcus Armistead already and at eighteen was still growing. And it was obvious he hated that even more than she did.

The first time he'd come to visit them with his parents, his disappointment had shown clearly when he was introduced to Jane. Now he hardly bothered to talk to her, though they often placed him next to her on a sofa. Mostly he sat silent, unless he was agreeing with everything their parents said. He always looked sulky – no, more than sulky, cruel even, behind those careful smiles and nods. It was strange how sure she was that he was a cruel man, or would be if given the chance. She doubted his parents gave him much chance to do anything but obey them, though. As her parents gave her little choice about anything. In that way the Rishmores and the Armisteads were very much alike.

She had been so lost in her thoughts that she jumped in shock when her mother walked into the bedroom.

'Jane, my dear, straighten your hair and come downstairs. How can you have got it into such a mess already? Your father wishes to have a little chat with you before dinner.'

Jane closed her eyes for a moment.

'Are you all right, dear?'

'Yes, Mama.' She went to the dressing table and tried to straighten her hair, but her hands were trembling, so her mother tutted and took the comb from her. When her mother did her hair it obeyed, even hair as straight as Jane's. Her mother couldn't add a column of figures to the same amount twice, though.

In the end Jane couldn't keep the question back any longer. 'Mama, is it Mr Armistead?'

Her mother smiled at her. 'Yes, dear. Had you guessed? You must be feeling very excited.'

'Excited? I hate him. I told you that months ago.'

The smile vanished and the hairbrush came down to rap Jane's knuckles sharply. 'I thought we'd agreed that you would do as your father wished in this? He knows what's best for you.'

'But you said you'd try to persuade him to find another man. You promised me you would.'

Her mother stilled then let out her breath in a long slow stream. 'I did try. But his heart is set on this match, I'm afraid.'

'I can't agree to it.'

'You have no choice.'

Her mother's eyes met Jane's in the mirror. 'We women can do nothing but obey our fathers, and later our husbands. It's what we promise in church: to love, honour and obey.'

'I haven't promised to obey anyone,' Jane muttered.

'The Bible says: "Honour thy father and thy mother, that thy days may be long upon the land which the Lord thy God giveth thee".'

Her mother always took refuge in biblical quotations when she could summon up no reasoned arguments. Jane should have known better than to expect any help from her.

When they got downstairs, her father was standing in front of the fire, warming himself and looking smug. 'Ah, my dear, come and sit down. We have some good news for you.'

She sat. Listened. Fought to contain her anger. Failed. 'How can you ask me to marry that horrible little man?' she burst out suddenly.

Samuel stopped speaking to gape at her.

'We shall be a laughing stock as a couple – and he dislikes me as much as I dislike him. He's *horrible*.' With a sob Jane closed her mouth on further angry words, knowing how much her father hated hysteria.

He swelled visibly with outrage. 'Are you daring to question my decision?'

'When it comes to the man with whom I shall be spending the rest of my life, yes. I won't marry Marcus Armistead, Father.'

'You will do as you're told, young lady!'

'No, not in this.'

'Jane, dear,' her mother remonstrated.

She swung round. 'Why can you never stand up to my father? You know I'd be unhappy with that man. He's—'

'Silence!' her father roared suddenly. 'He's an Armistead and a suitable match for you and that's all you need to know. You will obey me in this as in everything else.'

Jane shook her head stubbornly. 'No. Not him. Anyone but him.'

He stared at her for a long, fraught moment, before making an angry sound in his throat and saying, 'Then you will be confined to your room on bread and water until you come to your senses. No, not to your room. To the smallest bedroom in the house, with no books save the Bible.' He turned to his wife. 'See to it.'

'Samuel, dear, perhaps—'

'*Take her out of my sight this minute!*'

Jane debated refusing to go, then shrugged and walked upstairs.

'Why are you doing this?' her mother whispered. 'Please, Jane. Come down and apologise. Your father has your best interests at heart.'

'No, he doesn't. He has his own interests at heart.'

She was too proud to make any further protest as her mother escorted her to the small rear bedroom that was never used because it was too small for guests. It looked out on to the moors and was furnished only with a narrow bed and chest of drawers.

It took a week for her to realise that her father meant what he said, a week of stifling boredom and gnawing hunger. In the end she decided she might as well obey him. She was merely a pawn to be used in his business agreements. If she'd had any money at all, she'd have run away, but her father kept her jewellery in his big safe and when she went out with her mother it was to shops at which they had accounts, so she had only a few coins of her own.

Jane was trapped, and furiously angry about that.

Smiling in anticipation Marcus rode through the moonlit darkness to Northby, which was not far away from Moor Grange if you took the track across the moors. His grandfather had bought the house from its impoverished aristocratic owners thirty years previously and his parents behaved as if they had been born and bred as lords of the manor in Padstall. The other county families did not deal much with them, however. They knew everyone's pedigree and, as far as they were concerned, the Armisteads had none.

Marcus was wearing an old brown cloak and as he approached Northby he pulled his hat down to hide his face. He left his horse at the livery stables and went straight to the back door of the alehouse, taking great care not to show his face. He didn't want word getting back to the Rishmores that he'd been in Northby for purposes other than courting their daughter.

A maid gave him a message from George and summoned the lad who had been waiting to guide him to where the girl was waiting. Eagerness throbbed through Marcus as he strode along. He was looking forward very much to mastering Emmy Carter and satisfying his needs with her. If she learned to please him, he would set her up as his mistress – until he tired of her, as one always did.

He was taken to a cottage on the outskirts of town, a small

building standing on its own. There was a lamp hanging on a hook outside the door.

'This is it,' said the lad, accepting a sixpenny piece with a grin that showed crooked teeth which even the moonlight could not whiten. He strolled off, whistling tunelessly.

Marcus rapped on the door. 'Is she here?' he asked when George opened it, unable to contain his eagerness.

'Aye. But there's a bit of a problem.'

'What do you mean?'

'She's not willing. I had to tie her up to get her here.'

Marcus found that thought piquant. Very. 'But no one knows? She didn't make a public fuss?'

'Nay, I soon shut her up. No one knows but us and her mother.'

'That's even better. I prefer the unwilling ones, actually. They're so much more satisfying to subdue.'

George frowned at him. He'd heard that tone before and distrusted it. 'We'd better get summat straight, then. If you harm her in any way, you'll have me to answer to.'

Marcus scowled at him. 'What concern is that of yours, fellow?'

'It's very much my concern. That lass is one of *my* girls now an' I look after my own. I mean it. If you mark or damage her in any way, I'll not only make you sorry you were born, I'll do to you exactly what you've done to her. Exactly.' He watched with satisfaction as Marcus shivered. 'And think on! You may be rich, but you can't watch your back every minute of the day and night.'

There was a moment's complete silence. Marcus was furious that a low fellow like this should speak to him in such an impudent manner, but he was also intimidated by George, who was a very large man with big fists and a battered face that said he'd been in a lot of fights. 'Why should I want to damage her?' he asked lightly. 'If I'm to take her under my protection I want her to keep her looks.'

Relieved, George clapped him on the shoulder. 'Well, if you want her in your keeping, you'll have to deal with me. I'm her protector now. I've got ambitions for my girls. A fancy whore-house in Manchester, mebbe.'

Marcus was disappointed by the restrictions, but decided it was probably for the best. In the past he'd been a bit careless and lucky to get away with it. It had cost him quite a bit to pay off the last girl's relatives for her injuries.

George jerked his head upwards. 'She's waiting for you in the front bedroom. I left her tied up. Thought you'd like to untie her yourself. Or not.'

With a smile Marcus moved towards the narrow stairs only to be halted by a large hand clamping down on his shoulder.

'Just a minute, Armistead. I'll have the money first.'

'You'll have it when I'm satisfied.'

George dragged him back to the door. 'Now! Ten guineas I was promised for first go at her and you don't lay a finger on her without paying me. I know she's a virgin and you're not going to claim owt else after you've had your fun.'

'Oh, very well.' Marcus fumbled in his pocket and counted out the coins impatiently.

'Right then. I'll be back in a couple of hours to check everything's all right.'

In the lane George paused for a moment, wondering whether he should stay around to make sure things went to plan. He'd didn't really like forcing a lass, but he was sure Emmy would change her mind in the morning when he gave her a guinea – no, two – for her trouble. As he hesitated it started to drizzle so he moved on, shrugging. Let Armistead have his privacy. He had, after all, paid handsomely for the privilege. A few bruises never did anyone any harm. It was the way lessons were usually learned in this life.

Tied to the bed, Emmy heard voices below her but could not make out the words, only the rumble of George's deep voice and the thin, drawling sound of Marcus Armistead's lighter tones. She could not hold back a moan of terror when footsteps sounded on the stairs. Until now she had clung to the hope that there might be a chance to escape, or even that something might prevent Marcus from coming. But the last hope died in her as he reached the top of the stairs and stopped in the doorway to study her.

He smiled, a narrow, cat-like smile which looked strange on a man's face. 'That's how I like to see a woman: helpless and ready for me to please myself with.'

She summoned up all her courage. She had to persuade him to loosen her bonds. Allowing her voice to tremble as he started to walk towards the bed, Emmy begged, 'Oh, please, sir, don't hurt me! I'll do as you want if only you won't hurt me.'

Not even attempting to reply, he continued to smile as he shed his coat, then began to unfasten his waistcoat.

She knew what men looked like only too well, because few of them troubled to hide their need from a child, so the sight of him did not shock her. But the thought of him touching her made her want to be sick.

Breathing heavily, he leaned over her. 'Have you ever had a man before? I warn you, I shall find out. There's no hiding such a thing.'

She shook her head and tried to look as helpless and frightened as possible, but anger was simmering behind the fear. That someone should do this – and enjoy it! 'No, sir,' she whispered. 'My mother was saving me for someone special.'

'Then why did you fight me?'

'I'm afraid, sir. Some of the men – they hurt my mother.'

When he smiled she knew he meant to hurt her, too, and tried to hide an involuntary shudder.

He took off everything except his shirt, then ran his hands over her body.

She tried to twist away from him.

'I'm going to untie your legs, Emmy. Don't try to resist me because that'll make me angry. If you even try, I'll hurt you.'

She let out a long shuddering sigh and closed her eyes for a moment, then opened them and stared straight at him. 'If I do as you wish – in everything – will you pay me well?'

He gave a scornful snort as he realised she was no different from the others. 'Yes.'

'Will you set me up in my own rooms? Not let other men come near me?'

'If you please me, yes.' A heady sense of power filled him. This was the way to treat them. Keep them submissive, make them tremble. He hadn't set up a woman as his mistress before, but the thought of having one who depended on him for everything, whom no other man had ever touched or ever would touch, pleased him so much he felt a renewed surge of passion. 'If you really are a virgin,' he warned.

'Oh, I am, sir, I am.' Emmy swallowed and said, 'All right. I'll be good, sir.' She kept still as his hands roamed over her body because she could do nothing unless he untied her hands. She hadn't counted on how free he'd make with her, or that he would actually tear off her shift. She could not help whimpering once or twice, but strangely he seemed to like that. Lying still beneath his loathsome touch was the hardest thing she'd ever done in a life where hardship was a frequent bedfellow. To her surprise it took a long time for him to be ready, far longer than was usual with her mother's customers.

'That's a good girl,' he said softly, touching and tweaking at her body, smiling as she cried out involuntarily at a particularly sharp pain. 'Very well. I'll untie your arms now and see how you keep your promise to behave yourself.'

As he untied her, she cried out as if her limbs would not work, though George had given her time to move them a bit before tying her to the bed head. She pretended to rub her arms. 'Pins and needles, sir. Sorry. Ow!' Lowering her eyes, she estimated distances and then grabbed the pewter candlestick she'd decided on from the chest of drawers beside the bed and smashed it against the side of his head. As he cried out, she brought it down again, twice more. It was heavy and after the third blow he did not move but lay sprawled across her on the bed with blood flowing copiously from the wounds she had made on his scalp.

Knowing she had no time to waste, she shoved his plump white body away, not dressing herself until she had tied him up with the same strips of cloth that had bound her. 'See how you like it for a change,' she muttered.

By the time she had finished he was groaning and his eyelids were fluttering, so she snatched her clothes from the floor and flung on her skirt and torn bodice hastily, clutching the other things to her chest as she moved to leave.

Just as she got to the door his voice rang out, sharp and high with anger. 'You little bitch! You'll pay for that.' He began to struggle.

She turned to shout, 'You're wicked, you are! *Wicked!*' Then ran down the stairs, praying that George was not waiting outside.

No one stopped her as she half fell through the door and began to stumble down the lane. Once she fell over and winded herself, but dragged herself to her feet and carried on, desperate to get as far away from here as she could.

Suddenly she sobbed in relief. She was at her own end of the town, just a little beyond the bottom of Weavers Lane. She wondered if she dare risk getting some of her possessions from the cottage, then realised she'd have to, because her money was there, still hidden in the lining of the frayed travelling bag Mrs Tibby had given her. Without that she'd have little chance of escaping.

When she bumped into a warm body at the dark corner where the track opened into Weavers Lane, she screamed in shock and terror, thinking that George had caught her.

Chapter Eight

In the darkness at the corner of Weavers Lane a voice exclaimed, 'Emmy? It is Emmy Carter, isn't it? I thought you'd left Northby.'

With a sob of relief she clutched Jack Staley. 'I got away from him. Oh, Jack, can you help me? *Please*. I have to hide somewhere. They'll be looking for me.'

It was so wonderful to have her in his arms that for a moment Jack could not speak. For once, just this once, he dared to lay his cheek against her hair. Then her words sank in and he became aware that she was only lightly clad on this frosty night and was trembling uncontrollably. 'What's happened? Has someone hurt you?' If so, he would find them and punish them.

Emmy forced herself to move away from him, though she longed to stay in his arms. 'I'll tell you later. I have to hurry, they'll be after me. I need to get my things from the cottage and then find somewhere to hide.'

'I'll help you in any way I can, of course I will.' He fell into step beside her, not pressing for an explanation but determined not to leave her until he was sure she was safe. It galled him that he daren't take her home but he could guess what his mother would say if he did.

At the cottage Emmy stopped for a moment to get her breath, feeling upset to see it looking so dark and abandoned. Then, as someone walked briskly down Weavers Lane towards them, she gasped and clutched Jack. 'They mustn't recognise me.'

'They'll think it strange if we run into an empty cottage. Pretend we're kissing. If we look like a courting couple, I can keep most of you hidden.' He took her in his arms and bent over her. He didn't mean it to happen but somehow the pretence became reality. As his lips met hers, cool with the night air, he groaned in his throat and wrapped his arms more closely around her, kissing her tenderly, showing her how much he loved her.

Emmy nestled instinctively against him. The touch of this man seemed so clean and normal, it was as if his gentle kiss began to wipe away the dirty feeling of Marcus Armistead on her skin and that other equally dreadful feeling that, like her mother, she was soiled now for Marcus had touched her in places only a husband should see.

The man strolled past, laughing softly and calling out, 'Eh, you young lovers!'

Once his footsteps had faded they drew apart, staring at one another shyly in the light of the street lamp, then she took his hand and led the way round to the back of the cottage without a word. Even his hand felt good in hers, warm and strong but not holding on too tightly, so that she could remove hers any time she wished. Only she didn't wish to do that. What she really wanted was to stay beside him for ever.

For a moment joy flared through her as she realised how much she loved him. Despair swiftly followed. She couldn't stay with him. She understood his situation and knew only too well how any mother would regard the daughter of Madge Carter.

But it was hard to let go of Jack. Very hard.

Bending, she retrieved the back door key from under a stone. She couldn't turn it in the lock because her hands had begun to tremble so stood there, teeth chattering, and let him take the key from her.

When he had opened the door, he waited for her to lead the way in, but she could not move as reaction hit her. While she had been escaping she had pushed it aside. While Jack had been holding her she had felt safe. Now the memories of what had happened flooded through her in a dark wave of shame and misery.

Scooping her up, Jack carried her inside. 'Emmy, tell me. Let me help you.'

There was no furniture so he took her to sit on the stairs that ran up between the kitchen and the front room and there, cradled against him, her shamed blushes hidden by the darkness, she told him how her mother had helped George Duckworth to capture her – and sobbed as she did so. A mother should protect her child, not give her to a man to ravish, even a mother like hers. In a voice that faded and wobbled as she gulped back the tears, she told how George had taken her to the little cottage and left her tied up there for Marcus Armistead's use.

Jack held his anger back, saying nothing, just making low, soothing noises as she stumbled through the explanation. Only when she had faltered to a halt did he growl, 'Armistead deserves to be hanged! Nay, it'd be too good for him. And I'd not have thought even George Duckworth would force a lass like that. We should go and report this to the constable.'

Emmy gave a snort of what was meant to be scornful laughter but it turned into a sob. 'I daren't tell anyone. Marcus Armistead is rich. No one's going to take the word of Madge Carter's daughter against his, are they? Anyway, if I go to see Mr Makepeace, George will know where I am and he'll be waiting for me. I need to get away from Northby, and quickly.'

Jack let a little of his anger escape in another low rumble of sound. 'You're right. I wish you weren't but you are. Armistead has been a regular visitor at the Rishmores' recently an' folk at the mill say he's going to marry their daughter.'

'I pity her, then!'

'Aye. I feel sorry for her, too. I deliver messages to the house sometimes an' she allus looks unhappy, but that doesn't stop her being polite to me.' You noticed things like that when you were delivering messages to rich people's houses and places of work. There were some who treated you like dirt.

They sat on in silence, bodies warm against one another, but Emmy knew she couldn't stay much longer and tried desperately to pull herself together. 'I've got to leave town, Jack. If either of them catches me . . .' They might finish what they had started and that would destroy her, she knew it would.

'I've been trying to think how best to help you,' he said slowly. 'What you really need is protection. If you set off for Manchester alone and on foot they could easily find you on the road tomorrow and there's nowhere much to hide on that track over the moors.' He snapped his fingers suddenly as the solution came to him. 'Parson Bradley! I'll take you to him.'

'But he's a friend of Mr Rishmore's.'

'Aye, but he's also a decent chap who really cares about ordinary folk like us and doesn't look down his nose at anyone. If we tell him only that you have to escape from George Duckworth, who is trying to drag you into your mother's trade, I'm sure he'll help you – and get Mr Rishmore's support if necessary. Parson and his wife have helped several lasses to find decent jobs in service and they've done a lot for lads like me, too, teaching us to read and to think for ourselves. They might even know those ladies of yours in Manchester.'

'Are you sure – quite sure – that he and his wife would help me?'

'Oh, yes.'

Emmy hesitated, very conscious of time passing. This cottage would be the first place George would come and look for her when he found Armistead. Since she couldn't think of an alternative, she let Jack's certainty about the Parson guide her. 'Very well. We'll go and see Mr Bradley. But I'll wait outside and if he doesn't want to help, you can signal to me. I can still get a long way from Northby before morning and I'll make sure to hide somewhere during the daytime.'

In silence they left the little house, locking the door carefully behind them. Jack carried her bag of possessions and insisted she take his arm, for she was still shaken by occasional fits of shuddering.

By the time they got to Parson Bradley's house Emmy was feeling dizzy with reaction and lack of food, but was trying to hide her weakness from Jack. She might have known he'd notice.

'You all right?'

'Yes. Of course I am.'

'No, you're not, lass, but if you can just keep going as far as the churchyard, I'll leave you in the porch of the church hall. It'll keep the wind off you a bit and you'll be out of sight there.'

When he had left her Emmy tried to find a sheltered corner of the porch but the wind was blowing strongly and seemed to be trying to scour out every crevice. In the end she sagged against the wall with her bag clutched to her chest, ready to run at the slightest sign that anything was wrong.

A figure appeared at the gate of the Parsonage and she tensed before realising it was Jack. She would have recognised his sturdy outline anywhere, even before he called out to her.

'Parson wants you to come in so he can talk to you himself.'

'What did you tell him?'

'That you're Mrs Oswald's former maid, escaping from George Duckworth who wants you to follow your mother's trade now you no longer have a job. That you're a good girl and don't want that. Parson has seen you attending church with your mistress and he's surprised she didn't take you with her. We'll have to tell him about Marcus Armistead, I'm afraid.' He picked up her bag and put his arm round her shoulders to guide her towards the house. 'Come on, love. You can trust Parson.'

But he felt bitter that he had to seek another man's aid for the young woman he loved. His footsteps faltered for a moment as he admitted to himself that he did love Emmy. Always had done, it seemed, from the first day he'd seen her. Had no right to, but couldn't help it.

At the kitchen door she hesitated. It looked so cosy inside, with oil lamps burning brightly and a glowing coal fire in the huge modern kitchen range. Would someone who lived in such luxury understand enough about her sort of life to believe her story?

A buxom woman in a big white pinafore glanced at her curiously, but said nothing.

Mr Bradley was standing in the doorway at the other side of the room, looking at her with a steady, questioning gaze. He was not as tall as he seemed in the church pulpit, and looked plump, well-fed and a little rumpled. Why should a gentleman like him help someone like her? But as she hung back, Jack put his arm round her again and drew her forward, closing the door behind them with his foot.

The room they took her to was lined with books and Mrs Bradley was waiting there. Like her husband she did not seem as grand a lady tonight as she did in church. Wisps of hair were escaping from her lace cap and her skirts were a little creased.

She moved forward at once. 'Come over to the fire, child. You must be chilled through. Goodness, how you're shivering! It's a bitter night.' She unwrapped the soft grey shawl from her own shoulders and cast it around the girl.

That simple gesture brought tears into Emmy's eyes. 'Thank you, ma'am,' she said, her voice husky with suppressed tears, clutching it round her neck. She felt as if she'd never get properly warm again.

'Sit down near the fire and tell us what happened, Emmy,' Mr Bradley said gently. 'Jack says someone has been trying to force you into immorality?'

'Yes, sir.'

'How old are you?'

'Seventeen, sir.'

'You look younger.'

'My mother has always told people I'm younger, so that,' she took a deep breath, 'her protector wouldn't try to force me to . . .' she broke off, not knowing how to continue in front of a lady, then finished lamely '. . . follow my mother's trade. I told them I'd never do that but he captured me and – and tied me up for a client to use.' Suddenly she was sobbing. 'I pretended to do as the man wanted, but there was a candlestick next to the bed and when he untied me, I hit him with it.'

'Did he – have his way with you?' Mrs Bradley asked.

'No, ma'am. But he touched me. It was horrible!' Sobs had punctuated her words. Now she broke down completely, sobbing hysterically, hiding her face in her hands.

'I think it would be best if I took her upstairs, my dear,' Mrs Bradley said to her husband. 'She's far too overwrought to question further tonight.'

Emmy shot her a terrified glance. 'No, I have to get away! Jack said you'd help me *get away!*'

Mrs Bradley's voice was firm. 'No one will harm you here, I promise you, or take you away from us.' She pulled Emmy up from the seat by the fire. 'Let's get you out of those torn clothes and find some hot milk for you.'

When the two women had gone, Parson looked at Jack. 'She's telling the truth?'

'Yes, sir. I'd stake my life on it.'

'Did she say who the man was?'

He hesitated. 'A gentleman, sir. He'd paid Duckworth to get the girl for him.'

'I can't understand why Mrs Oswald didn't take her maid with her.'

Jack could see no way of avoiding the truth. 'She couldn't. The man who wanted Emmy was Marcus Armistead. She doesn't think anyone will believe her word against his, so won't even try to lay a complaint.' He watched the Parson's face to see how he took this and as he'd expected, Mr Bradley immediately saw the implications.

'Ah. She's probably right, I'm sorry to say.' Gerald Bradley gave a muffled snort of irritation. 'Mr Rishmore is very eager for young Armistead to marry his daughter and that makes it – difficult.'

'But you believe Emmy, sir?'

'Yes. I've heard rumours about young Armistead's behaviour towards women. I dismissed them as exaggerations, but now . . .' He sighed. Rich men could get away with some terrible things. 'We'd best leave the girl in my wife's hands for tonight. She's very good with young women in trouble. Then we'll see if we can find her another place. We both saw for ourselves how well she cared for her former mistress.' He paused then asked with a frown, 'Why did Emmy come to *you* tonight?'

'She didn't. I was out for a stroll because my sister's baby was crying and I bumped into Emmy by sheer accident. I could see she was terrified and – well, I couldn't just leave her there alone and in trouble, so I brought her to you.'

Gerald stood up. 'You did the right thing. You'd better go home now, though. There's nothing more you can do. The girl will be quite safe with us, safe from *everyone* who wishes her harm. That I promise.'

As he walked home, Jack's arm felt wrong without Emmy

clinging to it. She had been warm and soft and had made him feel as a man should.

Yet he had to leave it to others to help her. That made him feel so useless. And the thought of her going away – eh, it was too much to bear. He was glad of the rain hiding his tears. Men weren't supposed to cry, but how could you help it when what you wanted most in life was being taken away from you?

It took Marcus nearly an hour to free himself from the pieces of cloth that vicious little bitch had tied him up with. He was furious with himself for believing her to be submissive, furious that George Duckworth had not warned him how deceitful the wretch could be.

The room was dark except for a small fire in the grate. He found the candle that had fallen out of the metal holder when she'd hit him and lit it in the fire, setting it back in the holder with an unsteady hand.

What was he going to do about this?

His first thought was to call in the constable and lodge a complaint against the girl for attacking and robbing him. They hung people for that. He'd like to see her hang!

But after a while, as his mind grew clearer, he abandoned that idea. If he made a complaint, he'd not only have to explain what he was doing consorting with a whore, but explain to his future father-in-law who was the local magistrate. No, he'd have to spin some other tale to account for his injuries tonight and find a way to pay back that cheating jade himself.

He walked through the town unsteadily, thumping on the back door of the alehouse. Covering his face with his muffler, he asked to see George. Used to gentlemen trying to hide their presence, the tapster who'd opened the door took him into a little room nearby and brought George to him.

'How can I help you, sir?'

Marcus uncovered his face. 'You can find that bitch and hand her over to me!'

George gaped at him. 'What the hell happened?'

'She hit me over the head with a candlestick and escaped. I'll have my money back from you, for a start.'

'I'd never have believed it . . . she's such a little thing.'

'She's a sneaking, lying shrew and she's not going to get away with this!' Marcus indicated the wound on his head and winced.

'I'll find her for you – and punish her, too,' George said confidently. 'She can't get far on foot. Do you want another lass for tonight?'

'No, I bloody don't. I'm going home now. I'll expect to hear from you – and soon.'

By now it was so late he had to knock them up at the livery stables. Since the moon was nearly full he took the quickest route home, the track across the moors. He had to knock up the grooms and then the servants at home, groaning and pretending to be more badly injured than he was. The sight of his bloodied face sent them running to fetch his parents.

'What happened?' his father demanded.

'Robbed. On the moors. Two men set on me, pulled me off my horse and took my money.' Marcus put one hand to his forehead which was swollen and painful. 'They knocked me unconscious, but when I woke up my horse hadn't wandered far, so I dragged myself up on it and came home.'

'What were you doing on the moors at that hour?' his mother asked.

Marcus scowled. Trust her to ask the awkward questions! 'Coming home from visiting a friend.'

If she asked what friend, he'd pretend to faint. But she didn't. She just gave him one of her measuring looks as if she had a fair idea what he'd really been doing and let the matter drop.

When Emmy woke the next morning she couldn't think where she was and sat up with a gasp, ready to flee. Then she realised she was in Parson's house next to the church and sagged back against the pillow in relief. From the sloping ceiling she guessed this to be an attic bedroom. Getting out of bed, she tiptoed across the wooden floor to the window. The back garden of the Parsonage lay beneath and to one side of it the church hall in whose porch she had sheltered the night before. Beyond that were the church and churchyard. Everything looked fresh and sparkling in the feeble winter sunshine and a line of washing was flapping in the breeze. Even the sky looked newly washed.

Mrs Bradley had been very kind to her last night, promising to find her a new position and saying they could use an extra pair of hands here in the meantime. But would they be able to protect her from both George and Marcus?

'I thought I heard you moving about,' said a cheerful voice behind Emmy. 'You certainly slept a long time. It's nearly ten o'clock.'

She turned to see a young woman a bit older than herself with dark hair and a rosy face, standing smiling in the doorway.

Emmy could only stare at her, feeling stupid and heavy-headed.

'I'm Cass, the general dogsbody here.' She smiled as she said that. 'I'll bring up some warm water and you can have a wash, then Cook'll get you something to eat. We've got your clothes dry and I've given them a bit of a press and mended the tears. I'll bring them up as well.'

Emmy slipped under the blankets to keep warm. When she heard footsteps again, she sighed, wishing she need not face the world yet.

Cass came in and deposited a ewer of hot water on the scuffed little table that had a blue and white wash basin on it, then laid Emmy's clothes carefully across the foot of the bed. 'There y'are. Just follow the stairs down two flights when you're ready. They lead straight into the kitchen. Well, mustn't stay chatting. There's allus a lot to do here.' She clattered off, humming as she went.

Emmy washed every inch of herself, trying in vain to rub the dirty feel of Marcus Armistead's hands off her skin. She could not understand why he'd spent so long just playing with her body. From what she'd seen and heard with her mother, men liked to get on with it and gain their release. But perhaps *he* wasn't like other men. She shivered and tried not to think about him, getting ready as quickly as she could, anxious not to seem lazy.

As she went downstairs she heard a piano tinkling some-where, the front door knocker sounding and voices coming from several parts of the house. How lucky people were to live like this! It must be wonderful to have company all the time. You'd feel so safe. She wondered if she would ever feel safe again and hoped Mrs Bradley would find her another position as far away from Northby as possible.

A plump, grey-haired older woman, whom she vaguely remembered from the night before, turned from stirring some-thing on the range, pushing her mob cap higher up her flushed forehead. Massive and comforting, she put an arm round Emmy's shoulders and guided her across to one end of the big wooden table. 'Sit there, love. Cass'll get you something to eat.'

So Emmy sat and watched what was happening in wonder. A pot of soup was bubbling at one side of a large range whose fire was glowing cheerfully in the centre. Cook began dismem-bering a plucked chicken while Cass brought Emmy a cup of tea and then went to toast a piece of bread for her on the fire.

'And give her a bit of that ham,' Cook ordered. 'Keep up her strength.'

Good as the food was, Emmy had to force herself to eat because she was still so worried about what was going to happen to her.

Mrs Bradley came bustling into the kitchen just as she was finishing her food and smiled at her. 'You look better this morning, dear. I've been talking to my husband and we think it'd be sensible for you to stay with us for a while. We can always use another pair of hands. Five shillings a week all found. Will that suit?'

Emmy hesitated. 'I don't want to sound ungrateful, ma'am, but hadn't I better get away from Northby as soon as possible?'

'Parson is having a word with Mr Rishmore about what happened. This Duckworth man will be told in no uncertain terms to leave you alone. You have nothing further to fear from him.' As long as her story is true, which I think it is, Prudence Bradley added mentally, but I'm certain I shall be able to tell if she's a decent girl after she's been with us a few days.

Emmy gulped. 'Are you sure?' There was still Marcus Armistead, only she didn't dare mention him.

'Of course I am.' She saw the anxiety in the girl's eyes and added in a low voice, 'And the other one won't dare come after you while you're with us. Now, if you've finished your breakfast, perhaps you could help Cass. Only light work today, Cass, till we're sure Emmy has recovered from her nasty experience.'

'Yes, ma'am.'

So began a blissful few days during which Emmy helped when and where she could, learning a few new skills as she went because what happened in a household where money was not in short supply was very different from what happened in a cottage whose mistress had to watch every farthing.

'She's a good little worker,' Cook told Mrs Bradley two days later.

'She's a nice, decent lass if ever I saw one,' Cass reported to her mistress the next day when questioned.

'I'd keep Emmy on here myself,' Prudence said to her husband that same evening, 'but I think she'll do better in a place where no one knows her background, which will take a little longer to find.'

He nodded absent-mindedly and she left him to his sermon, smiling to herself. Although she always made a point of appearing to consult him, he never overruled her 'suggestions' and in practice left running the household and dispensing acts of charity towards female members of his parish entirely in her hands.

Samuel Rishmore listened to what his Parson had to tell him, nodding thoughtfully. 'I know Duckworth. But we have only the girl's word against him and he keeps a very orderly house, so I am inclined to give him a severe warning to leave her alone from now on and then let the matter drop. The men must have somewhere to drink, after all.'

Gerald stared at him, feeling disappointed. He ventured a mild protest. 'But this was a grossly immoral act, and what about the gentleman to whom Duckworth sold her? What if he snatches other young women and exposes them to such attacks?'

Samuel's voice grew sharper. 'As I said, we have only her word for it and with such a mother we cannot place too much trust in what she says.'

'My wife considers her a decent, willing girl and a good worker,' Gerald said stiffly, refusing to back down.

'Then let your wife find the girl another place, which will solve the problem of what to do with her. I will have a word with Duckworth and I assure you he will not dare go near her again. Now, about the monument on my father's grave . . .'

Gerald Bradley knew when to draw back, even though he was sure Prudence was going to be angry at this lack of response, as indeed he was himself. Like many gentlemen in positions of power, Samuel Rishmore believed what was convenient and no one dared gainsay him. Life could be very unfair to the poor.

George Duckworth scowled at the rent collector who was explaining very emphatically that he would lose his alehouse and licence if he went near Emmy Carter again.

'You understand? Mr Rishmore himself told me to speak to you about this.'

'Aye, I understand. But she's a liar. I've had nowt to do with her.'

'That's as may be, but if Parson believes her lies, who are we to argue? Besides, I've seen you myself, watching her in the street. She's a bonny 'un, but you'd better forget about her, George, my lad, and get on with running your alehouse. There's other fish in the pond. Mr Rishmore is pleased you've heeded his last warning and stopped the fighting. You heed him in this as well and he'll let you be in your other activities, so long as you keep your girls off the main street. And I wouldn't say no to a glass of your best if there's any going. Thirsty work, collecting rents.'

George went to draw him a glass and managed to chat amiably enough, but when the rent collector had left he went stamping up the stairs, furious that his plans for bettering himself had received this setback. He threw open the door of Madge's room. 'Get out, you!' he roared.

She looked at him in puzzlement. 'George?'

'Get out of my alehouse and out of Northby, too. Within the hour.'

'George, no!' She flung herself at him and when he shook her off, clung to his legs. 'George, what have I done? I don't know what I've done.'

He scowled down at her and gave in to the temptation to kick her away from him. 'Brought up your daughter to defy me, that's what you've done. I've just nearly lost this place because of *her*. And without her you're no use to me. Look at you! Drunk all day now, you are, and don't even keep yourself clean any more. *Just bloody look at you!*' He dragged her across the room and thrust her face in front of the fly-specked mirror which cruelly exposed her bloodshot eyes, bedraggled hair and pallid skin.

She whimpered and tried to cling to him. 'George, don't send me away. *Please*. I'll do anything.'

'There's nothing you can do now. She ran off bleating to Parson about last night, the bitch. Well, I've had a bellyful of both you and your bloody daughter. Just make sure you're out of Northby by nightfall or you'll be sorry.'

He shoved her away from him violently, sending her tumbling to the floor, then stormed out, still seething with anger. Damn all interfering, sanctimonious bastards!

After a while he grew thoughtful. He'd had enough of this place now and although he hadn't enough money saved to do what he wanted it occurred to him suddenly that Marcus Armistead might be interested in a joint investment. It was worth a try anyway. Give that randy bugger the chance of girls easily available at any time and he might just be tempted into doing something a bit ungentlemanly. George grinned. Though the sod didn't always follow through, the girls told him – had trouble finishing off, as some men did.

Madge lay sobbing for a few minutes then heaved herself to her feet, muttering, 'It's not fair. It isn't *my* fault Emmy's like that. She takes after her father's side. Always has done. If they'd only treated us properly, there'd be no need for any of this.' She sneaked downstairs and stole a bottle of gin from behind the bar.

In between sips she packed her things, sobbing sometimes and muttering to herself.

An hour later a voice roared up the stairs, 'Are you still there?'

She yelled back, 'I have to pack my things, don't I? Aw, Georgie, please—'

'Get the hell out of here, you cheating trollop!'

She left the inn by the back door just as Marcus Armistead was slipping inside, standing back to let him pass and scowling at him.

He watched her go indifferently, then went to see George and ask whether the girl had been traced. But it seemed the stupid bitch had found herself protectors of another sort in the Parson and his wife who had the ear of Samuel Rishmore. 'Damnation!' Marcus picked up a glass and sent it shattering against the wall. 'I was looking forward to teaching her a lesson. Well, if you can't supply her, I want my money back.'

'Haven't got it. I had expenses getting her and hiring the cottage. I can only return five guineas, take it or leave it.' George turned to the slattern wiping over the tables. 'Has Madge Carter left yet?'

'Yes. But I feel sorry for the poor bitch,' she muttered, secure in her own position as highest-earning whore in this establishment. 'She can't help it if her daughter won't do as you want. You shouldn't have chucked her out like that.'

'That old woman leaving the inn was Emmy's mother?' Marcus exclaimed. 'Hell, she looks more like her grandmother!'

George cleared his throat. 'I was wondering if you'd be interested in a little business proposition? It'd give you access to a lot of other girls.' He watched Marcus's face carefully and grinned as he saw his companion's expression change. Aha! Caught you!

In the privacy of his own room, George explained what he wanted to do.

Marcus nodded thoughtfully, asked one or two questions, then said, 'We'll talk about it again next week. In the meantime I'll look into the situation in Manchester.' Now he had to go and do the pretty to Jane Rishmore, the mere sight of whom made his gorge rise.

He went outside and mounted his horse, still seething with fury every time he thought of the girl who'd escaped him. He hadn't been able to get her out of his mind, her and her pretty unmarked body. One day he'd make her sorry for what she'd done. Very sorry indeed.

Marcus would have thought no more of the old woman, but as he was riding across the tops on his way home he saw her by the side of the road, sobbing and wailing, clearly drunk. He reined in his horse to look down at her, smiling to see her brought so low.

'Give us a shilling, sir,' Madge begged, trying to smile at him enticingly. When he stayed where he was, she staggered across to clutch his stirrup and say, 'I can pleasure you, if you like, sir. I know how to make a gentleman happy.'

The thought of that sickened him. Who would want to touch an old hag like this? In a sudden spurt of anger he kicked her away as hard as he could.

Screeching in fury, too drunk to think what she was doing, Madge snatched up a stone and hurled it at him, catching the horse on its rump. 'You rotten devil! No wonder my Emmy didn't want anything to do with you.'

How the hell did she know that? Had she helped her daughter to escape?

The animal began to sidle nervously and when Marcus tried to hit it with his riding crop, he hit the old woman instead. It filled him with such savage satisfaction to hear that girl's mother scream in pain that he leaned sideways to swipe another blow at her. As the red rage he usually managed to control rose in him he gave in to it for once, kicking his feet out of the stirrups and jumping down from his horse the better to get at her. He cracked his riding crop down on her again and again.

At first she screeched and tried to fight back, but in a very short time she stopped doing anything but try to protect herself. Power filled Marcus. He felt strong and masculine. You didn't need to be tall to prove you were a man. You just needed to show women who was the master.

As she fell and lay moaning feebly, he abandoned the riding

crop to kick and beat her till she stopped making any noise at all. He continued even after she lay motionless.

Eventually the rage died down and he stepped back, panting as he wiped one arm across his forehead. It was a while before he realised how still the whore was. There was no sound but the chill wind whining softly across the moors and lifting his hair off his forehead – and no sign of movement at all from her. His horse was some distance away now, blowing uneasily through its nostrils.

He yelled, 'Away with you, you old hag!' That should have made her at least crawl away from him. What was she trying to do now, pretend he'd really hurt her? Well, she wasn't going to get any money out of him.

As he bent to roll her over on to her back he saw in shock that her eyes were open, staring blindly up at the grey sky. Her chest was still. She wasn't breathing. She was dead! 'No,' he whispered. 'No, she's faking. She must be.' So he shook her. But her body flopped around like a broken doll and in a sudden fit of disgust he hurled her away from him, watching her head bounce on the ground.

He backed away, horrified. 'No! Damn you, get up!'

But she didn't move.

At first he thought only of getting away, but even before he'd caught his horse, he realised that would not be wise. What if someone found out he'd done it?

Shuddering, he looked down at himself but there was no sign of blood, no sign that he had just beaten and kicked a woman to death.

He looked around, trying to work out whether there was anything to give him away. And of course he saw the hoof marks and footprints in the muddy ground around her body.

Muttering in annoyance, he led the horse on to stony ground quite a bit further up the track, tethering it to a gatepost and keeping a careful eye out for whatever farmer the land belonged to. But there was no one in sight. 'Thank God!' he muttered.

As he made his way back he tried to keep to rocky ground and leave no distinguishable footprints. After staring at the still figure, he stripped off his cloak and frock coat, even sacrificing his new waistcoat. He didn't want to touch *her* again. Couldn't. But he used the waistcoat to wipe the ground around her clear of hoofprints and footprints, walking backwards and smoothing the muddy patches as he went. It took him a long time and it was bloody hard work.

It was all *her* fault for accosting him like that. They shouldn't allow whores out in daylight.

When he got back to his horse it was fretting but he dressed again and re-mounted. He looked down at the muddy waistcoat, slung across the pommel now. It would have to be got rid of or the servants would ask why it was in such a state. He reined in and stared round, then remembered the old abandoned quarry and turned off along the stony rutted track towards it. He didn't even need to dismount to toss the waistcoat over the edge and laughed as it vanished from sight. By the time anyone found it, if they ever did, it'd be weathered beyond recognition.

As he rode slowly home, he smiled to think of what he had done. No one messed around with Marcus Armistead. He was a man to be reckoned with, a man who knew how to treat women. He felt good, happier than he had for a long time.

But he had better be careful next time the rage rose in him. If he could.

When he got home, he claimed a fall from his horse, something which had happened to him once or twice before.

His father was loudly scornful of his horsemanship at dinner that night, but when Marcus said he'd been coming back from calling on Jane Rishmore, the old fool shut up about the fall and wanted to know about that instead.

'I think we had a pleasant visit,' Marcus said. It had been purgatory. She'd barely said a word to help the conversation along and she'd looked worse than usual, great ugly lump that she was.

'Good, good. You'd better propose soon. I'll speak to Rishmore and see when he wants the wedding to take place. Easter might be a good time. What do you think, my dear?'

Eleanor nodded. 'A very good idea. A young man needs some responsibility to keep him out of mischief.'

What the hell did she mean by that? Marcus wondered. He

avoided her eyes and concentrated on his food. He was hungry tonight and the lamb was particularly juicy.

His parents continued to discuss the coming marriage for the rest of the meal until Marcus could have screamed at them to shut up. But he didn't dare because his bloody father still held the purse strings.

As he was getting into bed he again remembered the woman he'd killed, and smiled. One day her daughter too would find out that it did not pay to cross him. He would look forward to that.

Chapter Nine

Mrs Bradley came into the kitchen looking very grave. 'There you are, Emmy. Could I have a word with you, please?'

Exchanging worried glances with Cass, Emmy wiped her hands on her apron and followed her mistress along the corridor to the small sitting room in which parish business was conducted. Her heart was thumping and her hands felt clammy. What had happened now?

'Sit down, child.'

It didn't sound as if she was in trouble, but she was so terrified she was going to be turned off, Emmy remained where she was and burst out with, 'If I've done something wrong, Mrs Bradley, I didn't mean to and I'll never do it again, if you'll only tell me what it is.'

'Dear me, it's not that. This is about your mother, I'm afraid.' Again she gestured to the chair beside her.

'Oh.' Emmy's heart sank still further as she took the chair. Surely her mother wasn't causing more trouble for her? It'd be a long time before she forgave her for taking George's side, that was for sure. If she ever did. 'I don't want to have anything else to do with her, ma'am, and I'm really sorry if she's bothered you.'

'It's not that. Look, there isn't an easy way to tell you but I'm afraid your mother's dead, Emmy. She was found on the moors just outside town, lying by the side of the road. And, well – it seems someone had murdered her, beaten her to death.'

Emmy clasped the edge of her mistress's rosewood desk as the room wavered around her. '*Dead?* My mother's dead?'

'Yes. I'm so sorry. The constable wants to have a word with you later, to ask if you've any idea who might have done this.'

Emmy could only think of one person. 'It must be George Duckworth. Who else could it be?'

'That was what Constable Makepeace thought, but it's not possible. Mr Duckworth turned your mother out yesterday and sprained his ankle soon after she left. He was sitting in the bar for the rest of the day with his foot up, in full view of his customers, and then,' she flushed, 'he, um, spent the night with one of his – women.'

Emmy wasn't convinced. 'But who else would . . .' She broke off as she realised that only one other person wished her ill and might have tried to get at her through her mother. But surely Marcus Armistead could not have done such a thing? He was a gentleman, and would he even know someone as old and shop-soiled as Madge Carter? And he wasn't a very big man either. Her mother could have fought him off as Emmy had. Only – he'd hurt Emmy, had enjoyed doing it too. Maybe he'd planned the attack, taken her mother by surprise? Thoughts were whirling round her brain, but she kept seeing her poor mother – dying alone and in agony somewhere on the moors. And then remembering that Madge hadn't even looked at her when George had carried her out of the inn.

For all her faults, her mother hadn't deserved to be murdered. No one deserved that.

Mrs Bradley allowed the young maid a moment or two, then asked quietly, 'Is there something you know that might help, dear?'

She looked at her mistress. 'It was only a thought, ma'am. Nothing definite. I'd better not say. It concerns the gentleman who . . .' She could not finish the sentence, could only swallow hard and stare down at her tightly clasped hands.

'Hmm.' Prudence looked at her thoughtfully. 'I think you should tell Constable Makepeace everything you know and let him decide for himself whether it's important or not. I'll send you word when he arrives. If you wish to go to your bedroom until then, you may.'

'Thank you, ma'am, but I'd rather get on with my work. It's better to keep busy.'

Emmy walked slowly back to the kitchen and told Cook and Cass what had happened. 'Why am I not crying?' she asked in bewilderment. 'My mother's dead. Shouldn't I be crying?'

'Shock,' Cook said. 'It'll hit you sudden, then you'll bawl your eyes out.' Having offered that comfort, and being a woman of few words, she went back to her work.

When Cass passed she gave Emmy's back a friendly pat and smiled at her. It was comforting. In fact, Emmy found just being in that big warm kitchen comforting. If only she could stay here at the Parsonage! But she knew she couldn't. It was even more important for her to leave Northby now that someone had killed her mother.

She'd lost her dear mistress, then her mother, and now she was going to lose her only friend. You could not be much more alone in the world than she was. Once Mrs Bradley found her a job, she would probably never see Jack again. Life was cruel.

Eli Makepeace came to the Parsonage that afternoon and spoke gently to Emmy, with such kindness in his weatherbeaten face she decided to do as her mistress had suggested and tell him everything. When she told him the name of the gentleman who had paid George to kidnap her, he whistled softly through his teeth.

'Have you told anyone else about that, girl?'

'Only Mr and Mrs Bradley – oh, and Jack.'

'Would that be Jack Staley?'

'Yes, sir. I bumped into him when I was escaping from the cottage. He brought me here and agreed with me that it was better not to mention the man's name to anyone else.'

'Well, lass, he was right, more's the pity. He's got his head screwed on, has young Staley. You were right to tell me about it, but it doesn't do to set up the backs of the gentry unless you've proof. It's not fair, but it's how things are in this world.'

Eli chewed the corner of his lip thoughtfully as he studied her. He'd seen Emmy Carter about town with old Mrs Oswald and knew her to be a decent lass. Surprising, that, with a drunken whore of a mother but he liked to take folk as he found 'em, not let others tell him what to think. 'I can't see any reason why Marcus Armistead should have killed your mother, though, even if he is angry with you, so it's no use bringing him into it unless I find cause. I won't forget what you've told me, though, and I'll keep my eyes open.' It was surprising what you could piece together bit by bit sometimes.

She nodded, accepting what he had said. Her life had given her no reason to believe in the fairness of things, either. All you could do was look after yourself to the best of your ability. And sometimes even that wasn't enough to keep you safe.

When the constable had gone she sat on for a few minutes in her mistress's comfortable little sitting room, thinking about her mother. Emmy still couldn't take it in that she was really dead.

Mrs Bradley returned. 'Are you all right, dear?'

Emmy stood up hastily. 'Yes, ma'am.'

'My husband says they want to bury your mother the day after tomorrow. He'll hold a short service but it'll be a pauper's grave, I'm afraid.'

Emmy nodded. She had expected nothing else. And who but she would care that Madge Carter was dead?

'I'll find you some dark clothes to wear. You need some warmer things anyway.'

As she went back to her work, Emmy could not help thinking about her future. Some maids stayed with families all their lives, Cook said, and she should know because she'd been with the Bradleys for nearly twenty years. 'You put your heart into your work, my lass,' she'd advised, 'and you'll make a good life for yourself in service.'

Emmy intended to do that. But first they had to bury her mother – and bury the past with her, she hoped.

It was Martin Graslow who told his friend that his sister had been murdered, and how.

Isaac looked at him in shock and could not speak for a minute or two, then he swallowed hard. 'I must go to the funeral. I can't let them bury her without me. She was such a pretty little lass, our Madge was. My father used to think the world of her. I – I can't rightly take it in that she's dead.'

He went to see his employer as soon as he was feeling more himself. Time to make a clean breast of things. 'Madge Carter, the woman who was killed – she was my sister, sir.'

Samuel Rishmore stared at him in amazement. 'You never said a word about that when the woman came to work in Northby!'

'Well, it's not something I'm proud of. My father never spoke her name aloud from the day she ran away to the day he died. The reason I'm telling you now, sir, is that I should like to attend the funeral. I shall only need an hour off and I'll make the time up.'

'No need for that. You've more than earned an hour off. We'll be holding an inquest tomorrow afternoon. It's a clear case of murder, but I can't see us catching the criminal who did it. He'll be miles away now. A disgruntled customer, I should think. Makepeace tells me there's a daughter. Is she a whore too?'

'I don't know the girl, because we didn't associate with my sister, but I'm told the lass is not at all like her mother. She's working for Parson at the moment as a maid, it seems, but used to work for Mrs Oswald.'

Rishmore nodded. He remembered now seeing her in church and thinking her pretty. Too pretty. 'Well, you're her only relative now, so you'd better make sure she's all right. Let me know if there's anything I can do to help. We don't want her turning to the streets like her mother, do we?'

When Isaac went back to the office he sat down heavily behind his desk, forgetting to shut the door. There was something he had to do for his sister before he could bury her and her murky past.

After a few minutes' deep thought he went to the door and called Jack in. 'I want you to take the afternoon stage coach to Manchester and deliver a message for me, then wait for an answer. You'll be late back, I'm afraid, so here's some money for a meal as well as the fare. Make sure you're not late for work tomorrow, though.' He felt guilty about doing this in his own interests, but doubted Mr Rishmore would question the junior clerk's absence.

Jack was startled at this order, but the thought of going into Manchester excited him for he'd never visited the city. Carefully he memorised his instructions about delivering a message to a lawyer called Reynolds who had offices just off Deansgate, then went to catch the stage coach that passed regularly through Northby on its way to the city.

Jack hadn't believed it when people told him there were over a hundred thousand people living in Manchester, but as the coach creaked and rumbled towards the smoky mass he gazed out of the mud-splattered window in awe. On and on the city went, a great sprawl of buildings: houses of all sizes, terraces of workers' dwellings, mills with big smoking chimneys, workshops, man-ufactories, smithies, shops, innumerable public houses, and nearer the centre a few imposing civic buildings. And people everywhere you looked! Rich ones in their carriages, hawkers with trays hanging round their necks, people on foot, and beggars at the corners of the meaner streets. It made his head spin to see it all.

As the coach drove into the city centre it had to slow down to a walking pace because there were so many other vehicles on the roads – fancy carriages, gigs, carts, drays carrying heavy loads, men pushing handcarts, everything you could think of. And the people on foot were bustling to and fro as if their lives depended on them getting somewhere as rapidly as possible.

Jack had heard Mr Butterfield say how important a city Manchester was becoming, and he had read about it in Parson's newspapers, but it hadn't seemed real before. Now it was. And he was proud to see such progress, even though he'd not like to live here himself.

Once out of the coach he walked as briskly as he could through the crowds, following the clear directions he had been given by the head clerk. He delivered the letter and had to wait a few minutes for a reply, then was given another letter, its edges stuck down so hastily the sealing wax was smeared everywhere. He didn't waste time wondering what it might contain. Mr Butterfield did not confide all Rishmore's business to him and relied on his discretion. He made the most of the chance to see a bit of the city in the two hours before he could set off back on the last coach of the day.

When he got to Northby, it looked very small to him and almost deserted, only a few people to be seen by the light of the lamps the parish council insisted be kept lit until midnight in the centre of the town. He shivered as he walked briskly to Mr Butterfield's house and knocked on the front door, handing over the reply to what must be a very important message indeed.

Then he made his way home to the much smaller house that felt more like a prison each year. He hesitated outside the front door, listening to the sound of yet another shrill argument between his sister and mother. It had been wonderful to escape, if only for a few hours. He just wished he didn't have to go back inside again!

The day of the funeral was cold but fine, with an icy wind whistling through the streets and sucking the warmth from those who had no choice but to be out in it.

Emmy helped out in the kitchen, then at ten o'clock went up to the chilly attic to change into her new clothes, shivering in the raw air of the unheated rooms. The matching skirt and bodice fitted nicely, though she'd had to take the hem up. And the clothes hardly showed any signs of wear. Imagine people giving away clothes as good as these! She fingered the material, a sturdy dark grey wool that would keep her nice and warm, then swung the lighter grey woollen cloak round her shoulders and picked up the small felt bonnet with the new black ribbons on it.

When she went down Cook stopped work to stare at her and nod approvingly.

Cass came in and said, 'Eh, them dark colours suit you, Emmy love.'

'Who will be there to notice? There's only going to be me at the funeral.'

She walked across to the church with Parson, keeping her eyes cast down, relieved when he didn't say anything. She still hadn't wept for her mother and that made her feel so guilty.

The air inside the church seemed no warmer than that outside and Emmy shivered as they walked across the stone-flagged floor at the back towards the aisle. On Sundays they lit braziers in here to try to warm the place up, and usually she'd have been in the crowded back pews with enough people around to kept her warm. Today, with only a pauper's funeral taking place, the sexton hadn't bothered lighting any braziers and the empty church seemed larger than usual as their footsteps echoed around them.

Automatically she moved towards a rear pew.

'You must sit at the front today, my dear,' Parson said in his kind, plummy voice.

It made everything feel even more unreal to follow him towards the altar. She took the seat he indicated on the right side of the aisle and bent her head. She tried to pray for her mother, she really did, but no words would come.

The coffin was already standing at the front of the church. It looked small and the wood was roughly finished. The thought that her mother's battered body lay inside it made Emmy shiver again.

Parson, who had vanished to one side, now came out to the front in his vestments. He opened his mouth to speak then closed it again with a look of surprise.

The big door at the rear opened and shut again with a bang that echoed through the church and footsteps paced slowly along the aisle. Emmy didn't like to turn and stare so waited to see who this was. When a man joined her in the front pew, she glanced quickly sideways and saw in shock that it was the one her mother had said was her brother, Mr Butterfield who worked at the mill. He had always walked straight past them in the street, never showing by so much as the flicker of an eyelid that he recognised them, so she was astonished to see him here today.

He nodded to her, then sat down beside her and bowed his head for a minute in prayer.

The door banged again and another set of footsteps came along the aisle. Emmy could not help turning round to stare this time, even if it was bad manners, but the newcomer was a complete stranger, a man she had never seen before. Who was he? What was he doing here? Had he known her mother too? And if so, how had he found out about the funeral?

He and Mr Butterfield nodded to one another as if they were already acquainted, then he sat down in the front pew on the other side of the aisle.

Parson cleared his throat and began the service. It didn't take long and little of it registered in Emmy's mind. When it was over, the two men employed as gravedigger and gardener at the church came and lifted the coffin. She didn't know what to do next and looked questioningly at Mr Butterfield.

'We must follow them to the grave,' he said quietly. He stood up and went to wait at the end of the pew for her to lead the way out of the church, as if she were a lady.

The other man followed them in silence.

It was all so strange Emmy didn't know what to make of it, had given up trying.

To her surprise they didn't go to the back of the churchyard, to the spot reserved for paupers, but stopped near a newly dug hole.

'I could not see my sister laid in a pauper's grave,' Mr Butterfield told her. 'This is where the rest of the Butterfield family are buried, Emmeline.'

'Yes, sir.'

'You should call me Uncle Isaac.'

But she couldn't say that. It just didn't feel right. And she couldn't remember the last time anyone had called her Emmeline. Her mother had always said the name had been her father's choice, to match his own name, Emerick.

The Parson said some more words at the graveside while Emmy watched his surplice bell out in the breeze and wished he'd hurry up. That wind was sharp as knives and even in her new clothes she was finding it hard not to shiver. Besides, what did words matter? They wouldn't bring her mother back, would they?

'Emmy!'

She realised Parson was looking at her as if he expected her to do something. Panic filled her. She should have been paying attention. What did they want?

'You should throw some earth on the coffin,' the stranger prompted. He bent to pick up a little moist dark soil, so she did the same, and when he gestured, she threw it into the hole. It seemed a pointless thing to do and it dirtied her hand, but both men did the same thing, after which Parson did some more praying.

When that was finished, he looked at the two men. 'If you need to talk to Emmy, you can be private in my study.'

'Thank you,' the stranger said. 'We do need to talk to her.'

Remembering the last time she had been alone with a stranger, Emmy hung back. 'I don't want to go with them, Mr Bradley.' And then the tears came. Tears for the mother who would never know that her brother had cared enough for her to come to the funeral and pay for a proper burial. Tears for Mrs Tibby, whom Emmy was missing dreadfully. Tears for herself, too, because she was not only alone in the world, but was suddenly very afraid of what these men might want with her.

'She won't understand till she's settled down,' Parson said. So they took her back to Mrs Bradley, who sat with her till she'd grown calmer then accompanied her into the Parson's study when she confessed she was afraid to go alone.

'This gentleman is Mr Reynolds, a lawyer,' Parson said. 'He has your mother's will and has brought some things for you.'

Emmy could only gape at him. She had never expected her mother to make a will. You only did that if you had something to leave people. For the first time she wondered if some of her mother's tales of better times were true. She had never quite believed them, knowing how Madge always embroidered the truth and saw things as she wanted them to be instead of as they were.

The lawyer placed a cardboard box in front of Emmy. 'Your mother left you everything she owned – but sadly she'd fallen on hard times so this is all that remains: a locket and some papers she wanted you to have.'

All Emmy could think of to say was, 'Thank you, sir.'

'The locket belonged to your father's grandmother. It's a pretty piece.'

She didn't want anything from her father's family, because if they really were well-off and had sent her and her mother away after her father died, she'd never forgive them for condemning her to a life of shame. But she didn't dare refuse it. Taking the box, she put it on her knee. The lawyer had a narrow face and kept talking over her head to the other men as if she didn't exist, occasionally throwing disapproving glances in her direction as if he didn't like what he saw. She didn't know why that annoyed her so much, but it did. She sniffed away the tears that were still threatening and tried to listen, but could not seem to concentrate on the words, only stare from one man to another.

Her uncle was looking tight-faced and angry now. Well, she hadn't asked him to come today, had she?

In the end it was Parson who spoke to her. 'We've been discussing your future, Emmy, while you were – composing yourself.' He leaned back in his chair, clasping his hands across his plump belly. 'At seventeen you are very young to go out into the world alone. You have just escaped from serious trouble and we do not want you facing other temptations.'

'Mrs Bradley said she'd find me a position, sir. Away from Northby. I'm sure I'll be all right once I have a place. I'm a good worker and I won't let you down.'

'It would be better if you had someone to keep an eye on you, a family member, until you are older,' Mr Butterfield replied.

He didn't say, *So that you don't follow the same path as your mother*, but that was what he meant, Emmy thought resentfully. 'I've been on my own for a while now, sir – Uncle, I mean – working for Mrs Oswald. I don't *need* anyone to keep an eye on me, I just need a job. I'm not like my mother and I'm never going to be.'

'Very laudable,' Parson said. 'Yes, yes.' He glanced sideways at the stranger as if expecting him to speak and when he didn't, asked, 'Is that all you wish to say, Mr Reynolds?'

'Yes. Since Mr Butterfield is taking an interest, I feel the less said the better. My family does have some – concerns, but I feel today's decision will answer the case nicely.'

The long words meant nothing to Emmy. She wished they'd just let her get on with her work. She was determined to prove to Mrs Bradley what a good worker she was, determined to do everything she could to wipe out the past. She realised with a start that they were all looking at her again and glanced uneasily sideways at Mrs Bradley.

'She's still a bit upset and finding it hard to concentrate,' that lady said. 'Let me explain it to her.' She took Emmy's hand in hers. 'My dear, we don't feel you should be on your own. Life can deal very harshly with young women like you.'

'When I get another place, I'll not be on my own. You *said* you'd find me one.'

The mistress's hand patted hers firmly. 'Well, what we've decided will be better. Your uncle has kindly offered to take you into his own home.'

Emmy gaped at the stern man on her other side. 'But why?'

Isaac looked at her in surprise. 'Because I'm family. The only family you know now.'

'But I *don't* know you! And your wife won't want someone like me living in her house.'

'My wife knows her duty to the family, I hope.'

'And there are your daughters . . . they hate me, too!' Everyone stared at her as if she were telling lies, so she added desperately, 'They say nasty things to me in the street. I can't go and live with people who hate me.'

'She's overwrought,' Mr Reynolds said.

Emmy answered for herself. 'I'm not! And I won't do it.'

'You have no choice, dear,' Mrs Bradley said quietly. 'You're under age and they *are* your family.'

'Then where were they when we didn't have enough to eat? I don't want a family like that.'

Isaac looked at her in shock. 'Didn't have enough to eat?'

'Many a time!'

'All the more reason for Mr Butterfield to look after you now, young woman,' Mr Reynolds said firmly.

'What do *you* know about it?' she flung at him. 'It's none of your business what I do, you're only the lawyer.'

Everyone looked at Mr Reynolds as if expecting him to say something else, but he didn't.

Emmy felt as if her head would burst with the anguish of this day.

'I think you should go with Mr Butterfield, dear,' Mrs Bradley urged. 'It really is the best thing for you.'

'No, it isn't. People in Northby will know about my mother and say I'm like her. I need to get away, make a new start.'

Parson spoke, his voice sharper than usual. 'That's ungrateful, Emmy. They're your family.'

'They still hate me.' Why could he and his wife not understand that?

Mr Butterfield looked at her and for a moment his face softened. 'I don't hate you, Emmy. I hate what my sister became, but that isn't the same thing at all.'

Then Mrs Bradley said in that no-nonsense tone of hers, 'Emmy, that's enough! We've found you a good home and it's all settled. Besides, Mr Rishmore himself wants to make sure you're properly looked after. He's taking an interest in your welfare and you would be foolish to go against his wishes. His support offers you excellent protection from the other things you fear.'

Emmy looked from one to the other and closed her lips on further protests. But she knew this wouldn't work out. And she was afraid of going to share a house with Lal Butterfield. Terrified. Lal was so much bigger and stronger than she was.

Chapter Ten

'Why did that man come to my mother's funeral?' Emmy asked suddenly as she and her uncle walked slowly up the hill from the church.

'Mr Reynolds? Well, um, on behalf of your father's family.'

'The Carters should have come themselves. I hate them. It's all their fault my mother had to earn her living like that. Why could they not look after her when my father died?'

'Because she had lived in sin with him before they were married. They never forgave her for that. And I think you should know: your father's name wasn't Carter. Your mother changed her name after he died, because of what she was doing.'

She stopped walking to stare at him in surprise. 'What was his surname, then?'

'His family would rather keep that secret. They don't wish her shame to be known.'

'Their shame, too. She didn't like doing it, you know.' Anger warred with tears and she fell silent as she fought for control.

Isaac sighed. 'It's our fault as well, I'm afraid. The Butterfields didn't help her, either. I shall always regret that.' After a few more paces he pointed ahead, 'That's where we live.'

Emmy stared at the Butterfields' comfortable villa, four stories high if you included the attics above and the cellar below, one of a pair of semi-detached houses at the upper end of Weavers Lane, where the better class of folk lived. Only a hundred yards north of the church, it felt like a hundred miles away from the bottom end of the street with its squalor and tumble-down houses, its seedy inhabitants and furtive passers-by.

Here folk walked sedately, nodded to one another, called greetings or stopped for a leisurely chat. They spoke to her uncle and stared at her in curiosity when he simply nodded back without stopping to introduce her. He was carrying her bag of clothing and personal possessions while she held her mother's box in her arms, clutching it to her chest as if it could protect her. Only it couldn't. Nothing could protect her now that they'd forced her to stay in Northby where no one would ever quite trust her. She breathed in deeply and slowly to hold back the tears that still threatened to overwhelm her.

Her uncle opened the front door and led the way inside, calling, 'We're here, my dear.'

There was the murmur of women's voices from the front room. The door opened and Lal stood there, looking scornfully at Emmy before closing the door carefully behind her and saying in a low voice, 'Mother says to take her up to her bedroom because Mrs Moston has called.' She stared at the box in Emmy's hand as if trying to assess its contents, then went back into the front room.

Isaac looked helplessly at Emmy then gestured towards the stairs. 'I'll lead the way, shall I?' Not waiting for an answer, he strode up stairs so thickly carpeted that his feet made almost no sound. Emmy looked down the long narrow corridor also covered in a carpet runner that led towards the back of the house then followed him, feeling strange and cut off from everything she knew.

He stopped on the first landing to say, 'You're in the attics because all the bedrooms on this floor are occupied' Opening a door, he disappeared through it.

Emmy followed him in silence up another set of stairs, narrower and steeper, with a worn carpet on them. Here the walls were in need of painting and it was much colder.

'This is your room, Emmy.' His tone was apologetic.

She went reluctantly inside. The bare boards were unstained

but clean – well, bare boards were no hardship to her. The room was larger than any she'd had before, but no effort had been made to make it feel welcoming and the bed was narrow and hard-looking. The only other furniture consisted of a rickety chair and a tin trunk.

'I suppose you're meant to put your clothes in there.' Isaac went over to the trunk and lifted the lid. 'Yes, see, it's empty. But we'll have to find you a rug and a proper wash stand.' He pulled out a silver pocket watch and consulted it. 'Dear, dear! I really must get back to the mill. I'm sorry to leave you. Why don't you unpack? I'm sure someone will come to fetch you as soon as Mrs Moston has gone.'

When his footsteps had faded away and the front door closed, the silence seemed oppressive. Emmy turned round in a circle, then did it again as she surveyed her new room. Mrs Bradley had provided far more comfort for her maids than these people were providing for a relative, but if you looked on the bright side, at least there was no one sharing this room with her. She went to try the bed and it felt as hard as it looked.

Something bumped against her thigh and she looked at the box of her mother's papers which she had set down beside her, remembering the way Lal had stared at it. What if Lal took her locket away? It was the only thing Emmy had from her father. She could not bear to look at it yet, for her emotions were still raw from burying her mother and she was still angry with her father's family lawyer for disposing of her like this. What right had they to interfere in her life now when they hadn't helped her before?

Emptying the contents of the box on the bed she looked round for a hiding place for them, getting up to inspect the room more carefully. Nowhere in here. She tiptoed out into the big open attic space outside her room, which had some trunks and pieces of old furniture piled in corners. Not in those, either. Anyone could find things in there.

A door opened and closed downstairs and she stopped to listen, her heart pounding as if she were contemplating a crime, but there was no sound of footsteps coming up here, so she continued her inspection. The walls sloped to the ground at one end and the plaster had crumbled away near the bottom. She picked up the bag of papers left by her mother, which she would read later, when she could face what she didn't doubt were more shameful details about the past. She slipped the locket into it and pushed it between the slats of wood showing beneath the rotted plaster. She could poke her finger through and reach it if she wanted to get it out, yet from only one step back you couldn't tell it was there if you didn't know what to look for.

She sighed in relief then realised she had to put something else in her box. In the bedroom she hastily fumbled in her bag of possessions and found a piece of embroidery and a few skeins of thread that Mrs Oswald had given her. They would have to do. Tears came into her eyes as she stared at the embroidery. Mrs Tibby had been trying to teach her fine needlework, but this was her first piece, clumsily done and grubby-looking because she'd had to pull her stitches back a few times.

After putting it into the box she took everything else out of her bag, folding her clothes and laying them neatly in the trunk, then setting out her soft felt house shoes beside it, ready to change into. She put the cardboard box on top of the trunk, then wondered what to do.

The front door opened, there was a murmur of voices, it shut again. Her room was at the rear of the house, so she couldn't see who came and went. She expected her aunt or cousins to come up for her then but time passed and still nothing happened. What were they doing?

The church clock struck the hour then the half-hour. Tired of sitting there with nothing to do, Emmy wandered out into the attic again. There was a larger bedroom opposite hers but it didn't look as if anyone used it because the bed was not made up.

At last she heard footsteps on the stairs so went back into her own bedroom, standing beside the window facing the door. No need to tell her that her aunt didn't want her here, she thought bitterly. They were making it all too plain.

A very plump lady whom she recognised from church puffed her way across from the top of the attic stairs and stood staring at her from the doorway. Lal and Dinah were visible, smirking behind her as if expecting to enjoy themselves.

Emmy's aunt was fashionably dressed in full skirts and her sleeves were so wide at the top that they made her look even larger. She was wearing a fussy, frilled cap on her head which had bunches of ribbons to each side of her face and did not suit her. She stared at Emmy in a chill, assessing way. 'So you're that woman's daughter? I never thought I'd see the day when I'd have to give house room to someone like you.'

This open malice was far worse than Emmy had expected, but she said nothing.

'I am *not* pleased to have you living in this house, girl, and I shall *never* regard you as a member of my family, whatever my husband says! However, Mr Rishmore wishes you to live with us so we must make the best of things. You will work hard and earn your keep, believe me, and you will behave yourself. Do I make myself plain?'

'Yes, Aunt Lena.'

'Show me what you've brought with you.'

Emmy looked at her in puzzlement.

'I wish to make sure you are not bringing anything dirty or distasteful into this house.'

Why should she expose all her pitiful possessions to this woman and her two grinning cousins? She made no move to open the trunk. 'I have the outfit I'm wearing, which Mrs Bradley gave me, and another like it, but my summer dresses are rather worn and too small for me.'

The slap her aunt administered took Emmy by surprise, sending her reeling onto the bed and making her head ring.

'I said to show me what you've brought with you!' her aunt cried.

Lal and Dinah tittered but a glare from their mother silenced them instantly.

'That is your first lesson in obedience, Emmy. Now, show me what you have or I shall fetch my strap.' The resemblance to her elder daughter, both in voice and behaviour, was striking. She was much bigger than Emmy and much fiercer, too, so the girl gave in and opened the tin trunk.

Her aunt pulled everything from it, scattering clothing across the bed and floor, poking through her spare chemises and petticoats disdainfully. 'You're badly equipped and I suppose they'll be expecting us to clothe you decently on top of everything else! Still, you're so small I dare say I can find you some of Dinah's cast-offs.' She took a step backwards. 'I shall give you five minutes to put your things away in the chest then you are to come downstairs. Lal, Dinah!' She led the way out again.

At the door Lal paused for a moment to smile at Emmy: the smile of a cat who has a bird trapped and is looking forward to tormenting it.

When they had gone Emmy closed her eyes and willed the tears not to fall. She had never experienced such hatred in her whole life and was shaken by it. Her cheek still stung where her aunt had slapped her. What was she to do? The only word she could think of was *endure*. At least until her life had settled into some sort of pattern again. She'd done plenty of that before, but had been so happy with Mrs Tibby that this new life seemed a dreadful prospect. She stopped folding things for a moment, deciding that if things did not go well, she would find a way to leave. At least she still had the coins she had sewn into her petticoat. She had been going to run away, so it would not be much different, but she would *not* stay with people who hated her and slapped her for nothing!

When she could delay no longer Emmy went downstairs, her stomach churning with nervousness. As she walked along towards the rear of the ground floor, she passed three doors on the right but they were all closed. At the end of the passage was an open door which led into the kitchen. There she found her aunt and Dinah preparing food, while Lal was visible in the scullery beyond washing dishes.

Her aunt found her jobs to do and kept her busy until the church clock struck half-past twelve, then Dinah looked at her mother and asked, 'Shall I set places for us all?'

'Certainly not! *She* isn't going to be eating with us.' Her aunt turned to Emmy. 'Go into the scullery. Lal will bring your food to you there.'

The meal Lal brought in was adequate but plain. Soup that would have been better for a ham bone to give it savour and stale bread, followed by a wizened apple. Lal slapped it down on the scullery bench.

'I have nothing to eat it with.'

'As far as I'm concerned you can lap it up like the animal you are!' Lal hissed.

But even as she spoke, Dinah appeared. 'You forgot her cutlery.' Her gaze was more curious than hostile but she said nothing as she turned to follow her sister back into the kitchen.

Emmy was aware of them staring at her from the kitchen as she ate. How cruel to put her in here only a few yards away!

When she had finished eating the housework began again. Thanks to Mrs Tibby, Emmy was able to do most of the tasks they set her. When she wasn't sure what they wanted, she asked. It became obvious that her aunt and cousins did all the house-work and cooking, but tried to hide this from their neighbours, though apparently a scrubbing woman came in twice a week.

Emmy felt she'd acquitted herself well, but she had not received a single word of praise and once or twice Lal had pinched her as she passed, savage nips that left bruises on her arm.

As evening approached the three Butterfield woman tidied themselves up and went to sit in the little parlour to wait for the master of the house. They left Emmy in the kitchen, keeping an eye on a pan of potatoes and another of hearty lamb stew.

The front door opened and Emmy heard her uncle's voice. He sounded tired.

In the front hall the two girls greeted their father and fussed over him, taking his outdoor clothes and hanging them up for him, then joining their parents in the small parlour partway along the corridor.

Their voices echoed clearly down the corridor.

'Where's Emmy?' he asked.

'In the kitchen where she belongs,' Lena said.

'Don't you think she should join us here in the evenings, my dear? We cannot leave a relative sitting in the back room like a maid.'

'If you knew what it's been like you wouldn't say that. She's afraid of work, that girl is –'

Emmy gaped in shock.

' – and she has no idea how to do housework. We've had to show her everything, haven't we, girls?'

'Yes, Mother.'

'And she's bone idle! Did she think she was coming here to be waited on? She may have fooled an old woman, but she won't fool me. We all work hard, as you well know, my dear Isaac, and have no intention of letting her loll around in idleness.'

By this time Emmy's eyes had filled with tears. She almost went along the corridor to protest, but there were three of them and it would only be her word against theirs.

Sinking down on a chair, she dashed away a tear. It was going to be far worse than she had expected here, but she wasn't going to give them the satisfaction of seeing her weeping.

A smell of burning brought her out of her reverie, as did the eruption of her aunt into the kitchen, shouting, 'Can I not even trust you to keep an eye on a pan of potatoes, you stupid girl?' But Lena Butterfield smiled as she pulled the pan off the hot part of the cooking range, as if she was pleased with what had happened.

Again Emmy ate her meal alone.

Jane Rishmore stood motionless while her mother watched the maid who served them both fuss over her dress and hair.

'Thank you, Peg. You may go now.'

Jane turned away from the mirror, saying nothing. This dress was in the height of fashion, but was as unflattering as everything else she possessed, because her mother had no sense of taste or style and yet insisted on choosing everything her daughter wore.

'Are you all right, my dear?'

'No. You know I'm not, Mother.' Jane had done with pretending. 'I'm dreadfully unhappy and I hate Mr Armistead – *hate him!*' Her voice had risen in spite of her resolution to stay calm and tears were welling in her eyes. She went across to her drawers and fumbled blindly for a handkerchief, dabbing the moisture from her cheeks and taking several deep breaths.

Her mother sighed. 'Your father is quite determined on this match.'

'I know.'

'There will be compensations, I promise you. You'll have your own house, servants – children, too, one day.'

'And that's supposed to compensate me for having to live with that nasty little man?' For there was something about Marcus that revolted Jane, something evil. Which was a strange fancy for a young woman who was usually the least fanciful of beings.

As her mother continued to gaze anxiously at her, Jane heard the sound of carriage wheels outside the house and took a deep breath to pull herself together. 'Hadn't we better go down?'

They went to sit in the parlour where the master of the house was waiting impatiently for them.

'Does she not have any brighter clothes?' he demanded, staring disapprovingly at his daughter.

'Well, no, dear. You said you preferred us to dress quietly.'

'There's a difference between dressing quietly and dressing like a damned dowd! We're not still in mourning.'

Jane saw her mother wince and the determination grew in her not to let a husband treat her in this openly scornful way. Her mother wasn't very intelligent, but she was well-meaning and her father had no right to show impatience with her. After all, he had married her for her money and been richly recompensed. Jane thought about Marcus Armistead, who was much smaller than she was, and it occurred to her suddenly that nothing could prevent her from defying him once they were married. She didn't need to act in the subservient way her own mother did. Of course, she knew the main reason why her mother was always so apologetic. Because she hadn't given her husband a son.

Would Jane have similar difficulty in producing an heir for Marcus Armistead? She considered this thoughtfully as she waited for the maid to show him in. She would like to have children, but it worried her that she didn't understand exactly what married couples did to get them. When she'd asked, her mother had flushed and told her it would be up to her husband to enlighten her, and had then made an excuse to leave the room.

'Ah, my dear Marcus!'

Jane watched her father go forward to greet their guest, who then came to clasp her mother's hand and pass on his mother's regards. As he turned to Jane, she saw again how much shorter than her he was and a sudden savage joy filled her. If she did fight back, this little man would not easily best her. She straightened up to her full height, though her mother had ordered her to stoop a little, and had the further satisfaction of seeing Marcus scowl at her.

'Do sit down, Jane!' her mother said hastily.

She did so, smiling. At a gesture from her mother Marcus sat beside her. Even sitting he was shorter than she was.

After a few civilities her father said bluntly, 'Mr Armistead wishes to speak to you, Jane. We'll leave you two young folk alone for a few minutes.' He waited impatiently for his wife to get to her feet then hurried her out of the room.

Jane stared down at her clasped hands. When Marcus reached out to take one of them she let him, but made no attempt to clasp his in return and after a moment he let the limp hand drop.

'You are looking very – charming today,' he managed at last.

'I don't think so. This colour doesn't suit me. My mother chose it.'

'Well, you have a very – fine complexion, so that doesn't matter.'

' "Lancashire fair women", don't they say?' she replied. 'My skin is certainly light, but I would prefer fresh air and rosier cheeks only Father doesn't approve of my going walking on the moors.'

Marcus breathed deeply then began again, 'My dear Miss Rishmore – Jane, that is – you must know that I have grown – um – fond of you.'

'Have you? I hadn't realised. I thought it was my father you came to see on behalf of yours.' She distinctly heard a growl of anger in his throat. It gave her immense satisfaction. She gazed at him limpidly, her eyes not leaving his, and this seemed to make him uncomfortable. When he rose abruptly to his feet she gazed down at her hands again.

'My dear Jane, you must surely realise why I am here?' he said in exasperation.

'Yes.'

'Yet you give me no encouragement!'

'Why should I? Our fathers have decided what is to happen. I've had no choice in it. Have you?'

He blinked. 'Well, it is usual in our circles to marry for convenience, is it not?'

'Whose convenience?'

'That of all parties.'

She did not dare go as far as telling him she loathed the very thought of marrying him, so pressed her lips firmly together and waited for him to continue.

He spoke rapidly as if determined to give her no chance to interrupt him. 'My dear Jane, given our families' joint expectations, I sincerely hope you will do me the honour of becoming my wife?' He paused expectantly.

She had to force the word out. 'Yes.'

'You have made me very happy.'

She could not hold back a snort of disbelief.

Ignoring it, Marcus sat down again beside her. 'My father is to provide us with a house in Padstall village. I should like to show it to you.'

'My mother and I will be very happy to drive over to see it.'

'Good, good.'

Silence deepened between them and she was relieved when the library door opened and footsteps come towards them.

Marcus rose and took up a studied position in front of the fire. As his host came in he said, 'I am happy to tell you, sir, that your daughter has agreed to become my wife.'

Jane thought he sounded resigned more than anything. His smile certainly faded within seconds and he did not again look directly at her or even address a remark to her.

Her father came across to pat her shoulder and say 'Good girl!' in exactly the same tone as he used with his dog.

Her mother followed to give her a fluttery kiss.

They sat on and made stilted conversation for a minute or two. Jane said nothing. Why should she help them in any way?

Her father soon tired of this and said impatiently, 'Well, I must be getting back to work.'

Marcus stood up. 'And I too have duties which call, sir.' He rode back to Padstall feeling thoroughly depressed. He'd got through the proposal as well as could be expected, though he'd swear the stupid female had grown another couple of inches since the last time he'd seen her. As he passed the spot where he'd killed the old whore he reined in his horse for a moment and smiled. The deed was something he took a certain amount of secret pleasure from, for it showed he was not a man to be trifled with.

It came to him suddenly that there must be ways of disposing of a wife if she displeased you and that thought cheered him up considerably. As did his father's approval when he returned to report that he was engaged to be married.

The next day Jane went to visit her old nurse, a Scottish woman who had been pensioned off to a small back-to-back cottage in a narrow alley off Weavers Lane. She took a basket of food with her because she knew her father gave Aggie only five shillings a week to live on.

When they were both seated in front of the fire Jane came straight to the point. 'I've had to accept Marcus Armistead, Aggie.'

'I knew your father would make you, lassie.'

'Yes. But, Aggie, I need to know now what happens between a man and wife. You can't let me face it in ignorance. Not with a man like him.'

Her nurse stared into the fire and sighed. 'Your mother has forbidden me to tell you anything. It seems you've been asking her as well.'

'She won't know.'

The two looked at one another and Aggie said suddenly, with tears in her eyes, 'Och, lassie, I'll miss you sorely.'

'If it's at all possible I'll bring you to live with us once I've settled in. I'll have to wait and find out about that, though. I can't promise you anything until I see how things – work out.

But whatever happens, I will continue to help you.' She looked at the old woman expectantly. 'So tell me about it. Please.'

'Well, it's like this . . .' Aggie explained simply and straight-forwardly how children were made.

Jane sat there in amazement, staring into the fire as she listened, unable to believe that her father actually did this to her mother. 'I hadn't realised it was so like animals,' she said at last. 'Does it – hurt?'

Aggie shrugged. 'Depends on the man. If he's skilled he can make it pleasant for a woman. If he doesn't bother it can be uncomfortable. It's not normally painful, though.'

'I don't think I can bear Marcus Armistead to touch me like that.' Jane shuddered.

'You've no choice, hen.'

Determination rose in her. 'We'll see about that. Maybe he won't *want* to touch me.'

'Oh, he will. He's young enough to need it regular.' Aggie paused and looked sideways at her young lady, then said, 'I'd better tell you the rest.'

'What do you mean?'

'Your intended has a reputation with the ladies. They say no woman is safe with him, that his mother employs only old and ugly maids, that he visits houses of ill repute. Some men are like that. Always needing it. So he *will* want to touch you, I'm afraid.'

'I'm still bigger than he is.'

'Och, lassie, you can't keep him off by force. It's his *right* to have you in his bed. The church says that and so does the law.'

'Is there no way women can live without men?' Jane demanded bitterly.

'Only if they have money, hen. And men don't often give that to a woman. It makes them too independent.'

'I certainly have none, though my father has given me some expensive jewellery now that I'm engaged to be married. Part of my dowry, he says. I'd rather have had half its value in money and gone away to live quietly somewhere.' She sighed and changed the subject to her wedding clothes.

When she went home, she was very thoughtful. Marcus Armistead was *not* going to have things all his own way after they

183

were married, whatever his behaviour was like with other women. But perhaps later she could find some way to strike a bargain with him and keep him away from her bed? Surely he'd prefer women who were not reluctant to have him touch them?

She'd have to bear him a child or two first, however. Tears rose in her eyes. She didn't know how she was going to bear being married to him. Even to have him touch her hand made her feel uncomfortable.

Chapter Eleven

Tibby Oswald stood by the window of her bedroom in the Grange staring across the moors. They looked as bleak today as she felt, with rain sweeping across them like ragged swathes of dirty gauze and black clouds racing to shed more moisture on the damp, rain-darkened land. She was extremely comfortable in her old home and though she missed Emmy, at first had loved being back here, waited on hand and foot. But now she was feeling the lack of a suitable occupation to fill her time.

She looked down, stroking the material of her skirt. The new clothes had been provided only to suit her station as an Armistead of Moor Grange, not to give her pleasure, but she did enjoy wearing them. There were several simple but elegant gowns for the daytime and a real silk dress for evenings. She had forgotten how soft silk was against the body.

Now that the novelty had worn off, however, and the friendly dressmaker from Northby had stopped calling for fittings, Tibby was feeling lonely. She kept wondering how Emmy was, but didn't like to ask Eleanor because her sister-in-law would think it strange to take such an interest in a maid. And since they attended the local church in Padstall village, she didn't see dear Mrs Bradley any more either.

Claude wanted to take over her tiny income and manage it. What difference could such a small sum make to a man as wealthy as him? That was the only time she had stood up for herself, for she had refused to sign a piece of paper giving the annuity into Claude's keeping and leaving it to Marcus when she died. It had made him furious and she had been unable to hold back the tears. Eleanor had overheard the end of their conversation and said brusquely that it was a great deal of fuss about nothing, so Claude had let the matter drop after that, thank goodness.

Tibby hadn't mentioned the other money sitting in her savings account at Northby Bank or the few items of silver still lying in the vault there unsold. She had written to Mr Garrett to ask him to keep her money and possessions safe and not to give them to anyone but her. She had also begged him not to reply to her because she was quite sure Claude checked all the letters that came to the house, though not those that went out, and would want to know why she was receiving one from the bank.

He was out most days, thank goodness, managing his various ventures or meeting gentlemen of similar stature in the Manchester business community. Some of the so-called business meetings brought him home unsteady on his feet and with slurred speech, but no one commented on that, least of all his wife. In fact, her sister-in-law seemed to regard Claude with cool tolerance and he always appeared slightly uneasy in her company, doing as she asked without a quibble when she spoke in a certain tone of voice.

Eleanor was polite enough to her. You could not fault her on that. But she was cool and distant in her dealings and had made it plain Tibby was not welcome to join her in receiving daytime callers unless expressly invited and was to dine with the family in the evening only when no guests were expected. The maids let Tibby know about that, knocking on her door to say, 'I'll be bringing you up a tray tonight, ma'am.' It was a further humiliation, she felt, to be told this by a servant.

As for her nephew Marcus, he treated her like a half-wit, speaking slowly and mockingly when he did condescend to notice her existence. And she had seen the hot way his eyes devoured any young female he encountered. She could understand Emmy's wish to stay out of his clutches far better now and, although she was sure Eleanor would have allowed it, she would not even ask to bring her former maid here.

While this lack of affection between members of the family reminded Tibby of exactly why she had run away to marry her dearest James, it also reminded her of the girl who had been brave enough to do that. When she compared her younger self with the timid old lady she had now become, she felt downright ashamed. Age made you frail in more ways than one, it seemed.

She could not run away again because she had little money, could not walk far without assistance and had nowhere to go. In fact, her world had dwindled to a comfortable room where maids popped in now and then to suggest a tray of tea or to help her get ready for bed. There was not even anywhere close enough to walk to and the gardens were presided over by a surly fellow who would barely give you the time of day, let alone discuss the flowers she loved so much. Tibby's only entertainment was to read the novels Eleanor supplied her with, which was the only human weakness her sister-in-law seemed to have, or to watch the comings and goings in the stable-yard below the wing where she was housed.

'There must be a way to escape,' she muttered, then realised she was talking to herself again, something which had made Claude stare at her suspiciously the other evening. She would have to guard against that. But the thought of getting away from this velvet prison went round and round in her head for the rest of the day. Not that she could see a way to do it, but dear James would have said, 'Let it go round. Maybe it'll find a new turning one day.' He had been so sensible and had made her feel sensible too.

That evening she was told the family wished her to dine with them, so she asked for help with her hair, dressed carefully and walked downstairs on the arm of one of the capable middle-aged maids because the stiffness in her hip was no better for soft living.

'We have excellent news for you, my dear Matilda,' Claude said over dessert, examining the port wine in his glass against the excellent light shed by the ornate colza oil lamps and nodding in approval of it.

She waited to be enlightened, silver spoon poised over her fine china dish.

'Marcus is soon to be married – to Jane Rishmore.' He raised the glass in a silent toast to his son.

Tibby saw Marcus's sour expression and was intrigued. Was he not pleased about his betrothal, then? 'I'm sure she must be a delightful girl. I shall look forward to meeting her.'

'She's invited to dine here with her family tomorrow evening,' Eleanor said. 'You must join us, Matilda – as long as it's not too much for you?'

'I'd be delighted to join you. I find myself in much better health these days.' Tibby took a deep breath and ventured to make her first small stand against the way they treated her. 'And I should like a small glass of port as well, Claude, if it's not too much trouble? I find it very fortifying.' Her heart was pounding in her chest as she waited for a response.

He waved a hand and the maid served her.

'Make sure a decanter of port is kept in Mrs Oswald's room from now on,' Eleanor ordered.

Tibby enjoyed the port and began to wonder if she was imagining restrictions on her life where there were none. When the meal ended Claude told Marcus to escort his aunt to her room, but she declined hurriedly, saying the maid's pace suited her infirmity better.

That brought her a thoughtful stare from Eleanor, who then frowned in Marcus's direction.

The following evening Tibby was again escorted downstairs by the maid. 'It's good news, is it not, that Mr Marcus is to marry?' she said, feeling desperate for conversation.

The maid sniffed. 'Good news he'll be leaving and us maids will be safe to walk about the house.' Then she realised what she had said and gasped in dismay. 'Oh, I'm sorry, Mrs Oswald. I don't know what came over me to say that.' She did know, though, an encounter with Marcus on the back stairs which had made her flee shrieking to the safety of the kitchen and had filled her with outrage that he would so treat a woman old enough to be his mother. Though if she'd borne a son as nasty as him, she'd have smothered him at birth, 'deed she would.

'It's all right, dear. I shan't tell anyone what you said. And I'd guessed what he was like anyway.'

'Thank you, ma'am.'

'I do wish you'd call me Mrs Tibby. It's the name I prefer. And you're Katy, are you not?'

But they were now descending the main stairs and the maid said only, 'Yes, ma'am. But Mrs Armistead prefers to address us by our surnames. Mine's Beggley, if you please.'

No sooner had Tibby settled in a chair in the drawing room than the visitors' carriage drew up outside. A cold draught swept in from the hall as the front door was opened and Claude turned to fix his son with a stern glance and say, 'Make sure you speak pleasantly to Jane tonight. You hardly said a word to her last week.'

'Of course, Father.'

The Rishmores greeted Tibby politely then seemed to forget her existence. Eleanor made sure Jane sat next to Marcus on a sofa and the two pairs of parents stared at the ill-matched pair in obvious satisfaction.

To her surprise Tibby liked the look of Jane Armistead, who might not be a beauty but had clear, steady grey eyes and an intelligent look to her. You could tell so much from the eyes. Mrs Rishmore's were pale blue and vacuous, and she looked to be a foolish creature. She had topped her corkscrew curls with one of the fashionable silk dinner berets Tibby had read about in Eleanor's ladies' magazines but had never seen until now. The beret was far too large for Mrs Rishmore's narrow face and the vivid colour did not suit her, either. Jane was wearing a bright pink gown, which was also wrong for her, and the poor girl was far too tall for Marcus. He was bound to feel that, being such a short man, very like Tibby's own father in appearance.

Jane's expression remained tight and controlled and she contributed little to a conversation with her betrothed. Marcus was unable to hide his impatience with this.

At table Jane let out a muffled yelp and Tibby guessed that Marcus's hand must have strayed under the table. A minute later he gasped and glared at his fiancée. What had Jane done to him? Tibby wondered in shocked amusement. Pinched him hard where it hurt a man most, she hoped.

She was glad to see the young woman standing up for herself, and it was a further impetus to make Tibby do something for herself as well. She was going to try, she really was. She could not go on living this lonely, useless life.

The mere thought of taking action made her feel better than she had since her arrival here.

Emmy found it hard at first to believe the spiteful tricks the three Butterfield women played on her. They had soon convinced Isaac she was lazy and stupid, good for nothing, the true daughter of her feckless mother, though sometimes she thought she saw a look of embarrassment in Dinah's eyes and certainly her younger cousin did not play such nasty tricks on her as Lal.

The only time Emmy was allowed out of the house was when she went on errands for her aunt, and she was not entrusted with money, simply told where to go and what to ask for. The goods were then charged to the Butterfields' account.

As she was coming back from the nearby farm from which her aunt bought eggs, she stopped in the lane to stare across the gardens between her and the rear of the Butterfields' house. Tears came into her eyes at the thought of re-entering it. Lal and her mother had been particularly unkind to her that morning. How she was to endure it for much longer she did not know.

A young man turned the corner, whistling, and she saw it was Jack, so turned her head quickly to hide the tears.

'Don't you speak to old friends now, Emmy?' he asked in such a gentle tone that it drew a sob from her. 'What's wrong?'

When she turned to face him she felt a tear trickle down her cheek, then another.

He said simply, 'Tell me!' and she poured out the tale of what her life was like now. The only self-control she exerted was to speak in a low voice and keep her distance from him. She longed for him to take her in his arms, to hold and comfort her as he had done on that dreadful night, but he was as far beyond her reach as he had always been. Further. For her aunt would not allow her to have friends of any sort, she was sure.

Jack stood there aghast at her unhappiness, knowing he must

not touch her because someone might walk past and then her reputation would be blackened. 'Is there nothing you can do about it?'

She shook her head. 'Mr Rishmore wishes me to live with my mother's family.' She was thinking of running away, only how to smuggle her few possessions out of the house and get away without being recaptured were puzzles she had yet to solve.

He made a bitter sound in his throat. 'Mr Rishmore thinks he runs everyone's life.' After a moment's thought he added, 'Your uncle's quite kind, though.'

'Kind? He does nothing to help *me!*'

'Maybe he doesn't understand what it's like for you.'

'Or doesn't care!' The church clock struck the half-hour and she took a shaky breath. 'I'd better go or she'll say I've taken too long and slap me again.'

Back at the mill Jack finished his next task and went to return the ledger to Mr Butterfield's office, saying casually, 'Could I ask how Emmy is, sir?'

'My niece?'

'Yes. I thought last time I saw her she was looking unhappy. She must be missing the old lady very much.'

'She has reason to look unhappy. She is a lazy young madam, and I should be grateful if you would stay away from her.' The constant anxiety that Emmy would do as his wife feared and fall into sinful ways, bringing down Mr Rishmore's wrath on the Butterfields' heads, made Isaac add, 'The last thing we want is for her to become interested in young men.'

Jack drew himself up. 'As you know, I can't even consider young women in that way, sir, and I think you do Emmy an injustice in comparing her to her mother. She was always very hard-working and behaved decently when she worked for Mrs Oswald, though she had plenty of freedom to do otherwise if she'd chosen. And she was running *away* from immorality when I found her and took her to Parson Bradley, so I don't know why you should be worrying about her in that way.'

'I can only repeat, her happiness is not your concern and I would be grateful if you would stay away from her.'

But Isaac found this conversation disturbing because he had been so busy at work that he realised he had not paid his niece much attention.

Jack went back to his work, unsure whether he'd done any good mentioning Emmy or made things worse for her. After further thought he decided to speak to Parson Bradley about her as well. And if neither of them would do something, then he must!

That evening Isaac studied his niece as she served them their meal then went off to eat hers in the kitchen, something that still made him feel guilty. Jack was right, she did look unhappy. And was that not a bruise on her cheek? When she returned to clear away the soup bowls, he noticed another on her arm. Yet she didn't seem clumsy, and in fact had his sister's graceful way of moving.

Even as he watched he was shocked to see Lal stick her foot out, trying to trip her cousin. But Emmy avoided it as if she'd been expecting something like that. When she'd gone back to the kitchen, he frowned at his daughter. 'Why did you do that, Lal?'

She stared at him in surprise. 'Do what?'

'Try to trip Emmy.'

'I didn't.'

'I saw you do it.'

'It was an accident.'

He thumped the table, indignant that she should look him in the face and lie like that. 'Go to your room this minute! I will not have a daughter of mine lying to me! And if I see such spiteful behaviour towards your cousin again, I shall punish you severely.'

His wife waited until Dinah too had gone up to her room after the meal before saying reproachfully, 'I didn't think to hear you taking your niece's side against your own daughter, Isaac.'

He hesitated. It was usually wisest not to anger Lena. But once again he remembered the unhappiness in every line of his niece's body, the unhappiness that a stranger had had to point out to him before he'd noticed it. 'Lal was behaving badly, my dear. What sort of person would play such tricks on another? But what annoyed me most of all was that my own daughter would lie to me and *that* is why I sent her to her room. And how did Emmy get those bruises, pray? I would not like to think she was being ill treated here.'

'I slapped her face for impudence today,' his wife said complacently.

'What did she say to make you do that?'

'What does it matter what she said? Do you not believe me? Is that girl more important to you than your own wife and daughter now?'

Her voice was dangerously close to hysteria and her emotions had been very uncertain lately, so he said nothing more. But he lay awake for a long time in his lonely bedroom worrying, determined to keep a more watchful eye on his family's behaviour towards his niece from now on. While he did not wish to give his sister's daughter any opportunity to misbehave, he did not like to think of her being bullied or slapped so hard for what could only be minor offences. He was glad he no longer shared a room with his wife. He wished he didn't have to share a house with her, either.

Two days after the Rishmores' visit to Moor Grange, a note was brought across inviting the Armistead ladies to call upon the Rishmore ladies to discuss wedding details.

'I'm sure you won't want to come, Matilda,' Eleanor said. 'I'll give them your apologies.'

Tibby saw this as another opportunity to make a stand. 'I'd love to come, actually. I'm feeling so much better that I'm finding the days dragging a little. And I've been thinking I'd like to get out and about a bit. Would there be any objection to my going out for rides in the carriage – when it isn't needed, of course?' She waited with pounding heart for a curt refusal or a scornful remark, for Eleanor didn't mince her words when she was angry with her menfolk.

'There is usually a vehicle of some sort free. I'm pleased you feel able to get out more.' Eleanor paused then added with another frown, 'You're not a prisoner here, you know, Matilda. Surely we haven't made you feel like that?'

She gathered her courage together. 'I have felt a bit confined, I'm afraid. This house is so isolated and – well, I miss having my own place more than I'd expected.' She blinked her eyes rapidly to dispel the moisture. 'There is something about running a home and garden, even a humble one, that fills the hours nicely and offers many small pleasures. If I'd had only a very little more money, I don't think I'd have grown so worn down. And I miss my maid as well. Dearest Emmy was such a comfort to me.'

After thinking this over for a moment or two, Eleanor said slowly, 'If you like, after the wedding I'll see if I can persuade Claude to find you somewhere else to live. Maybe a little house in Northby – or Rochdale perhaps?' After all, it wouldn't cost much and it'd save them the embarrassment of not quite knowing what to do with Claude's sister whenever they had guests. And although her husband wouldn't care whether Matilda was unhappy or not, Eleanor found she did.

Tibby stared at her, hands clasped at her chest, eyes brimming with tears. 'Do you really mean that? I'd so love to live in Northby again!'

'Of course I mean it. But first we must get Marcus wed. Maybe then he will not be so – troublesome.' Eleanor's expression became closed again and she changed the subject firmly to the arrangements for their coming visit to the Rishmores.

Parson Bradley frowned at Jack who had come up to speak to him after the Sunday classes had finished. 'Are you sure of this? I mean, sure Emmy is not exaggerating?' He found it hard to believe that respected members of his congregation like the Butterfields would engage in active cruelty towards their orphaned niece. Though, on the other hand, Lal was not a very likeable young woman and he'd noticed she didn't seem to have any friends and was only ever seen with her sister.

'I'm pretty sure of it, sir. Emmy was crying when I saw her

and she had a bruise on her cheek. I think they're ill treating her.'

'I'll speak to my wife. She may be able to help.' But Gerald Bradley wasn't sure whether they dared do much. Samuel Rishmore had made his wishes very plain. The girl was to live quietly with her family and be trained in decent ways. It didn't do to cross the mill owner when he was hell-bent on dispensing charity.

When Gerald confided in his wife, Prudence looked at him in dismay. 'I was afraid of this!'

'You mean, you knew about it?'

'I guessed it might happen. Mrs Butterfield was furious that the girl had to live with them. She's told all her friends that Emmy is beyond redemption and she fears the worst. Someone asked me only the other day if I'd found the girl lazy, but I soon set them straight about that.' She sighed. 'I'll go and call on Mrs Butterfield, but I don't hold out much hope of being able to do anything. I doubt that woman will listen to anything I say.'

In fact, the visit was very short and within minutes Lena was bristling with indignation. 'The girl is bone idle, and she's a liar too if she's complained about us!'

'She hasn't said a word to us.'

'Then why are you questioning me about her like this?'

'Because I can't help noticing how unhappy she looks when she comes to church and I hear others say you're not satisfied with her work. Yet I remember how cheerfully and willingly she worked in my house.'

'She was trying to impress you, no doubt. But *we* have had the dubious pleasure of her living with us for several weeks now and I assure you we have found her seriously lacking in skills, manners *and* moral fibre.'

Prudence looked at her, certain now Mrs Butterfield was telling lies. Emmy's household skills were excellent, and no one could completely change character in so short a time. 'I'll be happy to take her back, then, if you're dissatisfied with her.'

'She is part of our family now, for good or ill,' Lena said, very much on her dignity, but spoiled it by adding bitterly, 'and besides, Mr Rishmore has made it only too plain what he expects.'

*   *   *

A week later Emmy bumped into George Duckworth in town. When she tried to walk past him, he caught hold of her arm, saying, 'Hold on a minute!'

Heart thumping, she said, 'I don't want to talk to you. Let go of me!'

'I just wanted to say I was sorry about your mam, that's all. And,' his eyes raked her body as if she had no clothes on, 'if you get fed up of being respectable, you can still come to me and I'll help you get away from Northby.'

'I'll *never* get fed up of being respectable,' she said fiercely, trying to pull her arm away from him and failing. 'Let go, will you?'

'Is this man bothering you, lass?' a voice asked behind her, and Emmy sagged in relief as the grip on her arm loosened.

'Yes. I don't want to speak to him and he won't let me past.'

'You run along, then.' When she had hurried away, Constable Makepeace looked at George and said, loudly and distinctly, 'If anything else happens to that girl I'll come knocking on your door first, believe me.'

'I was just saying I was sorry about her mother.'

'Bit late for that, isn't it? Are you sure you had nothing to do with killing her?'

'No, I bloody didn't. Killing isn't my style, as you well know, Eli Makepeace!'

'Who do you think did it, then?'

George shrugged. 'Who's to say?' He turned and walked away. Bloody Makepeace! Well, if his negotiations with Marcus Armistead worked out, he'd not be seeing the sodding constable for much longer. George smiled. He'd *make* things work out.

Lal had seen Emmy speaking to George and then the constable's intervention. She rushed home to tell her mother about it, putting the worst possible interpretation on the scene.

It had been a frustrating day and Lena's head was thumping. Indeed she had not felt well for months. 'That girl must have a lesson she'll not forget,' she said. 'She's just come in. Fetch her to me.'

Lal went to the kitchen, smiling in anticipation.

Dinah was uncertain whether to stay or leave, and worried about what her mother might be planning to do now. She did not dare protest, but their bullying of her cousin sickened her.

Emmy's heart sank at the mere sight of her older cousin. She did not ask what the other girl wanted, just waited for whatever unpleasantness Lal was about to unleash upon her.

'My mother wants to see you. Now you're really in trouble!'

'I haven't done anything.'

'That's not what Mother thinks.' Lal sauntered out to take up a position behind her mother's chair from where she could watch everything. Her mother's temper had been very chancy lately and they'd all suffered. It would be good to see it vented on her horrible cousin.

'You were seen talking to George Duckworth today,' Lena said coldly.

'*He* was talking to me. He wouldn't let me pass. I *hate* George Duckworth.'

'I don't believe you. I think you're planning some immorality that will shame us all in the eyes of this town.' Lena turned to her daughter. 'Lal, fetch me the kitchen scissors.'

Intrigued, Lal hurried off.

Lena stared at Emmy who was beginning to feel nervous. How was her aunt planning to humiliate her now?

Lal came back with the scissors.

'Come and kneel at my feet, Emmy.'

She didn't like the look in those eyes or the scissors in her aunt's hand. 'Why? I'm not going to let you beat me for something that isn't my fault.'

Lena bounced to her feet, cheeks burning red with fury. 'Do you dare defy me?'

'I haven't done anything wrong.'

As Emmy took a step backwards, Lal ran to stand in front of the door to prevent her leaving.

Lena grabbed Emmy by the hair, shoving her to her knees. As she started to drag her across the room, she called, 'Help me hold her, Dinah!'

Her younger daughter did not move, just stared at her in fear.

Emmy fought with all her strength, but two strong women were too much for her and soon she found herself held down by Lal, with her aunt holding her head back by the hair in an uncomfortable position.

She saw something flash, heard the snipping sound and saw a chunk of her hair fall to the ground. She could not help crying out in shock.

'Mother, no!' Dinah cried, rushing forward. 'Don't do this!'

'Shut up, you fool! How else are we to ensure her obedience?'

Sobbing loudly, Dinah ran out of the room. She could not bear to watch them ill treating her cousin any more, simply could not bear it.

Screaming and struggling Emmy fought, but the two women laughed and taunted her as her hair was chopped off, ragged chunk by ragged chunk.

When they had finished, Lena dragged her across to stand in front of the mirror. 'Remember this. I'll do it again if you so much as look in George Duckworth's direction.'

Lal was nearly choking with laughter. 'You look like a convict woman now. Ugly! Everyone will laugh at you.'

When Isaac got home that night there was no sign of Emmy, but his wife and Lal both looked puffed up with satisfaction. He wondered wearily what they had been doing now. As Lal went to fetch the food, Dinah suddenly burst into tears.

'Is something wrong, my dear?'

'Ask them what they've done to Emmy,' she sobbed, and ran from the room.

He froze and looked at his wife. 'Done to Emmy? What does she mean?'

'I've made sure she won't disgrace us. You'll see how in the morning.'

'I wish to know now.'

'I've sent her to her room. She is not to have any supper.'

The gloating smile on Lal's face sickened him suddenly. And when his wife followed her pronouncement that Emmy was to go hungry to bed by piling food on her own plate, Isaac suddenly had to know what they'd done. He pushed his chair back.

'Do finish your meal, dear,' Lena said.

'I'm going to see Emmy.' He turned to leave the room, ignoring her shrieks to him to come back this minute. He picked up the lamp from the hall table and carried it upstairs.

When he knocked on his niece's door, she screamed.

'It's only me,' he called, and pushed the door open. What he saw made him stand gaping in horror. They had cut off her hair. How could they have done such a thing? And why? It was no more than an inch long and Emmy had several more bruises on her face and arms as well as scratches. She must have tried to fight them off.

She was sitting up in bed and when she saw him staring at her, began to sob. 'Don't let them touch me! I didn't do anything wrong!'

As he took a step forward, she cowered away from him and horror filled him that she should have been so severely ill treated under his roof. 'No one will hurt you any more, I promise you,' he said gently. 'Stay here and I'll be back in a little while.'

He went downstairs to demand, 'What on earth has the girl done to deserve such treatment, Lena?'

'She's been talking to George Duckworth. Lal saw her and Eli Makepeace had to intervene to send her on her way.' She glared at her husband. 'This is the final warning as far as I'm concerned. Someone has to bring that young woman into line. And if I fail, I shall insist on her being sent to the house of correction.'

'But why did her speaking to George Duckworth make you cut her hair off? How could you be so cruel to a young woman as to do that? You've made a public spectacle of her.'

Lena searched for an explanation which would convince him. 'Because it was the best way to teach her a lesson and ensure that our own daughters remained safe, untainted by her.'

She looked so unrepentant, so sated with pleasure at her own actions, that Isaac knew he had to get his niece away from her. His wife had been behaving strangely for a while, ever since she entered the change of life, but this was arrant cruelty. 'The poor child won't even be able to go out of the house like that.'

'Oh, won't she? She'll do as I tell her, believe me, and will run my errands as always.'

He heard Lal sniggering and glared at her. 'I forbid either of you to touch or speak to Emmy again. I never thought to see the day I'd be ashamed of you, Lena Butterfield, but I am today. Deeply ashamed. This was a vicious and unprincipled act.'

With a sniff of disdain she lifted her fork to her mouth and continued to eat. Suddenly his anger spilled over and he picked up her plate, hurling it into the fireplace where it smashed and scattered food everywhere. 'If you ever touch that girl again, I'll give you a taste of your own medicine and do exactly the same to you!'

For a moment Lena gaped at him, then her face turned bright red and she shouted angrily, 'Don't you dare speak to me like that! I am your wife!'

'Which makes what you've done even worse. Did you really think I would condone such cruelty?'

As she opened her mouth, anger contorting her face, he could not bear the sight of her and moved towards the door. 'Do not go near that girl again. You and Lal may both wait for me in the back parlour when you have cleared up this mess. I shall not want any food because I'm too disgusted to eat. And I warn you: I have not finished with this matter yet.'

He left the room, slamming the door behind him, something he never did normally. He kept seeing his niece's swollen, tearstained face and then Lal's ugly expression of triumph. He could guess who had helped hold Emmy down. And the contrast between the two girls suddenly brought home to him one of the other reasons why Lena had done this. Her own elder child was plain and plump while even when she was tired and unhappy Emmy had a sweetness to her face that made her very attractive. No young men had ever tried to court Lal, or even talk to her after church, because her ugliness came as much from her character as from her features.

As did her mother's.

Standing there, Isaac bowed his head and acknowledged that

his marriage had not been a good one. He would have been far happier without Lena and her money, and had been badly advised by his father who had arranged the match. At best he and Lena existed in a state of mutual tolerance. He doubted even that would be possible from now on.

He went back upstairs. 'It's me again, Emmy.' As he went inside, pity overwhelmed him and he reached out without thinking to pull her towards him and try to comfort her, but again she shrank away, as if expecting a blow. 'Child, child, I'm not going to hurt you!' She began sobbing, shaking with the violence of her emotions, and this time she allowed him to fold her in his arms and shush her gently.

As he patted her back, he wondered what to do. First discover the truth, he decided. Then find her somewhere else to live. When she had calmed a little, he asked, 'What were you doing with George Duckworth, Emmy?'

'He stopped me in the street and wouldn't let me pass. I was trying to get away from him. Constable Makepeace saw what had happened and made him let me go.'

He was pleased there had been an independent witness and decided to speak to Eli before he did anything else. If life had taught Isaac one thing, it was to be sure of his facts before he acted.

'You wait here, my dear,' he said. 'I have to go out, but I won't be long.'

Emmy glanced over his shoulder, fear on her face.

'They won't come near you, I'll make sure of that.'

On the landing he found Dinah waiting for him, also weeping. He put his hands on her shoulders and asked, 'What happened exactly, dear?'

When she told him, relief surged through him that she had not taken part. Perhaps there was hope for this daughter. He did not feel there was much for Lal.

'Come down with me now and get your cousin something to eat, then stay with her till I return.'

'Yes, Father.' She hesitated. 'Mother will be angry with me, though.'

'I shall deal with her. But I'll wait until you've gone up to Emmy before I leave.'

He watched Dinah carry a tray upstairs then left the house. He did not come back for over an hour, by which time his anger had grown into a towering rage. When he opened the door to the back parlour Lena looked up and he saw her expression become apprehensive.

'It's as I thought,' he announced. 'Constable Makepeace has confirmed that Lal lied about the meeting with Duckworth and Emmy was telling the truth.'

His daughter began to sob noisily. 'It's not true. It's not true,' she wailed.

'And you're *still* lying. Go to your room this minute!' he roared. 'I shall speak to *you* in the morning.'

When she had gone, he turned back to his wife, willing himself to calm down. 'I went to Parson Bradley's house to seek their help. I'm taking Emmy there tonight. I don't trust you with her. In fact, I doubt I'll ever trust you again.'

'What! How *could* you shame me so in front of the Bradleys? I shall never be able to hold my head up in church again.'

'You've shamed yourself by your cruel behaviour to my niece, Lena.'

He might have been speaking to a stranger, his voice had become so chill and measured. That frightened her more than anything else.

'I shall make sure that from now on I am master in my own house, and since Lal must be taught better manners than you have managed, I intend to send her away to school. Mrs Bradley knows of a place where the discipline is fair but firm. We'll find another school for Dinah who suffers from her sister's bad example and bullying ways. At least she did not join in your cruelty today.'

By this time Lena was weeping, not tears of remorse but of anger, alternately raging at him and begging him not to do this to her. He left her to her hysterics.

Upstairs he found Emmy sitting on her bed with Dinah beside her at a little distance. His niece stared at him apprehensively. 'It's all right, Emmy. You won't be hurt again.' Isaac turned to his daughter. 'Go to bed now, dear. Thank you for sitting with your cousin.'

When Dinah had gone he studied his niece again. The bruises on her face stood out lividly and he wished he could let them fade before he took her to the Bradleys, but did not dare leave her in his wife's care a day longer.

'Mrs Bradley has invited you to go back to her, and once your hair has grown and you've recovered from this ill treatment, she and I will find you another place away from Northby.'

Emmy stared at him, her eyes huge in a face chalk-white where it was not bruised.

'My dear, are you all right?'

She nodded.

'Do you need any help packing?'

'We're leaving tonight?' She whispered the words as if afraid to believe what he had said.

'Yes. And Emmy – I'm sorry I didn't realise what was happening. I'm ashamed that I haven't taken better care of you, deeply ashamed. I hope from now on you'll let me visit you sometimes, so that we may get to know one another? Before she – turned to immorality, I was very fond of my sister.'

Emmy felt too spent to do more than nod and turned with relief to her packing. 'It won't take me long – Uncle Isaac.'

Which he took to mean she forgave him, and that hope brought moisture to his eyes.

Chapter Twelve

Prudence Bradley was waiting for Isaac to return and opened the front door herself. 'What have they done to you?' she asked in an outraged whisper, gathering the shivering girl to her capacious bosom and glaring at Isaac. She led Emmy straight through the house. Her husband stared in shock at the battered waif with shorn head who had been a rosy bustling young woman the last time she'd been here.

'You can deal with Mr Butterfield, Gerald!' she snapped. 'I have better things to do.'

In the kitchen Cook and Cass bit back exclamations and looked to their mistress for guidance.

'I think Emmy will be the better for a nice hot bath,' she told them, 'and a bowl of your excellent soup, Cook. She has been ill treated, as you can see, but we shall enjoy the privilege of comforting her and nursing her better.' She gave Emmy another hug. 'Now, my dear, you really must stop weeping because you're quite safe here and need never go back to that woman.'

But Emmy could not stop and in the end they abandoned the idea of a bath, fed her warm milk and brandy, and simply put her to bed with two hot bricks wrapped in flannel.

Prudence herself sat by the bed, talking comfortingly of how glad they were to have her here and how Cass needed some help. She wasn't sure Emmy heard any of this, but she could see that her voice was having a soothing effect. When the girl fell asleep she went down to the kitchen and looked at her servants, tears welling in her eyes, for once uncertain what to say.

'It's disgusting!' Cook declared, not troubling to be deferential. 'I'd never have believed it if I hadn't seen it with my own eyes. What did that poor lass do to deserve such treatment?'

'She did nothing, I'm sure. The woman has been beating her for a while, it appears. There are bruises all over her poor body.' Prudence swallowed hard, for she was still horrified by it.

Cass wiped a tear away. 'Did you see her eyes? Haunted, they looked.'

Prudence sniffed and nodded. 'I'm sure you'll both help me to make her feel wanted and appreciated, but it'll take a while for her hair to grow again so we'll let her stay inside the house for the time being.' She wondered if the scars on the girl's spirit would ever be erased; wondered also how any woman could call herself a Christian and do something like this.

In the Parson's study the two men sipped a glass of port together, for it was clear that Isaac was deeply upset by what had happened and that recriminations were the last thing he needed.

'I'm to blame,' he kept saying. 'Emmy was placed in my care and I didn't look after her properly.'

In the end Gerald said frankly, 'Mr Butterfield, I have seen my share of inhumanity and can never understand how some people behave. The important thing is that you have discovered what was happening and brought Emmy to us. If anyone can help her recover it's my dear wife. And *you* can make sure that your wife doesn't hurt her again.'

'There's something else worrying me,' Isaac admitted, studying the glass of port intently and forgetting to drink it. 'What about our own girls? I – I fear Lal is cut from the same cloth, and indeed I've always known that she can be,' he hesitated over 'cruel', then substituted, 'spiteful. But perhaps there is still hope for Dinah, who is much gentler and who refused to take part in this shameful act.' He stared into his glass then said slowly, 'I'm going to send them both away to different schools, as your wife suggested. I'm not a rich man, but if I can find somewhere where they can teach Lal to respect her fellow human beings – or at least to behave in a seemly manner – and another place which will allow my Dinah to be herself, surely it's the best thing I can do for them?'

'I'm sure it is. But what about Mrs Butterfield? What shall you do about her? This was not a . . .' Parson hesitated then said it '. . . rational act.'

'I don't know. Lena was never easy to live with, but since she got to a certain age, her mood and temper have changed for the worse.' Only to the Parson could he have admitted this. 'I even fear for her reason at times.'

'If Prudence and I can help in any way . . .'

Isaac shook his head sadly. Lena was his cross to bear, and anyway would spurn the offer of help.

The wedding of Marcus Armistead and Jane Rishmore took place in the parish church of Northby at the end of March with all due pomp and ceremony. The pews seemed to Tibby to be overflowing with Rishmores: tall, well-built people with loud voices for the most part. The Armisteads were less well endowed with relatives and lacking in inches in comparison to this race of giants, but they made up for that by dressing splendidly.

Tibby smiled down at the finery dear Eleanor had provided for her: a full-skirted gown in navy blue cashmere trimmed with navy satin and cream lace. It had Donna Maria sleeves, full to the elbow, then tightly fitting to the wrist, and she was very pleased with how she looked. He bonnet was huge and, to her eyes, overtrimmed. She had surreptitiously removed some of the decorations the night before, and to her relief Eleanor did not seem to have noticed. She also possessed a new full-length cloak of thick, soft wool, made in the current winter fashion with a matching elbow-length cape, a very practical garment that had kept her snug and warm during the church ceremony.

But however fine the clothes, it was still painful for her to walk. Her hip had been very bad this winter and sometimes in the early mornings she almost wept with the pain of starting to move on it. When she went out in the little carriage she didn't often get out for a walk, because it was such a trouble to get back in again, but she greatly enjoyed the change of scenery. She had visited Mr Garrett at the bank twice now to make various financial arrangements. Such a gentlemanly person!

The bride was wearing the most unflattering dress you could possibly imagine for a woman like her and Tibby blinked in shock when she saw it. Stark white did not suit Jane, who would have looked better in cream or soft blue, and the elaborate hairstyle with its piled curls embellished by a profusion of beads, braids and bows made her look so much taller than Marcus that she was like an adult standing next to a child when the two of them took their places at the altar.

Marcus looked grim throughout – and angry. Tibby prayed he would calm down before the night. It could be hard for a gently bred girl the first time and she did not think her nephew would be a considerate lover like her dear James had been. It was wrong, very wrong, to coerce young people into unsuitable marriages.

After the ceremony the guests drove back to Mill House in their various carriages and were then entertained to a sumptuous meal. The Armisteads left the gathering a little earlier than planned because the weather had turned and snow was threatening. There wasn't going to be a honeymoon, at the groom's suggestion, but Jane and Marcus would spend the first night alone in their new house, with the servants banished from the place till morning.

Which might have been done out of delicacy by another man, but struck Tibby as sinister where her nephew was concerned. But dear Jane had agreed to it with her usual calmness. Such a kind girl. Unlike Marcus, she wasn't too proud to talk to his aunt and even seemed to enjoy an old lady's company and conversation.

As the newly-weds were going out to their carriage a flurry of sleet swept down on them and they abandoned farewells to scramble inside the vehicle.

'Drive on or we'll be snowed up here!' Marcus yelled to the coachman, and the vehicle lurched forward.

Jane studied her husband surreptitiously. He looked sour-faced and was making no attempt to converse with her. She was rather pleased with the result of her first essay into choosing her own clothes, for although she had instinctive good taste, she had gone against it and knew she could not possibly have looked worse than she had done today. She only hoped her strategy would help deter him from paying her too much attention.

After a while he turned to look at her. 'That hair arrangement doesn't suit you.'

'It's the latest fashion.'

'Well, I don't like you making yourself look taller. You're too tall already. Make sure you keep your hairstyles low in future.'

'I shall arrange my hair as I please,' she said.

'*What did you say?*'

She saw his fists bunch up and thought for a moment he was going to hit her. Shock held her still for a few seconds, then she decided that if he did she would hit him back. She knew some men beat their wives, but no one was going to do that to her. 'I shall dress to suit myself and my station,' she told him.

He grasped her arm then, his fingers digging in cruelly, and tried to pull her to her knees opposite him, but she was too big and resisted his attempt, so he let go and glared at her. 'You'll do as you're told! Did you not just promise to obey me?'

'I meant my promise to obey as much as you meant yours to love and cherish me.' She let her own anger show. 'Let's be truthful now, Marcus – we neither of us wished for this match.' As his scowl deepened, she added, 'And if you try to hurt me, be sure I'll hurt you back. I'm big enough to give you a good fight for your money.'

He stared at her in shock then said in an outraged tone, 'You're a woman. It's your *duty* to do as you're told.' Her mother was so meek always and Jane had said very little in company, so he had not expected this defiance.

'I'm bringing you a large enough dowry to do as I please,' she said dryly.

'We shall see about that.'

'We shall indeed.'

After a few moments' silent fulmination he threw at her,

'You should be grateful someone has agreed to marry you, so tall and ugly as you are.'

She gave a bitter snort of laughter. 'They had to *force* me to marry you, Marcus. I'd far rather have stayed unwed. And so would you, if you tell the truth.' She softened her tone, trying to sound more friendly. 'Can't we come to an agreement? This marriage was devised to get an heir for your family and to cement our two families' business links. If we produce a couple of children for them, there is no reason why we should not each go our own way thereafter. And keep to our separate bedrooms.'

'If you think I'll stand for you cuckolding me −'

'I've no intention whatsoever of doing that. I find the idea of relations between men and women distasteful, if you must know. But I shall not object to your having mistresses so long as you allow me to sleep alone and don't touch me once I'm with child. I can make sure your home life is very comfortable or extremely uncomfortable, and I'm not the sort to give in to bullying.'

He studied her sourly, admitting to himself that what she said made sense. Did he want to wake up to her scornful talk and ugly face for the rest of his life? No. Did he even want to bed her? No again. Though he would do it to get an heir, since that was expected of a gentleman in his position, as well as being a sign of manhood. 'I shall require you to submit to me in bed until you are with child,' he warned, 'and to show respect towards me in public.'

'If you keep our agreement, I shall appear the most dutiful of wives − as long as you show respect towards me in front of others as well.'

'And in bed?'

'I shall allow you to do what is necessary.'

'I'll think about your suggestion. But first,' he leered at her, 'let's see how dutifully you behave yourself tonight.'

She hoped her apprehension about this did not show. She was dreading the coming ordeal, absolutely dreading it. She hated even to touch his hand.

At the house he unlocked the door and ushered her inside with a mocking wave. 'You're far too big for me to carry over the threshold.'

The hall was chilly but there was a fire in the parlour and she went to warm herself gratefully.

'I think we'll go to bed right away,' he said, coming up behind her and grabbing her breasts, which were at least big enough to tempt a man – as long as one didn't look at the face above them.

She struck his hand aside. 'That hurts.'

He smiled. 'I know. And so will the bedding, it being your first time.'

'I'm not prepared for you to hurt me when it's not necessary,' she said, mistrusting the look in his eyes.

'What do you know about that?' He stared at her, eyes narrowed. 'Your father assured me you were untouched and innocent of what was to come.'

'I am untouched, but I have taken care to inform myself of what happens. Only a stupid woman would climb blindly into a marriage bed and I am not stupid.'

'Then get upstairs and show me how clever you are,' he sneered. 'It's up to a wife to *please* her husband in bed, and do as he wishes.'

Why did he keep saying that? 'Rather, it's up to a husband to initiate his virgin wife into the ways of love,' she countered, knowing no other decent word for it.

'Love!' He let out a shout of braying laughter. 'What has that to do with anything? You don't suppose a man could love *you*, do you?'

'Or that I could become fond of you.' She turned and made her way towards the stairs. 'Give me a few minutes to get ready.'

He laughed and followed close on her heels. 'I'll get you ready myself. I'm very fond of taking a woman's clothes off.'

Taking a deep breath and praying for the strength to endure what was coming, Jane led the way upstairs.

It was even worse than she'd expected. He was rough and inconsiderate, and he literally ripped her clothes from her body, becoming very excited in the process. In fact, he didn't show the signs of masculine readiness that Aggie had told her to expect until after he'd hurt and frightened her. And then it was all over very quickly.

When she was sure he'd finished, she got out of bed.

'Where are you going?' he asked in a sleepy voice.

'To my own bedroom.'

He bounced up into a sitting position. 'I want you here to warm my bed tonight. I might want to do it all over again.' He smiled to see her shudder.

'I won't sleep with you tonight or ever.' Because she didn't trust him. She had sent a carpenter across to the house secretly to make sure there were bolts on the inside of her bedroom door, strong ones. Just as she'd made sure all her clothes were unflattering and held herself as tall as she could whenever he was around. 'If you need me again, you can knock on my bedroom door.'

Gathering the rags of her wedding dress around her, relieved when he did not follow, she stumbled along the corridor to her own room followed by the sound of his mocking laughter.

Before she got into bed, she washed him off her skin, then knelt to pray more fervently than she had ever prayed before that she would get with child quickly.

In such a small town Samuel Rishmore found out very quickly that his head clerk had disobeyed his orders about his niece and did not scruple to ask him why.

Embarrassed, Isaac explained what had happened.

Samuel looked at him in sympathy. 'Some women can turn strange when they get to a certain age, and they are over-emotional creatures at the best of times.' His own wife was missing their daughter so much that he had been subjected to moods and floods of tears ever since the wedding. Margaret was, she said, worried about how strained Jane looked, and indeed he too could see that his daughter was not happy in her marriage, though that would no doubt sort itself out as the couple grew used to one another.

So he accepted Isaac's explanation with the warning, 'As long as the girl is decently taken care of! I'll not have her abandoned and falling into sin.'

'No, sir. Indeed not, sir. She is to work for Parson for a while.'

'Ah, that's all right then. Mrs Bradley is an estimable woman.'

When Isaac went back to his office he sat staring into space for so long that Jack, who could see him through the open doorway, ventured to ask, 'Are you all right, sir?'

'What? Oh. Yes. Yes, of course.' After further thought, he said, 'My niece has moved back to stay with the Bradleys until a suitable place can be found for her. I discovered that you were – um – correct about her unhappiness and I'm grateful you mentioned it to me.'

Jack nodded and made no comment. The whole town knew that Mrs Butterfield had run mad and cut off all her niece's hair, and that poor Mr Butterfield had been forced to send his daughters away to school to get them away from her cruel ways. He had seen Emmy in the Parsonage garden wearing a cotton bonnet and thought it shocking that anyone would cut off her beautiful hair.

He felt better to know she was all right, but it made him unhappy that he could not be the one to help her. He hoped she would meet some man who was free to love her and give her the happy home she deserved.

No, he didn't. It might be selfish, but he could never hope for that!

It was April before Emmy recovered her spirits and that was partly due to the arrival in the Bradley household of a puppy of uncertain parentage which had followed the Parson home one day, sneaking along quietly behind him, stopping when he stopped, not barking or making a noise, just following him determinedly. It was dirty and infested with fleas, all its ribs showing, and clearly it had not eaten properly for a long time. And yet it had an intelligent look to it and he simply could not bring himself to drive it away, which would almost certainly be a death sentence.

He fetched his wife to the door and they considered it together as it sat shivering and wagging its tail tentatively outside.

'What do you think, my dear?' he asked.

'I think this poor little creature is exactly what Emmy needs to draw her out of her sadness,' she replied, smiling down at it. 'I shall ask her to care for it for me.' She went through into the kitchen. 'Ah, Emmy, I wonder if you could help me? Can you spare her for a few minutes, Cook?'

'Of course, ma'am.' Cook was still upset at Emmy's listlessness. Though the girl's hair had grown into short curls like a cherub's and she had regained her former prettiness, she still looked thin and haunted, as though a strong breeze would blow her away.

Prudence led the way to the front of the house. 'Emmy, a dear little dog has followed Parson home and we can't bring ourselves to turn it away. Come and see!'

At the front door the dog had lain down, as if exhausted, his head on his crossed front paws but his eyes still watchful. When the two women approached he dragged himself to his feet and essayed another wag or two. He looked equally ready to flee for his life or collapse.

'Do you think you could wash him for us and give him something to eat?' Prudence asked. 'Parson and I have taken quite a fancy to him.'

'No wonder!' Emmy plumped down in front of the dog and gave it her hand to sniff. Talking softly and moving slowly, she stroked the emaciated creature and when she felt she had gained his trust, picked him up very gently. He gave her a quick lick on the hand and sighed. She smiled down at him then looked at her mistress, cradling him in her arms. 'I'll be happy to look after him, Mrs Bradley. I love animals, even though I've never been able to have a pet of my own.' But her attention was really on the dog and she began talking to it as she walked back to the kitchen with it.

The two Bradleys exchanged wry glances.

'It seems we have acquired a dog,' he said.

'What shall we call it?'

'What else but Hercules? After all, he has just accomplished the very difficult task of bringing a smile to Emmy's face.'

In the kitchen Cook stopped work to gape at the dirty little creature. 'Get that thing out of here!'

'Parson brought him home and the mistress wants me to bath him and look after him.'

Cook opened her mouth, then shut it again as she saw the tender glow on Emmy's face. 'Well, *you* will have to look after it. I haven't time. Though I'll find it some scraps once you've bathed it.'

'And perhaps a bowl of milk now?' Emmy begged. 'Just to make him feel at home.'

'Oh, all right. But take him through to the laundry. Can't have him under my feet.' She rolled her eyes at Cass. 'What next?'

'Listen to her,' Cass said softly. 'She sounds happier than she has since she came back.'

They heard Emmy talking to the little animal as she cared for it, laughing as it splashed her and tried to wriggle out of the basin she was using for a bathtub.

'Eh,' said Cook, mopping her eyes with a corner of her apron. 'Trust the mistress to find a way to help her. She was born to be a parson's wife, that one was.'

Everyone in the household turned a blind eye when Emmy smuggled Hercules up to her bedroom that first night, and after that, since he did not make messes inside the house, it became openly accepted that he should sleep up there on an old blanket.

Prudence got tears in her eyes as she listened to the girl talking to the dog in a low voice and saw her playing with him, laughing aloud as she threw a stick for him to fetch, a game both of them seemed to love.

When Isaac came to call that Sunday afternoon, Emmy introduced him to the clever little dog and for the first time relaxed fully with her uncle, seeming to welcome his company and quiet talk. He went away with his heart lightened, feeling that the harm his wife had done was at last unravelling. And since he had received a cheerful letter from Dinah only the day before, saying how much she was enjoying school and the company of the other girls, he felt life was back on course. There had been no letters from Lal, not even to her mother, something Lena kept blaming him for. He was not surprised. Lal had not gone to school willingly and he had chosen a strict establishment for her, one used to dealing with wilful girls.

After spending a pleasant howl with Emmy, he went home to a silent house, to spend the rest of the day with his head buried in a newspaper before attending Evensong. His wife refused to come to church with him any more and spent most evenings staring into space, not even pretending to embroider or read. Recently she had turned morose rather than aggressive and since the incident with Emmy would not even venture out of the house, saying people were staring at her. She paid little attention to her housekeeping duties, either, so he had had to hire a sensible older woman to come in three times a week to 'help out' and do the shopping. Evening meals on other days were very haphazard affairs.

In fact, his life was bleak indeed these days and he was missing Dinah very much.

Eleanor could see that her daughter-in-law was unhappy in her new life and blamed it on Marcus. Her son had always been very selfish and self-centred. But then few women married the perfect man, did they? She certainly had not.

When she found Claude in a good mood one day, she broached the question of finding a cosy little cottage for his sister.

His smile faded instantly. 'Why the hell should we pay out good money for a cottage when there's a whole wing unused here?'

'Because it's awkward for me having Matilda here,' she said. 'I've done my best and so has she, but she simply doesn't fit in with our friends. And if I don't invite her to join us, people talk, you know. If we set her up in a little cottage somewhere, she could make a life of her own and we could be seen as being generous without suffering any inconvenience. If we found a place in Northby I could call in to see her when I visit Margaret Rishmore, which should satisfy the gossips.'

He growled under his breath and sat slapping one hand idly up and down on the arm of his chair as he thought this through. 'She'd need servants.'

'Just one maid and someone to help in the garden occasionally. The girl who used to look after her could come back, I'm sure. Mrs Bradley tells me she's looking for another place. Matilda talks about her often and seems very fond of her.'

'You want my sister to leave, do you, then?'

Eleanor shrugged, a delicately expressive gesture. 'I must admit I should prefer such an arrangement and I think it would make her happier, too. She's lonely here.'

'Have it your own way, then! I'm not sorting out any of the arrangements, though.'

'Of course not. Women do these things so much better than men. And as to the cost?'

'Spend as little as you can get away with. I'm not throwing money at her.'

'I shall be most frugal.' He was frowning in thought, so Eleanor waited for him to speak.

'If there's a suitable cottage for sale, it might be best to buy a place for her. I don't like putting money into other men's pockets. Afterwards, when it's not needed, we can rent it out.'

'What a good idea! Trust you to turn this into a sensible business arrangement.' She smiled to see his smug expression then went to break the news to Matilda. What Claude considered a small amount of money to live on would seem lavish to a woman who had managed on two guineas a month previously, she was sure.

Tibby stared at her sister-in-law in disbelief. 'You mean – Claude has agreed to let me have a house of my own again?'

'Yes. I told you he would once the wedding was over.'

Tibby burst into tears.

Eleanor went to put an arm round her. 'Are you not pleased? You don't have to leave if you don't want.'

'Pleased? I'm delighted!' Tibby blew her nose. 'I can't believe it's happening.'

'There's even better news.'

Tibby blinked at her, unable to conceive of anything better.

'Emmy hasn't found another place and I'm sure she'd come back to you if you want her.'

She then had to hold the old lady and rock her until she'd stopped weeping.

'So happy!' Tibby kept saying through her tears. 'So very kind of you.'

In the end Eleanor said bracingly, 'Then if you're happy, kindly stop weeping all over my new gown and help me plan what to do.'

Chapter Thirteen

When Mrs Armistead next came to call on Mrs Bradley, whom she had known before her marriage, Emmy asked Cook if she could run out and speak to the coachman waiting outside. 'I just want to ask him if Mrs Tibby is all right.'

'Still miss her, don't you?' Cook asked indulgently, waving a hand in permission.

The coachman condescended to inform the young lass that Mrs Oswald was keeping well, though she was having trouble walking.

'Would you give her my regards, please?' she asked. 'I'm Emmy. I used to be her maid.'

He smiled down at her, thinking how pretty she looked and wondering if the tales he had heard were true. Her hair was hidden beneath a cap but it did look very short. 'Of course I will, lass,' he said.

As Emmy turned towards the house, there was a tapping on the window and she saw her mistress beckoning from the front parlour. She hurried inside to find Mrs Bradley waiting in the hall. 'I'm sorry, ma'am. I was just asking the coachman about Mrs Tibby. Cook said I could.'

'Come and ask my visitor about her instead. Mrs Oswald's sister-in-law will know much better than the coachman how she's keeping.'

Emmy followed her into the parlour, feeling apprehensive. What was all this about?

Eleanor studied the girl, remembering her from last time. 'I've come to ask you if you'll look after my sister-in-law again? She needs a new maid.'

Emmy stared at her in dismay, not knowing what to answer. There was nothing she'd like better than to go back to Mrs Tibby – nothing! – but the thought of meeting Marcus Armistead again, of living in the same house as him, terrified her. What if he decided to pay her back for hitting him over the head? What if he captured her again?

Eleanor frowned. 'I'd have thought you'd have jumped at the chance.'

Mrs Bradley came to put an arm round Emmy. 'I'll explain to Mrs Armistead, my dear. Just tell me – if we can sort out that little problem of yours, would you like to work for your old mistress again?'

'Oh, ma'am, there's nothing in the world I'd like more.'

'Wait for us in the kitchen, then.' When the maid had gone, Prudence turned to her visitor. 'I don't know how to explain this tactfully, so please excuse my being blunt. Late last year Emmy caught the attention of your son Marcus.'

'Ah! No need to explain further.'

Prudence sighed. 'I'm afraid there is. You see, he arranged to have her kidnapped and she had to hit him over the head before she could escape. She's now afraid to go anywhere near him.'

Eleanor froze. She knew Marcus was promiscuous, but not that he would stoop to such lengths. She also knew how unhappy Jane was with him. Even in the short time since their marriage, her daughter-in-law seemed to have grown thinner and more nervous. It was hard to believe the worst of your own son, but Eleanor prided herself on facing up to things. After all, her own husband had been unfaithful to her many times, so why should she be surprised that the son took after him? What was there about the Armistead men that they needed so many women? She didn't think Claude would force an unwilling one into his bed, however, though sadly she did believe that of Marcus.

'I shall ask my husband to have a word with our son and warn him to stay right away from the girl. But Tibby finds life at

Moor Grange lonely, so we're going to find her a cottage in Northby. Emmy will have no need to see Marcus again.'

'But will *he* stay away from her?'

Eleanor smiled grimly. 'He is dependent upon us for money. If we tell him to do so, he will listen, believe me. And if we find Matilda a cottage in Northby, perhaps you and your husband could also help keep an eye on things? I doubt Marcus would want to be seen in this town being unfaithful to Samuel Rishmore's daughter.'

'No, you're right.' Prudence had forgotten that.

When Emmy found it was possible to go back to her dear Mrs Tibby, she wept for sheer joy. 'I can't believe it!' she kept saying. 'I can't believe how lucky I am!'

'Eh, it fair warms your heart,' Cook muttered to Cass, blowing her nose vigorously. 'It's about time that lass had some happiness.' Then she made up for this display of human weakness by being very sharp with everyone for the rest of the day.

Mrs Tibby came to call at the Parsonage the following day and Prudence left her and Emmy alone together to chat about their plans. When she came back, she found them both misty-eyed.

'What am I to do with you, Emmy?' she teased. 'Shall I find you another maid, Mrs Oswald, one who doesn't weep all over you?'

'Never!' Tibby reached out to take hold of Emmy's hand and beam at her kind hostess. 'And I hope you'll come and take tea with me once I'm settled in, Mrs Bradley?'

'It'll be my pleasure.' She looked at Emmy. 'There's just one other thing: what are we going to do about Hercules?'

Emmy's face fell.

'I don't think he'll be happy with anyone else. Should you mind, Mrs Oswald, taking a dog as well as a maid?'

Tibby had already been introduced to Emmy's new friend and although she had been nervous of Hercules at first, had soon realised he was a loving creature. 'I should be delighted to have him,' she said at once.

She went home with such a smile on her gentle face that it

did the coachman's heart good to see her, it really did. They all wished Mrs Oswald well in the servants' hall.

Jane watched surreptitiously through the window, almost groaning in relief as Marcus got into the carriage they hired regularly from the village inn. She was delighted that he would be gone for several days because she was finding his presence more wearing on her nerves than she had expected. If she had realised how very difficult he would be to live with, and how viciously unkind, she would have continued to defy her father about marrying him.

Marcus boasted regularly to her of his other women, comparing her unfavourably to them and taunting her with her inability to produce an heir. It didn't seem to occur to him that he might be the one at fault because he could not always manage to complete the act – which he also blamed on her. It had occurred to Jane, though, and very forcibly.

She had intended to bring Aggie to live with her but had changed her mind about that, explaining frankly to her old nurse how unkind Marcus was. 'He'd soon realise he had another way to hurt me by hurting you, and he'd enjoy that very much indeed. He can be – creatively cruel.'

As the carriage vanished into the distance, Jane turned with a sigh to wander through the house which was now wonderfully quiet. The minute Marcus left everything seemed to settle down, as if even the walls sighed with relief to be rid of his presence. By the time he returned she would know whether she had to endure his nightly assaults for a further month. A tear trickled down her face at that thought, but she told herself not to be so stupid. What good would tears do?

She decided to go and visit Aunt Tibby to cheer herself up. She had grown very fond of her husband's aunt and the walk to the big house would cheer her up. Indeed, going for long walks was her favourite pastime now.

Jane found the old lady in high spirits at the prospect of moving into a cottage of her own and returned home feeling jealous. What would she not give for somewhere like that, a place truly her own where no one would disturb her peace?

That made her draw in her breath suddenly. Would it be so impossible? How much did one need to live simply? She must discuss that with Aunt Tibby on her next visit. There must be a way to escape from here. She knew she could not face a lifetime of Marcus Armistead.

But dare she do it? Leaving her husband would destroy her good name.

Jane smiled wryly at the thought. What did her good name matter when staying with him for the rest of her life would destroy her utterly? She was quite sure of that.

As the carriage jolted along towards Manchester, Marcus stared sourly across the fields. He was relieved to be out of that miserable box of a house, where there was only his horse-faced wife to enliven the monotony. He was already sick of being married to a woman who was as much fun as a corpse in bed and big enough to fight him if she didn't like what he was doing. And he loathed being dependent on his father's goodwill.

Well, today would see the latter start to change, at least. He was on his way to meet George Duckworth to finalise plans for setting up their little business together. He snickered at the thought. A high-class brothel! George said they would not only make a great deal of money, but Marcus would be able to try out the stock whenever he wanted. Now that would be — interesting.

His father would throw a fit if he knew what Marcus was doing, but he wasn't going to find out. What was the use in harping on the importance of the Armistead name when he kept his only son perpetually short of money?

Marcus left the carriage at an inn and took a cab for the rest of the journey, not wanting the driver from the livery stables to tattle about where he had gone. The house George had found for them was on the edge of a slum area and not nearly as big as Marcus had expected, but it was only a starting point after all. Even before he knocked the front door opened and his partner stood there grinning at him.

'Well, Marcus lad, so you're here at last.' George wondered if the silly young fool knew how ridiculous he looked in a cloak with two capes and a collar on top of them. The top hat was, of course, the tallest style available. As if that would make a small man look taller. In fact, all this outfit did was make Armistead look as wide as he was high.

'Fetch my bag in, will you?' Marcus ran lightly up the steps. 'And I'm Mr Armistead to you!'

George bit off the words, 'Fetch it your bloody self!' and did as he was asked. One day he'd pay back this snivelling rich man's son for all the petty insults, but not yet. For the moment, Mr Marcus bloody Armistead was going to help George make his dreams come true.

Marcus wandered down the hall, peering into each room. 'It needs decorating.'

'Well, a'course it does. I'll find folk to do that cheap.'

'I'm not made of money, you know. Be sure you don't spend foolishly.'

George breathed deeply. 'We'll do it on the cheap, I promise you, an' start off with just a couple of girls. Soon build up to more if you play your part and spread the word among your rich friends. I've got one lass interested in working for me already.'

Marcus brightened. 'You have?'

Talking genially, George took him through to the back.

When Marcus had left he strolled round the house again on his own. Pity Madge had been killed. She'd have been perfect here to help train the young 'uns. And he missed her more than he had expected. She'd always been able to make him laugh. No one else could do that quite like her. If he ever found out who'd murdered her, he'd make them sorry, by hell he would!

Jack walked slowly home from the mill, glad the weather was milder and the evenings growing longer. It had been raining earlier, but a fitful sun had now come out and he smiled up at its cheerful light. Not really warm yet, but getting warmer by the week. Once it was summer he would resume his early Sunday scrambles across the moors, however much his mother complained. A man had a right to some pleasures, after all.

It seemed a perfect end to the day that he should meet Emmy on his way back, taking the young dog for a walk. It had grown quickly with good food, but was still clumsy. You could see at a glance, though, that it had a nice nature and was willing to be friends with the world. He smiled as he watched it gambolling along, then his eyes went back to Emmy. Her hair had grown into a fluffy mass of curls around her face and it suited her. She had lost that haunted air which had so worried him and he thought her the loveliest creature he had ever seen. Not artificially lovely like some of the rich women who visited the Rishmores, but with a loveliness that glowed inside her, that needed no fancy clothes to enhance it.

When she saw him, her face brightened and she came hurrying across the street. Jack waited for her but as she stopped beside him he could not think what to say, so patted the dog, using it as an excuse to linger.

'He's growing. And you, are you – well?' he managed.

'Oh, yes, thank you. Very – um – well.'

Silence hung between them, a silence heavy with all the things he would have liked to say to her and, he hoped, she would have liked to say to him. There was a new self-consciousness in their meetings lately.

She broke it by smiling up at him and saying, 'I have such good news, Jack! Mrs Tibby is to have a cottage of her own again in Northby and I'm to go back to work for her.'

'Eh, I'm delighted for you.'

'And would you believe it? We're to live in that house on Weavers Lane at the end of Cross Alley – Chad's Cottage they call it, for some reason, no one knows why. I've always liked the look of it, but it's been lying vacant for months so it needs refurbishing before we can move in.'

How stupid to feel jealous of an old lady! Jack thought, but could not help it. He felt quite overwhelmed by how pretty Emmy was when she was happy like this.

'I thought I'd have to leave Northby,' she went on.

'Well, I *wanted* to go away. But now that's all changed.' She lowered her voice to say, 'Mrs Tibby's brother is going to tell his son to keep away from me, too, so I shan't have to worry about *him*.'

'Good, good.'

'And Hercules is to come with us because Mrs Bradley says she hasn't time to look after him and is sure he'll pine for me. Oh, if only we could move in straight away!'

'Are you going to Moor Grange to look after Mrs Oswald till then?'

Some of the happiness faded from Emmy's face. 'No. Marcus Armistead lives in the nearby village and visits regularly, so Mr Bradley thinks it's better if I don't go there.'

'If that man ever tries to hurt you again, you know you can always come to me for help.'

'I know.' She looked up at him, loving the steady way his dark eyes met hers.

'I wish I could do more for you, Emmy.'

She shook her head. 'You have your own family, and even if you didn't,' she hesitated, then said in a rush, 'I haven't changed my mind about marrying. No one will ever forget what my mother was.'

'You could marry someone from another town or go and live elsewhere.'

She shook her head decisively. 'No. I'd still have to tell the – the person about my mother. I couldn't keep something like that a secret. And it'd probably probably drive him away or make him suspicious of me. Better I stay unwed, with only myself to worry about.'

'Any man worth his salt would see that you're not like your mother . . .' But she had withdrawn from him, was nodding and walking away. And he could only stand and watch her go. It felt as if the sun had gone behind a cloud and he was surprised when he looked up to see that it was still shining.

Sighing, he turned towards his home where there would be arguments between Meg and his mother, his little niece grizzling – poor Nelly was sickly and seemed to fret a lot, and the other children would be demanding his attention or squabbling with one another. He didn't know which was worse when he wanted a bit of peace for himself.

By May the new cottage was ready and Emmy went there to receive the furniture Mrs Armistead was sending across from Moor Grange. As she waited for the men to arrive she walked from room to room, longing to come and live here. There was a proper hall with a front parlour to the right and another room behind it where she and Mrs Tibby could sit cosily in the evenings. That way the parlour would do them credit, always spotless and ready to receive guests. In the kitchen a Yorkshire range had been newly installed. Such a modern miracle! It had a fire in the middle with an oven at one side and a boiler for heating water at the other side, with a tap to draw it off. Just imagine being able to get a bucket of hot water any time you needed one! She was taking lessons from Cook on using a range.

When the furniture arrived Emmy helped the men from Moor Grange decide where to put it, then after they had gone rushed round the house, trying the new chairs and marvelling at how comfortable they were, touching each piece of furniture. After that, in a fit of furious activity, she made up Mrs Tibby's bed with the linen that had been sent – such fine smooth sheets and such thick feather beds to lie on, even for her! She had never felt so happy in her whole life.

But still, just occasionally, she experienced nightmares in which she relived that dreadful time when George had captured her and Marcus Armistead tried to rape her. She kept telling herself not to be silly, that it was all over and done with, but the nightmares kept returning and she would wake screaming to find Cass or Cook standing by her bed shushing her. In her uncle's house, Lal or Dinah had shaken her roughly awake whenever this happened and told her to stop caterwauling. And once or twice her aunt had slapped her for waking everyone – as if she'd done it on purpose!

She would have to warn Mrs Tibby about the nightmares or they would come as a great shock. She didn't know whether her mistress was aware of what had so nearly happened, but there would be no hiding it from her once they were living together.

Emmy shook those sad thoughts away. She was not going to let them mar her present happiness. The nightmares would pass. Mrs Bradley said they would. And indeed, they came far less often now.

That reminded her suddenly of the package she had hidden in her uncle's attic. She had been too distraught to think of it when she left and since then there had always been something more important to do. After all, she didn't want to wear the locket and if truth be told, she didn't want to read her mother's papers. She was sure they'd only contain unpleasant news. No, they could stay where they were until she needed them. No one ever did more than sweep the floor up there. They'd never notice them.

A noise from outside alerted her and she went rushing to the front door to see the Armistead carriage draw up and Mrs Armistead get out. Emmy rushed to help her get Mrs Tibby down and together the two women eased the old lady across the pavement towards the house.

Tibby stopped for a moment on the doorstep to stare along the street. 'Oh, Eleanor, it's as nice here as I remember. It'll be so convenient to have a proper pavement outside. The mud used to be dreadful at our other place, didn't it, Emmy?'

'Yes, ma'am.'

'And we're nearly in the centre of the town. I'm sure I'll be able to manage such a short walk, as long as we take it slowly.'

Inside the house Tibby allowed them to seat her in the best parlour and felt a bit annoyed when Eleanor asked Emmy to fetch some tea. It was *her* home, after all, and *her* place to do that. And it might be ungrateful but she wished her sister-in-law would leave them alone now. She wanted to talk to Emmy, find out what had happened to her. She was sure it was more than Mrs Butterfield cutting off her hair. The girl looked years older and there was an unhappy shadow in her eyes for all her smiles and chatter. Something very serious must have happened and they were not going to keep it from her.

When Eleanor had at last been driven away, Tibby said firmly, 'Come and sit in here with me, Emmy.'

'But don't you want me to unpack for you?'

'Not yet. We'll do that together later. I want to talk to you now.' She stretched out one hand. 'And don't pretend they haven't hurt you badly because I know better. I can see it in your eyes, my dear child.'

With a sob, Emmy sank down on the rug at Mrs Tibby's feet and poured out her tale of woe. The familiar hand was on her hair, stroking, offering unspoken comfort. Not even Mrs Bradley knew all the details of what had happened, but somehow she could say anything to Mrs Tibby, anything at all.

When the tale ended, when all the questions had been asked and answered, she blinked up at the dear old face and gave a half-laugh as she mopped her eyes again. 'How dreadful of me to greet you like this!'

'There's no need for pretence between us, Emmy dear. As I shall not pretend about how painful my hip has become. I fear I shall not be able to walk at all if this goes on.'

'Then I'll be your feet and look after you. Or we'll get a bath chair and I'll push you round town.'

Mrs Tibby brightened. 'We could do that, could we not? I need not become a prisoner here, need I?'

They sat together for a long time, age-spotted hand in firm young one, then Mrs Tibby stirred. 'Time to inspect my new kingdom.'

They made a slow tour of the little house, so different from their old one, just as Emmy felt like a very different person from the one who had left the other house only a few months before.

By the time Marcus returned from visiting his friends, Jane suspected she was with child. When she saw the carriage she rushed up to her bedroom to dress her hair as unappealingly as she could before he saw her, then took a deep breath and walked composedly downstairs. He looked exhausted, but with such smug triumph behind his weariness that it made her wonder what he had been doing. Nothing good, she was sure.

'Heavens, you get uglier every time I see you,' he said by way of a greeting.

She was tired of humouring him 'So do you. When you speak so nastily, it seems to be reflected in your face.'

He took a threatening step towards her, hand upraised.

She retreated hastily behind a chair. 'I'm with child! You'd better be more careful how you treat me from now on if you don't want me to lose it.'

He stopped dead. 'I was beginning to wonder whether you were barren as well as ugly. Well, your ability to conceive a child is about the only thing I know in your favour. Make sure you look after yourself properly from now on.'

'I shall not come to your bedroom again until afterwards,' she reminded him.

'Think I want you there?' Then he frowned. 'But I shall need somebody to warm my bed. I'm going to bring in a girl to serve my needs. We can tell everyone she's a maid.'

Jane was horrified. 'I shall not allow that!'

'You will, you know. It's that or you sharing my bed.'

'But we have an agreement.'

He snapped his fingers in her face. 'That for your agreement! And after the child is born, we'll do things my way. I insist on being master in my own house.'

She did not allow herself to become agitated, for the baby's sake. Later she left him sipping a glass of brandy – he seemed to be drinking much more recently – and went up to her own bedroom, bolting the door behind her as always and sitting gazing bleakly out across the moors. Even to get children she did not think she could share his bed again. It had been so wonderful while he was away.

As for bringing in a girl to serve his needs, well, if it kept him quiet she supposed she would put up with it. For the time being.

She had never thought herself capable of wishing for someone's death, but she wished for his. Every time she was forced to share his bed, every time he hurt her, she prayed fervently that he would die, preferably slowly and in agony. If that made her wicked, she could not help it.

If only she could run away and never see her husband again!

But if she left here, how would she live? That was the main problem. She stared down at her hand and noticed the gold bracelet gleaming at her wrist, which reminded her of the leather-covered box filled with jewellery her father had given her. That jewellery was worth a great deal of money, and she did not need to live richly. Mrs Tibby had managed on a very small amount of money, after all.

Could she really escape from him?

Jane clasped her hands together at her breast and closed her eyes to contemplate the wonder of a life without Marcus, then she opened them again and drew in a deep, shuddering breath. It would have to be carefully planned – very carefully indeed – but she had nearly seven months to do that.

She did not even want to take his child with her. She wanted nothing of his.

Part Two

Chapter Fourteen

At Chad's Cottage Emmy was happier than she'd ever been in her whole life before. She and her mistress were together again and had no worries about money. What more could you want? She didn't let herself think about that. For someone like her this was as much as you could expect from life. The other was – impossible.

She watched indulgently, sometimes feeling like a mother with a shy child, as Mrs Tibby began to enjoy a social life, receiving other ladies and calling on them, too, on her better days. Mrs Armistead came to visit them whenever she called on the Rishmores, usually accompanied by her daughter-in-law who was expecting a child in January. Jane always behaved in a friendly manner towards Mrs Tibby, but from what Emmy saw as she brought in a tea tray there was a look of strain behind the calm smiles and conversation. Well, was it any wonder, married to Marcus Armistead? She felt sorry for the poor young lady, she really did.

But the days when Mrs Tibby could walk into town grew fewer as time passed, and it was bitter-sweet for Emmy to see her beloved mistress growing slowly weaker, more and more incapacitated by her twisted, swollen limbs, and sometimes breathless for no reason.

Mrs Tibby really needed a bath chair now, but she always made some excuse when Emmy raised the matter, saying there was plenty of time for that later. She remained cheerful in spite of her painful hips, saying she had a lot to be thankful for and must not complain about growing old.

Another bitter-sweet pleasure for Emmy was to go to church which her mistress rarely missed, even in bad weather. From the rear pews Emmy would watch Jack Staley singing in the choir or see him outside afterwards when the weather was fine enough for them to linger in the churchyard. She had long since stopped pretending to herself that she didn't care about him.

But she cared too much to encourage him.

That decision was reinforced each Sunday as she waited quietly on her own for Mrs Tibby, standing at the edge of the crowd in the churchyard. Few of the other servants, except for Cass, did more than nod to her and some of them very ostentatiously avoided her

But her uncle spoke to her sometimes and had begun calling on them both. Mrs Tibby enjoyed his company and Isaac seemed to enjoy hers. Well, the whole town knew how hard it was for him at home nowadays and how strangely his wife was behaving. No one had seen Lena Butterfield outside the house for a while and a woman went in every day now to help – every day but the Sabbath.

Emmy could not help noticing that occasionally young women from the congregation tried to flirt with Jack. This made her feel jealous even though she never saw him do more than respond politely and coolly. Usually he brought his mother, brothers and sisters with him to church, and his mother clung to his arm, scowling at any young woman who dared to come near. Mrs Staley had to go home on her own, however, and leave Jack to teach in the Sunday reading classes, so he would occasionally come across to speak to Emmy after her departure. She treasured those conversations, short, impersonal and public though they were.

His sister Meg never attended church, but Emmy saw her now and then in the street with a frail-looking little girl toddling beside her. Meg nodded as they passed one another, not stopping to talk but not looking in the least scornful either. Emmy never saw her linger to gossip with anyone. She was about a year older than Emmy, but looked older, and her expression was always tinged with bitterness except when she was talking to her child. Then sometimes her face would light up and she would look almost beautiful.

'What a pleasant outing it makes and didn't the choir sing well today?' Mrs Tibby would say as Emmy escorted her slowly back from church. 'And we have several things to read this afternoon, thanks to dear Eleanor. Isn't it kind of her to send us their old newspapers and ladies' journals?'

Once a week they read the *Manchester Guardian*, which was becoming very popular in the north. It didn't matter to them if the news was a week old, or even a month, because Manchester seemed very remote from Northby. The city the newspapers described was not the same world as the one Emmy had grown up in. The slum streets and that ragged, hungry child now seemed very distant and strange to her.

Mrs Tibby settled down after luncheon with *The World of Fashion*. 'Oh, look, Emmy. Just see what the ladies in London society are wearing. I shouldn't want to wear such a ridiculously large bonnet, I'm sure it'd give me a headache.' And a little later, she clicked her tongue in a comfortable way. 'Turbans, indeed! You wouldn't need an umbrella if you wore this one because it's wide enough to keep the rain off.' She chuckled and held the magazine out.

Emmy obediently studied the illustrations, agreeing that it would be difficult to walk with so many layers of petticoats and that one couldn't do any housework in the huge sleeves currently in vogue. She thought them ridiculous but had developed a habit of agreeing with whatever her mistress said.

When Mrs Tibby's head began to nod, Emmy took the magazine gently from her and tiptoed into the kitchen where she sat idle for once, spinning her own dreams. Then she realised where this was leading and picked up the magazine. But she simply couldn't get interested in what the gentry were wearing.

King George died on June 26th, a month after they had set up house together, and the news took only two days to reach Northby. Mrs Tibby immediately insisted they draw the parlour curtains as a sign of respect. 'He was not always a good man,' she told Emmy, 'but he *was* our monarch.' Then she brightened.

'But King William is a married man, which is much more respectable, and I'm sure Queen Adelaide will be an example to us all, though how sad it is that she has not been able to rear any children.'

In September of that same year the Liverpool and Manchester Railway was to open and it was much discussed in the town. Mr Bradley was in favour of progress and had told his congregation about locomotives and railways during one of his rather un-orthodox sermons, ascribing such inventions to God's loving care for his people.

He insisted on going to see the opening himself and took Jack with him. For this he had to win Isaac Butterfield's permission, but the head clerk was a more lenient man nowadays and gave it gladly, saying a young man should be a part of such a momentous occasion and he would enjoy hearing about it all when they returned.

The two men hired a trap and set off very early on the morning of the fifteenth to be there for the start at twenty to eleven. However, they came back in rather more sombre mood and Parson's wife, who would talk to a maid just as easily as to a mistress, told Emmy the following day when they met outside the draper's shop that a gentleman had been killed during the opening ceremonies. A Mr Huskisson had been knocked down by the train.

'Could he not see it coming and move out of the way?' Emmy marvelled. She had seen sketches of trains in the news-papers and knew they were much larger than stage coaches. Jack had explained that there was a front part called a locomotive where a coal fire burned to heat water in a boiler and provide steam – though how that could drive a huge vehicle full of people was beyond her understanding. The locomotive appar-ently pulled several carriages, only they weren't really carriages. They looked as if someone had glued two or three stage coaches together. So how could you possibly miss seeing something that big coming towards you?

'It seems he didn't see it coming – or misjudged the speed,

my husband thinks. Trains sound very dangerous to me for they can travel at a speed of twenty-four miles per hour, perhaps more. Can you imagine that? How it must bump you around!' Prudence shook her head disapprovingly. 'But my husband insists railways are the way of the future and says we shall all be riding on them within a few years, travelling more easily than we ever have before. And he is intending to travel to Liverpool one day by rail, just for the experience. I don't contradict him, but *I* have no intention of ever entrusting myself to such a monster. Why, I've heard the sparks from the engines set crops alight and terrify the poor animals in the fields.'

'I can't imagine why I should ever need to ride on a train,' Emmy agreed. 'Where would I want to go anyway, when I'm so happy where I am?'

Mrs Bradley's expression softened into a smile. 'And so is Mrs Tibby. You're looking after her very well, my dear. But you do realise that she's – well, getting very frail?'

As if Emmy didn't know that! 'Yes. But I try to enjoy each day as it comes. And Mrs Tibby looks after me, too, you know. I could barely read and write when I first went to work for her.' She saw with relief that this had distracted her companion from sad thoughts because education was one of Prudence Bradley's pet enthusiasms.

'The day will come when everyone will learn to read and write, girls as well as boys. That's far more important than travelling at breakneck speed. We are to have a proper school in Northby soon, you know. The Church is to build it and the Government will pay money towards the schooling of every child in town, no matter how poor. Now *that* is what *I* call progress!'

One Sunday after church Jack made his way across to Emmy as she was waiting for her mistress to finish chatting to a friend. 'Did you know that George Duckworth has left Northby?'

She stared at him in surprise. 'Are you sure?'

'Oh, yes. He's sold his alehouse to his cousin, Gus Norris, and taken two of his regular girls with him.'

'He's probably going to set himself up somewhere more profitable, then,' Emmy said lightly. 'He used to talk to my mother about "moving up" and "serving the gentry".' Only to Jack could she have said this. There was nothing they could not tell each other about. 'But thank you for letting me know. I shall sleep sounder knowing he's not in town.' Though he had not tried again to speak to her in the street, George always nodded in a familiar way whenever they passed one another. She ignored him completely, of course. She was not afraid of Gus, the carter who had brought them to Northby. He was large but not devious and did not make her feel nervous as George did, even now.

She only wished Marcus Armistead would suddenly move elsewhere as well for she still saw him watching her from a carriage sometimes, a rather shabby vehicle for a rich man to use. But she confided her fears about him to no one. At least he had not come to visit his aunt. He could stare as much as he wanted so long as he didn't come near her.

As he often did, Jack seemed to read her mind. 'Are you still worried about Armistead?'

She looked up at him, so tall and sturdy, and the rest of the world seemed to fall away as if there were only the two of them. 'Yes,' she said simply. 'I always shall be. Until I can go to live somewhere he can't find me. If anything happens to Mrs Tibby, that's what I shall do.'

'Don't—' Jack broke off, hesitating, then said in a rush, 'Don't leave without saying goodbye.'

But she couldn't even promise him that. She knew she might have to flee suddenly when her mistress died and didn't intend to involve Jack in any more of her troubles. 'I shan't leave as long as my mistress needs me,' she said, stepping back. They had talked for long enough. She didn't want tongues wagging about them.

He raised his hat and half turned, then looked back at her and what he could not put into words was in the look he gave her. She hoped her feelings had not shown as clearly in her own face.

When they got home Mrs Tibby said thoughtfully, 'That young man cares about you, you know, Emmy.'

She did not need to ask which young man. 'There can be nothing between us.'

'Why not?'

'He has his mother and family to look after, and besides, I could never marry.'

'You can't let that stop you. I ran away with James, my dear, because I loved him so, and I'm not afraid of dying because I'm sure I'll be reunited with him.' She sighed reminiscently, then reached out to take Emmy's hand and say earnestly, 'Don't throw away the chance to encourage a good man, my dear.'

The following week a carriage drove past Emmy and stopped. She thought nothing of it but continued walking along the lane, thinking about the things she must purchase at market. Then she drew level with the vehicle and realised with a shock that it contained Marcus Armistead. The window was open and she was closer to him than she had been since that dreadful night. For a moment she froze, terror shivering through her as he stared out at her, then she hurried on.

Behind her he called out, 'One day!' and Emmy broke into a stumbling run.

She never went out alone at night after that, not even at dusk, and if she saw the shabby carriage in the distance she tried to keep out of sight until it had passed. But there were few turnings off Weavers Lane, and if she couldn't get out of the way she would stare straight ahead as she walked past the carriage and try to hide her fear.

She said nothing about these encounters to her mistress or about the fear of him which had returned to sit like a stone in her belly. She didn't want to spoil Mrs Tibby's quiet happiness in any way.

Jane went into labour in February 1831. Things progressed so rapidly and easily that her son was born a mere three hours later, long before his father came back from Manchester where he had spent a number of nights recently, to his wife's relief.

The baby so resembled Marcus that Jane could not take to the infant as she knew she ought to. She claimed more exhaustion than she felt and asked them to take the child to the wet nurse she had insisted on hiring.

When they had gone she blew out the candle and huddled down in bed, enjoying the feel of her now slender body. She stared at a narrow shaft of moonlight which had penetrated one side of the heavy velvet curtains and admitted to herself that the moment had come to act on the plans she had made. But for the first time she wondered if she'd have the courage to carry them through.

She took a deep breath. She *had to* leave him.

As a first step she insisted on getting out of bed the very next day, scandalising the entire household by this action.

Marcus came into her room to protest as she stood by the window, struggling to open it. 'Why are you out of bed? You're jeopardising the health of our future children by your foolish behaviour!'

'Poor women continue working and I can see why. I feel very well, but if I have to lie in bed any longer I shall start imagining myself ill out of sheer boredom.'

'And they tell me you haven't wanted the babe brought to you,' he went on.

'It's the wet nurse he needs at the moment, not me.'

'You may not be feeding him, but surely you want to hold him?'

She did not wish to antagonise Marcus at the moment, so smiled brightly and said, 'Of course I do.' It worried her that he continued to stare at her across the room. When he gave one of his almost-smiles, the smile of someone with mischief in mind, she tensed.

'Since you are feeling so well, understand this, my dear wife. I shall not tolerate any more unwomanly independence or disobedience.' He paused, his smile broadening. 'And we shall be sharing a bedroom every night once you have recovered fully. If I have to hire a strong man to help me control you.'

She was horrified at this threat and could not hold back a sharp response. 'Then you'll definitely have to force me to your

242

bed screaming every night. The only time I shall willingly share a bedroom with you again, Marcus, is when you're dead and I'm keeping a final watch – as a dutiful widow should.'

His face contorted suddenly in rage. 'Or perhaps it's I who will be keeping watch over *your* dead body.' One more child and he would seriously consider getting rid of the bitch. He had no intention whatsoever of spending his life shackled to such an ugly and unmanageable female. Afraid of saying it to her, so deep had the hatred grown, he spun on his heel and walked out.

Jane did not move for quite some time. This conversation had made her utterly certain she must leave. She could tell what he intended as clearly as if he had spoken it aloud. If she stayed, he would one day kill her. And you couldn't guard yourself every minute, not even if you were bigger than your husband. Poison could be put into anything you were eating.

She had even been tempted to rid herself of Marcus. That was what hatred did to you. But she had settled instead on running away for she did not wish to kill, even in self-defence.

Was her husband really capable of it?

After a moment she nodded. Yes, she was quite sure he was.

Three days later Jane watched from her usual vantage point at the bedroom window as Marcus left the house on business. He would never discuss what he did with her, telling her that a woman would not understand the activities of a Manchester merchant. Of course she could! Such men sent consignments of Lancashire goods round the world, acting as middlemen, taking a small profit here and another there. She had heard her father talk several times about John Owens, a gentleman who was apparently making a fortune for himself in this way. She could have done the same thing herself easily enough after listening for years to her father and his colleagues talking over dinner, but of course no one would deal with a woman.

Soon afterwards she got dressed on her own, then sum-moned her maid to say she was going for a stroll in the gardens and perhaps out on to the nearby moors. 'I'll be back in an hour or so, Hellie.'

'Oh, Mrs Armistead, you shouldn't leave the grounds on your own. It's too soon!'

'I shall come straight back if I feel at all tired, I promise you. But I'm desperate for some fresh air.'

Since walking was an old habit of Mrs Armistead's no one worried when she did not return straight away. However as the hours passed Hellie grew anxious and went out to look for her. She was nowhere in the gardens and the gardener said he had seen the mistress go out through the little gate and over the brow 'an hour or two gone'.

By lunchtime the two maids and cook-housekeeper were getting really worried, though the young woman whom the others referred to scornfully as 'Mr Armistead's maid' mocked their anxiety. As one o'clock struck on the hall clock with no sign of their mistress still, they decided to send a message across to Moor Grange. The master's mother would know what to do, they were sure.

'She's turned her ankle and can't walk,' Hellie kept saying. 'That'll be what's happened. My mum did that once.'

They waited for an hour for an answer, worry deepening by the minute.

'She's been murdered,' Cook said finally with dark relish. 'It'll be some rascal on the tramp. He'll have beaten her to death and thrown her body into the quarry. Someone killed an old woman on the moors a few years ago, I remember it clearly.'

Hellie shivered. 'Oh, don't say things like that! It'll be dark soon and then how shall we find her?'

When Eleanor arrived in person at half-past two she expected to find Jane waiting for her. She had been so sure that all the fuss was about nothing she had not hurried. Her daughter-in-law was fond of taking long walks and it was a fine mild day for March, so Jane had probably just gone too far and had to rest before returning.

But she had still not returned and the whole household was

in a twitter, all work suspended, so after checking that her grandson was being properly cared for by the wet nurse, Eleanor went up to Jane's room and searched it thoroughly.

She summoned the maid to help her and it was Hellie who thought to check her mistress's jewellery. As she opened the leather-covered box, she let out a shriek. 'It's all gone! She's been murdered and robbed. Oh, my poor mistress!' She began to sob.

'Stop that noise!' Eleanor took the box from her. Not every item was missing. Jane's wedding ring lay in solitary splendour on the velvet pad in the top compartment. 'Does she usually leave her wedding ring in here?'

Hellie shook her head and the two women looked at one another in consternation.

'If someone had stolen her things they'd have taken this as well. Jane must have done this herself.' After a moment Eleanor said quietly, 'Go and wait in the kitchen until I call you. And say nothing of this if you wish to keep your place here.'

'Yes, ma'am.' Hellie, who was fifty and as plain as the other maids Jane had engaged, went to sit in the kitchen. She kept her mouth firmly shut and scowled at the master's flibbertigibbet who was lolling around drinking a cup of tea. What was the world coming to when someone like that was employed openly in a gentleman's household? Not that the master was much of a gentleman in her opinion, though the mistress was a nice lady and had to put up with a lot, poor soul. But to leave the wedding ring behind like that! Surely her mistress had not run away? If she had, what would the master do about it, eh? He'd be furious, that's what, and would probably take out that anger on the servants. She'd beg Mrs Armistead not to let him turn her off without a reference, that's what she'd do.

When the bedroom door had closed on the maid Eleanor had no compunction about searching every drawer and cupboard again. But she could find no clue to indicate what had happened. She went down to the parlour and from there to Marcus's smoking room, searching with equal thoroughness but with the same result. Jane had definitely not left a note. Only the ring. And its message seemed all too clear.

245

Going back upstairs she stood staring out of the window at the village below, wondering what to do and facing up to the fact that her daughter-in-law had run away. Was Marcus such a monster to live with, then?

He must be.

What had he done to Jane to drive her to this?

With a sigh Eleanor went downstairs again to write a note to her husband and another to Samuel Rishmore. After some hesitation she decided not to send for Marcus until later. She had no doubt they would find Jane before too long – a woman could not vanish into thin air, after all. Perhaps she could insist the couple come to live at Moor Grange from now on, so that she could keep a better eye on things and offer Jane a little support? Not to mention keeping an eye on their grandson.

Samuel arrived first, just before dusk, and Eleanor told him the bald facts, not attempting to hide her fears about her son's behaviour and his daughter's unhappiness.

He stared at her in shock. 'You mean, you think our Jane's just – run off? Left her husband and child?'

'I fear so.'

'She's gone mad, then. Women do that sometimes after they've had a child.'

'I don't think so. I saw her yesterday and she seemed in full possession of her faculties. In fact, she looked better than she had for a while.' And that thought made Eleanor even more certain that her daughter-in-law had indeed run away. Knowing Jane, it would have been carefully planned. For the first time it occurred to Eleanor that they might not find her and she sucked in her breath in shock.

Samuel glared at her. 'I'm not having it said that my Jane has broken her marriage vows and run off like a loose woman.'

'We shall not be able to hide the fact, I'm afraid.'

'Then we'll say she wasn't in her right mind because of the child.'

Eleanor did not argue. It would be easy enough for her to set rumours circulating to contradict such a statement and she intended to do just that. She already felt guilty for helping bring about such a disastrous marriage and was definitely not going to add to that guilt by allowing them to malign the poor young woman. If she did, Marcus might lock Jane up in an asylum once they found her. It had been done before by cruel husbands.

When Claude joined them it was after nightfall and he was in a sour mood at having to leave a convivial evening with friends. His reaction was the same as Samuel's. They must tell everyone Jane was in low spirits after bearing her son Charles and had been behaving irrationally. 'And why the hell haven't you sent for Marcus?' he asked his wife. 'Didn't you think *he* needed to know?'

'I thought that since she might have run away from him, we could work out some way to help her when she was found before sending for him. I see you do not agree.' Suddenly, listening to the two men plotting how to keep the news a secret, not even considering that Jane might need help more than condemnation, she hoped her daughter-in-law really had been clever enough to get away. But she did not say that or openly argue with Claude who was bright red with anger.

Marcus did not arrive until well after midnight and like his father he was furious, threatening to beat his wife within an inch of her life when she was found and to teach her a lesson she would never forget.

Eleanor retreated to a corner of the parlour and watched them. Both fathers were on Marcus's side still, she could see, though Rishmore said firmly that there would be no beating of his misguided daughter. 'If I consider it necessary for her protection, I'll take her to live with me again,' he stated as his son-in-law ignored him and continued to rant.

'Sir, she is in my charge now,' Marcus said. 'You would have no legal right to do that.'

Samuel stared at him through narrowed eyes. 'If I thought you were beating my daughter, I'd find a way.'

Marcus had an ugly twist to his mouth sometimes, his mother decided, watching. She would not fool herself about her son from now on. What's more, if she ever saw a way to help her daughter-in-law, she would do so. In the meantime she said quietly, 'Until we find Jane, I think the baby and its wet nurse

247

should be brought to Moor Grange where I can keep an eye on them.'

All three men agreed instantly, almost absent-mindedly, then the two Armisteads went back to making angry comments about women and their irrationality while Samuel sat frowning at them.

Feeling exhausted and upset, Eleanor left them to it.

No one on the regular stage coach from Manchester to London thought anything of the young fellow who sat so quietly in a corner, wrapped in a heavy cloak and looking white and wan. When he mentioned in a hoarse whisper that he was recovering from the influenza, they took care to keep as far away from him as possible, relieved that he was not sneezing all over them.

In London he strode off down the street with his small valise swinging in his hand.

Two days later a lady wearing the flowing black veils of recent widowhood took a house in a small village in Hertford-shire. She and her elderly maid settled down to live together very quietly and frugally, working in their garden, attending church every Sunday and borrowing books from a circulating library to enliven their peaceful evenings.

The maid told everyone that her mistress had lost not only her husband but also her only child in a carriage accident. Such a tragedy. And the late Mr Barrow had been a rather foolish young man where business matters were concerned, so sadly her mistress was now living in straitened circumstances.

But Mrs Barrow must have been a trifle homesick for the north because it was noticed that she still found the money to take the *Manchester Guardian* every week.

When several days had passed without news of Jane and with no sign of a body, Samuel Rishmore reluctantly agreed to the printing of handbills and posters offering a reward for anyone giving information which might lead to the discovery of his missing daughter. His wife had drawn a likeness of Jane only the previous year which, unlike most of Margaret's sketches, actually bore a resemblance to its subject. The printer used it to make a woodcut and again, chance made it turn out well.

'That's her to the life, the jade!' Marcus snapped when he saw it. 'If that doesn't find her for us, nothing will.'

The posters were sent out far and wide across the county.

A pawnbroker in Manchester studied one of them and decided that the young woman who had brought in a rather fine pearl necklace a few weeks ago was probably the one they were looking for. He smiled as he tore the poster down from the wall outside and threw it away. He did not intend to say anything. If his customer really had been this Mrs Armistead, it would do him no good to have her found. If she stayed lost no one would come to retrieve the necklace she had pawned and he would make a fine profit for himself by selling it.

'Clever lady, that one,' he muttered as he went back inside his shop to study the necklace again. She had known exactly what the piece was worth and what she could expect from him for it. She had been prepared to go elsewhere and had started to walk out before he gave her the price she was asking. 'I bet they don't find her,' he said as he put the string of pearls away to wait for his next trip to London where he had acquaintances who would take it off his hands, no questions asked.

As day succeeded day with no news, Samuel Rishmore grew so difficult to live and work with that his wife kept out of his way as much as she could.

Claude Armistead alternated between anger and long dinners with colleagues in Manchester at which he could drown his sorrows and forget about his damned daughter-in-law.

Marcus soon made an excuse to return to Manchester to deal with some 'pressing matters', leaving Charles, in whom he took almost no interest, to Eleanor's care.

George Duckworth had to tread carefully around his partner

249

for a while, though Marcus was more angry at the humiliation of having a wife run away from home than about losing Jane.

It was Margaret Rishmore who thought to go and see Jane's old nurse to ask if she knew anything. But the old woman had apparently left town some three weeks before the birth of the baby.

'Poorly, she was,' the neighbour said. 'Told me she wanted to die where she grew up, somewhere in the north I think. Near Carlisle. Or was it near Lancaster? I misremember. You could ask her cousin, who still lives in the next street.'

Margaret went into the next street and found the cousin, from whom she obtained Aggie's address. She didn't tell Samuel about her visit or show him the piece of paper. She rolled it up and hid it among her embroidery silks which no one but she ever touched. She was quite sure Aggie was involved in her daughter's disappearance. She remembered Jane once showing her a badly bruised back and begging for her help in escaping from Marcus and his cruelty. She hadn't dared do anything. Now she wished she had.

Margaret prayed every night that her daughter was all right and that her jewellery had brought in enough money for the two women to live on in decent comfort.

And she kept the address secret. She had failed her daughter once, but would not do so again.

After his first rage had died down Marcus came to the conclusion that Jane had done the best thing for him in running away, though of course he didn't admit that to anyone. Having a missing wife actually suited him far better than being widowed because no one could press him to remarry. He had provided his father with the grandson he wanted, so Claude continued to pay him an adequate allowance and left him mostly alone.

And George was proving a very efficient partner. They were making a steady profit from their 'little house of pleasure' as Marcus liked to call it, though its official name was The Red House and they had used that colour in the furnishings. Good idea of George's, that.

On his occasional visits home Marcus watched from a distance as his aunt declined in health and her maid bloomed. If Emmy had been pretty before, she was beautiful now, glowing with happiness, and he could not stop thinking about her, wanting her. He'd arranged for a man in Northby to keep an eye on her and the fellow assured him there was no sign of anyone sniffing around, though she did talk to that Jack Staley sometimes after church. But they weren't walking out together. Definitely not. And she never left the house at night.

So the likelihood was that Emmy Carter was still a virgin.

And one day Marcus fully intended to finish what he had started.

Chapter Fifteen

On September 8th Claude Armistead dropped dead in Manchester while drinking a loyal toast to the new King on his Coronation Day. His colleagues, who were as far gone in drink as he was, did not at first realise that he was dead and continued to drink around him until one of them tried to rouse him from where he lay slumped on the table.

When they realised Claude was dead they laid him on a sofa with a handkerchief over his face and drank a solemn toast to him as well.

The following morning half of them were still there, some awake but rather glassy-eyed, others with their heads pillowed on the table, snoring gently. After much discussion two of them drove to Padstall to give the widow the sad news and those remaining summoned a local undertaker to deal with the body.

He seized his opportunity with enthusiasm and carried the corpse away, installing it in one of his more expensive coffins. He then drove it slowly to the deceased gentleman's home in his best glass and iron hearse drawn by four glossy black horses. In this the coffin was displayed for all to admire, with its fine polished wood and gleaming brass fitments.

The two gentlemen arrived at Moor Grange first.

Eleanor listened to them in stony silence. Damn Claude! Could he not have died decently at home, instead of at a drunken dinner?

'Thank you for informing me,' she told them with chill

courtesy. 'I presume you have made arrangements to have the body brought home?'

'Yes. Of course. The – um – undertaker fellow seemed very capable. He's bringing it here this afternoon. In a hearse. All done right and proper.'

'Thank you.'

His companion cleared his throat. 'Would you – um, like me to fetch someone to be with you? A relative? Close friend?'

'No. I can manage, thank you.' She had them shown out then informed the staff, who received the news in silence, except for the butler who offered her their condolences. She guessed from their expressions that they were already wondering about the security of their jobs, but soon that would no longer be her business.

After sending a groom with a message to the family lawyer, she indicated where the coffin was to be placed when it arrived, refused to have the curtains drawn all over the house – a foolish custom and what good did it do out here in the middle of the countryside? – and left them to it. In the nursery she dismissed the nursemaid and held out her arms to her grandson who gurgled in pleasure. Holding him and occasionally murmuring endearments, she paced up and down the nursery thinking about what she would do after she had buried her husband. The warm body snuggling against hers was a great comfort and little Charles was his usual sunny-natured self. It was a constant source of amazement to her that her son could have produced a child as delightful as this one.

Given her husband's choleric disposition, she had been pondering for years about what she would do if she were widowed and had mentally settled on moving to Cheltenham or some similar town, where she might meet other genteel widows and enjoy some civilised company after all her years living on the edge of these bleak moors. Bath was too hilly for her taste, but Cheltenham was fairly level and would be a delightful place for gentle strolls and visits to the shops. No one, not even her husband, had ever known how much she hated living at Moor Grange or how the wind irritated her nerves when it whined around the windows, spattering rain and hail against them in season and out.

Concealing her relief that this exile was about to end, she handed her grandson back to his nursemaid and went to change into some black garments.

Later that day her messenger returned from the lawyer, offering his condolences and affirming Mr Baird's readiness to be present after the funeral to read the will. Eleanor knew her jointure would be secure because her father had managed the legalities of that when she married. She was glad not to be dependent on her son but decided with some reluctance to offer to raise his child for him. As soon as she could, she would leave Padstall. She had done her duty and now intended to please herself for the rest of her life.

The undertaker turned up with the body before Marcus arrived from Manchester and Eleanor received the man alone, amused that he seemed to have a face made for his trade, with long drooping jowls and sad brown eyes. However, his solemn demeanour hid a sharp eye for business and she was much entertained by the perfectly tactful way he outlined, with much detailed description, the services he could provide for a gentleman's funeral and at what price.

After a while she cut short his wilder extravagances and hired him at a total cost of £150, which the estate would pay for and which, she was sure, would infuriate Marcus. For this she would be supplied with mutes, black horses, plumes and weepers, not to mention the glass and iron hearse to carry Claude ostentatiously to his final resting place. She had never seen the point of employing mutes – sad-faced strangers dressed in what seemed to her more like fancy dress costumes than suitable funereal garb – but people in their position had to make some sort of show, so she suppressed a smile and approved of two being added to the mourning procession.

Marcus arrived home just in time for dinner. As she sat down to eat with him, Eleanor saw that her son was already giving himself airs. He talked of little save what he intended to do with the money he had inherited and she listened with only half an ear because it had suddenly occurred to her that if she left the north, poor Matilda would be entirely at Marcus's mercy. She could not do that to the old woman and would invite her to come and live in Cheltenham, she decided. There must be cottages to rent there as well as here and she had grown quite fond of her husband's sister. The young maid could come with them, too. She was a good little worker. That would keep her out of Marcus's hands.

'I intend to settle in Cheltenham,' she told her son abruptly, interrupting his tedious monologue.

He looked at her sharply then nodded approval. 'An excellent idea, Mama. You have no doubt had enough of these stupid moors – as have I. In that case I shall definitely sell the house and move into Manchester.'

'And Charles? What shall you do about him?'

He threw her a startled glance. 'But I thought – you seem fond of him – aren't you going to take him with you?'

'If you will pay for his keep, certainly. But housing a child will require me to find a larger property than I would need on my own, not to mention hiring a nursery maid and extra laundry maid, so I shall expect you to cover those expenses.'

'Ah. Yes.' Marcus scowled, not wanting to give away any of his long-awaited wealth, but realising after very little thought that he had no choice. 'Very well. I shall miss him, of course, but it is important for him to be under a woman's care. My only condition is that if his mother ever turns up again, you do not allow her to see him.'

Eleanor inclined her head. She could not imagine that Jane would ever reappear – unless something should happen to Marcus, which was not likely. 'Then after the funeral I shall visit Cheltenham which sounds a pleasant place with a very healthy situation and much to see and do. After all, if the Duchess of York and the heiress to the throne consider it worth a visit, I believe I could be happy there.'

'I should come with you, I suppose.' He didn't want to. He and George were looking for new premises because the enterprise was flourishing and their girls were becoming very popular in certain circles. And now he'd be able to finance a rather special sort of place. He realised he had let his thoughts stray and looked across at his mother who had just cleared her throat to attract his attention.

'As I was saying, you need not come with me, Marcus. It's kind of you to offer, but I can manage perfectly well on my own. And you will be needed to deal with matters here.'

'Well, if you're sure . . .'

Eleanor wondered as he left the next morning what it would be like to have a son whom you could love. She had loved him as a baby, though even then he had grizzled a lot, complaining and whining and keeping the nursemaid awake night after night. But he had grown into a spiteful unlovable boy, the sort other children avoided and other parents did not invite to visit a second time. And as a young man he had become a nuisance, always pestering her maids whether they welcomed his attentions or not. She had been relieved to marry him off and, she thought sadly, would not worry if she never saw him again after she'd moved away.

Claude Armistead's funeral was held two days later. Carriages, local gentry and tenants followed the hearse to the little church in the village of Padstall, then returned at a decorous pace to the big house for refreshments.

Though it was a raw day and she was not in the best of health herself, Tibby Oswald was among them, accompanied by Mrs Bradley. Emmy remained in Northby, however, staying at the Parsonage.

After the funeral Marcus said to his mother, 'I don't see why I should go on paying for the old lady.'

'It will look bad if you don't.'

'I don't give a damn how it looks. If you care about her, *you* take her to live with you. The girl will soon find herself another position. She can come here till we sell the place, if she likes. We can always use another maid.'

'I'll see what Matilda wants to do,' Eleanor replied calmly. But she had not missed the sudden tension in his body as he'd mentioned the maid, however casual his words. It was a strange offer for him to make, since he never concerned himself with servants' welfare, and she decided that Matilda's fears about his intentions were probably justified.

257

It would be best simply to take Matilda and her maid with her to Cheltenham and let Marcus find out later that they were gone. Eleanor doubted he would pursue the girl there.

She returned to the north after spending a very pleasant two weeks in a hotel in Cheltenham. She had rented a charming villa within walking distance of the town centre and felt the air there exactly suited her constitution.

The northern landscape put on its bleakest face to greet her, with rain sweeping across the moors and turning the slate roof of her home black. She shivered. She was going to move south as quickly as possible.

The following day she went to visit Matilda and suggest her sister-in-law come and live with her in Cheltenham.

Emmy put her ear to the kitchen door and eavesdropped shamelessly on their conversation, tears of relief welling in her eyes as she heard what they were planning. This was the answer to all her worries. She would get away from Northby, away from *him*, and she was never going to come back again, whatever happened.

Over the next few days they began their preparations, but although Emmy tried to spare her mistress as much as possible, she could see that Mrs Tibby was struggling more than usual. Emmy was worried sick about her but said nothing, trying to maintain a cheerful expression and chatting as they sorted things out for the move.

And then, even before they could put their exciting new plans into operation, Tibby Oswald died. It happened very suddenly, only six weeks after her brother's death. She was sitting staring into the fire one evening and fell asleep as she did sometimes. When Emmy went to rouse her and suggest it was time for bed, she found that her mistress had died as quietly as she'd lived. The old lady had a faint smile on her face, so Emmy knew she could have felt no pain.

'I'm going to miss you,' she whispered as she closed Mrs Tibby's eyes. She wept a little, then put on her cloak and braved the windy night to go and tell Mr Bradley what had happened. He would send someone to inform the Armisteads.

She and Mrs Bradley came back to the cottage together to lay out the old lady with loving care. Cass followed shortly afterwards to spend the night there with Emmy.

As she lay in bed, unable to sleep, Emmy could not help thinking that this would change things for the worse. She knew it was ungrateful to regret that her mistress had not died *after* they had moved instead of now, but she was so afraid of Marcus Armistead she could not help it. He was now head of the family, a rich man. And he had stopped his shiny new carriage to stare at her as he passed her on the street only the other day. She felt quite sure he would come after her.

'Once Mrs Tibby has been buried,' she said to Mrs Bradley, 'I shall have to leave Northby quickly.'

The Parson's wife stared at her, eyes narrowed. 'Because of Marcus Armistead?'

'Yes.'

'Are you sure he's still – interested?'

'Yes. He's been stopping the carriage and staring at me for a while now. He did it only last week.'

'Drat the man! You'll need to find another place, then. I shall be happy to provide you with references, my dear, though I don't think I know of anyone who is looking for a maid at the moment. But there are employment agencies in Manchester, so I'm sure you'll easily find a position. We can go into the city together to make enquiries, if you like.'

'I don't want to go into Manchester. Mr Armistead does business there. I want to find a position as far away from here as possible. I was thinking of going to London and trying there.' The thought of travelling to the capital terrified her. What did she know about the south?

But the thought of falling into Marcus Armistead's hands terrified her even more.

Marcus drove into Northby the day before the funeral. He called first on Mrs Rishmore with a message from his mother, then went to a small cottage on the outskirts of town to discuss a certain matter with the man who was keeping an eye on Emmy Carter for him.

He smiled all the way back to Moor Grange. Now the old lady and his parents weren't around he could put his plans into action. Soon, Emmy Carter, very soon now! he gloated as he was driven back across the moors.

As he passed the spot where he had killed Madge Carter, he threw back his head and laughed. No one had ever suspected him. As they would not suspect him of abducting her daughter if he planned things carefully.

You only had to wait a little and everything came to you. He intended to become extremely rich before he was through. He had a far better grasp of business than his father and was not afraid to seize chances Claude would have rejected. Look how profitable the venture with George was, and there were other avenues open if a man was not afraid to tread the shadier paths.

As they turned into the drive of Moor Grange, Marcus's smile turned into a frown, however. His lawyer said it would be hard to find a buyer for a house so isolated and in such a stark, old-fashioned style. Why the hell his grandfather had bought this place he would never understand.

Mrs Tibby's funeral took place in Northby because the old lady wished to be buried next to her husband there, not in the small village church at Padstall where her brother and the rest of her family lay. It was a beautiful autumn day. The sun shone and birds fluttered around as if they were watching over the grave and knew that this was the old lady who had fed so many of them in her back garden, delighting in their antics as her body grew weaker and her life more restricted.

Emmy went to the funeral with Mrs Bradley. The family was represented by Marcus Armistead and when his eyes rested on her, it made her shiver to see the gloating expression in them.

After the coffin had been lowered into the grave people began to move away. Emmy, who had lingered to say a private farewell, saw Mr Garrett approaching her.

'You'll miss her,' he said in his sympathetic way.

She nodded, trying hard not to weep again.

'What are you going to do now, my dear?'

'Find myself another place in service.' She glanced over her shoulder towards where Marcus was standing beside his carriage watching her. 'As far away as possible from Northby.'

He followed her gaze. Everyone in town knew what Marcus Armistead was like, but it disgusted John Garrett to see that he was behaving in such an unseemly manner at his aunt's funeral. 'Is that young fellow annoying you?'

'He'd like to, but I shan't give him the chance. I shall leave town as quickly as I can, and in the meantime I'm staying with the Bradleys.'

'Could you come back to the bank with me, do you think? There are some things we need to discuss.'

She fell into place beside him, wondering what he wanted but relieved to have an escort.

At the bank Mr Garrett ushered her into his office. This brought back memories of that first visit with Mrs Tibby and Emmy had to blink away more tears. Mr Garrett fussed with some papers to give her time to pull herself together.

'I'm sorry, sir. I was just – remembering the first time we came here.'

'Well, this time I have some good news for you. I asked Mr Baird, your employer's lawyer, if I could tell you myself.' His voice was gentle. 'Did you know that Mrs Oswald had left you everything she owned?'

Emmy gaped at him in shock, unable to form a single word.

'There will be the two guineas a month from her annuity and also her furniture and savings, as well as five small pieces of silverware. With that as a dowry, you could consider looking for a husband instead of a new place to work. You might be safer that way.'

She stared at him. 'Don't Mrs Tibby's things go back to the Armisteads?'

'No. They were hers to leave as she chose. She made the will before she went to live at Moor Lodge, and when she came back to live in Northby she told me she didn't want to change a thing. Her nephew is rather annoyed about it, but he can do nothing.'

John spent some time going through the exact details then sent for some tea.

Emmy nodded and replied, but was still struggling to take it all in. She now had what seemed to her a great deal of money. She didn't have to earn it. It would be there every month. She felt dizzy at the mere thought. Two guineas was not quite enough to live on if you had rent to pay, but enough to make a big difference to a young man's earnings, certainly, so that he could still look after his mother, his brothers and sisters and . . . The banker's voice interrupted her thoughts.

'Can you come and see me again tomorrow? There are papers to sign. Would ten o'clock be all right?'

'Yes.' But she would ask Mrs Bradley if Cass could walk across town with her.

'Shall you be staying on at Chad's Cottage, Emmy?'

'No, sir. I'm staying at Parson's house. It seems – safer.' Marcus Armistead had lived mainly in Manchester since his wife's disappearance, but every now and then he came over to Northby. Emmy looked out of the window, dismayed when she realised dusk was falling. 'Oh, dear! I had meant to go straight back to the Parsonage with them today.' She tried to smile at him and failed. 'I don't know why I feel so nervous, only it's getting dark and . . .'

He was astonished at the way her voice shook with fear. 'I'll walk back with you, if you like, though I think you're making too much of Marcus Armistead's – um – interest in you. He is a gentleman, after all, and will surely not try to force his attentions on you?'

'He paid someone to kidnap me once, but I got away. I had to hit him quite hard to do that, and I don't think he's ever forgiven me for it.'

John Garrett stared at her in shock. 'Kidnap you! But wasn't there something you could have done about it afterwards? Told Constable Makepeace at least?'

Emmy let out a mirthless laugh. 'I *did* tell him. But how could I have proved anything? Who would have believed the word of a maid against that of a gentleman, especially a maid with a mother like mine? They'd have said I was making it up.'

262

She tried to smile and failed. 'But the Bradleys believed me, thank goodness, and they're helping me. I'm going to look for a job as far away from Northby as I can get. Mrs Bradley will give me references. When I get a new place, can you help me make arrangements about the money?'

He nodded then went to put on his overcoat and place his top hat firmly on his head.

As they walked up the lane towards the Parsonage someone stopped to greet Mr Garrett near the mouth of Dyers Alley, so Emmy stepped back to let them chat.

She realised with a shock that a dark figure was standing behind her in the shadows at the mouth of the alley, but before she could cry out, the man covered her mouth with his hand and started dragging her backwards. If the attacker hadn't stumbled and let his hand slip for a moment, he'd have succeeded in getting her away before anyone realised what was happening. But just for a moment his hand did slip and she seized the opportunity to scream loudly then bite him for good measure as he tried to shut her up.

A voice called out from the street and footsteps pounded towards them. With a curse Emmy's attacker threw her at the leading figure and ran off down the alley.

Emmy and Mr Garrett fell to the ground and as they struggled to right themselves the gentleman who had been talking to the banker stood beside them, muttering, 'I can't believe it! Attacking you right in the middle of town. Whatever is the world coming to?' He stared after the retreating figure then turned to help them up, still shaking his head and glancing over his shoulder occasionally to make sure no one sneaked up on them.

'Are you all right, Emmy?' Mr Garrett asked as he brushed down his coat.

'Yes, sir.' But she wasn't. She was terrified. If she couldn't walk down the main street safely, it was even more imperative she leave than she had realised.

'Let's get you back to Mrs Bradley before we talk,' Mr Garrett said, setting a brisk pace.

As usual the Parsonage was a haven of warmth and safety.

Parson questioned Emmy about her attacker, but she had seen nothing beyond a shadowy figure. 'He was a big man,' she kept saying, 'very big, with a muffler over his face.'

'It can't have been Armistead, then.'

But she felt utterly certain it had been done for Marcus Armistead.

'We shall have to make sure you never leave the house on your own,' Mrs Bradley worried. 'It's even more important now that we find you a position away from here quickly and that no one knows where you have gone.'

'Actually, I may be able to help. I know a lady who is looking for a reliable maid,' Mr Garrett said. 'And Emmy hasn't told you her good news – Mrs Oswald left everything to her, a small income and all the contents of the cottage. I know my client was hoping Emmy might find herself a husband with it.'

As Mrs Bradley looked at her, Emmy could feel herself blushing. She was relieved when no one said any more about that. It could not be. Money would not wipe out the shame. Nothing would.

But when she went to bed that night she wept bitterly, trying to muffle her sobs in her pillow, not only for herself but for dear Mrs Tibby whom she still missed dreadfully.

She was not surprised when Mr Bradley told her the following afternoon that it could not have been Marcus Armistead who had attacked her since he had gone on from the funeral to dine with the Rishmores. As if he'd do the deed himself!

Well, he wasn't going to get his hands on her again.

The following morning was Sunday. After the service Jack came up to Emmy openly in the churchyard. 'How are you keeping? You look strained. I know you'll be missing Mrs Oswald, but is something else wrong?'

'It's been a difficult time.' Did he know about the attack or the money?

'We need to talk, don't we?' he asked, smiling down at her.

That smile always made her feel as if her bones had turned to wax and were melting inside her. Her heart began to thump and she could only stare at him. How fine and upright he was! How different from Marcus Armistead with his sneering face, plump body and cruel mouth! She glanced sideways to see Mrs Bradley nodding and smiling encouragement at her.

'Can we go and sit in the churchyard?' Jack asked. 'That will be quite respectable, I'm sure.'

His soft voice robbed the words of any offence and she could not help smiling at him. 'What about your Sunday classes?'

'Parson has found someone else to take them today. He had a word with me before the service – about you.'

'Oh.'

Jack offered her his arm and led her through the churchyard to the wall at the side where there was a bench. There they were in full view of anyone walking past, yet had the privacy to speak without being overheard. He brushed some dirt off the bench and waited until she was seated to take his place beside her.

'I've been thinking all through the service. Parson told me about the money you've inherited, you see, and hinted at what it could mean for us. He's right.' Jack gave her a wry smile. 'Though that makes me sound as if I only care about you because of the money, and it's not so. Say you believe that, Emmy. Say you understand how difficult it is for me, with my mother and the children to look after.' He took her hand.

She stared down at their joined hands as she said, 'I know it's not so, Jack.'

His sigh of relief was so loud she looked up and smiled.

He had meant to talk sensibly, lead up to his question gradually, but the words he had dreamed so often of saying came pouring out: 'You will marry me now, won't you, my little love?'

For a minute she nearly said yes. But she had gone over all this in bed the previous night. The money had changed the situation in only one way. Her own past and the shame of being the bastard-born daughter of a whore would not be wiped out by an annuity. And added to all that was the threat of Marcus Armistead.

No, to marry Jack would be to put him in danger. She loved him far too much to do that.

'I can't.' She had to swallow hard after she had said the words because Jack's face showed both disappointment and surprise.

'You must, Emmy!' His voice broke on the words. 'I can't bear it if you don't. I've been a good son for years, but surely I've a right to some happiness of my own now?'

'At the expense of your mother's,' she pointed out, her voice sounding thin and unlike her usual tones even in her own ears.

'My mother will grow used to it. Once she comes to know you, she'll realise how good and kind you are. Emmy, we can't let other people keep us apart – not when there's no need.'

She shook her head, trying to keep her voice level even though her throat had thickened with tears. 'You and your family would suffer if you married me.'

'We'll move away from Northby, then. Somewhere no one will know about your past.'

'If that were all, perhaps we could do it – if your mother agreed.' She felt a tear trickle down her cheek. 'Will she?'

He bent his head and a sigh escaped. 'I doubt it.'

'And then there's Marcus Armistead. Even if we were married, you couldn't guard me all day every day, Jack. I think the man's mad. He's been whispering threats to me from his carriage for a while now, or just sitting in it smiling at me. And he'll succeed one day if I stay in Northby. I've lived in the slums of Manchester, Jack, where life is cheap, and I know what people will do for money.' Jack had lived all his life in a small, quiet town. He'd never understand how little value a human life could have.

'If he touched you I'd kill him.'

'And then they'd hang you. Your father was shot dead for machine breaking. Your brother was transported. They'd say violence runs in your family and blame you, not him, because he's a *gentleman*.' She paused for a moment, waiting to let her words sink in, seeing the moment when Jack understood exactly what they'd be facing if they married.

He looked at her, misery in his eyes.

'Don't say anything. Just walk back with me to Parson's house and then go home to your family. Be glad you have them.' Because she had no one and never could have.

At the Parsonage gate he stopped and took both her hands in his. 'If you're ever in trouble, you'll come to me, won't you?'

She nodded, not daring to try to speak.

'And if I think of a way round this, I'll come to you.'

She shook her head. There was no hope for them.

'One kiss?' His voice was rough with longing.

Again she could only nod.

So he bent his head and took her in his arms, brushing her lips with his, then deepening the kiss until it felt as if they had touched one another's soul.

As they pulled apart the tears spilled out of her eyes and with an inarticulate murmur she ran inside.

He didn't even try to brush away his own tears as he walked home. Hadn't his whole life shown him that the rich could do as they pleased? That he could not have what he wanted most without hurting those he loved? But not even his father's death and his brother's transportation had been as painful as losing Emmy.

One evening George went up to check why Peggy had not come down with the other girls who were waiting for clients of The Golden Swan, his newest business venture with Marcus Armistead and a much bigger place than the first one. He found her room empty and, although she was normally the tidiest of girls, her possessions strewn all over the place as if someone had ransacked it.

Worried, he checked all the other attic bedrooms quickly but found nothing, then glanced at the stairs that led to the upper attic. No, Peggy couldn't be up there! Still, it wouldn't hurt to check. They'd had an intruder once.

He found Peggy's battered body lying on a blood-spattered bed in the 'quiet room' at the top of the house, the one they used for men with strange tastes. She was tied to the bed and the ropes had bitten deep into her wrists, as if she'd struggled desperately to escape. Why had no one heard her? When he looked into her mouth he found bits of lint and realised she must have been gagged.

It took him a few minutes to pull himself together because he'd had a fondness for poor Peggy who'd reminded him of Madge Carter. Then he started thinking. And worrying. Marcus Armistead had been the last one to see her. Surely he hadn't done this?

Not wanting to upset the other girls just as customers would be starting to turn up, George went downstairs and said he could find no sign of Peggy. 'I'll give her what for when I see her.'

His partner came in later and George took him into the office to say baldly, 'Peggy's dead, been murdered.'

'What? How can she be? I visited her myself earlier today.' Marcus smiled reminiscently. 'She's a most obliging young woman.'

'Was, not is,' George corrected.

'How did she die? Who killed her?'

'Some bastard tied her up then beat her to death – broke her neck, it looks like.'

'Did she not cry out? Surely someone must have heard something?'

'She was only a little woman. He had her tied up and gagged, poor little bitch. I can't believe such a thing could have happened inside my house.' Just when they were doing well, when he was so proud of running a clean and orderly business that served only gentlemen.

Marcus began tapping his fingers on the arm of his chair. 'Some villain must have sneaked in. We'd better get a guard for the back door as well as the front. What are we going to do about this?'

George stared at him in surprise. 'What do you mean? Report it to the authorities, of course. This is murder.'

Marcus raised one eyebrow. 'George, my friend, do we really want them involved? They might close us down.'

'Not with a gentleman like you involved.'

'But the last thing I want is to be publicly associated with The Golden Swan, you know that. It'll stop me bringing my friends here. And they spend freely.'

George stood scowling at the floor, seeing his fine new business destroyed. It didn't take much to get a place a bad reputation – and its owner with it. He made an exasperated noise in his throat. 'We'd better get rid of the body quietly, then.'

Marcus nodded. 'I think you're right. You'll have to do it, though. I don't know this area and,' he grimaced down at himself, 'I'm not exactly the strongest of men.' With hardly a pause he went on, 'Now, about Saturday, I'm bringing . . .'

It was only as George was wrapping up the body that it occurred to him that Madge had died in almost exactly the same way, beaten to death, and he stopped what he was doing to frown at poor Peggy's battered face. Surely it couldn't have been the same person who killed them? No, of course it couldn't. What was he thinking of? Madge had died on the moors near Northby. That was miles away from here.

Then the thought came unbidden: Marcus visited Northby sometimes and he had been here earlier today. George shook his head. No, Marcus was an undersized fellow. Any woman could fight him off for long enough to scream. It had to have been someone bigger, someone who'd taken Peggy by surprise. Besides, why would Marcus damage his own business? No, it didn't make any sense at all.

George disposed of the body by leaving it on some waste ground in the small hours of the morning. He couldn't hide the fact from the other women that Peggy had vanished suddenly, or that he had gone into the girl's sleeping quarters in the lower attics and packed up her things himself. 'Found herself a protector, the lucky bitch,' he told them.

But although they did not question this openly, they did a lot of muttering to one another and stopped talking when he went near them for the next few days.

The youngest of his girls, another rather small woman, ran away a few days later.

None of the others would say why.

Still sure the girls knew something, he took one of them aside and offered her ten guineas to tell him.

'Ten guineas and a coach ticket to London,' she insisted. 'And not a word of this to Mr Armistead. What's more, you're to put me safely on the coach yourself.'

He hated to lose her. But he also hated not knowing what had happened and worrying that it might happen again. He *needed* to know. 'All right.'

He didn't believe what she told him at first. But the more he thought about it, the more the pieces fell together.

When he was putting her on the coach, she turned and kissed his cheek. 'You're all right, George, but that other fellow is poison. Get rid of him. He'll bring you down.'

But he couldn't get rid of Marcus Armistead who had sunk a great deal of money into this enterprise. And if he challenged him, who knew what Marcus might do? The rich could get away with all sorts of things.

Did nothing in the world ever go sodding right?

He'd have to bide his time and see what else he could find out, but he wasn't going to put up with any more murders, by hell he wasn't! George didn't like anyone upsetting his girls – anyone at all.

And if it really was Marcus doing it, well, rich men could go missing as well as poor little whores. But before he did anything he had to find some proof.

Chapter Sixteen

Jack went home burning with resentment and despair. Of course his mother saw something was wrong and sent the others to bed early.

'What's wrong, son?' she asked, laying one hand on his shoulder.

Only as she spoke did he look up and realise they were alone. 'Is it bed time already?'

As he started to get up, Netta pushed him down again and sat beside him on the wooden settle his father had made for them. She kept hold of his hand, clasping it tightly in hers and looking earnestly into his eyes, not saying anything.

From the front room he could hear Meg murmuring to her little daughter. From upstairs the creaking of beds showed that the children were not yet asleep. He sighed as he studied his mother's face. She was looking older recently and her hair was fully grey now with none of the rich brown colour left. Why had he not noticed that change? He could remember her hair shining in the sunshine once and his mother smiling at the world with her hand linked in his father's arm. Not only his younger brothers and sisters, but memories like that, together with the pity he now felt for her, were what tied him to her, even though Meg said he was a fool to give up his own life.

The old resentment against his father surged up again and with it a strong desire to be left alone. 'Go to bed, Mam. Leave me be.'

She shook her head. 'No. Something's upsetting you. I've never seen you so low before, son. Is it –' she hesitated '– a woman?'

He nodded, then said in a tight voice, 'It's all right, you don't have to worry. She won't have me.'

Netta's mouth fell open in shock. 'You've asked a lass to wed you without telling me? Who is she? Do we know her?' When he didn't answer, she asked in a sharper tone, 'What did you think would happen to the rest of us if you got married?'

'I'd worked it all out and –'

'Well, I'm not having it!'

Anger surged up in him. 'It's not just your decision, though, is it? And it's more than time you thought about *me* and what *I* need. I'm not without a man's natural feelings, you know. I'd like a wife and family of my own. I've wanted it for years and well you know it.'

She pressed one hand against her mouth, moaning behind it. 'It's *her*, isn't it? Still her. The whore's bastard!'

'Don't *ever* talk about Emmy that way!' Jack jerked his hand away and went to stand with one foot on the brass fender. As he stared down into the dying embers of the fire, he said more gently, 'Emmy's not at all like her mother. Do you think Parson would have her living in his house if she wasn't a decent lass? You've never even given her a chance.'

Netta's tone became piercingly shrill. 'Parson can have who he wants in his house, but that one's never coming into mine! Never! If you bring her across the doorstep, I'm leaving.'

Meg's voice interrupted them from the doorway that led to the tiny hall. 'She'd never leave. She's bluffing you, Jack, been doing it for years. If you want to get wed, you do it. I'll welcome your wife with open arms. An' we'll manage, too. It's not just you bringing in the money now. There are my wages coming in as well, and Shad's, an' Ginny's looking for work.'

Netta spat the words across the room. '*Your* wages, Meg Pearson! You're a fine one to talk! It's not just wages but another mouth to feed, a child to care for, that you've brought us. You can only work because I look after your Nelly. You're one of the burdens our Jack carries – an' so do I.'

Meg gave her a bitter look. 'I more than earn my keep and Nelly's, and well you know it. You take most of my wages every week. Don't think I don't know about the money you've got saved under the floorboard now. I've seen you putting coins in there. We all know about your little hiding place, actually, Jack as well.'

Netta folded her arms across her chest. 'Well, someone has to think of the bad times. What if you came home with another babby in your belly? What'd happen to your wages then?'

'The only baby I've ever had was born to my husband, an' he's the only man I've ever had as well. If Ben hadn't died I'd not have come home at all. Do you think your nagging makes for a happy home? And when will you admit we're not lacking food in our mouths or clothes on our backs?'

'It doesn't matter what we've got now. Good times don't last, and I deserve a bit of comfort after the hard life I've had.'

Meg made a scornful noise in her throat. 'You don't deserve anything, Mam, an' what's more, you've no *right* to prevent our Jack from marrying the lass he loves.' She turned to him and asked more gently, 'It's Emmy Carter, isn't it? I've seen you looking at her in church. She has a sweet face an' I don't blame you for wanting to live with someone who knows how to smile. You call Mam's bluff, our Jack. Bring your lass home and tell *her* she can like it or lump it.'

'Don't let her talk to me like that!' Netta wailed, clutching his arm.

But for once he was unsympathetic. Meg was right. They would manage somehow if he married. Especially with Mrs Oswald's money behind them. He had to persuade Emmy to marry him, not for the money but because he didn't think he could live without her. 'Go to bed now, Mam. It's getting late.' Then he went back to staring into the fire.

Sobbing, Netta stumbled up the stairs.

He thought he was alone until he heard the soft sound of Meg's felt slippers on the stone-flagged floor. She came to stand beside him and laid one hand on his shoulder, a light butterfly touch. The hand was removed almost immediately. Funny, he thought, Meg doesn't like to touch anyone now except for her child.

'It *is* Emmy Carter you care for, isn't it?' she repeated.

He nodded.

'And does she care for you?'

He smiled. 'Oh, yes. I'm sure she does.'

'Then don't let Mam ruin your life, Jack!'

'How could I bring Emmy home to that?' He jerked his head towards the back bedroom where his mother slept with Ginny. 'She'd make our life a misery.'

'She makes everyone's life a misery anyway because she has to have someone to cling to. First Dad, then you. An' yet she can't even be kind to them when she's got them.' Meg sighed and stared bleakly into the dying fire. 'I'd get out if I could see any way to do it, Jack.'

'Where would you go?'

'I don't know. I'm a good worker, but there's Nelly. I have to be able to look after her.' She smiled wryly. 'Any road, I won't leave you on your own with Mam – well, not unless she drives me mad with her moaning and nagging. Eh, I'll be no good for work in the morning if I don't get some sleep.' She yawned and padded off towards the front room where she and her child slept.

Jack stood there, losing himself in his thoughts again until the embers sighed and settled still lower, making him realise how late it was. He went up to the bedroom he shared with Shad and Joe. They were asleep, huddled together in the middle of their bed. He got into his own, but it felt cold and lonely.

It was a long time before he got to sleep and Emmy's face filled his dreams.

The following day when everyone was at work, Netta Staley left her granddaughter with a neighbour and went to the Parsonage, knocking on the back door and asking to see Emmy.

Cass called out, 'It's Jack's mother to see you, love. Go and sit in the garden with her for a few minutes. It's a mild day and you've been looking downright peaky since that attack.'

So Emmy went outside, hoping desperately that his mother had come to tell her it was all right for her and Jack to marry. But the expression on Mrs Staley's face burst that small bubble of hope almost immediately. 'You'd no need to come. I've already refused him,' she said wearily.

'I'm here to make sure of that.' Netta glared at her, arms akimbo. 'How he can even think of wedding such as you, I don't know. You look like your mother. I used to see her playing in the street when she was a little lass. All the lads used to look at her even then, she was that pretty. But she was rotten inside! An' so are you. It's born into women like you an' I'm not having a decent lad like my Jack caught in your snares. I'll kill you myself first. They might hang me, but at least he'd be safe then.'

So virulent was the hatred on her face, so vicious her tone, that Emmy took an involuntary step backwards.

'Think on!' Netta said, moving forward to thrust her face close to Emmy's. 'My Jack's not for such as you. An' that's all I have to say.' She turned on her heel and strode out of the garden.

Emmy stood there for a moment or two, shaken by the encounter, then returned to the house, feeling quite wretched. 'I'll go and dust Parson's study,' she said, her voice breaking on the last word. She fled from the kitchen.

'What's that dratted woman been saying to her?' Cook wondered aloud. But she was making a cake and did not dare let her attention wander.

A few minutes later Gerald Bradley went into his study for a book and found Emmy there, clutching a feather duster and sobbing quietly but despairingly. 'What's wrong?'

But she couldn't answer him, she was weeping so hard.

He guided her towards a chair and she went with him like a limp rag doll, almost collapsing on it. 'Tell me what's wrong, child? Has that man come after you again? Surely he wouldn't dare do anything while you're in my house?'

She shook her head blindly.

'Tell me,' he insisted.

The words came slowly at first, interrupted by sobs, then the story gathered momentum and she unburdened herself to him.

After she'd finished he sat with his head bowed, then sighed and looked across at her. 'I think you've made the right decision, Emmy,' he said at last. 'It hurts now, I know, but you're young still and one day, when you're living somewhere else – a place where people don't know about your mother – you'll find a man who doesn't have Jack's problems.'

She stared at him, misery clamping itself around her like a leaden shell. 'I've loved Jack Staley for years, since soon after we came to Northby. I know I couldn't love anyone else.'

He didn't smile, though he knew from experience that life had a way of changing black to grey. 'Well, we won't argue about that. Why don't you go up to your room and lie down for a bit, my dear? You look exhausted. I'll send Cass with a cup of tea, and my wife will no doubt come up to see you when she returns.'

For once Emmy nodded and did as he suggested. Today she could find no solace in hard work because Netta Staley's words kept echoing in her mind: *I'll kill you myself first.*

When Prudence came in from her shopping, Gerald told her what had happened and she shook her head in dismay. 'That girl is still grieving for Tibby Oswald, still recovering from the attack, and she shouldn't have to put up with anything else. If Mrs Staley comes round here again, I'll give her a piece of my mind.'

Jack called at the Parsonage on his way home from work, unaware of his mother's disastrous visit. He felt desperate to see Emmy again and make her realise they'd find a way to work out their problems.

She refused point-blank to see him. She wanted to – oh, how desperately she wanted to talk to him, just one more time! But she was too afraid of weakening.

★   ★   ★

The following day John Garrett came round to say that the lady he had mentioned, a widow in comfortable circumstances, was still looking for a maid and would be happy to give Emmy a trial.

He and the Parson put their heads together and worked out a way to get the girl out of town without anyone knowing that she was leaving or where she had gone.

When they said Emmy must tell no one what they were doing, she shrugged. 'Who is there to tell?'

'Don't you at least want to write a farewell letter to Jack?' Prudence asked quietly as she was helping Emmy pack her things.

'There's nothing more to say. But if you see him, you could – tell him I'll always think of him fondly.'

Prudence patted her shoulder. 'All right, dear. I'll do that. And if you're ever in trouble, if this job doesn't work out, you're to come straight back to us. You'll be safe in this house, at least.'

But Emmy was determined never to return to Northby

Mr Garrett was to take her across to see Mrs Dalby in his own carriage and, as planned, she crept out of the Parsonage to join him before it was light, after giving Hercules one last cuddle.

Once inside the comfortable vehicle she sat back and closed her eyes, relieved when he didn't try to start up a conversation. No one saw them go and the coachman, who had been with his master for many years, was sworn to silence.

They drove to Blackburn and left both carriage and driver there, pretending they were going somewhere in the town so the coachman wouldn't even be able to let slip her destination accidentally. Mr Garrett hired a vehicle from a nearby livery stable to take them on the last part of their journey while Emmy waited outside.

'You've thought of everything,' she said gratefully. 'I don't know how I can ever repay you.'

'You don't need to repay me. I'm happy to help you – and I think Mrs Dalby will be more than happy with your services. She's a kindly soul, if a bit fussy.' A little later he asked, 'What shall I do about your money?'

Emmy stared at him, so tired from lack of sleep that she couldn't for a moment think what he was talking about. 'Oh, Mrs Tibby's money. Could you keep it for me, please? I shan't need it while I'm with Mrs Dalby.'

'Very well. If you do need it, you have only to find another bank where it can be paid and ask them to contact me. I'm acquainted with most of the bank owners in this part of Lancashire and can arrange to have the money paid to you quarterly anywhere in the county.' When she didn't reply only nodded as if she was not really interested, he left her to her thoughts.

The village of Carbury, where Mrs Dalby lived, lay between Blackburn and Preston. It rained heavily all the way there so that the carriage trundled along slowly and mud splashed up against the windows.

Emmy's thoughts brought her close to tears several times, but she didn't want to meet a new mistress with a face swollen by weeping, and anyway, what good would it do? She had to make a new life for herself now and all the tears in the world wouldn't bring Jack back to her.

Cynthia Dalby sat waiting in her comfortable parlour, hoping this girl would prove more satisfactory than her last two maids. John Garrett and a parson's wife had both vouched for her, and Mrs Bradley has written of the great devotion Carter had shown towards her previous mistress. Cynthia sighed, bored by her own company. No one had come calling on such a rainy day and her son rarely drove across from Manchester to see her. If he'd marry and settle down, she might move to live near him and his family. She'd like to have grandchildren, but Edward laughed whenever she raised this matter, saying there was plenty of time for marriage. She suspected he had a rather hedonistic nature, unlike her late husband. Though at least Edward worked hard in the bank in which he and his uncle were now partners.

When she heard the sound of carriage wheels and hooves smacking down wetly on the muddy ground then stopping outside her house, she got up and went across to the window, watching through the lace curtains as John Garrett got out and turned to help the girl down. She looked to have a pretty face, which was not always a good thing in a maid, but there was no time for more than a brief glimpse because the two of them hurried towards the shelter of the front porch.

On days like this Cynthia wished she had not chosen to come and live in her old home in the village where she had grown up after her husband died. She should have stayed in Manchester where there was so much more to see and do and rented a house there. But she still had friends in the neighbourhood and could be sure of their support. She went and seated herself by the fire, waiting for her maid to show the visitors in.

'Mr Garrett,' Babs announced, not leaving the room until she had studied the young woman accompanying him.

Cynthia didn't reprimand her because she was always a little nervous of Babs who was an excellent worker but of an independent turn of mind. She noted that the new girl knew her place well enough to stand with hands clasped and eyes lowered just inside the door while Mr Garrett came across to greet his hostess.

'My dear John, it's been a long time since we've seen you,' Cynthia said. 'Too long. You and your wife must come and stay with me soon and I shan't take no for an answer.'

'As soon as our latest grandchild is born, Cynthia, my dear.' He kept hold of her hands and now held her at arm's length to study her face. 'You're looking well.'

'I am well, though I still miss Henry.' She looked over his shoulder. 'Well, aren't you going to introduce your companion?'

'Of course, of course! This is Emmy Carter.' He beckoned and she came a little closer.

'Are you a good worker, Carter?' Cynthia asked.

'I believe so, ma'am. Though I shall have to learn your ways, shan't I?'

Cynthia decided this was not impertinence, simply a direct way of speaking. A bit like Babs. She sighed sometimes for the meek maids of her youth. 'What duties did you perform for your last mistress?' She did not miss the sadness this question brought to Carter's face and watched with interest as the girl answered. She had a horrible accent, not at all refined, but kind eyes which looked at you directly. And the way she spoke of her late mistress pleased Cynthia, too.

'Very well, my dear. We'll give you a try.' She rang a bell. 'Babs, please take Emmy to the kitchen and give her some refreshments. And you may bring in the tea tray now.'

When they got to the kitchen the other maid and an older woman who must be the cook both stared openly at Emmy.

'Well, you're a pretty one, and no mistake. She don't usually hire pretty ones,' said the cook.

'What's your first name? Mine's Babs and Cook's Mrs Porter, but she prefers to be called Cook.' As she was speaking Babs was pouring boiling water from the kettle standing on the big modern range into two teapots, one china and one earthenware. She cast an expert eye over the tray of cups and small cakes. 'I'll just nip this through to the missus, then we'll have a sup ourselves. Sit down and warm yourself, love.'

Emmy sat down on one of the wooden chairs and stared around her. The house was smaller than the Parsonage but just as luxuriously appointed. It had a Leamington kitchener, a wonderfully modern appliance Emmy had seen advertised in the newspapers. How conveniently it was arranged! A saucepan was simmering to one edge of the hob and the kettle was standing on a trivet on the table waiting to be refilled.

Cook gave her a half-smile but said nothing, continuing to knead a big lump of dough with muscular hands and rhythmic movements that Emmy found soothing.

Babs came bustling back in. 'There, that's the mistress settled for a while. Eh, take your outdoor things off, love. Mucky old day, isn't it? We hang our cloaks over there. Now, let's have our tea before it gets stewed.' While she was talking she poured out three cups, setting one down beside Cook. 'All right if we have some of your scones?'

The woman nodded. 'Take yesterday's, though.'

Babs got out a big butter dish and a smaller dish of jam. 'Help yourself, Emmy. We all eat well here. Cook's a dab hand at baking. I never saw a better.'

'And you'll never meet a lass as knows how to get her own way better than Babs here,' Cook laughed.

When she'd drunk a cup of tea and eaten a scone, Babs looked at Emmy. 'Well, tell us about yourself, then. Who have you been working for and why are you changing places?'

'My mistress died.' Emmy blinked hard because tears still welled in her eyes every time she had to say that.

Babs' voice softened. 'Fond of her, were you?'

Emmy nodded, taking a sip of tea to give herself time to control this stupid tendency to weep.

'Well, it's not every mistress as makes you feel like that. I've had some terrible ones, I can tell you. Mrs Dalby's all right. A bit fussy and under the thumb of that son of hers – though luckily he don't come to visit us very often so he don't interfere all that much – but she has a kind heart and feeds us generously. I can't abide a mean mistress. I left my last place because of the poor food. I'm not a pauper and I don't eat fish head soup for anyone, and so I told her.'

Emmy gaped at her. 'You told her!'

Babs tossed her head. 'Of course I did. Where would they be without us? I'm a good worker if you treat me right, and if you don't treat me right, I'm off.'

Emmy had never met anyone of her own class who seemed so confident and began to look forward to working with this young woman. Babs was older than she was, probably about thirty, not pretty, but lively, with an infectious smile and bouncy black curls. She was plump, but it suited her. You simply couldn't imagine her thin. 'What will my duties be?'

'You an' me will share the cleaning, I suppose, but she likes us to fuss over her as well. She likes someone to go shopping with her and read the newspaper to her – her eyes are getting worse, but she won't wear spectacles. Too vain. I'm no good at reading aloud. Well, it gives me the pip, squinting at an old newspaper does. We have a scrubbing woman, so there's no heavy work. Well, I wouldn't be here if I had to do the scrubbing myself. I did it when I was first starting out as a maid, but I'm past that sort of thing now.'

Emmy found that if she kept nodding and murmuring agreement, Babs would do most of the talking. The warmth and cheeriness of the kitchen were very comforting and she began to hope that if she gave satisfaction, she could settle into a quiet life here for a while.

Babs took her upstairs for a lightning visit to her new bedroom, a small place in the attic but decently furnished. Emmy unpacked her aprons and indoor shoes then went down to start work, happy that her mind would be taken up with learning her new duties.

It wasn't until she was getting ready for bed that misery swept over her again. She had lost not only Mrs Tibby but Jack. She had resolved to shed no more tears, but could not prevent a few from sliding down her cheeks.

She lay wakeful, listening to the rain still falling outside, and its soft pattering sound lulled her to sleep eventually.

But she dreamed of Jack.

Back in Northby he was also wakeful. He had found out that Emmy had left the town, but no one would tell him where she had gone or how she had managed to leave without anyone seeing her go.

Isaac commented on her departure in the office the following day. 'I hope my niece has found a good place. Mrs Bradley told me they'd decided it would be safer to tell no one where she'd gone. That poor girl's had too much to bear.' He sighed. 'I'd have liked to say goodbye before she left, though. I've grown quite fond of her.'

Jack got on with his work, but he was upset that he had lost his chance to persuade Emmy to marry him. Mr Bradley had been adamant that her leaving was the best thing for them all. Jack wasn't so sure.

Luckily Mr Butterfield had some new jobs for him which entailed his going into Manchester to deliver messages. Jack tried not to let his distaste show when he found that some of the messages were to Marcus Armistead's rooms, but to his relief he was too lowly to be shown in to see that gentleman and only had to wait in the outer office for replies then carry them back to Northby. Which suited him just fine. It surprised him they didn't use the post for this, but like his father, Mr Rishmore didn't trust the postal services since they had once lost some important letters, Mr Butterfield said. And anyway, with a messenger, they could be sure of getting an immediate reply.

Travelling into Manchester was tiring and the coach rumbled along so slowly the return journey seemed to take for ever. By the time he got home Jack wanted only to eat and seek his bed.

But as the days passed he could not help being aware of the increasingly acrimonious bickering between his mother and Meg. Sometimes he would sit with his eyes closed in front of the fire, trying to let their sharp words pass over his head. Other times he would go out for a glass of ale. Once or twice he was driven to shouting at them both to be quiet.

On the first Sunday after Emmy had gone, Jack came out of the church hall after taking his reading class and noticed her dog lying in the back garden of the Parsonage, looking dispirited and thin, with a dull coat. As he was staring across at the poor creature, Mr Bradley came out of the church hall and joined him.

'He's fretting for her. Nothing we've said or done seems to have cheered him up.'

'Perhaps I could take him for a walk?' Jack offered. He certainly didn't feel like going home yet and he felt a certain sympathy with the animal.

He took Hercules up the back lanes to the edge of the moors, it being a fine day, and sat there, stroking the animal's head and running its silky ears through his fingers. For some reason this made him feel closer to Emmy and after a while the dog sighed and pressed itself against him, as if it too needed the comfort.

After that he took Hercules back to the Parsonage and persuaded him to eat.

'Look at that!' Cass marvelled. 'He's really taken to you, that dog has. Poor thing still sleeps by her bed.'

Jack broached the idea to his mother of bringing Hercules home to live with them, but she refused point-blank and slapped Joey when he added his pleas. After that Jack went to see the dog several times a week at the Parsonage, spending even less time at home and ignoring his mother's complaints about that.

'You can't have it every way!' he snapped one evening, goaded beyond endurance. 'You deny me the girl I love, you won't even let me have a dog. This place feels less like a home every day.' As he went out, he slammed the door hard behind him.

Meg smiled. 'You've gone too far, Mam. You're losing him.'

Netta raised her hand.

'If you hit me, I'll hit you back twice as hard. And if I catch you hitting my Nelly again, I'll take a stick to you.'

For the next few weeks Jack kept an eye open for Emmy whenever he went into Manchester. He didn't know where she'd gone, but remembered her talking about the ladies at the Mission, so it seemed as if the city was the most likely place. Once he saw a young woman who looked a bit like her from the back and rushed across the road, nearly getting trampled by a cart horse in the process and causing the driver to brandish his whip and swear at him.

When it wasn't Emmy, Jack had to stand still for a moment and pull himself together before he could move on.

What if he never saw his darling girl again? How would he bear it?

The following Sunday after church he stopped Mrs Bradley and asked if she'd heard from Emmy, hoping she'd tell him more than her husband who kept saying it was God's will and all for the best.

'No, I'm afraid not, Jack. She didn't dare keep in touch, thought it better to make a completely new life for herself.' But the young man looked so anguished that Prudence could not help adding, 'She asked me to tell you she'd always think of you fondly.' She laid her hand on his arm. 'Emmy thought it was safer for those she loved if she went away, as well as for herself. Never doubt that she cared for you.'

He was miserable enough to let his feelings show. 'If she really cared about me, she'd have stayed and we'd have faced things together.'

'It wasn't only the danger, Jack. Your mother came to see her. Cass could see them talking from the kitchen and she said your mother was – well, shouting. And Emmy was very upset when she came back into the house.'

'I didn't know. My mother never said a word about it.' How could she have done that?

He made his way home, completely forgetting about his Sunday School class because he had to know what his mother had said to drive Emmy away. He stopped dead in the street as the idea came to him and with it a sense of determination and purpose – he was going to look for Emmy and persuade her to marry him. However long it took.

The decision lifted his spirits slightly and the anger carried him rapidly down Weavers Lane towards his home.

When Jack burst into the house in a towering rage, the rest of the family stopped what they were doing to gape, this was so unlike him.

'What's wrong, love?' Meg asked.

'Where's Mam?'

'She hasn't got home from church yet. You know she sometimes stands around talking to one of her friends on the way back. Didn't you pass her? And what about your classes?' As he would have swung round to leave the house again, she caught hold of his arm. 'Wait! Don't go out like that. What's the matter?'

'Let go of me!' But he didn't shake her off, just looked at her, anger warring with misery on his face.

'You kids stay here in the kitchen,' she called out. 'Keep an eye on our Nelly.' Taking Jack's arm, Meg drew him into the front room, which she had made her own. 'Tell me, love.'

He let out a deep, shuddering sigh. 'Mam went to see Emmy just before she left. In one of her rages, Mrs Bradley said. And really upset her.'

'Mam's getting worse. You should have heard her going on at me this morning because I wouldn't let her take Nelly to church.' Meg hesitated. 'She's been hitting Nelly again, too. I don't think I can stand much more of that, Jack. I don't want my child to grow up in an unhappy house. If Mam's not angry, she's fretting and worrying. Either way we get no peace or happiness. I reckon she was born to be miserable.'

He put his arms round her. 'Oh, Meg, don't go. I can't bear to lose you too. You said you'd stay.'

'That was before I found out what else Mam had done.' She hesitated, then told him, 'I've been seeing this fellow, just talking to him a bit, going for walks, getting to know one another better, like. He seemed nice. Then suddenly he began avoiding me. He works near me an' I often used to see him on the way home. So I waited for him after work on Friday to ask what was wrong.' She bent her head, fighting tears. 'He told me Mam had been to see him, to warn him off, to tell him the family would never accept an Irish Catholic as a husband for me.'

'Aw, Meg!' Jack put his arms round her and held her close.

'I'm sorry.' She wept against him. 'I'm supposed to be comforting you, not piling my troubles on your shoulders as well.'

'We can comfort one another.'

He heard the sound of the front door and turned quickly, putting her gently aside. 'That's Mam!'

He went into the back room and found Netta untying the ribbons of her bonnet, a smile on her face for once. 'Eh, Jack. I didn't think you'd be home yet. What happened to your class? I've just been talking to Mrs . . .' Her voice trailed away as she saw his grim expression. 'What is it? What's wrong?'

'You'd better come into the front room,' he said. 'Me and Meg both need to talk to you.'

She tried to edge away. 'I'm dying for a cup of tea. Can't it wait?'

'No, it can't.' Jack guided her into the front room, not letting her pull away, then closed the door and stood with his back against it. 'What did you say to Emmy just before she left?'

'Me? Why should I say anything to that one?'

She was avoiding his eyes and he could tell she was lying. 'Mrs Bradley told me you'd been to see her. Their cook saw you shouting at Emmy. *What did you say to her?*'

Netta pressed her lips together for a moment, then shrugged. 'I told her I'd kill her if she tried to wed you. And I meant it, too.'

Breath whistled into his throat and shock prevented him from speaking.

'Mam!' Meg gaped at her. 'Mam, I can't believe you'd do a thing like that. How could you?'

Netta folded her arms and scowled at them both. 'I could do anything to save my son from ruining his life.'

Jack let out a harsh laugh. 'Have you forgotten, Mam, that I'm a felon's brother? That my father broke the law and was shot dead in the street? How am I any better than Emmy?'

But Netta Staley was not to be swayed by any arguments. 'That lass is rotten inside, just like her mother,' she shouted. 'And so I told her. I'm *glad* I did if it's driven her away!'

'You're a wicked old devil!' Meg burst out. 'You've been interfering in my life, too, haven't you? What did you say to Liam Kelly?'

'I said what I had to. You're not getting mixed up with an Irish Catholic. You married unwisely once and look where it led you, but you're not doing it again. You're still only twenty. What do you know about life? You'd be better not marrying again. We're doing all right as we are.'

Meg didn't even try to hold back the tears. 'Liam's a good man, but he won't even speak to me now! If you ever interfere again in my affairs, I'm leaving, I swear it.'

'And where would you go?' Netta jeered. 'You've got a daughter to think of now. You can't just walk off when you have a child.'

'I am thinking of her. That's another thing – you've been hitting her again. Did you think I wouldn't notice the bruises?'

'She keeps falling.'

'No. *You* keep hitting her.'

Netta burst into tears and tried to push her way out of the room, but Jack refused to step aside. 'Son, don't let her talk to me like this,' she begged. 'I did what was right for us all. Me and the childer.'

'You allus say that.'

'Well, it's true. You can't *afford* to get wed.'

He laughed at the irony of that, though it went on for too long until he felt a hand on his arm and saw Meg staring at him in concern. He turned to his mother. 'That's just it. You didn't let me finish telling you: Emmy Carter's got money of her own.'

Netta stared at him, one hand at her throat. 'What do you mean by that?'

'Mrs Oswald left everything to her – two guineas a month Emmy gets. Every month. She doesn't have to lift a finger to earn it. As long as she lives it'll be there, then she can leave it to her children. And there's other money saved in the bank as well.' He looked at her pityingly. 'We could *easily* have afforded to get wed, me and Emmy.'

'I don't believe it! She's lying to you.'

'Go and ask Mr Garrett at the bank, then. Or Mr Bradley. It's all true.'

There was silence in the room, the only sounds the ticking of the clock and the murmurs of the children next door.

In the end Netta sniffed and repeated. 'The money doesn't change anything as far as I'm concerned. She's a whore's daughter and no one will ever let her forget it.'

Jack closed his eyes for a moment because her expression was so triumphant. She didn't care that she'd hurt him, didn't care about anything but herself. 'Well, I'm going to warn you now, Mam, and for the last time: you'd better not interfere in my life *ever again* or I'll up and leave you.' He looked across at his sister, at the tear marks on her cheeks, and added heavily and emphatically, 'And don't interfere in our Meg's life, either. She's young enough to marry again, and good luck to her. It doesn't matter whether the man is a Catholic or a Maharajah from India – it's her choice, not yours.'

Netta said nothing, staring from one to the other, scowling, biting on her knuckles.

Jack's expression did not soften as he turned towards the door. 'What's more, I'm going to look for Emmy and when I find her, I'm going to marry her. And neither you nor Marcus Armistead nor the King himself is going to stop me!'

Chapter Seventeen

But before Jack could start looking for Emmy, his little niece fell ill. Meg didn't dare take time off work to care for her daughter because Roper would have found someone else, but she grew increasingly worried at the careless way her mother was looking after the child and the two of them had several rows about it.

When Jack came into Roper's pawnshop on the afternoon of the fourth day of her daughter's illness, Meg clasped one hand to her breast, unable to speak for the terror that clutched at her heart.

After one loving glance towards her, Jack said to the pawn-broker, 'My sister's needed at home. Urgent.'

Roper looked at him, glanced sideways at Meg, then nodded reluctantly.

She walked outside then took her brother's arm to stop him. 'What's wrong?' He didn't at first answer and she said, 'Jack?' But she didn't need him to tell her. His expression said it all.

'I'm sorry, love, but Nelly died this afternoon. Mam sent our Joey to fetch me, but it was too late to do anything by the time I got home. I'd have sent for the doctor but . . .' He let the words trail away and put one arm round his sister's shoulders to hug her close.

'Why didn't she send for me?' Meg asked, her voice muffled by his chest.

'I don't know.' He shook his head helplessly.

His sister pulled away and wrapped her arms round herself,

staring blindly into the distance. 'Then I'm leaving Northby as soon as we've buried her. I should have done something sooner. Mam's been neglecting Nelly and I'll never forgive myself.'

'The child was never very strong, love. No one could have loved her any more than you did, but I don't think she could have lived to grow up, I really don't. She was very frail.'

'I know. I always knew.' The words were whispered, but anguish rang through them. 'If Mam had taken more care, though, I might have had more time with Nelly. And I might have fewer regrets now.' Meg couldn't go on for a minute, then beat one clenched hand against her breast. 'Well, Mam's lost a daughter as well. Not that she'll care about that.' She could feel tears welling in her eyes, but there was a stony weight on her chest and tears couldn't melt that, so she dashed them away impatiently. What good did it ever do to weep?

Jack tried to hug her again, but she stood passively in his embrace. For a moment they were motionless, then she reached up to touch his cheek fleetingly with the back of her hand. 'You're a good brother, Jack.' She began walking again. 'I won't stay in the same house as Mam after we've buried Nelly – and if *she* doesn't dip into her savings to pay for the funeral, I'll break open that damned money box of hers myself.'

A little later she suddenly stopped walking again and burst out, 'To think my little love's last days were made miserable by scoldings and slappings – just as our childhood was – that hurts me, Jack.'

He looked at her in puzzlement. 'Mam didn't hit us that much.'

'Not you lads, but she certainly laid into us girls. Especially when she was vexed at Dad.'

'I didn't know. Why didn't you say?'

'What could anyone have done? Even Dad couldn't control her.'

As they drew near home, Meg stopped again and said in a tight, hard voice, 'Will you go and see Parson Bradley for me, Jack? Ask him to hold a proper service for Nelly, just a short one, I'll pay. I want proper prayers to send my baby on her way. And she's *not* having a pauper's grave! I want a proper coffin, too.'

Tears were running down her cheeks but she didn't seem to notice them. Jack brushed them away with one fingertip and she stood there like a hurt child and let him do what he would.

'Yes, love,' he said soothingly. 'I'll see Parson for you. But first I'll take you home, eh?' He began to guide her along, his arm round her shoulders.

When they got back Meg went straight into the kitchen, stopped to gaze down at her dead child, who was lying on the settle, then picked her up and carried her into the front room.

'What's she doing?' Netta whispered to Jack.

'Saying goodbye to her daughter.'

'I lost two mysen,' his mother said sourly. 'You can't risk getting attached to 'em, not till you're sure they're going to live.'

He had forgotten the way she'd never seemed to care about the little ones. Now he realised why. She got on with cooking the tea, though he doubted he'd be able to eat anything. She wasn't crying, didn't even look sad, just busy.

'I've to go and see Parson,' he said abruptly and went out again. He was finding it more and more difficult to bear his mother's ways. Why had he not realised how much she'd always favoured the lads? First Tom had been her favourite, now it was him. Her clinging love was a heavy burden – too heavy.

After he'd seen Parson, he called in at the mill to let Mr Butterfield know what had happened and ask if he could have some time off work. He wanted to be there to comfort Meg. Mr Butterfield tutted sympathetically and said of course he could.

On his way home Jack went to scrounge some pieces of wood and borrow some tools from his neighbours to make a coffin and began to work in the back yard of their house. It was a rough affair, because he wasn't very good at woodworking, but he wanted to do it himself.

Meg nodded when he brought it in. 'Thanks.' She put her soft shawl inside it to lay the little girl on.

'Shouldn't you keep that for yourself?' Jack asked gently.

She shook her head. 'I want something of mine to be with her. I want her to lie comfortably.'

He was worried that she kept talking as if the child were still alive, so when she showed no signs of going to bed after tea, he sat with her in the front room. Their mother banged around in the other room, scolding the children, then one by one they went to bed.

Meg didn't speak much, but spent a lot of time staring at the pale face in the coffin, sometimes closing her eyes and sighing. Jack had feared for her reason earlier, but the gaze she turned on him occasionally was not that of a madwoman, just one who was angry as well as ravaged by sorrow.

At one point he fell asleep and woke with a start to find Meg staring at him. 'Sorry,' he croaked, his mouth all dry.

'Nay, you've stayed with me when I've needed you. I shall allus be grateful for that, love. Why don't you go and make us both a cup of tea?'

It was a relief to have something to do.

After that they sat in silence again. It seemed a very long time until it grew light.

The others were subdued when they came downstairs.

'I don't think they'll want me to take time off work to come to the funeral,' Shad said. 'I'd like to, but I don't want to lose my job.'

'There's no need for you to do it. But go and say goodbye to Nelly.' Meg didn't even look at her mother, but when Netta would have followed the children into the front room, she barred the way. 'Not you, Mam. You've done enough to her. I remember you slapping her face last week. It makes me want to slap yours now.'

Netta fell back a step, her mouth open in shock, then looked at Jack. When he jerked his head, she went back into the kitchen, muttering under her breath.

'I don't want her coming to the funeral, either,' Meg said.

So he went out to tell his mother and when she began to speak angrily about 'ingratitude' and to weep, he told her sharply to be quiet. Her tears were for herself. They always were.

In the end there was only him to accompany his sister to the church because his mother refused to let Joey go. Jack came home from work to carry the coffin, which was so small it hurt him every time he looked at it.

Meg walked along the street beside him, her old faded

woollen shawl pulled tightly round her. Once she bumped into an old woman, but didn't seem to realise what she had done, let alone offer an apology.

The woman looked down at the tiny coffin and stepped back, her face shadowed by some grief of her own.

During the short service Parson spoke gently, using the kindest words he could find to comfort the young mother.

'Thank you,' Meg told him after the coffin had been laid to rest. 'I'm grateful to you.' Then she turned and walked away.

Jack threw him an apologetic glance and raced after his sister. 'Hold on! What's the rush?'

She reached up one hand to pat his cheek. 'I know my own way home, lad. You get off to work now.'

'You'll be all right?'

'Aye. Of course I will.'

When he got home from work, though, Meg had gone and so had some of Netta's savings.

As his mother talked of ingratitude and theft, something snapped inside him. 'Our Meg didn't take it all, did she? She had a right to some of it. She'd earned it.'

'That was *my* money!' Netta yelled, slapping one hand down on the table. 'An' I could lay a charge of theft with the constable about her taking it.'

'It's not just yours, it's our family's money. I've earned my share of it, too, and Meg's more than welcome to that. And if you so much as mention the constable again, I'll take the children and move out, leave you to your nastiness.'

Her face was red with fury. 'You've allus cared for her more than you do for me! It's a shame when a poor widow woman can't get a bit of love from the children she's slaved for—'

Jack strode out, ending up at the local alehouse for want of anywhere else to go. He sat in a corner and gazed into his beer. He enjoyed one glass, but never fancied a second and today didn't really fancy this one, except it gave him an excuse to sit here. His father had drunk heavily and stumbled home after the alehouses closed. Jack would think shame to make himself foolish with drink. He couldn't see how it helped.

Some fellows from the mill greeted him, but they left him alone when he only nodded briefly in response. They'd know about little Nelly. Everyone knew your business in a small town.

It was a relief to be out of the house, though. It gave him time to think about how to start his search for Emmy. He was definitely going to look for her. And find her. However long it took.

And after that he was going to look for Meg.

Emmy settled in quickly at Carbury. She found her new mistress very different from Mrs Tibby but pleasant enough to work for and she thoroughly enjoyed the other maid's company, though Babs lectured her a lot at first. Emmy had not realised how apologetic she had always been about herself. And, as Babs said, why? She was honest and a good worker.

Babs taught her to laugh, too, in spite of the way she was missing Jack. Babs even made Mrs Dalby laugh sometimes.

In early December, when Emmy had been there for a month, a letter arrived which threw the household into a great fuss. Mrs Dalby's son, Edward, was coming to stay for a few days.

Babs rolled her eyes. 'It's all a lot of to-do about nothing. *Master Edward* never stays for long and spends half his time visiting old friends and relatives. She loves to see him, though, and it'll put her in a good mood for days.'

'What's he like? And why do you call him "Master Edward" like that?'

Babs grimaced. 'Because for all he's over thirty, he's spoiled and acts like a child half the time, wanting this, wanting that. He never seems like a grown man to me somehow. He's not half as nice as his father was, that's for sure, an' he talks in a plummy way, looks down his nose at us servants. He's not married and the mistress is always trying to find him a wife. Fair makes me laugh, that does. You'll see. There'll be lots of visitors while he's here – 'specially them with unmarried daughters – but I've heard him say he don't intend to wed till he's forty an' too old to have

296

a good time.' She sniffed. 'We all know what sort of a "good time" he means, don't we?' She winked at Emmy.

'He doesn't pester the maids, does he?'

'Bless you, no. Just let him try. I'd soon give him what for.'

But Emmy looked at Babs's plump face and frizzy hair, then across at Cook, solidly built and approaching fifty, and the old fear came creeping back. She wished she'd been born plain. It'd make life a lot easier.

Edward Dalby arrived the next day. He was tall and lean, with features that looked too wide for his face, so that he was all eyes and mouth. When he smiled he looked a bit better, Emmy thought, but it worried her that he kept staring at her.

'I don't want the mistress thinking I'm trying to encourage him,' she muttered to Babs as they cleared up the kitchen together on the second evening of his stay.

'He has been gawping at you,' Babs agreed, frowning. 'The mistress hasn't had a maid as young and pretty as you before.' She studied Emmy, head on one side. 'You're a right lovely lass, though you allus look a bit sad.'

Emmy shrugged. 'I'm still missing my old friends.'

'Or one old friend in particular?' When Emmy's colour deepened still further, Babs teased, 'I don't know why you don't go back to that fellow of yours, I really don't.'

Emmy hesitated, then asked in a voice that shook slightly, 'You don't think Mr Dalby will try anything on, do you? Only he makes me feel nervous the way he looks at me.'

Babs considered this, lips pursed. 'I don't know. Never seen him like this before, I must admit. Tell you what, though, you can come and sleep in my room while he's here. We can put your mattress on the floor and the mistress need never know about it. Cook won't say anything.'

The next night the maids were late going to bed because of all the extra work of a dinner party. As Emmy was about to get undressed, Babs said, 'Psst! Listen.'

A moment later they heard footsteps creeping up the attic stairs.

Emmy froze. 'Babs!'

Her friend made a shushing sound and they continued to

listen as someone – it could only be Mr Edward – opened the door of Emmy's room.

A minute later the same footsteps were heard going back down the stairs.

'Well, I'll be blowed!' Babs muttered. 'The cheek of it. In his mother's house, too. You'd better sleep in here till he goes, love.'

'I shan't feel safe while he's in the house.' Emmy could not believe this was happening to her again. What had she ever done to encourage these attentions? Who did these men think they were to pester her like this?

'Oh, you'll be all right in the kitchen during the daytime. He never comes back there.'

But after Cook had gone out for her morning constitutional, which only snowy weather ever prevented, the mistress sent Babs to buy some embroidery thread, then went out shortly afterwards herself to call on a friend who lived just down the road.

Realising she was alone in the house with *him*, Emmy began to worry.

Not long afterwards she heard footsteps coming along the passage towards the kitchen. Glancing wildly round for something to defend herself with, she saw the meat mallet and put it near her.

He came in whistling. 'Ah, Emmy, how about making me a cup of tea?'

'Certainly, sir. If you'd like to wait in the parlour, I'll bring it through to you.'

His voice became softer. 'But I'd rather wait here with you. You're the prettiest thing I've seen in years. It's a pleasure just to look at you.'

She swallowed hard. 'I don't like it when you talk that way, sir.'

'Of course you do! All girls like to be told they're pretty. And you're wasted working as a maid. Haven't you ever thought of doing something else?' He took another step towards her, his voice low and persuasive. 'I could set you up in a nice little house in Manchester and we could have some fun together. There's lots to see and do there. I'd be generous with you.'

'No, thank you. I'm a respectable girl.' She moved back but he followed. When she bumped into the table and could go no further, she begged, 'Don't, sir. *Please!*'

'Why, Emmy, I do believe you're nervous. I'd never hurt you, surely you realise that? I want to love you and—'

As he took yet another step, she snatched up the meat mallet and held it threateningly in front of her, shouting, 'I'm *not* like that.' But her hand was shaking because this had brought back the memory of the night when Marcus Armistead had her trapped in the bed.

Edward Dalby stopped moving and frowned at her. 'You're trembling,' he said, sounding surprised.

She couldn't move, felt panic-stricken and kept seeing Marcus's face, not Mr Edward's.

'Emmy, it's all right. *Emmy!*'

His voice was so loud, she jumped in shock and saw with relief that he'd taken a couple of steps back.

'Look, I didn't mean to frighten you. You can't blame a fellow for asking, but I'd never do anything you didn't want. Come and sit down a minute, you're as white as a sheet.'

She shook her head. She wasn't going an inch closer to him and she wasn't putting down the meat mallet till he'd left.

At that moment Babs breezed into the kitchen, carrying a small parcel and talking even before she got through the door. But her voice trailed away as she took in the scene in the kitchen and the terror on Emmy's face. She rounded on Edward Dalby, crying, 'Shame on you, Mr Edward! Look how you've frightened her. What have you been doing to her?'

'I haven't laid a finger on her, I only –' he shrugged and tried to make a joke of it '– offered to set her up in a nice little house in Manchester.'

'Your mother's maid! Very gentlemanly behaviour, that is.'

'There's no harm done and no need to tell my mother. She'll take it the wrong way. Just as Emmy did. It was *meant* as a compliment.'

'That sort of offer isn't a compliment to a decent girl,' Babs told him roundly, going to stand between him and Emmy and glaring at him. 'And now, sir, if you'll leave the kitchen, we'll get on with our work. And we'd be grateful if you didn't climb the attic stairs tonight.'

He flushed and turned round, feeling annoyed to have been treated as if he'd done something wrong. It *was* a compliment to offer to set up a common girl like that. And if Carter had had any sense she'd have accepted and made some good money for herself. He was always generous with his mistresses.

His anger mounted as Babs treated him with icy disdain from then onwards and Emmy avoided going anywhere near him. In the end he decided to leave a day early.

Jack thought long and hard about how to find Emmy. In his lunch hour he went to see Parson, but Mr Bradley refused to tell him where she was, except to say she'd found a new position and was safe. He also added a lecture about it being for the best.

Jack said firmly, 'It's not for the best, sir, and I shall never get over her.'

Outside he paused to stroke the dog. Hercules got excited every time he saw Jack, but was still moping. Giving the dog a final pat, he made his way down Weavers Lane to the bank, utterly determined to find Emmy.

He looked so fierce as he insisted on seeing Mr Garrett that the teller gave in and took him straight through to his master.

'I'm looking for Emmy Carter,' Jack said without preamble. 'I want to marry her. I think you know where she's gone.' He had found out that the banker had left town before dawn on the same morning as Emmy had vanished. Gentry never set off at such an early hour. It had to be connected.

'Jack, believe me, I sympathise with you, but I can tell you nothing. I won't break my promise to Emmy and besides, Parson and I feel she has done the right thing – the *only* thing – for everyone concerned.'

Jack glared at him. 'I don't happen to agree and I'll find her with or without your help because I'll not stop looking until I do.' He turned and walked out, furious that they were conspiring to keep him from Emmy.

As he hurried back to the mill, he saw a carriage coming

down the hill and in it Marcus Armistead. The man was looking so smug and self-satisfied that Jack stood and scowled at the vehicle. It wasn't fair that a wicked fellow could get away with ruining honest folk's lives, just because he was rich.

An hour later Mr Butterfield placed a hand on his shoulder. 'What's wrong, Jack?'

He sighed. 'They know where Emmy is and they're trying to keep me from seeing her.'

'There are other young women, you know,' Isaac said gently. He held up one hand. 'I know, I know. First love can be very painful. But there are other reasons for marrying, reasons that make more sense financially.' He stared into space and dropped the first hint. 'I myself have two daughters, both of whom will have decent dowries to bring to the young man who marries them. A thousand pounds each.'

But Jack didn't even hear what he was saying. He thought vaguely that it was kind of Mr Butterfield to try to cheer him up when everyone knew the head clerk has his own troubles. They said his wife was up half the night sometimes, yelling and shouting. That he had to give her laudanum to calm her down.

Edward Dalby was relieved to get back to Manchester, but could not get the pretty maid out of his mind. The cheek of it, turning down a good offer like that! And treating him as if he'd done something wrong in making it. The annoyance festered and one evening, when he was drinking with a few of his friends, it spilled out.

Marcus Armistead laughed. 'Why don't you simply take matters into your own hands and kidnap the girl? Once the deed is done and she finds out how much you're willing to pay her, she'll soon change her tune.'

Edward was a bit startled by this suggestion. 'That's a bit thick, isn't it? I mean, this is England, not the Barbary Coast. You don't go round kidnapping girls and forcing them into your bed.'

'Then stop moping and find yourself a more willing mistress,' Marcus replied, thinking him a fool. 'In the stews of Manchester there are dozens of pretty girls who'd be more than willing to accommodate you. And some of them are nearly virgins.'

The men round the table burst out laughing.

'Go to The Golden Swan,' one advised. 'They've got the best girls in town there, willing to accommodate all a chap's needs.'

'Bit pricey there, what?' another said.

'Worth it, though. Dashed obliging girls.'

Edward sighed. 'Trouble is, I can't get Emmy out of my mind.'

Marcus stiffened. 'Emmy?'

'Yes. That's what she's called.'

'Light brown hair, curly, big blue eyes, trim figure, very pretty indeed?'

'Yes.' He stared at Marcus. 'You sound as if you know her.'

'Mmm. Surname's Carter, isn't it?'

Edward thumped the table. 'That's the one! How the hell do *you* know her?'

Marcus grinned. 'Because she used to be my mistress. Her uncle took her away from me and hid her somewhere. She didn't go with him willingly, either.'

'Doesn't sound like the same girl. She started to tremble when I tried to kiss her. She definitely wasn't making that up.'

Marcus laughed for a very long time, then shook his head. 'She's still at it then, egging fellows on without seeming to. That's how she caught me. Best little actress in town, that one is.'

'Then what the hell is she doing slaving for my mother?'

'Who knows? Perhaps she's trying respectability for a change. After all, it's not every girl who can have a second try at being a virgin, is it?' He let the laughter die down and changed the subject easily. The rest of the evening passed in drinking and then half the members of the group made a visit to The Golden Swan.

Marcus made sure to leave the whore house at the same time as Edward Dalby and walk to the cab rank with him. 'I've been thinking about what you were saying. Look, Emmy's not the sort of girl I'd like to have working for my mother. Are you sure you should leave her there? I mean, if she goes off the rails again, well, your mother could be seriously embarrassed by her behaviour.'

'I'd never thought of that, but you're right. I'll write to Mother straight away. No, better still, I'll go and see her this weekend.' The idea caught Edward's fancy, for he was still smarting from the way the two maids had treated him.

The following Saturday Edward Dalby arrived in Carbury unannounced and when Emmy opened the door she gasped in shock at the sight of him.

'You may well gasp, young lady!' he said, grabbing her by the wrist and dragging her into his mother's parlour.

Mrs Dalby uttered a squeak of shock and pressed one hand to her breast when her son erupted into the room, dragging a protesting Emmy behind him.

He threw the girl to her knees on the rug and stood over her, enjoying the fear on her face. He'd teach the bitch to reject his offer like that!

'It's come to my attention that this young woman is no better than she ought to be,' he announced dramatically, folding his arms.

Emmy scrambled to her feet and retired behind the sofa. 'It's not true, Mrs Dalby! I don't know why he's saying this.'

'Edward dear, do you have to be so violent? You've given me palpitations now. Emmy, go and fetch me some of my cordial and then bring us some tea. Edward, sit down and let us talk about this quietly. I'm sure you're mistaken.'

'No, you don't.' He moved to prevent Emmy leaving the room. 'She's going nowhere, Mother, until I throw her out of your house.'

Emmy was getting angry in her turn. 'Why are you saying this? It's not true. You don't know anything about me.'

He laughed. 'Oh, don't I? Well, does the name Marcus Armistead mean anything to you?'

She froze, staring at him as that hated name echoed in her head. She couldn't believe Marcus had managed to track her down and was still trying to ruin her.

Her expression convinced him that Marcus had been telling the truth and his anger flared even higher. 'You see, Mother! She does know him.'

'He—'

'Be quiet, you slut! To think that *my mother* employed a creature like you in her house.'

Mrs Dalby stared at him in horror. 'Edward dear, how can you be sure? I promise you, Emmy has done nothing but work hard and cheerfully, and I simply can't believe—'

'I know because she used to be his mistress. Her uncle took her away from him and put her back to work with you.'

His mother stared at him then looked at Emmy, her expression uncertain.

'It isn't true,' Emmy said, loudly and emphatically. 'Marcus Armistead tried to kidnap me and I hit him over the head when I escaped. Since then he's been pursuing me to get his revenge.'

'*Marcus Armistead?*' Edward laughed loudly. 'I rather think if my friend had kidnapped you, you'd have stayed kidnapped. He's a very smart fellow, not to mention a respected member of Manchester trading circles and a gentleman of property. And you, young woman, are leaving this house immediately.' When his mother would have spoken he held up one hand. 'No, Mother. Father is no longer here to protect you and it's my duty to keep an eye on things.'

'But it's nearly dark and she can't—'

'She'll be quite at home on the streets at night, believe me.' Besides, he intended to follow Emmy and make his offer again, rather more forcibly this time. She might be a bit more grateful and if she wasn't, he might just take Marcus's advice.

'He's lying to you,' Emmy said to her mistress, tears of mingled anger and shame streaming down her face that she should be treated like this. 'But if you believe him, I'll go back to Parson Bradley's house. I beg you to let me stay here till morning, though, ma'am. I'm *not* at home on the streets, whatever your son says.'

But Edward was furious at being contradicted in front of his mother and annoyed that Emmy had stopped cringing away from him. He wanted her afraid and grateful. So he grabbed her shoulder and frog-marched her out of the room, saying loudly, 'Out, you!'

After a moment's shock she began to struggle and scream, 'Help! Help!' feeling sure he meant no good.

Babs erupted out of the kitchen followed by Cook, to watch open-mouthed as Edward tried to force the still screaming Emmy up the stairs.

Mrs Dalby tottered to the door. 'My cordial!' she gasped.

'What's he doing to Emmy?' Babs demanded, ignoring her mistress's request.

'Taking her to pack her bags, throwing her out. It appears she's – well, not a good girl.'

'Emmy Carter? I don't believe it. And I'm not leaving him alone with her, either, not if you dismiss me for it. Your son, ma'am, tried to creep into her bedroom last time he was here – against her wishes. This is just to get his own back on her for refusing.' Babs ran up the stairs before her astonished mistress could stop her.

Cook went back into the kitchen to pour out a glass of her mistress's 'cordial' which consisted of brandy and raspberry vinegar.

When she took it into the parlour, Mrs Dalby asked hesitantly, 'Do *you* think Carter is respectable?'

'Yes.'

'But Edward seems so *sure*.'

'Well, me an' Babs know her a bit better than he does.'

Upstairs Babs arrived in time to see Edward Dalby making free with Emmy's breasts while her friend struggled desperately to get away from him. Babs grabbed his arm and dragged him away, shouting, 'How dare you? Who do you think you are?'

'I'm your employer, that's who, so if you want to keep your job, go away and mind your own business.'

Babs stood between them, hands on hips. 'No, you're not! Your mother's my employer. And if she's going to allow her son to make free with us maids, I'm leaving anyway.'

'Don't be stupid. I know this one's been someone's mistress before she came here.'

'It's not true, Babs, I promise you,' Emmy said. 'Marcus Armistead's lying out of revenge.'

'I prefer to take the word of a gentleman to that of a slut like you.' As Edward moved towards Emmy, Babs stepped between them again, so he took a step backwards and pointed one finger at Emmy. 'Pack your bags, you. You're leaving here tonight. And I'm watching everything you pack to make sure you're not stealing anything.'

'Is your mother letting you do this?' Babs demanded, shocked rigid. 'Turning a decent girl out on the streets!'

'My mother will do as I say.'

'In that case, I'm leaving too. Here, love, let me help you pack, then you can come and help me. He can't rape two of us at once, can he? If he tries, I'll hit him on the head with the chamber pot.' Suiting the action to the words, Babs picked the object up from under the bed and brandished it at him.

Spluttering with indignation, Edward retreated to the doorway. Things were not going as he'd expected.

Emmy gave Babs a grateful glance then began to throw things into her bag anyhow. She didn't know what she'd have done without her friend's help. When everything was packed, Babs brandished the chamber pot again and said, 'Get out of our way, you.' The two of them carried out the bag and a bundle, edging past him as if he was a dangerous animal, and went to Babs' room to pack her things.

'Where are we going to go?' Emmy whispered.

Babs put her mouth close to her friend's ear. 'I've got an old auntie lives at the other end of the village. We can sleep there, though there's only the floor. But at least we won't have any unwanted bed companions.' She was thoroughly enjoying the drama and meant exactly what she said. After fifteen years in service she had money saved and enough confidence in her own worth to defy anyone who ill treated her.

When her things were packed she stared aggressively at Edward. 'You can either help me down with my trunk or wait for a cab driver to come and help me, but I'm not leaving Emmy alone with you, not for a second. You're no gentleman, that's for sure.'

'I'll help,' he said sulkily. He was beginning to think he'd gone a bit overboard and wanted the two of them out of the house as quickly as possible before they could plant any doubts in his mother's mind about what he had done. Maids were two a penny, after all. She'd soon find others.

The bumping noises brought Mrs Dalby out of the parlour. 'What are you doing in your outdoor things, Babs?' she asked in shock.

'I'm leaving, ma'am. And I'd be obliged if you'd give us our wages before we go. We've both worked hard for you and I don't think you're the sort of mistress to cheat us out of our earnings.'

'*Leaving?* But why are *you* leaving? It was Emmy my son said must go.'

Babs drew herself up. 'I'm not working anywhere that young men can make free with the maids. When I went upstairs just now he was holding Emmy prisoner and touching her breasts.'

'She's lying, Mother!'

'I saw you doing it myself,' Babs declared. 'And Mrs Dalby knows I don't tell lies.'

Cynthia Dalby turned bright red, gasped and put one hand to her throat.

Babs jerked one shoulder scornfully towards Edward. 'First your son tries to force his way into poor Emmy's bed, now he's getting her dismissed. At night! After dark! How does he think she'll find a room at this hour? It's disgusting and I didn't think it of you, Mrs Dalby, I really didn't.'

'But I—'

Edward interrupted his mother. 'I was going to go with her and make sure she was safe.'

'*Safe!* With you? Hah! She'd be safer with a wild tiger than with you.' Babs went to put an arm round Emmy. 'Well, I'm not leaving her to his mercy, Mrs Dalby, and I'm not staying in a house where us maids aren't safe from men like him – or from being dismissed when we've done nothing wrong.'

'Babs, don't,' Mrs Dalby begged in a quavering voice. 'We can talk about this in the morning.'

'I couldn't sleep for worrying he'd come creeping into my

room.' Babs slammed open the front door. 'You run down to the cab stand, Emmy love, and ask old Alf if he'll come and pick us up.' She scowled at Edward. 'I'll make sure *he* doesn't follow you.' As Emmy left, she turned to her mistress and said coldly, 'Our wages, if you please, ma'am.'

Cynthia Dalby tottered into the parlour, her head spinning so much from an unaccustomed second glass of her cordial that she could not think what to do. She opened her bureau and fumbled for her purse.

Edward followed her to demand, 'You're not going to pay them, surely?'

'They've done the work so they've earned the money.' She counted out the coins and took them into the hall. 'Could you . . . come and see me on Monday, please, Babs? After Edward has left?'

'If I'm still in the village, I may do,' Babs conceded, sure they'd both get their jobs back once her mistress had had time to think things over. 'As long as you promise faithfully that *he* won't molest me.'

Cynthia threw her son an angry glance. 'Edward won't be here on Monday.'

The village cab came clopping to a halt outside and Alf jumped down, all agog to see what was going on. It'd take something shocking to drive Babs Meeson out of her comfortable position at this hour of a Saturday night. He'd known her since she was a girl visiting her auntie and if there was trouble, he knew whose side he was on. As soon as he saw Edward Dalby and the way Babs avoided going near him as she walked down the hall, he said, 'Been pestering you, has he?'

'Yes, he has,' said Babs, loudly and defiantly.

'His father was just the same. Came after my Bet once, he did, but I soon told him where to get off, gentleman or no.'

In the hall Cynthia heard every word and breathed in deeply before reaching for her cordial again. She had known her husband was not faithful, but not that his behaviour was such common knowledge in the village.

As the cab horse clopped away, Edward came back into the

house and slammed the front door behind him, saying loudly, 'Good riddance to the pair of them!'

His mother scowled at him. 'You'd better leave first thing in the morning, Edward. And don't return until you have learned to behave in your mother's household. Even your father, for all his faults, never attacked my own maids.'

'But—'

She raised one hand. 'I do not intend to discuss this further. In fact, I'm going to bed. I shan't get up tomorrow until you've gone.'

Marcus Armistead sent the groom to Carbury, where Edward's mother lived, to look for Emmy. Denny took a room at the alehouse and found out that the girl his master had described was indeed working for old Mrs Dalby. His instructions were to follow her if she left the village; otherwise just to keep an eye on her. Easy work, this.

The second evening he saw her come for the village cab, looking upset. Intrigued, he swallowed the last of his ale and loped along after the cab to the Dalby house, two streets away. The driver went inside then came out carrying some luggage. Two women left the house, the pretty one his master fancied and a hard-faced older piece who turned to shout, 'People like you should be taken out and hanged!' at a gentleman standing in the doorway with arms folded before she let Alf close the cab door.

Denny continued to follow the vehicle, giving thanks that the horse was elderly and only willing to plod. It stopped at a cottage on the outskirts of the village and the driver helped the women carry their possessions inside. The observer could not get close enough to overhear what they were saying, but decided there was nothing further likely to happen that night so went back to the alehouse. To his delight Alf came in a bit later for something to warm his bones. Judicious questioning revealed that the two women had left their jobs and gone to stay with the older one's aunt.

Someone came to shout for a cab just as Denny was getting

the questioning round to why exactly the two maids had left their mistress at this hour on a Saturday night. When Alf had left, he grinned as he ordered another glass of ale. This was better than working in the stables, by hell it was! In the morning he'd take up position near the cottage early on, to make sure the young woman didn't leave without his knowledge. In the meantime, he'd enjoy the local ale.

Chapter Eighteen

On Sunday morning, as soon as her son had left, Cynthia summoned Cook and asked her to fetch Babs and Emmy back. 'They need have no more fear of my son. He will not be coming back here for quite some time.'

'We can send the lad from next door to fetch 'em,' Cook said. 'I have my work to do if you want any food preparing today.' She was very much on her dignity and knew her mistress was terrified she would leave as well.

'I'd be most grateful, Cook. Thank you so much.'

When the lad brought the message, Babs winked at Emmy and sent back word that they could not come until the following day as they still had not recovered from the dreadful shock of being treated so badly.

Emmy listened in amazement to the confident way Babs dealt with the message boy. She didn't know what she would have done without her friend and wished she were even half as sure of herself. She felt safe with Babs in charge and that suddenly reminded her of how her mother had often used the word. *Safe!* She had experienced a distinct lack of safety in her own life now and so far all she had done was run away.

Was there a better way to deal with it?

What had made her mother turn to selling her body? Emmy wondered suddenly. Had she been driven to it by men like Marcus Armistead and Charles Dalby? And who had killed her? How many nights had Emmy lain awake wondering that? Was it, as she suspected, Marcus Armistead or just a passing stranger? And would they ever find out?

After Babs had sent the boy away she put an arm round Emmy, giving her a quick hug. 'You look like you've lost a guinea and found a farthing, my girl. Cheer up! We've got a day's holiday today and then tomorrow we'll let Mrs Dalby persuade us to go and work for her again.' She chuckled. 'I bet she even raises our wages.'

Emmy said quietly, 'I shan't be going back to her.'

'What? Why ever not?'

'Because her son knows Marcus Armistead and will tell him where I am.' Suddenly she had a longing to tell the full story to someone. 'Could we go for a walk? I need to ask your advice. If you don't mind, that is?'

'Good idea. You've been looking as miserable as a wet week this morning.' Babs raised her voice. 'We're going out for a bit of a stroll, Auntie.'

They put on some warm clothes and walked along the lane before climbing a stile to cut across the nearby meadows. The countryside was softer round here than at Northby and the weather was quite mild for December. It made Emmy wonder what the rest of England was like.

They found a sheltered bench and sat on it while she told her friend how she'd been driven away from Northby. When she finished she looked up, expecting to see disgust in the other woman's eyes, but found only sympathy. 'I thought you'd despise me,' she said shakily.

'Why should I? You haven't done anything wrong, love. And you shouldn't go round acting as if you have something to be ashamed of, either. It was your mother who misbehaved, not you. If that Jack fellow wants to marry you and you love him as much as you say, I think you're a fool not to do it. I'd have snapped his hand off if it'd been me.'

'But his mother said she'd kill me rather than see me marry him.'

'She wouldn't really do that – unless she's insane.' Babs wrinkled her nose in a wry smile that was peculiarly her own. 'She's just trying to frighten you away, love. And don't you think your Jack would have something to say about such a threat?' She let that sink in, then said thoughtfully, 'You'd better not let her live with you, though. She sounds a right old misery-guts.'

'You've been such a good friend to me, Babs. I've needed someone to talk to for ages, someone more like myself. Mrs Bradley is lovely, but she doesn't understand things like you do because she's never known what it's like to be poor.' Emmy gave a tremulous smile then it faded and she added in a low voice, 'There's still Marcus Armistead, though. He's a real threat to both Jack and me.'

'Yes. But with a parson and a banker on your side, the two of you should be safe enough from him.' She frowned, thinking over what Emmy had said. 'What about that lawyer fellow who came to Northby after your mother died? You said he knew your father's family. Maybe he could ask them to help you find somewhere else to live. After all, they won't be sorry to hear you're getting wed to a decent young chap, will they? Try asking them. They can only say no, after all.'

'I don't want anything from them!'

'What was in those papers of your mother's?'

Emmy looked at her in surprise. 'I don't know. They're still hidden in the attic at my uncle's. I decided to leave them there. I doubt they'll contain any good news.'

Babs shook her head with mock severity. 'You should have checked, though. You never know. It seems to me that what you need, my lass, is to take charge of your life and make it go where *you* want. And the first thing is to marry that Jack of yours if you love him so much.' She nudged her friend and grinned slyly. 'I'm right, aren't I? You do love him?'

Blushing, Emmy nodded.

'You're not like me, love. I never did want to marry. Had enough of kids when I was helping bring up my brothers and sisters. It's hard work being the eldest of ten, I can tell you. But once I'd got used to how things work in service, I stopped letting anyone mess me around, whether they were my employer or not. I'm really happy with my life now. I don't work for anyone as treats me badly, and if they try anything on, I leave.

313

Believe me, employers need us as much as we need them. I tell them straight out when they're interviewing me that I'm an excellent worker, none better, but I'll only stay with them if they treat me right and feed me properly. If they don't like that, I find someone else to work for. I've been with Mrs Dalby for three years now. She suits me, but I never did think much of her son and I think even less now. If she lets him start pestering her maids, I'm off for good.'

Babs let those ideas sink in, then continued, 'So if you're not coming back to Mrs Dalby's, what exactly are you going to do, love?'

'I'm going back to Mrs Bradley and . . .' Emmy took a deep breath as she put her dearest wish into words '. . . I'm going to talk to Jack and see if we can work something out. Like you said, there are people on our side. Besides, I've missed him dreadfully since I came here. The thought of not seeing him again, well . . .' It had become too much to bear.

Babs crowed in triumph. 'Now you're talking a bit of sense, my girl.' She frowned. 'But we don't want anyone stopping you on your way back. We have to get you to Blackburn safely first and then across to this Northby of yours.' She tapped her forefinger against her lips as she considered the problem, then held the finger up and waggled it triumphantly. 'I know! Let's go and see a farmer friend of mine. If he's sending any loads into Blackburn tomorrow, he can take you with him.'

Arm in arm the two women strolled back to the village. Emmy didn't even notice that a damp breeze was blowing, presaging rain, because she felt a growing determination to take charge of her life, just as Babs had done.

And this new turn in events seemed meant to be when they found that the farmer was taking a load of potatoes into Blackburn the very next day and would be happy to give her a ride.

Lenny was an older, fatherly sort of man and she felt quite safe with him, but Babs was still frowning. 'I think we'll disguise you as well. Better safe than sorry, eh?' Then she chuckled suddenly. 'How do you fancy being great with child, Emmy

Carter? I'll borrow a cushion and we can tie it under your clothes.'

Jack spent his half-day on Saturday making inquiries, and by playing the lovelorn suitor desperately wanting to find his young woman, make up an alleged quarrel and marry her, he eventually persuaded Mr Garrett's coachman, who was of a sentimental nature, to tell him where they'd gone.

When he got home he told his mother what he was doing. She looked at him in horror. 'No! Son, don't do it!'

Knowing it had to be said sooner or later, he said sternly, 'I'm still upset about you driving Emmy away, and I haven't forgiven you for that. You've done the opposite to what you intended as far as I'm concerned. You've made sure that I'll *have* to leave you, because I'm going to marry Emmy whatever anyone says or does, and I'm not having her living with someone who makes everyone's life a misery.'

When Netta began to sob he raised his voice: 'Stop that!' She continued to sob, so he shook her lightly, just enough to get her attention. 'Listen to me, Mam. I'll make sure you're all right, but Emmy's done nothing wrong and there's no reason on earth why I shouldn't marry her.'

'But—'

'I haven't finished. You've also driven Meg away and I won't be able to forgive you for that till I bring her back. She'd lost her husband then her child. You should have been looking after her, comforting her. Instead you never stopped nagging her. You've a lot on your conscience, Mam, and I hope you can live with it if any harm comes to our Meg. As soon as Emmy and I have sorted our lives out, I'm going to look for my sister and bring her home as well – to *my* home, not yours.'

'But—'

'I don't want to hear any excuses because there's nothing you can say or do that'll make me change my mind. You've made your bed and must lie in it. I'll make sure you're all right, but I won't be living with you after I've married Emmy.' He stood up. 'Now I have things to do.'

He left his mother sobbing, but her tears had lost their power to move him. He should have been firmer with her before, but he'd been young himself when she became his responsibility.

Leaving the house, he went next to knock on Mr Butterfield's door. The Chief Clerk opened it himself, in his shirt sleeves and looking harassed. 'Jack! What's wrong?'

'I need to speak to you, Mr Butterfield. About Emmy. Can I come in?'

'Haven't we had enough talk of that creature in this house?' a woman's low, throbbing voice demanded from behind them.

Jack stared in shock at Lena Butterfield, who was wearing a stained house dress with her hair hanging down over her shoulders in tangles. He'd heard she'd gone a bit strange, but now he could see for himself that something was very wrong with her.

Isaac closed his eyes for a moment as if gathering his strength then led his wife back down the corridor. 'Go and sit in the kitchen, my dear. I shall only be a minute.'

'But Isaac—'

He closed the door on her and came back to wave Jack into the front parlour, which looked dusty and unused, with no fire in the grate. 'My wife is not well, I'm afraid. I hope you will not mention to anyone the state she's in?'

'Of course not, sir.'

'Even Lal and Dinah don't know how bad she is.' He sighed then glanced sharply at his visitor. 'What brings you to see me on a Sunday, lad?'

'Emmy.'

'She's not in trouble?'

'I hope not, sir, but my mother has helped drive her away – and Marcus Armistead has, too. I can't live without her, so I need to go after her and persuade her to marry me.'

'But how shall you find her? You said Mr Bradley refused to tell you where she was.'

'I've spoken to Mr Garrett's coachman who says he took his

master and a young maid to Blackburn. His employer was gone for three hours then came back alone. So they can't have gone far, can they? I'm going to Blackburn and I'll stay there until I find Emmy. I came to tell you I won't be at work tomorrow and perhaps not for a few days.' He hesitated, then added, 'And if I lose my job for it, I'm sorry, but Emmy's more important to me than anything else in the whole world.'

Isaac wished either of his daughters had the power to attract a principled young man like this. 'Wait a minute.' He left the room and came back a short while later to press some coins into Jack's hand. 'I could do nothing for my sister, but maybe I can help my niece.'

Jack looked down at his hand, startled to see some gold coins. 'I can't take this!'

'You must. My wife did Emmy a serious wrong and it's been on my conscience ever since. I'll also tell Mr Rishmore I gave you permission to take time off work. If he dismisses you then he'll have to dismiss me too.' Isaac gave a wry smile. 'And I think he values me too much to do that. I am rather useful to him and he would find it difficult to replace me.'

Jack's voice was roughened by emotion as he shook the hand Isaac Butterfield held out and thanked him.

'And when you get back I shall be happy to be seen in public with my niece, if that helps. Now, how shall you get to Blackburn?'

'I thought to hire a trap and leave early tomorrow morning.'

'Excellent idea. You can give my name as surety at the livery stables.'

Jack went away with a warm feeling inside him. Surely with her uncle on their side Emmy would change her mind about marrying him?

Marcus Armistead was also making his way to Blackburn that Monday, but he drove there in the luxury of his own coach, arriving by mid-morning. He was so impatient to find Emmy he had not been able to resist following his spy. The thought of getting his hands on her drew him like a magnet. Soon, soon he would have her in his power and this time she would not get away.

Funny how he could not forget this woman when usually they meant little to him. One was much like the other in bed, he'd found.

He took a room at a large coaching inn which seemed to promise reasonable comfort and then told his coachman to drive him to Carbury. 'If we find that young woman, we shall bring her back with us, willing or not. You'd better stop and buy some rope in case we have to restrain her.'

The man looked at him uncertainly. It was one thing to chase a willing piece of skirt, and good luck to anyone who could have as many women as his master did, but he drew the line at kidnapping which carried stiff penalties in law. 'Sir, I don't like the thought of . . .'

Marcus glared at him. 'You can either do as you're told or find another job. Immediately.'

The coachman bit back further comment, but he was beginning to worry about the wild look in his master's eyes. He should have got himself another position when the old master died, he really should.

In Carbury Denny was quickly found and confessed that Emmy Carter had vanished off the face of the earth. Marcus fell into a rage, shouting and hitting out at both men with the lead-weighted walking stick he habitually carried for protection, then sending them out to hunt for the girl.

But it was in vain. No one had seen her and the villagers were getting suspicious of Denny and his questioning. The other maid was back working for Mrs Dalby so they couldn't question her.

'If you ask me, there's a conspiracy here, sir,' Denny said gloomily. 'They've helped her get away.'

Marcus felt anger mounting inside him again and ordered his coachman to get the horses put to and drive him to Blackburn. 'She must have left Carbury by cart or on foot, and neither of those methods will get her very far. She'll have to pass through Blackburn if she's going back to Northby, and where else would she go?'

If they didn't find her now, he'd wait for her to turn up in the village and make some new plans. Their meeting was only postponed.

Jack found himself a modest room in Blackburn and left the horse and trap at an equally modest livery stable for the night. Dumping his bag in his room, he spent the rest of the day visiting the other livery stables in the town centre. No one remembered a Mr Garrett or a pretty young woman hiring any vehicles a few weeks previously, and he grew more and more depressed. There had to be some way to find out where she'd gone and this had seemed the most promising path of enquiry.

What if he didn't find her?

The mere though made him stop walking for a moment. Then he shook his head and began moving again. He would find her! Someone must have seen her.

But the rest of his inquiries led nowhere and as darkness began to fall, he turned to walk slowly back to his lodgings, feeling miserable. Then, in the gathering dusk, he saw a man he recognised – he didn't remember from where exactly, but he knew that face. He turned to follow the fellow through the streets, which were still crowded enough to slow him down.

The man went into the yard of a coaching inn and disappeared from view up the stairs of the inn. Jack stayed in the tap room, which had a view of the staircase, ordered a glass of ale and waited. A few minutes later he saw the fellow come down looking sour-faced. To his delight, the man came up to the bar to demand a glass of ale. Something had clearly upset him. Jack edged a bit nearer and watched as the man got talking to another customer.

'Bloody masters,' he said, draining his glass and banging on the counter for another. 'Want you to perform miracles, they do.' He tapped his forehead which bore a large bruise. 'Thumped me, he did, just because I didn't find out what he wanted. If the wench he's looking for has disappeared, Mr bloody Armistead will just have to manage without her for another day. She won't be able to hide for long. He's got enough money to hire a dozen fellows to search for her, he has.'

When the conversation moved on to a discussion of horses, Jack left his own full glass behind on the bar and moved towards the door.

The thought that Armistead was still pursuing Emmy made him furious. Who did the fellow think he was to flout the law like this? Well, she seemed to have given him the slip for the moment, but she was in great danger and he needed to find her before anyone else did.

Racking his brain to think of another way of tracing her, he almost walked past the pregnant woman with the shawl over her head who had been standing outside the inn. It was she who touched his arm.

'Jack? Is that really you?'

He spun round, unable to believe it could be her. But it was. '*Emmy!* I've been looking for you everywhere. No one in Northby would tell me where you'd gone.'

She glanced round as if terrified. 'I've just seen *his* groom. I wanted to book a seat on the coach to Northby, only I daren't go inside the inn now.'

Jack put his arm round her shoulder, sighing in relief. 'Let's get away from here, love.' With a shaky laugh he held her at arm's length, nodding towards the swollen belly. 'What's this? Rather sudden, isn't it?'

He clearly hadn't even considered the idea that she could really be pregnant. Emmy smiled up at him and whispered, 'It's a cushion. Babs thought it'd make a good disguise.'

'She's right, whoever she is. It's an excellent disguise. Especially with your hair hidden under that shawl.'

They walked at random, not saying anything, but somehow her hand found its way into his and its warmth made him feel better than he had for a long time. He stole a glance sideways and as he saw her looking up at him, his feet stopped moving and he drew her towards him. Heedless of the passers-by, he cradled her against him and said firmly, 'We belong together, Emmy Carter, and you know it. Let's not have any more silliness about my mother or yours. We're going to get wed if I have to drag you to the altar.'

'Oh, Jack! I was coming back to Northby to say I'd changed my mind. You're right, we do belong together. There wasn't a night I didn't fall asleep thinking of you or a day when I didn't feel the lack of you.' She spoke simply and from the heart. 'I love you so much, Jack.'

'And I you, Emmy lass. I always have done, I think, right from the first time I saw you fighting off those damned cousins of yours.'

Someone bumped into them and Jack looked round. 'Eh, what are we doing standing in the street like this? They may still be out looking for you. We'll have to find you a room or . . .' He hesitated, then asked, 'Do you trust me, love? If so, we'll go back to my lodgings and you can share mine. I'll tell them you're my wife and you've come back from your sister's earlier than I'd expected.' He looked deep into her eyes. 'You know I'll not lay a finger on you until we're wed, don't you?'

She nodded. 'I know, Jack.'

Together they walked back down the street, his arm round her shoulders, her head leaning against him. No one gave them a second glance. Young couples expecting children were nothing unusual in those parts.

In the bedroom, however, she hesitated. Even with Jack she felt nervous. 'I think Marcus Armistead left me with a fear of men,' she confessed suddenly. 'It's not that I don't trust you, it's just that I can't seem to forget how he used me . . . touched me.' She shuddered, wrapping her arms round herself, making no move to lie on the bed, though she was clearly exhausted.

Jack hesitated, wondering how best to deal with this. He dare not let his anger surface, the almost ungovernable rage that filled him every time he thought of what Armistead had done to her. 'Do you think if you lie under the bedcovers and I lie on top of them, you'll feel safe?' he asked. 'If not, I'll sleep on the floor.'

'Let's — lie on the bed.' Emmy untied the tapes that bound the cushion to her and tried to make a joke about it, but could think of nothing. Removing her shoes, she slid into bed fully dressed and lay there feeling horribly nervous.

Jack waited till she had sighed and relaxed just a little bit, then kicked his shoes off and sat down on the edge of the bed. 'Are you sure?' he asked.

She nodded. 'You can't sleep on the floor. It's too cold.'

Careful not to touch her, he got into bed, lying as close to the edge as he could manage and pulling just the quilt over himself. He sighed. She looked so afraid. Did this mean she would not want him to touch her when they married? Had that man ruined her for a normal life?

Her voice was hesitant in the darkness. 'I think I'd like to hold your hand, Jack. Would you mind?'

His heart lightened a little and he fumbled for her hand, finding it cold as he took it in his big warm one. After a few minutes had passed he whispered, 'Eh, lass, I can't believe I found you tonight.'

But she didn't answer and when he listened to her slow breathing he realised she had fallen asleep. After they were married he'd teach her not to fear him, he vowed, teach her to enjoy his embraces. If it took years. So he kept hold of her hand and soon he was asleep too, a smile lingering on his face. Half a loaf was better than no bread to a starving man, after all.

A few streets away in a much larger and more comfortable bedroom Marcus Armistead lay awake for far longer. How could Emmy Carter have vanished like this? He considered finding himself a woman for the night but for some reason he didn't want anyone but *her* these days. It was infuriating and very frustrating.

She'd pay dearly for treating him thus! He'd make sure of that.

She couldn't hide from him for ever.

Chapter Nineteen

Prudence Bradley glanced casually out of the window and what she saw sent her rushing into her husband's study. 'Come quickly! Jack's brought Emmy back and they both look – strange.' Well, Emmy looked to be with child, but this couldn't possibly be in the short time since she'd left Northby.

Gerald looked up from his sermon with a frown. 'I thought your protégée had decided to make a new life for herself? A decision I agreed with absolutely. Jack has other responsibilities.'

Prudence waved one hand dismissively. 'Oh, rubbish! They love one another and it'd be shameful to keep them apart. Besides, he's done more than enough for his mother who's always complaining about something and quite sets my teeth on edge. It's about time he thought of his own needs for a change.' She whisked out of the room and hurried into the kitchen in time to see Cass open the back door and shriek in delight.

'You're back!' Then she noticed Emmy's stomach and gaped at it. 'What's happened?'

Emmy looked down. She had forgotten the pillow. 'It's not real, just a disguise.' She had sat in the trap on the way here with her false belly poking out and her face and hair hidden under a shawl. Jack had rubbed dirt on his face, slouched in his seat and pulled his hat down over his eyes. When Marcus Armistead's carriage had overtaken them on the road to Northby they had both held their breath because he had two men with him. But it had driven straight past without anyone recognising them.

Emmy noticed her former mistress standing at the other side of the kitchen and smiled at her. 'Oh, Mrs Bradley, it's wonderful to see you all again!'

Before she could cross the room there was a yelp from outside and Hercules pushed past Jack's legs to burst inside ahead of him. The dog immediately began jumping up at her, yelping, barking and trying to lick her face or any part of her he could reach. In the end she knelt down and clasped him in her arms, laying her face against his pointed furry head for a moment, enduring more licks but gradually calming him down. 'I missed you, boy. Have you been good while I was away? And who told you to come in here, eh?'

Jack was pleased to see her open joy at being reunited with the dog, but his smile faded a little as he realised she could not touch him with the same freedom – or let him touch her.

'Don't I get a proper greeting as well?' Mrs Bradley demanded in mock anger, hands on hips.

Emmy stood up, feeling suddenly uncertain what to do next, but Prudence gave her a big hug, after which Cass did the same and even Cook came across to pat her shoulder and say gruffly, 'About time you came home, young woman.'

Home? thought Emmy wonderingly. Yes, Northby did feel like home now.

'Well, Jack,' Prudence said quietly, guessing by his expression that he felt left out, 'you found her then?'

'Aye. Well, she found me, really, Mrs Bradley. She was already on her way back.'

'You'd better come through and tell me and Parson exactly what's been happening.' She put one arm round Emmy and led the way. Hercules pushed in front of Jack again, desperate to stay next to his beloved owner.

'Eh, she looks like she's seen some hard times lately, doesn't she?' Cass murmured to Cook when they had gone. 'But I wish someone would look at me the way Jack Staley looks at her.'

'Stop sighing for what you can't have, my girl, and make them some tea. They look chilled to the marrow.'

*   *   *

In the front parlour Jack stood behind Emmy, keeping very close to her as they waited for Mrs Bradley to fetch her husband. Emmy turned her head to smile at him and he laid one hand on her shoulder. The dog pressed itself against her, smiling as dogs do when they're with their favourite people, its tail thumping against her skirt in a regular rhythm. Occasionally he would swipe a lick at her hand.

Silly to be jealous of a dog, Jack thought. But he was. For all the time he had spent comforting the dratted animal while she was away, it had completely ignored him today.

As Prudence rushed into the study for a second time Gerald set down his pen and asked, 'Well, what's happened to them?'

She tugged at his hand. 'We're about to find out. Why are you still sitting there? Come and join us. From the way Emmy and Jack are looking at one another, I think there's going to be a wedding soon.'

He held her back to warn her, 'I'm not sure we should encourage this. It won't be easy for them, you know. All the love in the world won't solve the problem of Mrs Staley and the children, not to mention that other man.' But in spite of an uneasiness he could not shake off – an unusual state of mind for such an unimaginative man – he got up and followed his wife out.

Once everyone was seated in the parlour, Emmy explained what had happened to her.

Jack took over then to say, 'We want to get married as soon as we can, sir. Will you call the banns for us?'

'Yes, of course. But where are you going to live?'

'Mr Rishmore usually has a cottage or two vacant.'

'You're not going to live with your mother, then?'

'No, sir. That's not possible. She can be rather,' he hesitated over a choice of word and settled on, 'unreasonable about some things, including Emmy. I'll make sure she's all right, though.'

'Can you afford to run two households?' Prudence worried.

'I have Mrs Oswald's money,' Emmy put in. 'We'll manage, Mr Bradley.'

'I'm already twenty-one, and I'm sure Mr Butterfield will give his permission for Emmy to marry, if you need it,' Jack added.

After a moment's hesitation over the wisdom of this, Gerald gave in. 'Very well, then. I'll call the banns on Sunday for the first time and in three weeks you can get married.'

Prudence smiled as she watched the engaged couple exchange loving glances.

'Can I stay here until then?' Emmy asked hesitantly. 'I'll help in the house. I won't be a burden.'

'Bless you, of course you can,' Prudence said warmly. 'It'll be very useful to have another pair of hands over Christmas. And while you're here we'll make you a pretty dress to get married in, one that you can wear for best afterwards. Three weeks will soon pass.'

'She'd better stay close to the house,' Jack said. 'Armistead was in Blackburn and passed us on the road back.'

'You saw him again today?' Gerald asked, shocked.

'Oh, yes. And he had that groom with him, the one who does his dirty work.'

'Oh, dear.' Prudence looked to her husband for guidance, but he seemed at a loss for words.

After a moment or two's silence Jack stood up. 'I'd better get back to the mill and find out if I still have a job.' He turned to Emmy. 'You won't go out on your own? Promise me?'

She shivered. 'I promise. But when I do go out, I'm going to hold my head up proudly.' She looked round at them all. 'It's taken me a long time to realise that I'm not responsible for my mother's sins, and from now on I'm not going to let people treat me as if I'm like her.' She intended to follow Babs' example and stand up for herself. It wouldn't convince everyone, but it would make her feel better, she was sure.

Gerald did not think it would be so easy to change people's attitudes but he said nothing to Emmy, merely called after Jack, 'May I just have a word with you?' In his study he asked abruptly, 'How are you going to protect Emmy after you're married?'

Jack sighed. 'I don't know yet. We may have to leave Northby altogether.'

'I hate to say this, but that might be the best thing for all concerned.'

'I'd do it tomorrow if it weren't for my mother. I'll still need to keep an eye on her and the kids, you see. She can't manage on her own, never has been able to, and she's not always kind to them. And there's Meg as well. What if my sister comes back and we're not here? She nearly starved last time she was on her own. I want to try and find her, if I can. She was that unhappy after Nelly died . . .' His voice trailed away.

Gerald Bradley clapped him on the shoulder and watched him go. A fine young man, that. He would still have a word with Eli Makepeace about Emmy's safety, though.

At the mill the first person Jack met crossing the yard was Mr Rishmore, who stopped and scowled at him. 'Don't expect to be paid for the days you've been away, young man!'

'No, sir, I don't. I'm really sorry. It was very urgent business that took me away.'

Samuel's scowl did not lessen. 'Business to do with that young woman, I gather? Did you find her?'

'Yes, sir. And brought her back to stay with Parson until we can be wed.'

'You're a fool then. You could have had one of Butterfield's daughters and a thousand pounds into the bargain.'

Jack gaped at him because this had never even occurred to him. He didn't need to think about it, though. 'I wouldn't have been happy with Lal or Dinah – and I couldn't have made them happy, either, sir. It's always been Emmy for me. I just didn't think we could work things out.'

Once, Samuel would still have believed Staley was making the wrong decision and tried to talk him out of it, but since his own daughter had run away, he had begun to wonder if some differences could not be bridged by marriage; if indeed money was not the most important thing, as he had always believed before.

As for young Armistead, he was not proving a steady business partner like his father and had tried to push Samuel into some rash decisions, one of which had been distinctly unethical. Samuel was considering severing all connection with him.

Nor did Marcus seem to be regretting the disappearance of his wife. He refused to speak Jane's name and had not made much effort to find her after the first week or two. Once, when Samuel had insisted on discussing what they would do if she returned, Marcus had said frostily that he would not have her back under his roof now or let her near their son.

But what had upset Samuel most of all was the information given him by Eli Makepeace that Marcus Armistead had a bad reputation where women were concerned. When Samuel had pressed for more details, Eli had said a friend who was an officer of the law in Manchester had told him Marcus was part-owner of a house of ill repute there. Samuel still felt appalled every time he thought of this. A gentleman simply did not get involved in immoral dealings. And when Eli had hesitated, then added that Armistead was also known to beat women, Samuel had been speechless with shock. Had he beaten Jane? Was that why she had left him?

His son-in-law had not once travelled down to Cheltenham to see his little son, so Samuel and Margaret were making plans for a trip there in the spring. His father had not believed in taking holidays, but Samuel found the idea of seeing another part of the country appealing and was studying guide books to find out what sights he might profitably see in the south while he was down there. His wife said she only wanted to see her grandson, but they could not spend all the hours of the day imposing on Eleanor Armistead.

He realised he had been standing lost in thought and that Jack was looking at him in puzzlement. 'You'd better see if there's a cottage free, then,' he said gruffly and strode off towards his office.

Jack was surprised and relieved for he had not been at all sure Mr Rishmore would allow them to rent from him for all his brave words to Mr Bradley. He crossed the yard more slowly than his employer, reluctant to go indoors again after his days of freedom. After a last longing glance up at the sky, he pushed the heavy door open and went inside.

Isaac Butterfield looked up from the side office and smiled at the sight of his assistant's happy face. 'You found her?'

'Yes.' Jack explained yet again what had transpired.

'So Armistead is still making things difficult for her,' Isaac muttered. 'The man must have lost his reason to pursue her like this when she's made it plain she doesn't want him. Thank goodness she escaped from him last time. We must make sure he doesn't capture her again.'

In the corridor Samuel, who had been coming to ask Isaac something, stood like someone carved from stone. *Marcus* was the man who had kidnapped that young woman? He stretched out his hand to push the door open, then let it fall again. He did not intend to discuss this in front of Jack. He would ask Isaac to stay behind after work and question him then.

He went back into his office, but could not settle. After fidgeting for a while, he got up and left the mill without telling anyone where he was going. He needed to find out the truth of all this.

Eli Makepeace looked up in surprise as Mr Rishmore strode unannounced into the small building that was used as lock-up, police station and magistrate's court. From the millowner's expression something was very wrong.

'We need to talk in private,' Samuel declared. As soon as Eli had closed the door of his office he said, 'I need to know – was my son-in-law the one responsible for kidnapping Emmy Carter?'

Eli stared at the town's most influential citizen, chewed one corner of his lip and wondered how much he dared say.

As if he had read the other man's mind, Samuel added, 'I want to know the full truth and I think you're the best one to tell me.' He grimaced. 'You should have said something sooner, man.'

'It's just that I have no real proof, sir.' In measured tones, Eli went through the information he had gathered.

Samuel's expression became increasingly grim as the facts, deductions and theories were laid before him. 'The housemaid was absolutely certain sure that Marcus had beaten my daughter?'

Eli nodded, feeling sorry for the millowner. He himself had seen Jane Rishmore on her wedding day and had never forgotten how unhappy she'd looked.

'If even half of this is true, I'll never forgive myself for forcing her to marry such a monster,' Samuel said in a voice that cracked as he spoke. He covered his eyes with his right hand for a moment as guilt flooded through him. It seemed to him now that he had deliberately looked the other way about this, ignoring his wife's hints that 'poor, dear Jane has a lot to put up with', ignoring even the evidence of his own eyes. He would regret this until the day he died. 'If only I could find Jane,' he muttered at last, his voice thick with emotion. 'What if she's in want? She could come back and live with us. I'd protect her.'

'Better not try to find her yet, sir,' Eli said gently. 'The law would be on the husband's side unless anything were proven.'

'But surely we can . . .'

'At the moment we can prove nothing. As I've pointed out, these are mostly my deductions and suppositions. I believe them to be true, but they wouldn't hold up in court. And if we said anything, we'd alert Armistead to the fact that we suspect him, whereas if we keep our suspicions to ourselves, he may grow careless. You can be sure I'll be ready for that. In the meantime you must act normally with him.'

'*Act normally with him*! How can I, now?'

'You have to, for Emmy Carter's sake.'

Samuel stared down at his tightly clasped hands for so long that Eli wondered if he was all right.

When he looked up, he said slowly, 'Eli, I'm truly grateful for your honesty today.'

'It was more than time we had a chat, sir. I'm worried about Emmy Carter coming back to Northby. If Armistead is still obsessed with her, she's in great danger and Jack Staley can't be with her every hour of the day.'

After work Jack made his way home with the greatest reluctance. His mother glared at him. 'You're back then.'

'Yes.'

When he didn't say anything else, Netta smirked. 'I knew you wouldn't find her. She'll have getten hersen another protector by now.'

'I did find her, and brought her back to stay with Parson.'

She began to clatter some dishes around, muttering, 'Well, at least you haven't brought her here, that's one relief.'

Shad, Ginny and Joe, who were sitting at the table, stopped eating to stare from their mother to their elder brother.

Jack glanced at them and saw that Ginny, who was always soft-hearted, had an anxious look on her face while Joey was huddled close to his sister. Shad winked at Jack, an expression of sympathy on his face. He never said much, but didn't miss much, either, and the look he cast at their mother was distinctly unfriendly.

Jack took a deep breath. Might as well get it over. 'I'm happy to tell you all that Emmy and I are getting wed as soon as the banns have been called and you're all invited to the wedding.'

A plate smashed to the ground. 'No! You can't do it!' his mother exclaimed shrilly, heedless of the shards of pottery around her. 'If you bring her back here, I'll walk out of the door and throw myself in the river.'

Anger rose in Jack as he suddenly remembered old quarrels between his mother and father. She had used such stupid threats then until in the end his father had laughed at them – and her. 'Go and do it, then,' he snapped. 'I shan't stop you!'

She put one hand up to her throat, opened her mouth then closed it again.

'Can we really come to the wedding?' Shad asked.

Jack turned to him. 'Of course you can, lad. In fact, I want you all there.'

Netta found her voice. 'They'll not!'

'How will you stop them, Mam?'

'I'll tear up their clothes afore I'll let them.'

He stared at her, aghast, realising this was the sort of threat she *would* carry out. She had once ripped up one of Meg's bodices because she said it was indecent. 'Right then, we'd better settle a few matters. Is there food for me?'

His mother nodded sullenly.

'Then serve it. And afterwards, leave washing the dishes. I've other things to tell you. I'm not having any more of these stupid threats of yours. You drove Meg away, always nagging her. You're not doing that to these three or to my Emmy.' Jack sat down and folded his arms.

The others finished their meal in silence. His mother pushed her food around her plate, then shoved it away from her and muttered something.

Afterwards Ginny stood up to clear the table, glancing anxiously towards her mother who was now weeping silently.

Jack said gently, 'Sit down again, Ginny love.'

His mother stood up. He'd seen that trick before, too. 'You as well!' he roared. 'Or I'll bloody well tie you down.' He sounded just like his father. He knew now why Jem had shouted a lot, by hell he did.

'Emmy's in trouble. Bad trouble. A rich man wants to use her like her mother and has already tried to kidnap her. Only she doesn't want him, she wants to marry me, and that's what we're going to do.'

'Let him have her, Jack. You can't afford to get on the wrong side of someone with money,' Netta begged.

He was sickened by her selfishness. 'How can you say that?'

She stared back at him defiantly. 'Because I'm thinking of you.'

'Well, I'm looking forward to the wedding,' Shad said. 'And if Mam lays a finger on any of my clothes, I'll rip hers up for her in return.'

Ginny gave Jack a shy smile. 'Your Emmy's lovely. I've seen her in town.' She looked nervously at her mother, then, in response to a nudge from Shad, said in a rush, 'I'd like to come to the wedding.'

Joey looked from one to the other, bewildered by the anger that was crackling between Jack and their mother.

Shad continued to talk quietly. 'I'm right glad for you too, Jack lad. And with what me an' Ginny earn, you won't have to give Mam much. If you can pay the rent here, I reckon we could manage the rest all right.'

With a sob, Netta rushed upstairs.

Jack looked at his brother gratefully. 'Thanks for your support, lad.' He smiled at them all. 'An' Mam can do as she pleases, but I want you three to come and meet Emmy properly after church on Sunday.'

'Is she as nice as she looks?' Ginny ventured.

'She's the kindest, prettiest lass in the world,' he said, a besotted smile on his face at the mere thought of his darling.

After Jack's return, Isaac thought long and hard, before deciding that he must see his niece. It was more than time she knew the truth about her parentage.

He was admitted to the Parsonage and was allowed to see Emmy on her own. 'Are you all right, my dear?'

'Yes.' Her face looked soft and happy. 'You know that Jack and I are going to be married?' She indicated that he should sit beside her on the sofa.

'He told me. I'm pleased for you.'

Her joyful expression clouded a little. 'We have to hope that Marcus Armistead will stop pursuing me.'

'He cannot be so stupid as to continue now that people know about him.'

She was not sure of that, but she did not intend to let fear of Marcus stop her marrying the man she loved. 'What did you want to see me about?'

'Your father.'

She stiffened and drew away from him. 'I don't want to know about him.'

'It's more than time. Please listen to me. You remember the man who came to your mother's funeral?'

'Mr Reynolds, the lawyer?'

'Yes. Well, he's also your uncle.'

She stared at him in shock. 'Why did he not say?'

Isaac shrugged. 'The Reynolds wanted nothing more to do with you and your mother after your father's death.' As she opened her mouth, looking angry now, he held up one hand. 'Let me finish. Your mother was married to your father, though she did not marry him for several months after they ran away together, which upset both families. I believe he married her because she was expecting his child – and of course that child was you. So your name is really Emmeline Reynolds and—'

'No! I want nothing to do with them. Nor will I ever take their name.'

'Emmy, my dear—'

Her expression was fierce now, her voice low and passionate. 'If they had looked after her after my father died, my mother would not have had to turn to a life like that. She was no more capable of looking after herself than a – a butterfly!'

He was silent, acknowledging to himself the truth of this, then said sadly, 'I should have done more, too. She was my sister.'

She nodded, the look she turned on him unusually severe.

'Did you never read those papers Douglas Reynolds gave you, Emmy?'

'No.'

'They contain your mother's marriage lines.'

She gave a mirthless laugh. 'They're still in your house, actually, hidden in the attic.' She explained.

'I'll bring them to you.'

She shrugged, not really wanting them – not wanting anything to do with her father's family, even angrier now that she knew the truth. 'The only thing I'm glad about is that I'm not bastard born. For Jack's sake.'

And even when her uncle Isaac retrieved the package of papers, she didn't open them, didn't want to. Let the Reynolds keep their secrets. She was Emmy Carter now.

Emmy settled in quickly at the Parsonage, finding the hours flying past as she shared the work and chatted to the others. In the evenings she started sewing some underclothes with Cass's help. She had intended to make herself a new dress, because she had enough money to buy some material and wanted to look nice for Jack. But Mrs Bradley brought out from her stores of cast-offs from rich friends a dress in fine blue wool that was so beautiful Emmy accepted it at once. It had hardly been worn and was of the finest quality material. The colour was so lovely it made her feel happy just to touch its soft folds. It had been made for a much taller and stouter woman so needed quite a few alterations, but Cass helped her work on it.

Two days after their return, Jack turned up at the Parsonage during his midday break and took Emmy to see the two cottages belonging to Mr Rishmore that were vacant. Neither of them was really suitable. The better one was too far outside the village for safety and the other was damp and very dark, situated in the middle of one of the narrow streets that ran parallel to Weavers Lane.

'It'll have to be this one,' Emmy said at last when they had walked round the four small dark rooms in silence. 'We can whitewash the walls. It'll look better then.'

Jack looked round and grimaced. 'I doubt it. And it'll still be damp. Eh, I wanted something better for us, love. The other place was far nicer, but here you'll be surrounded by neighbours.'

She looked up at him, her eyes troubled. 'I'm bringing danger on you just by being here.'

'No.' He tugged her into his arms, not holding her too tightly which always made her tense, and for once she rested her head against his chest and sighed. 'I can't bear the thought of losing you, darling Emmy,' he murmured into her soft shining hair. 'If we have to move away, we'll go together.'

'And your family?'

'Are not in danger like you are.'

'I don't want to take you away from them – or from a good job. And I don't really want to leave Northby.'

He laughed, a bitter sound. 'I'd be glad to find some other job.' When she looked up at him in surprise, he confessed, 'I'm not made to be shut up indoors. The noise of that mill drives me mad while the office is like a – a cage. Sometimes I feel like running out of it and never going back.'

'But what else could you do?' she asked with a frown.

'I've allus had a dream to run a little shop and be my own master. You can pop in and out as you please if you're your own master, walk to the door and just enjoy a bit of sun on your face. And there's no damned machinery pounding away. Eh, that'd be the life!' He sighed. 'Only you need money to start up and buy the stock – and I'd need some experience before I'd know how to run a shop properly. I have none and no chance of getting any, so I don't know why I even think of it.' He smiled ruefully. 'Well, you can't stop yourself dreaming, can you?'

'I have the money, Jack. Mrs Tibby's savings. And we could sell the silver, too, if that's not enough.'

He smiled down at her. 'If we didn't have this threat hanging over us, maybe we could do summat like that, but as it is I think you're safer here in Northby, where Parson and Eli Makepeace can keep an eye on you, than among strangers. And you'll have Hercules, too, don't forget. He'd soon let you know if someone tried to break in.'

Emmy didn't say anything else that night, but she was beginning to feel depressed. Not once since her return had she dared go out alone and things wouldn't change overnight just because she had a wedding ring. Marcus Armistead was not only evil but obsessed. When he had held her prisoner his eyes had had a wild light which had frightened her far more than the horrible way he had touched her – and those staring eyes haunted her nightmares still.

Samuel Rishmore called Isaac into his office. 'Where's Staley going to live after he's married?'

'There's only the cottage on Bates Road.'

'What about the place Mrs Oswald used to live in? That's still empty.'

'It belongs to the Armisteads.'

'Marcus is selling everything and intends to settle in Manchester permanently. There's someone interested in buying Moor Grange but they don't want all the other little places so he offered them to me. Go and see Armistead's man of business. Tell him I'll buy them all if he'll push the sale through quickly.'

Isaac stared at him. 'That's very kind of you.'

Samuel shrugged, his expression bleak. 'I hope I am learning a little kindness. If ever I find my daughter again, I pray we can lay the past to rest and live happily together.' He shook his head. 'Jane must have planned things very well to have got away with no trace.'

'She always seemed a clever little lass when she used to come into the mill to see you. If she'd been a boy . . .'

'Yes. I didn't give her enough credit.' Samuel changed the subject firmly, unused to baring his innermost thoughts. 'How are your own daughters?'

'Dinah's very happy at her school and doesn't want to come home even during the holidays, because of her mother. I miss her. Lal's unhappy, but her one visit home was such a disaster, I haven't let her come back again. I fear she's too like her mother.' Isaac bowed his head as he admitted, 'I may have to find somewhere to put my wife away, somewhere they'll care for her properly. She's growing increasingly strange in her behaviour. Not really rational at all now.'

They stood there in silence for a few minutes, two ageing, unhappy men who had shared an almost-friendship since they were both lads.

Isaac went into Manchester the very next day and spent an hour with Marcus Armistead's head clerk, a man he disliked on sight but who was only too eager to do business with him. When he returned to Northby he was able to report that a price had been agreed and they had been granted permission to take immediate possession of Chad's Cottage.

When the banns were called that first Sunday, the congregation buzzed like a hive of bees as people heard that Jack Staley was to marry Emmy Carter. The buzzing grew even louder and was accompanied by shocked looks as Mr Rishmore and his wife paused briefly outside the church to wish the young couple well, and then Isaac Butterfield lingered to talk to them for quite some time.

From a corner of the churchyard Gus Norris watched the young couple sourly. He'd already sent word to Moor Grange that the lass had come back to the Parsonage, but this new development would have to be reported as quickly as possible. He'd best go across to Padstall that afternoon. Why the hell did a rich man like Mr Armistead, who could have any number of women, want this unwilling one so much that he'd risk kidnapping her? It didn't make any sense.

What's more, if Mr Rishmore himself approved of the match, Gus didn't want to get involved in any funny business that might upset his landlord. Unfortunately, though, George Duckworth knew too much about him and he didn't dare go against his cousin's orders.

Hiring a nag, he rode despondently over the tops to Moor Grange. Once there he left a message with the snooty butler, who said his master was in Manchester and he'd send the message on. And the old bugger didn't even offer Gus a wet of ale to see him on his way back.

Two weeks before the wedding Jack turned up at the Parsonage in the afternoon, beaming so broadly that Cass, who had let him in, gaped at him in surprise, for he usually wore a rather serious expression.

Emmy heard his voice and came running down the back stairs with the dog close behind her. 'It's such a fine day I thought we could go for a stroll,' she said, carefully avoiding the word 'walk' which always sent Hercules into such paroxysms of yelping delight that it prevented any further conversation. She didn't intend to take the animal with her this time as she wanted to talk quietly to Jack about what they would need for their new home.

'Has something happened?' she asked as they walked down the Lane. 'You look full of news.'

He nodded. 'I am.'

When he didn't speak, she poked him in the ribs. 'Well, aren't you going to tell me what?'

'In a minute or two.'

They came to the place Emmy thought of as 'Mrs Tibby's cottage' and she stopped to look at it, as she always did.

When she would have moved on, Jack held her back and pulled a key out of his pocket, dangling it in front of her. 'Want to go inside?'

She stopped dead. 'How did you get the key? Doesn't this place belong to *him?*'

'No, Mr Rishmore's just bought it from him, and guess what?' He stopped at the door to beam down at her, then could hold back the news no longer. 'He says we can rent it if we want to.'

She gasped and tears filled her eyes.

'Is something wrong? I thought you'd be pleased!' Jack opened the door and guided her inside.

'Of course I'm pleased, you fool!' she said, wiping away a tear with the back of her hand and fumbling for her hand-kerchief. 'I'm crying for joy.'

He chuckled. 'Oh, well, if those are happy tears that's all right.' He pulled out his own crumpled handkerchief and wiped them away, then bent his head to kiss her. For the first time she gave herself to him gladly, pressing her body against his and kissing him hungrily. He did not dare prolong the kiss but his heart lightened considerably and he began to feel hopeful that if he continued to be patient with her, he'd gradually undo the harm Armistead had wrought.

When she pulled away, he offered her his arm. 'Shall we look round our future home, Miss Carter? The furniture is yours anyway, apparently, only you've never claimed it. Just look at it! Isn't it grand?'

She smiled as bitter-sweet emotions chased through her. 'I never thought I'd dare claim it.'

'Well, you can now. This place has just been sitting empty since Mrs Tibby died, apparently, waiting to be sold. We'll have to check what needs doing.'

She ran one fingertip across the dusty top of the sideboard, leaving a mark in the dust. 'I shall have to give the place a good bottoming. Oh, I shall treasure her things, absolutely treasure them.'

They spent a delightful hour examining every inch of the place, with Jack making plans for some necessary minor repairs.

'Oh, my love.' Emmy looked up at him misty-eyed. 'Things are going so well. Surely that man will stop trying to capture me now?'

'I hope so,' he said carefully, not wanting to mar her happiness, 'but I don't want you to take any risks, my darling.'

'No. Of course not.'

But her joy had visibly dimmed and he felt the old anger churning through him that one wicked man could make so many other people unhappy. Would this never end?

Chapter Twenty

The following day as soon as the main chores were finished at the Parsonage Mrs Bradley sent Cass to the cottage with Emmy to help her scrub it from top to bottom. The two young women chatted as they worked and by late afternoon had everything gleaming.

'I can't believe I'm going to live here again,' Emmy said, smiling round her. 'And with Jack.' It felt as if all her dreams had come true.

'After this you've got to stop doing any scrubbing,' said Cass as they were walking home. 'You don't want your hands looking all red when he puts the ring on, do you? We'll rub some of Cook's goose grease into them tonight. Eh, you're going to be well set up there, aren't you?' She realised her companion was not listening, however, and nudged her. 'What's up?'

'That man!' Emmy pointed with a finger that trembled. 'The tall one. He's the one who's been following me, watching me.'

Cass stopped dead, her mouth open in shock. But there was no one visible who matched Emmy's description, and although they'd been out together several times, she couldn't remember seeing anyone following them. 'Are you sure?'

Emmy saw the doubt on her friend's face. 'I'm not imagining things, Cass.'

'What does Jack say about it?'

'I haven't told him. He's got enough to worry about. Only, what's going to happen after we're married if this doesn't stop?'

'You have to tell Jack and Parson and—' She broke off as she saw another man in the distance and shrieked at the top of her voice, 'Constable Makepeace! Yoo-hoo! Wait for us.' Grasping Emmy by the arm, she rushed across the street and up the hill.

'Cass, stop! You shouldn't do this. There's nothing he can do to help,' Emmy panted, but her friend was bigger and stronger than she was, and she could not prevent Cass from dragging her over to the constable.

'There's a man been following Emmy!' Cass announced breathlessly. 'And she won't tell anyone about it, but I thought you should know.'

'I'm being careful,' Emmy muttered.

'Do you know who he is?' Eli asked.

'Gus Norris,' she admitted reluctantly.

'I might have known he'd be involved. Him and his cousin George are a pair of villains.' He looked at Emmy's anxious face and his expression softened. 'I'll have a word with him for you.'

'It's no use, I can't prove anything,' Emmy said despairingly. 'He'll just say I've made a mistake.'

'You leave it to me, young woman.' Eli lowered his voice and added, 'I'm keeping a careful watch on the Parsonage, and I'll be at your wedding, too.'

But she was regretting now that she'd ever come back and put Jack in danger. Why could no one do anything to stop Marcus Armistead? Was Gus Norris working for him?

She was still wondering whether she should run away again, for Jack's sake, when she fell asleep that night.

Eli went along to the Horse and Rider that evening and ordered a glass of ale. As the woman behind the counter teased him about honouring them with a visit, he smiled and nodded, noting who was there and seeing one man down his ale and leave hastily.

Just as Eli was draining his glass and debating going home for his evening meal, he saw Gus Norris come in. The man looked to be in a bad mood and when he saw the constable, hesitated visibly.

That lass wasn't imagining things, Eli decided. There's definitely something going on. If ever I've seen a guilty look, that's it.

But he merely set his glass down, thanked the woman for the ale and left without saying anything further. No use warning them he was on to them.

Two days later Emmy and Cass were taking in some washing, laughing and talking together in the back garden. Hercules had gone out on his own business, as he sometimes did. When her friend went back into the washhouse, where the fortnightly washerwoman was busy with the poss stick, to bring out the next load, Emmy continued unpegging the last few articles.

Suddenly a man jumped out from behind some bushes and grabbed her, clapping his hand across her mouth. He was wearing a muffler round his face, but she recognised him at once. Gus Norris. She struggled and tried to scream, but could do nothing against such a big, strong man, especially when another appeared to help tie her up and gag her. It was all done in a couple of minutes.

They carried her across the churchyard to a cart waiting in the lane beyond and threw her into the back of the vehicle, covering her with an old blanket.

She could only lie there, rigid with fear, as the cart drove off, unable to do anything, even kick away the blanket, because when she tried, a heavy body leaned on her so that she couldn't move. After a while, the weight was removed but by then they sounded to be outside the town, for the wheels had a more muffled sound to them.

Where were they taking her? How could no one have noticed what was happening?

The cart jolted and rumbled along for what seemed like a very long time. Emmy was too terrified even to weep. All she could do was pray that Cass had missed her. Surely, surely they would be looking for her?

Where were these men taking her? She could guess.

343

To Moor Grange.
To Marcus Armistead.

Cass came out of the laundry at the back of the house with another basket of clean washing. 'Emmy love, what do you—' As she saw the overturned basket and clean linen scattered across the grass she froze then dropped her own basket and began to screech at the top of her voice. She kept on screeching till the laundrywoman, Cook and Mrs Bradley all came rushing out.

'Emmy's gone!' she gasped. 'Look! She'd never have dropped the clean things. Someone's took her again.' She began sobbing.

Mrs Bradley ordered, 'Be quiet this minute!' and walked past the basket. There were scrape marks on the lawn and behind the bushes she found some large men's footprints. 'Stay where you are!' she tossed over her shoulder, swallowing her own fear and anxiety as she continued to examine the garden. There was no sign of Emmy, no sign of anyone. Only that line of incriminating footprints.

'Run and fetch Constable Makepeace,' she ordered, and gave Cass's arm a quick shake when the girl did not move. 'Hurry! Mrs Jonas, please go back to the washing, and Cook—' Her voice failed her for a minute and she looked helplessly at the other woman.

'I'll go back to my baking,' Cook said gruffly. 'Nothing I can do here.' But even as she was turning away, she had an idea. 'What about Jack Staley?'

'Oh, my, yes. We should let him know.' Prudence tried to think clearly.

'I'll send sexton's lad,' said Cook. 'He's allus hanging round.'

Prudence nodded and went to find her husband.

By the time the constable arrived, Gerald had joined the horrified group standing at the edge of the back lawn. A grave-faced Eli examined the footprints, following them across the almost bare winter earth of the vegetable garden. The trail led to the back wall of the churchyard. Beyond it was a little-used lane which led up to a track across the moors. But the ground there was too stony to reveal much, unlike the soft soil of the vegetable garden.

'They're bound to have taken her away in a vehicle, but where did they get it from?' he muttered to himself, then went back to the Parson. 'I have to get down to the Horse and Rider at once, sir. Can't stop to talk.'

'I'll come with you,' Gerald offered.

'No, best you stay here, sir. When Jack arrives, tell him what's happened and make him wait here for me. Don't let him do anything till I've seen him.'

He strode down the lane to the alehouse. The place was empty but a woman was wiping the counter in a listless way. 'I'm looking for Gus Norris,' Eli told her.

She stared round vaguely. 'He were here earlier, but he's gone out.'

'Was he on his own?' As she simply stared at him, he rapped out sharply, 'Answer me! Was Gus on his own?'

'No, he wasn't.'

Before she could speak another woman came through the door. Dorrie Milford had bought a half-share in the alehouse from George and had set up here with Gus. She had a hard, bitter face and a sharp manner and Eli did not trust her an inch.

'What's the matter, Constable?' she asked.

'I'm looking for Gus. He was in here earlier, apparently.'

'Well, he isn't here now, as you can see for yourself, so I'm afraid we can't help you.' Dorrie gestured to the barmaid to leave and began to turn away herself.

Eli said mildly, 'Running this place will be much more difficult for you if I don't feel you've co-operated with me.'

'And it'll be no life at all if someone hits me over the head one dark night,' Dorrie retorted.

'Who would do that?'

She hesitated, then sighed and lowered her voice. 'Someone rich enough to do as he pleases. Someone as is very friendly with the previous owner. And if Gus is involved it's because they forced him. All he wants is a quiet life – same as me.' She folded her arms across her breasts and said flatly and emphatically, 'I'm not saying another word apart from that because I daren't.'

345

Eli nodded, certain she was referring to Marcus Armistead which was no surprise. But it *was* a surprise to see how afraid she was of the man. This mystery was growing nastier by the minute. Not just the kidnapping of a pretty young woman, but a whole group of people afraid of Armistead. What had he done to inspire such fear?

When the sexton's son burst into the mill office, he rushed straight across to Jack. 'You've to come at once to the Parsonage. They've took Emmy!' Caught up in the excitement he didn't even notice Mr Rishmore and Isaac inside the other office, staring at him in shock.

Jack tossed his quill pen aside and thrust his stool away so violently it crashed to the ground. Isaac stepped out of his office. 'I'll come with you, Jack.'

'So will I,' Samuel echoed.

But Jack had already left at a run, pounding through the town without cap or coat, his feet thudding on the cobbles. He burst into the Parsonage by the front door, heading straight for the Parson's study. 'Where's Emmy?' he gasped.

When he heard what had happened, Jack spun round. 'I'm going after her.'

Gerald grabbed his shoulder. 'Not yet! Eli Makepeace said you were to wait here for him.'

Jack stared at him, anguish in his eyes. 'How can I just stand here when they've got Emmy? Who knows what they're doing to her?'

'Sometimes it doesn't pay to rush into things. Eli is a wise fellow. Wait for him, Jack.'

When the cart began to slow down Emmy moaned in her throat.

Her captor didn't say a word, just wrapped a cloth round her head so that she couldn't see where she was, then picked her up and tossed her over his shoulder like a sack of potatoes. She hung there helplessly, head down, as he strode across ground that seemed soft underfoot. She strained her senses, desperately trying to work out where she was. The country, definitely. There were no noises around them. Surely there'd be noises if this were the Grange? If it was another isolated cottage, she doubted she'd get away from Armistead a second time, and since she had made a fool of him before, she knew he'd be wanting his revenge. He'd hurt her, and enjoy doing it.

Terror roiled along her veins.

She could feel the soft ground give way to some sort of paving and a few seconds later there was the sound of a door opening. The man took little care with her and bumped her head on the lintel as he entered. With a gag in her mouth, she couldn't even cry out.

When someone took off the blindfold she saw that she was in a room with a barred window that looked out only on to a wall. An old woman was waiting for her, face impassive. There were two men with her, Gus and a stranger. The latter said harshly, 'Call out if she gives you any trouble.'

'She won't.'

When the men had gone the woman stared at Emmy as if she was a bit of meat on a butcher's slab. 'If you promise to behave, I'll help you relieve yoursen an' give you a bite of food. If you cause me any trouble, you'll go hungry and thirsty and can piss yoursen for all I care.'

Emmy swallowed hard. 'I'll behave.'

The woman loosened the bonds round her legs, then helped her use the bucket in the corner. 'Didn't think I were goin' to untie your hands an' give you a chance to escape, did you?' she jeered. 'He pays me well to keep an eye on his lasses.'

'Marcus Armistead, you mean?'

The woman slapped her across the face. 'If you say that name again, I'll gag you an' you'll get nowt to eat.'

Emmy said nothing more. She forced herself to eat and drink, telling herself she had to keep her strength up, though the bread was tasteless in her mouth and hard to chew, and the lukewarm black tea was a foul brew.

'What's going to happen now?' she asked.

The old woman shrugged and sat down, closing her eyes.

Emmy was left to sit awkwardly on the chair with her hands still tied behind her. After an hour, it was so painful she said, 'Please could you tie my hands differently? My arms are going numb.'

'The old woman stared at her, then went to the door. 'Need to do summat about her hands.'

The man she didn't recognise came in, yawning as if he had been taking a nap. 'What's up?'

'Her hands are going numb. You can tie 'em in front of her while I'm with her. She won't get away from me.'

Emmy could not help crying out when her hands were loosened and the numbness turned to a tingling that became very painful.

'Let her stay loose for a few minutes till her arms are all right.'

After a while they tied Emmy up again and dumped her on the chair. Time passed very slowly. It was dark now, with the moon appearing and disappearing from behind some clouds, its light adding to the single candle burning on the mantelpiece and the dull glow of a smouldering fire in the small grate.

Emmy did not see how anyone could possibly find her. Even if they went looking for Marcus Armistead they'd discover no sign of her with him. As the minutes dragged into hours, fear sat like a heavy stone in her belly, making her jerk at every sound.

One or other of the men peered into the room at regular intervals to check on her, but neither said anything. The old woman brewed some more tea and offered Emmy a drink when it had cooled down. 'I could put a few herbs in it. Calm you down a bit, stop you fighting him. Won't do you any good to fight and it'll only make him wild. He can be dangerous when he's angry.'

'No.'

'Suit yoursen. But them as took my advice got out alive an' whole afterwards,' she said as off-handedly as if she were chatting to a neighbour at the market.

After which Emmy felt even more terrified. What others? And surely Marcus Armistead wouldn't *kill* her?

Isaac turned up at the Parsonage shortly after Jack, accompanied by Samuel Rishmore. Prudence let them in and showed them into the parlour. 'We're waiting for Eli Makepeace to return,' she said, then went back to the kitchen.

Jack looked at his employer and the head clerk, too miserable to care what he said or did in front of them. 'If he's hurt Emmy, I'll kill him.'

'If he's hurt your young woman, the law will deal with him,' Samuel corrected.

'Armistead's rich enough to get away with it if we don't stop him ourselves,' Jack said bitterly. 'The law won't be any use to us.'

'I'll make sure he doesn't escape retribution, believe me,' Samuel promised. 'He hurt my daughter, too, you know.'

Both Isaac and Gerald stared at him in shock, but Jack hardly heard and went back to pacing up and down between the window and the door. The others did not try to stop him but exchanged anxious glances from time to time.

Jack saw the constable coming along the street and rushed out into the hall to fling the door open. 'What's happened?'

Mrs Bradley joined them without a word, looking as if she'd been crying.

Eli went to stand in front of the fire and warm his backside. 'Gus Norris was seen earlier today with a stranger, but he's left town. It's very possible he was the one who took Emmy. Dorrie Milford seems to know something but will only hint that a rich man is involved, for fear of retribution.'

'Armistead,' Jack growled. 'We should be out trying to find him, not wasting time like this.'

'Let the constable speak, lad,' Gerald put in quietly.

'I think it is Armistead,' the constable agreed, 'but I'd guess this has been very carefully planned and it'll be hard to prove that he's involved. I've asked around and no one seems to have seen a vehicle waiting in the lane.'

Prudence leaned forward on a sudden thought. 'Have you spoken to the grave digger? He was working in the churchyard earlier.'

'Can you send someone to fetch him?' Eli asked.

Samuel said quietly, 'My carriage is completely at your

disposal, Makepeace, and as much money as you need to hire other help. Can you send for my coachman as well, Mrs Bradley?'

She bustled out, glad to have something to do.

Eli nodded, thinking it through carefully. 'We need to check several things. I wonder, Jack, if you and Mr Butterfield would go into Manchester and see if you can find any sign of Armistead and Emmy there? Do you know where his office is situated?'

'Yes,' said Jack, bouncing to his feet.

Samuel held up one hand to stop him. 'I can give you his home address as well.'

Eli looked sternly at the distraught young man. 'I want you to do nothing except try to find him and stay near him. You can leave a message for me with the night watchman at his office.' He gave a tight smile. 'I've been making inquiries for a while now and have spoken to the watchman a few times. He isn't fond of Mr Armistead and has been as co-operative as he dares. Like Dorrie he's afraid. If I don't receive your solemn word that you won't confront Armistead, Jack, you're going nowhere. I'll lock you up to stop you if I have to.'

With the prospect of action in front of him, Jack felt the tension inside himself ease a little. 'I'll do nothing unless Emmy's in danger.'

'I'll be with him, Eli,' Isaac said in his usual calm, dry tone, 'and I shan't allow him to do anything rash, I promise you.' He pulled out his watch. 'If we hurry we can just catch the afternoon stage coach into Manchester.'

When they had gone, Eli admitted to the two gentlemen, 'It's my opinion we shall find the young woman out at Moor Grange or one of the nearby farms, but I wanted Staley out of the way. He's as strong as his father and I don't want him going berserk with Armistead.'

Cass knocked on the door and showed in the grave digger who seemed ill at ease in such company. However, he had not only seen a cart in the lane but had recognised the men on it.

'Ah!' said Eli softly, glad Jack had left. 'Who were they?'

'Gus Norris an' Bill Sully,' the grave digger said. 'He's got a smallholding out on the moors, Bill has, Nasty sod he is. Lives with his mother an' she's as bad. I thought better of Gus than mixing with folk like that.'

With some careful questioning, Eli found out where the smallholding was situated and sent the grave digger out to give directions to Rishmore's coachman when he arrived.

'Shall we go then, gentlemen?' Gerald asked.

'There's no need for you to come, Parson,' Eli objected.

'You may need every bit of help you can get,' he said quietly.

But first they had to wait for the carriage, pacing up and down while Eli stood very calm and collected, knowing some things could not be hurried. 'Ah, there it is!'

The men got quickly into the carriage while the grave digger gave directions to the coachman. At the last minute Hercules scrambled into the coach with them.

'I'm afraid you can't come with us, my lad,' Gerald told him.

Eli frowned. 'Wait! That's Emmy's dog, isn't it?'

'Yes.'

'Then he might be able to find her where we couldn't,' Eli said. 'Let him come with us. We just need something to tie him up with, if necessary.'

So after a short delay to find a piece of rope they set off, Eli in his usual thoughtful silence, Gerald stroking the dog absent-mindedly and Samuel lost in his own dark thoughts, wondering where his daughter was and how she was managing. The longer she was away, the more he worried about her.

Chapter Twenty-one

The night seemed to go on for ever to Emmy and when she heard a rider outside she didn't know whether to be glad or sorry that something was going to happen.

The old woman went to look out of the window. 'Ah. Wondered what was keeping him.'

Emmy could hardly breathe for terror. Surely this wasn't *him?*

Another stranger came in, breathless. 'That bugger Makepeace has been asking around at the alehouse in Northby an' he's out searching, so we'd better move her on quick.'

The terror eased just a little as Emmy realised she wouldn't have to face Marcus Armistead yet. And if people were looking for her, there must be a slight chance of rescue. She had to hold tight to that hope, had to. If only she could leave them a sign. They were whispering to one another, their backs turned to her, so she eased her handkerchief out of her waistband with her fingertips and flicked it to one side. She didn't even have time to see where it fell.

Gus stepped forward. 'Come on, you.'

'Just a minute!' The old woman stopped to pick something up and wave it at Emmy. 'You dropped this! Nice little handkerchief that is. Finder's keepers.' She stuffed it in her own waistband.

'Don't try anything like that again or you'll regret it,' Gus snapped.

Emmy swallowed hard and said nothing, but tears welled in her eyes and she thought for a moment she saw a look of shame in his. But if she did it was soon gone and she let out an involuntary grunt as he heaved her over his shoulder and started moving.

They shoved her into a carriage and this time Gus got in with her. The other two climbed up on the box and they set off. The bumping and jolting were so bad that Emmy was tossed about, but Gus did nothing to keep her steady, just continued to stare at her sourly.

Once they stopped and one of the men got down, calling farewell to the others. As the carriage set off again, Gus said abruptly, 'When we get there you'd be well advised to do as the gentleman asks. It'll go easier for you that way.'

He slumped down, hating to see the terror on her face, wishing he were anywhere but here. He was getting more than a bit worried about the fate of the other girls he had delivered to Marcus Armistead. One had not been seen again while others had left the district immediately afterwards, refusing to say what had happened to them but vowing never to return.

'I'll never do as he asks,' Emmy said fiercely. 'And I don't know how you can live with your conscience, doing something like this. I'll tell them who captured me.'

'By the time he's done with you, you'll be glad to keep your mouth shut, just like the others were.' But Gus sighed. He didn't like this, not at all. It was not his conscience that was worrying him so much as his sense of self-preservation. He didn't want to be involved in murder – or anything else that weird bugger did!

Jack and Isaac sat in silence as the stage coach rumbled along the Manchester road. The other passengers made no attempt to converse. In the flickering light of the single lamp suspended from the ceiling their faces looked weary and drawn.

It seemed to take longer than usual to reach Manchester, and when the coach arrived they had trouble finding a cab. Isaac waited with arms folded while Jack paced up and down near the cab stand, scanning the street. When at last they heard the sound of hooves and a cab came clopping round the corner, Jack heaved a sigh of relief.

Isaac stepped forward to say to the driver, 'I'm prepared to pay handsomely if you'll stay with us for the next few hours and, if necessary, lend us a hand. A young woman has been kidnapped and we're searching for her.'

'How handsomely, sir?'

'A guinea for the next four hours.'

The man nodded, giving them a tight smile. 'I'll stick with you, sir. As long as it's legal.'

'It is indeed.'

There were no lighted windows upstairs at Armistead's offices and it took a while to attract the attention of the elderly caretaker in the basement.

'Have you seen Mr Armistead?' Isaac asked.

'Ah. Left here about half an hour ago.'

Isaac took out a half-crown piece. 'Any idea where he might have gone?'

The caretaker stared at it and shifted his feet uneasily. 'Home, I suppose, sir. He usually does when it's late. I call a cab for him sometimes. Not tonight, though. He said he was in a hurry and would hail one down at the corner. Do you need his address?'

'I already have it.' Isaac handed over the coin.

But the manservant who answered the door at Marcus Armistead's house said his master had not been there since he'd left for his office that morning, and no amount of promised largesse would make him offer any suggestions about where else they could search.

'Let's go back to that caretaker,' Isaac said as they drove away. 'He may know something else.'

Jack nodded, containing his impatience only with difficulty.

At first the old man denied knowing anything else, but the sight of a golden sovereign on Isaac's outstretched palm made him hesitate and lick his lips.

'You won't tell Mr Armistead I said owt?' he asked in a hoarse whisper.

'No. I'll not even mention that we've seen you, I promise.'

'Well, he does sometimes visit a brothel. I think it's called the

355

Red House' The caretaker sniggered. 'It's a place for the gentry, they say.' He gave them the address in a low voice, looking over his shoulder as he did so.

'One more favour, my friend,' Isaac said. 'If Constable Makepeace turns up, will you tell him what you've told us? I've no doubt he'll show his appreciation as well.'

The man nodded.

Jack strode back to the cab, waited for Isaac to get in, then flung himself down next to him. 'If Armistead's got my Emmy there . . .'

'You'll do nothing. Eli is the man to sort this out.'

Jack looked at him sideways then clamped his lips together. If he had even the slightest hint that Emmy was inside this place, he did not intend to wait for anything or anyone.

The cab drove slowly along the dark streets, but although it was past midnight now, Jack felt alert and ready for action. He looked down at himself, glad of his big, strong body. Clenching his hands into fists he studied them, feeling anger swell his veins.

Samuel Rishmore's coachman stopped at the end of a rough track and leaned down to call to his master, 'It'll not do the carriage any good to take it down there.'

'Never mind the damned carriage, just hurry up!' his master shouted back.

Muttering under his breath, the man told the horses to walk on.

They bumped down a track that seemed made of potholes towards the dark cottage belonging to Bill Sully. When they arrived a dog somewhere began to bark hysterically and Hercules growled and pawed at the carriage door. There was no sign of the inhabitants of the cottage, although they could not have failed to hear the carriage approaching,

Eli told the coachman to turn the carriage round ready to leave, then looked at the Parson. 'Perhaps you could bring the dog with you, Mr Bradley? It'll know if Emmy's here better than we ever could. Mr Rishmore, I think you should accompany us, as Magistrate.' He didn't wait for an answer but went to bang on the front door, rubbing his hands together to warm them as he waited, his breath clouding the air.

It was a long time before it was answered by an old woman who was, as Eli didn't fail to notice, fully dressed.

'If you're lost . . .' she began.

'We're not. We're searching for a young woman who's been abducted. We've been told that your son is involved.'

'There's no young woman here. An' my Bill wouldn't do owt like that.'

'Then you won't mind if we search the house, will you?'

She scowled and stayed where she was. 'You've no right to do that. No right at all.' As Samuel Rishmore stepped out of the shadows, however, she gasped and took a quick step backwards.

'As Magistrate, I have every right to search for a missing person,' he said curtly. 'Stand aside if you please, my good woman.'

Even as he was speaking Gerald Bradley felt Hercules began to pull on his lead, his nose down, and as Mrs Sully fell back, the dog dragged him inside the house, moving to and fro, yipping softly. The animal led them to a chair and began barking, looking round at them as if he wanted to tell them something.

Exchanging a quick glance with the Parson, Eli moved forward. 'Was she here, lad?' He caught sight of something on the floor under the nearby table and moved forward to pick up a piece of rope. When he held it out to Hercules, the dog began to bark furiously.

Eli turned to the householder. 'This is the young woman's dog. He knows her scent. I think she's been here.'

'No, she ain't.'

The dog moved so suddenly he pulled the leash out of the Parson's hand. He began to leap at the old woman, who struck out at him, trying to keep him away.

As soon as he was sure the dog wasn't trying to bite her Eli held up one hand to prevent anyone intervening, trying to understand what Hercules was doing. He saw a scrap of white material poking out of the woman's waistband. The dog seemed to be concentrating on that. Stepping forward, he tweaked it

357

out. 'Was this what you were looking for, lad?' he asked gently, holding it out.

Hercules grabbed at it, whining in his throat and looking at them again.

'It's a handkerchief,' Eli said grimly. 'And it's got an E embroidered on the corner.'

Gerald took it out of his hand to examine it. 'My wife teaches girls to embroider like that. I can't swear to it, but it's very likely Emmy's handkerchief.'

'Found it at the market in Northby,' the old woman said. 'Don't know who it belonged to afore.'

Eli changed tack, utterly certain now that Emmy had been kept prisoner here. 'Where's your son?'

'How should I know?' She leered at him. 'Out with a woman, I should think.'

'Or maybe he's on the way to Manchester, taking the girl to Marcus Armistead?'

For a moment fear showed on her face, further confirmation that they were on the right track. Eli turned to the others. 'I'll just check the rest of the house, but it's my guess they've already left. We'll follow them to Manchester.'

Samuel Rishmore looked at Mrs Sully as they were leaving. 'If I think you're involved I shall not hesitate to charge you with assisting in an abduction.'

She gave him a resentful look, turned her back on them and began to poke the fire. 'Shut the door after you.'

Outside they found the carriage facing the way they had come, ready to leave. Around them was a stark moonlit landscape of black and white. As the others got into the vehicle Eli gave instructions to the coachman then clambered in after them. Reaching down, he patted Hercules on the head. 'You're a good boy.'

The animal whined softly in its throat and settled at his feet as the carriage jolted on through the darkness along the rough moorland tracks. Eli could not see any possibility that they would arrive in time to save Emmy from whatever Armistead had planned, but he didn't say so. The other men were equally silent, their expressions grim.

As they regained the Manchester road with its more level surface, Samuel opened the window to yell, 'Drive as fast as you can!'

Emmy felt the change in the road surface and later saw through the carriage window the lights that suggested they'd reached Manchester. 'Where are we going?' People could just vanish in some parts of the city, she knew from her childhood.

'Never you mind.' Gus was still in a sour mood, unhappy with being forced to participate in this evening's work. 'Just you remember what I told you an' do as the gentleman asks.'

'And just you remember that I'll never do as Marcus Armistead asks. Never.' She saw an even more worried expression settle on his face and added, 'I think he killed my mother. Will you let him kill me as well?'

His mouth fell open. 'It were a tramp as killed your ma.'

'I don't think so, and neither does Mr Makepeace. He'll find me, you know. He won't give up. He'll know who's arranged all this.'

The thought of the constable pursuing them worried Gus more than anything. 'If you don't shut up, I'll gag you again!' he said roughly. But although she didn't speak she kept her eyes fixed on him and he cursed the day he'd ever got involved with Armistead. If Gus's cousin had been part of this there might be some hope for the lass, because George wouldn't let things go too far. But Armistead had made it plain that George was not to know what was going on tonight.

After jolting through the streets for a long time, they came to a halt.

'Where are we?' Emmy asked.

'Shut up, I told you!' When the carriage door opened, Gus nudged Bill. 'Keep an eye on her while I check it's safe to take her inside.' By which he meant that George wasn't around.

Emmy could see that they were in a back lane behind a big house that was full of light in spite of the late hour, and this puzzled her still further.

The man on the rear door told Gus that George was out at

the front, talking to the customers, so he beckoned urgently and Bill, who was a much smaller man, staggered across carrying Emmy.

'Give her here!'

As Gus reached out for her, she jerked sideways as hard as she could and although this made her fall to the ground, it also delayed them a little.

'What did you do that for, you stupid bitch?' Gus demanded, itching to slap her but not daring to because Mr Armistead liked them unmarked and untouched. He heaved her across his shoulder and carried her into the kitchen, groaning as he saw his cousin had come through to the back.

'What's going on here?' George demanded.

'Delivery for Mr Armistead,' Gus told him and started to move on towards the back stairs.

'George, don't let them take me!' Emmy begged. 'He'll kill me for sure this time.'

He stared at her in shock. Madge's girl! What the hell was going on? He rounded on the doorman. 'How come no one told me she was expected?' As the man looked uncomfortable, George had a sudden thought and asked, 'Has this happened before?'

The man avoided his eyes and shrugged. 'He likes his extra pleasures kept quiet does Mr Armistead. Not for me to tell the owner no, is it?'

'I'm the owner, too,' George declared angrily.

The doorman shrugged again.

Another voice interrupted them. 'Ah, I see my little parcel has arrived.' Marcus walked into the room, smiling to see Emmy Carter so helpless. This time she wouldn't get a chance to escape.

Although he was much shorter than the other men there, he dominated the group with his air of confidence and his well-tailored clothes. They were used to doing as the gentry wanted and in a place like this, the gentry sometimes wanted strange things.

'Take her up to the top attic,' Marcus ordered. 'And if she tries to make a noise, gag her.'

George stood chewing the corner of his lip, then shrugged

and let them go. But he was not happy about this situation. He had not forgotten the girl who'd been murdered or the one who had left for London. 'Don't make too much noise and don't hurt her,' he told his partner as they carried the girl through.

Marcus smiled.

George did not like that smile. Not at all. He turned on his heel and went to the front of the house, waited a few minutes then ran lightly up the stairs the customers used. In the attics where the girls slept he opened the door that led to the small upper chamber, then jerked back quickly and slipped into a nearby room as someone started to come down the stairs towards him.

When Gus had gone George opened the door again and tiptoed quietly up into the roof space. Moving carefully, he squeezed behind some boxes near the door of the room Marcus was using, knowing there was a peephole in the side wall. He set his eye to it, grimly determined to make sure that his partner didn't go too far.

And if what he discovered confirmed certain suspicions he had been nursing, then there were going to be some changes round here, some very big changes.

'Well, Emmy Carter, so I have you at last,' Marcus said, looking down at the bound girl on the bed. 'And this time you definitely won't escape.'

She said nothing, holding her fear at bay by sheer will-power.

'Nothing to say for yourself, girl?'

'They're looking for me. They'll find me, too!' she managed to say on a note of defiance.

He laughed. 'No, they won't. You'll only be here tonight and if you're still alive in the morning I'll have you moved again. I've done it before. It's not hard to fool people. Even my partner has no idea what I get up to.'

Outside George stiffened. *If you're still alive in the morning!* Was the sod planning to kill her? Oh, hell, what was he going to do about this? And who exactly was looking for her? Was this just an empty threat or was someone really on Emmy's track?

Marcus began to remove his outer garments. 'I'm going to enjoy this,' he said in a quiet conversational tone as he moved towards her.

Not too much, you're not, George thought. I'm not having you murdering Madge's girl. But he saw Marcus's sword stick on a chair and that worried him. He didn't intend to rush in and get himself stabbed.

The house the caretaker had sent them to was dark, with not a sign of life to it. Jack didn't wait for Isaac but jumped out of the cab and went over to some men lounging under a lamp post. 'I thought there was a whore house here,' he said, pulling a coin from his pocket. 'The Red House?'

One of them straightened up. 'There was. It moved.' He held out his hand.

'When you've told me where,' Jack said quietly.

'Why do you want to know? You're not the sort as uses a place like that. It's gentry only. But I can find you a lass as won't look down her nose at you.'

Jack forced a laugh. 'It isn't for me. Another time, perhaps. This one is for my master.' He jerked his head in the direction of the cab.

'Ah. That's different.' The man rattled off an address and held his hand out. 'They call it The Golden Swan now, though.'

Jack dropped the coin in it and went to tell the driver the new address. 'Do you know the place?'

'Aye. Going up in the world, aren't we?'

In the darkness inside the cab Isaac said quietly, 'Remember, when we get there you're not to go barging inside, Jack. *Jack?* Are you listening to me?'

'If I think Emmy's in there, I'm not going to sit and wait for another man to come and rescue her,' he said in a low, fierce voice. 'And if that bastard has touched her . . .'

Which made Isaac worry even more. Eli had sent them to Manchester specifically to keep the young man out of trouble, but if Armistead was here, Eli had guessed wrongly and they'd be right into the thick of things. It'd do Emmy no good to have her young man charged with assault by a man of means.

The large house they reached next was very brightly lit and in front of it a carriage had stopped to disgorge two drunken gentlemen.

'Go past and stop round the corner!' Isaac called up to their driver.

They drew up in the shadows near the entrance to a back alley. Jack reached for the door handle. 'I'm going to have a look round.'

'Jack, don't—' But Isaac was talking to himself.

Hugging the shadows and moving quietly Jack crept along the back alley. No mistaking which house he wanted. Only one place was lit up in every room. And outside the back entrance another carriage stood waiting. Why was it standing here when the others pulled up at the front? He sucked in his breath as it occurred to him that it might be Armistead's, concealed for a reason.

He was about to creep back to tell Isaac what he suspected when someone drew on a pipe, sending out a pungent cloud of smoke.

'I bet he's having fun in there,' a man said.

'Well, I feel sorry for the lass. He's a nasty sod, that one is.' Another puffing sound was followed by a second cloud of smoke.

'Ah, what's that to us?'

'It's our lives if he kills this one an' the law finds out, that's what it is,' the pipe smoker snapped.

Jack recognised the voice suddenly. Gus Norris! The new proprietor of the Horse and Rider alehouse in Northby. Emmy *had* to be here! Torn between forcing his way past the two men and breaking down the back door, or going back to Isaac Butterfield, he hesitated.

'It's bloody cold out here. I don't know why you won't wait in the kitchen.'

'I prefer it out here, cold or not!' Gus snapped. He could slip away from here if he had to.

His companion shrugged then turned towards the house.

With a laugh he pointed up to a skylight in the roof. 'Look, he's only just lit the place up. That's where he takes the special ones.'

There was the sound of footsteps moving towards the house and another voice asking, 'Who's that?' The back door opened and slammed shut. Which told Jack there was a man on guard there. He could definitely do nothing on his own, then. Moving very carefully he went back to the cab and told Mr Butterfield what he had heard, his voice breaking with anguish and fear for the woman he loved.

'We'll have to wait for Eli,' Isaac told him. 'I know it's hard, but you'll do more harm than good if you try to break in on your own.'

'How can I wait when Armistead's got her in there?' Jack thought hard for a moment then said, 'I'm going back. There has to be some way to get inside and help her.'

'Jack, no!' But again Isaac was pleading with thin air. He got out of the carriage, shivering as a chill breeze suddenly blew up. He looked at the cab driver, hunched up under his greatcoat, and debated going after Jack, but didn't move. His night vision was poor and in the darkness of that alley he would be like a man half-blind.

Jack crept towards the whore house again. There had to be a way to get into the place. There just had to.

George frowned as he watched Marcus take his time undressing the girl, poking the tender flesh and laughing as she winced and tried in vain to evade his marauding fingers. What a way to treat a pretty lass! Once, for no reason that George could see, Marcus slapped her across the face.

Something about Emmy's tearful, terrified expression reminded him suddenly of Madge. Eh, he still felt guilty about turning her out. He'd sent her to her death, there was no getting away from that. And now, if he didn't do something, her daughter was going to be badly hurt. Only how could he manage to prevent it? He needed a weapon, he decided, still worried about that sword stick.

Inside the attic Marcus was enjoying himself greatly and

about to add a further frisson to his pleasure. Emmy wasn't going to get away from him this time. He took a step back to prolong the moment and decided to indulge himself, take it the whole way. When the men moved her on to the next place, he'd wrap her in a blanket and tell them she was drugged. He'd done that once before.

Smiling and speaking in a light conversational tone, he shook her and said loudly, because she was weeping again and not paying attention, 'I killed your mother, you know. And before this night is through I'll have killed you as well.'

Outside George stiffened in outrage as the soft voice went on taunting Emmy and telling her exactly how it had happened with her mother. Time to put a stop to such doings once and for all. He felt like vomiting, especially when he thought of Madge and the way she had made him laugh sometimes before she got too deeply into the gin. Poor lass, you didn't deserve to die like that, he thought, all you wanted was a little kindness.

And your daughter doesn't deserve it, either.

Isaac could not sit still and began to pace up and down the street. When a carriage drew up outside the front of The Golden Swan, he did not think much of it until he saw Samuel Rishmore get out and turn towards the steps. Hurrying along the street, he called, 'Samuel, wait for me, old fellow!'

Samuel turned round and moved towards him. Mindful of the doorkeeper watching them he smiled and clapped Isaac on the shoulder. 'Thought you weren't coming.' In a low voice, he said, 'What are you doing here? You were supposed to be keeping Staley out of the way.'

'He wouldn't be held back.' Isaac's voice softened. 'The girl he loves is inside that place. He's keeping watch at the rear. Would you just leave her there if she were your fiancée?'

'No, I suppose not. Eli suggested I go inside and have a look round, pretending I'm not sure if I want a girl or not.' He grimaced. 'As if I'd even touch a harlot! While I'm doing that he's going to look round the back.'

'I need to speak to him, then. Jack went round there a few minutes ago and hasn't returned.'

'Damm!' Samuel turned and moved back to the carriage where the two men explained to the constable what had happened.

'You say there's a cab round the side?' Eli asked. 'Then this is what we'll do.'

Chapter Twenty-two

Jack crept up to Gus Norris and got him in a stranglehold before he could do anything. 'Tell me what's happening in there or I'll break your bloody neck,' he growled in the man's ear.

Gus stiffened for a minute, then squinted sideways at him. 'It's Jack Staley, isn't it? I knew your father, lad. You don't need to hold me. I won't do owt to stop you.'

Jack shoved him away, remaining watchful and ready to pounce again, but Gus stood there with what looked like genuine relief written all over his face.

'Where is she?' Jack demanded.

'Up yonder.' Gus pointed to the lighted skylight of the upper attic.

'With Armistead?'

The other man nodded. 'Aye.'

'How do I get to her?'

Gus shook his head. 'Buggered if I know. They've got guards inside, big fellows an' all. You'd have no chance of getting past 'em on your own. You'd better fetch help.'

'There's others on their way already. Only they might be too late.' Jack scanned the back of the house. It was a solidly built place and if a man were desperate, which he was, there were surely enough footholds and handholds to climb up to the roof. But he needed to get a start. The fancy brickwork didn't begin till well above a man's height. 'Is there a ladder anywhere? I reckon I could climb up to the roof an' get in that way.'

Gus followed his eyes and gasped. 'You'll never!'

'My lass is in there and I'm getting her out now, before it's too late.'

'It could be too late already. She's been in there a while.'

Jack's voice was quiet and deadly. 'Then I'll kill him.'

Gus swallowed hard. 'If I help you, I want your word you'll not tell Eli Makepeace I were here. I'll be off as soon as I've helped you up to the roof. That Armistead fellow's a mad bugger an' gets worse every time I see him. If I weren't frit of him, I'd not be here tonight, I can tell you.'

Jack stared at him. 'What do you mean, "every time"? You mean, he's captured other women before my Emmy?'

Gus nodded. 'I thought the first one was willing though she seemed to be drunk. But I realised later she were drugged.'

Jack could barely force the question out, so afraid did he feel. 'Was Emmy drugged?'

'Nay, there wasn't time. Constable Makepeace were after us.'

'How long has Armistead had her?'

Gus avoided his eyes, longing to get away, but not daring to make a break for it with this big fellow radiating anger and alertness. 'Twenty minutes, mebbe.' He winced at the anguished noise Jack made. 'Look, I helped George a bit with this place and there's an old ladder in t'shed. I'll help you carry it out.'

'And hold it steady while I'm climbing the first bit?'

'Aye.'

'If you do that, then I'll forget I've seen you tonight.'

'Thanks, lad.'

Keeping out of sight of the windows they got out the ladder, a flimsy wooden contraption, and carried it into the yard next door. This house was dark and with a bit of luck no one in The Golden Swan would see what they were doing. Jack turned to Gus. 'Remember, you're to hold it till I get up there or I'll recall your name very clearly indeed when Makepeace turns up.'

'I said I would, didn't I?' Gus hesitated, then added gruffly, 'Good luck.'

The third rung broke and sent Jack tumbling back down again. Cursing under his breath Gus controlled the ladder only with difficulty or it would have smashed to the ground. Grimly Jack started off again, going much more slowly and testing each rung carefully with his hands before trusting his whole weight to it. Another rung, this time near the top of the ladder, gave way as he tugged at it and for a moment he thought he'd lost his balance and would go crashing down to the ground, perhaps never to rise again if he fell from this height. Sweat beaded his brow as he struggled to keep hold of a narrow brick ledge. Only the fact that Gus was holding the ladder at the bottom made it possible for him to get his balance back.

When the ladder had stopped shaking, Jack rested his forehead against the next rung for a moment and felt cold sweat trickling down his face. He had to take it slowly. If he fell there'd be no one to help Emmy.

The next bit was tricky as he moved from the ladder to a window ledge, but he had a good head for heights and the skills he'd learned climbing trees as a lad and scrambling up and down the rocky slopes of the Pennine crags came back to him. He felt more alert than ever before in his whole life as he moved slowly from handhold to handhold. Blessing the person who had built the house with two storeys projecting at the rear to hold the kitchens and servants' areas, he climbed on to the roof of that and from there got on to the roof of the main house. Sucking in a deep breath, he made his way along the roof towards the whore house.

A tile cracked under his feet and he froze for a moment, terrified that it was going to give way beneath his weight. But nothing happened so he started off again. Light streamed from the skylight, guiding him, giving him the courage to continue. Half-crouching, he moved slowly and carefully up the roof tiles towards it, not allowing himself to think of the long drop to the ground. Emmy was there. He was the only one who could save her.

Marcus discovered to his dismay that his body had let him down and he could not yet finish using the girl. This happened to him sometimes, as it happened to all men, but it had happened more often lately. He turned away from her for a minute, wondering how he could revive his need. His eye fell on the brandy decanter and he went across to pour himself a glass.

He raised it to her in a mock toast. He liked it when they looked like that, helpless and terrified. Seeing her fear made the urge return to him and he smiled as he sipped again, then set the glass carefully down.

Before George could move to put a stop to Armistead's cruelty he heard a sound behind him. At first he couldn't place it, then realised someone was out there on the roof. Abandoning Marcus and the girl he moved quietly towards that part of the attic, bending his head as the ceiling became lower.

As he stood there concealed he saw the shadow of someone outside fiddling with the skylight. Who the hell was trying to break in? And how had they got up there? They must be mad risking a climb like that.

Mad – or desperate.

Here to rescue Emmy? What else could it be?

With a bit of luck, this person would put a stop to Marcus sodding Armistead's nasty little games and then George would take bloody good care such things didn't happen again on his premises. There were enough willing lasses around, as he'd discovered since opening up his first house in Manchester. Pretty lasses, too, especially those at the upper end of the market.

There had never been any need to force a lass with so many willing to earn money that way, and he'd long regretted that he'd captured Emmy and given Armistead the idea of doing it to other lasses. Though she was still one of the prettiest lasses he'd ever seen, George thought regretfully.

Jack tugged at the skylight and found it to be locked. Pulling his sleeve down over his hand, he thumped the side of his fist down on the glass. It cracked and a few pieces broke off and tinkled to the floor beneath. He waited to see if anyone had noticed, but when no one came to investigate he knocked enough of the splintered glass away to let him unscrew the lock.

Lifting the skylight, he eased his body inside till he was hanging by his hands and then dropped. It wasn't far, but he made a thud on the bare boards that sounded very loud to him.

He was up almost immediately, ready to defend himself. Light was coming from beneath a door, so he tiptoed towards it and as soon as he heard the voice inside the room he knew he had come to the right place.

He flung the door open to see Marcus Armistead advancing towards a bed where Emmy was tied up with most of her clothes torn off. Red rage surged up in him as Jack roared, 'Get away from her, you bastard!'

Marcus spun round and gaped in shock as he recognised the man Emmy was supposed to marry. How the hell had the fellow got in here? There were guards on both front and back doors. As Jack rushed across the room, Marcus flung a chair at him then scrabbled for his sword stick, twisting it open quickly to uncover the blade.

Jack growled in anger and snatched up the fallen chair, using it to keep Armistead away from the bed and Emmy.

For a moment there was a stand-off, then Jack began trying to push Armistead backwards. 'This is the last time you do this to a woman.'

Marcus jabbed, but the fellow was too quick for him, so he edged backwards, feeling behind him with his left hand for the doorway.

Jack let him do it. He wanted the fellow out of this room and away from the helpless Emmy. He kept his gaze firmly on the small man who was wearing only a shirt and whose face was now a sickly shade of white.

'Keep away from me or I'll have you arrested for assault,' Marcus panted, brandishing the narrow blade which was not much longer than a dagger.

'It'd be worth it to assault you.' Jack feinted with the chair and sent Armistead skittering back another couple of paces. 'What I'd really like to do is break your bloody neck, like they do with other vermin.'

371

Marcus raised his voice and yelled for help, sounding shrill and more like a woman than a man.

Watching them through the open doorway, George frowned. If anyone came up here now they'd think Jack Staley the criminal then Armistead would be free to hurt and kill other women. Suddenly Madge's face appeared in George's mind with a pleading expression on it. Was her killer to get away scot free? No, he bloody wasn't! He moved out from the shadows.

Marcus let out a squeak of relief at the sight of him and Jack froze. If he had to face two of them, and one a man as big as himself, he would have to stay in the doorway to hold them off when he was desperate to back into the room and release Emmy so that she could clothe herself again. 'I'll be with you in a minute, Emmy love!' he called.

'Very touching!' Marcus mocked, relieved that his partner was with him. Now he could have this fool arrested and they'd probably hang him for burglary and assault. He threw back his head and laughed, feeling power throb through him once more. Having Emmy whimpering beneath him was only postponed.

But George didn't move forward and his expression was as grim as Jack's.

Marcus's laughter faltered in the face of that stony stare. 'Deal with this fellow, will you? You're the one with the brute strength in our partnership.'

George took a step towards him, not even looking at Jack. 'You killed Madge,' he said. 'I heard you telling the girl. For no reason you killed a poor old sot that never did anyone any harm. Why did you beat her to death. *Why?*'

Marcus took a step backwards, suddenly nervous. 'I don't know what you mean. Of course I didn't kill anyone.'

'I was watching through the spy hole and I heard you boasting to her daughter about how you'd killed Madge. *Boasting* about it!' George spat on the floor and took another step forward, menace radiating from him.

Jack stared from one to the other, keeping very still.

Marcus skipped hurriedly backwards again. 'George, we'll discuss this later. I can explain everything. You've got to stop that fellow. He's trying to rob us.'

'He's trying to save his lass from you.' George moved forward again. 'I've done a lot of things in my time, but I've never killed anyone, an' there are only two things I really regret. One is capturing that lass and handing her over to you, and the other is turning her mother out that same day. If I hadn't Madge would still be alive. Well, I can't do owt about her, but I can stop you harming the daughter, by hell I can!'

Jack continued to watch them in horrified fascination. He did not dare turn to help Emmy until he was absolutely sure George was on his side. And he wasn't sure of anything yet.

'You were boasting to her daughter that you were going to kill her as well tonight when you'd finished with her,' George said, still in that quiet but emphatic tone, like a man reciting a lesson to a stupid child. 'What sort of creature kills a lass for sport? Only a madman.'

'I was just – trying to frighten her. That's all. I'd never kill anyone.' Marcus's voice was shaking.

Jack could see that Armistead was getting dangerously close to the top of the stairs and from the way George shot a glance along the floor, he guessed what the other man was trying to do. He didn't speak out to warn Armistead. He had never felt so coldly sure that someone deserved to die, that the world would be a cleaner, safer place without him.

With a suddenness that took even Jack by surprise, George yelled, 'You filthy pervert!' and rushed forward. Armistead yelped and stepped backwards into space. His shriek echoed in the enclosed stairwell as he tumbled and bounced down the steep stairs. Then there was silence.

George moved rapidly down after him and Jack crept forward to the top of the stairs to see what had happened.

Armistead was still alive, lying horribly twisted, still gasping out pleas.

Without a word George bent and gave the other man's neck a quick twist. The pleas were cut short. All sound seemed to have stopped.

With a faint gasp Jack moved backwards, feeling sick. He could not have done that. He did not think he could kill anyone in cold blood. But he was not going to let George know what he had seen, nor would he tell anyone else what had really happened. When rich men were in trouble, they could pay fancy lawyers to get them off any charges the police might bring. Poor men had to resort to subterfuge.

'He's broke his neck,' George yelled up the stairs. 'He's dead.'

Taking a deep breath, Jack yelled back, 'I saw him fall. I'll bear witness you didn't push him.' He had to stand very still for a moment and swallow hard against the nausea that threatened to overwhelm him. But he meant what he said. Other women's lives would be saved by what George Duckworth had just done, so he would not betray him.

Sound resumed very suddenly, pounding footsteps and a babble of voices. Jack went back into the attic room. On the way he picked up the sword stick.

Emmy sobbed in relief as she saw him.

'It's all right, my darling. Armistead's dead. Fell down the stairs and broke his neck.' He used the blade to cut the ropes that tied her to the bed, wrapped her in a sheet and pulled her close.

She was shuddering and shaking, and all he could do was hold her and murmur soothingly. He didn't know whether she'd ever recover from this, whether she'd ever want a man near her again, but even if he could never touch her as a husband should, he intended to marry her and cherish her for the rest of his life. His love for her was the most important thing in the whole world to him.

Footsteps made him look up.

Eli was standing in the doorway, his expression grim. 'Were you in time to save her, lad?' he asked in a low voice.

'I'm not sure,' Jack replied equally quietly.

Emmy raised her head to look at the constable. 'Is that man really dead?'

'Aye, lass,' he said gently. 'He fell down the attic stairs, it seems, and broke his neck.'

'He did,' said Jack. 'I saw it.'

She stared at him then began sobbing, this time from relief that she would never again have to fear Marcus Armistead. It was a while before she could calm down enough to explain this to Jack.

As Eli left the little room, Isaac came to stand in the doorway. 'Mr Rishmore's carriage is outside. He says you can use it to take her home, Jack. We'll do whatever is necessary here, then hire a carriage for ourselves.'

Jack looked down at Emmy. 'Do you want to go home now, love?'

She was lying spent against his chest. 'Yes. To Mrs Tibby's cottage. Just you and me.'

He picked a blanket up from the foot of the bed, wrapped her in it with infinite care, then lifted her gently into his arms, for her clothes were too torn to be of any use. 'Then that's exactly where we'll go, my little love.'

When they got out to the carriage they found Hercules sitting inside.

For once the dog didn't jump all over Emmy. It was as if he sensed her anguish and knew she needed treating gently. He pressed against her and risked only an occasional careful lick.

Watching the two of them, Jack thought that the dog's simple joy was doing her more good than anything.

But after a moment she turned back to him and whispered, 'I need you to hold me, love. I feel cold and lost. I need to know that you don't think I'm,' she sobbed, 'too dirty to touch now.'

So he took her in his arms, making shushing noises as he stroked her hair from her eyes. There was enough moonlight for him to see the bruise on her left cheek and the rope marks on her wrists. He wished Armistead had suffered before he died, as he had made others suffer.

While the carriage rumbled along the main road to Northby, the dog stretched out at their feet and Emmy said in a thread of a voice, 'I shouldn't feel glad that someone's dead, should I? But I do. I feel as if a burden has been lifted from me. We're safe now.'

After a while she dozed a little, only to wake with a gasp as the carriage began to make its way up the badly rutted lower end of Weavers Lane. When she saw it was Jack holding her she relaxed again.

'Nearly home now,' he said softly.

'Mmm.' She nestled against him.

He left her for a moment to open the cottage door, with

Hercules bounding inside after him. When he came back to the carriage Jack found Emmy sitting up staring out at their future home. In the moonlight it looked calm and pretty with its little garden and neat windows.

He looked up at Mr Rishmore's coachman. 'Can you wait?'

'Aye.'

'Home,' Emmy said as Jack carried her inside the cottage. She began to weep again.

Hercules pressed against her and she cuddled the dog to her, still sobbing.

'Will you be all right for a moment?' Jack asked.

She nodded.

He went out and asked the coachman to let them know at the Parsonage that he had Emmy safe in the cottage and would explain everything in the morning. Then he went back to shut out the world.

As if he knew his mistress was safe with Jack, Hercules vanished on a journey of exploration, nose down and tail wagging vigorously as he explored the house.

Scooping Emmy up into his arms Jack carried her upstairs to the bedroom they were to share – he hoped for the rest of their lives – and held her until she fell asleep again.

After a while Hercules returned to lie on the floor nearby.

Jack didn't sleep for a long time. Couldn't. Images of the night he'd just spent were still searing his brain. If only he could have got there sooner! How close he'd come to falling off that ladder on the way up to the roof! How high it had felt up there!

He realised at one point that he'd groaned aloud. Emmy didn't stir but the dog came to lick his hand and press its head against him, as if to reassure him that everything was all right.

Eventually Jack's eyes began to feel heavy and weariness weighed him down.

Waking suddenly, Jack realised it was morning and that Emmy was lying beside him staring at him.

'He really is dead, isn't he?' she asked in hushed tones. 'I didn't dream it.'

'He's definitely dead. I saw it myself.'

She let out a long half-groan, half-sigh. 'Then I can start to live properly again.' She looked at him very solemnly. 'I love you, Jack Staley.'

'And I love you, lass.'

'I can't wait for us to get married, to know that we really belong to one another.'

He nodded. 'There's nothing I want more than to make you my wife, my darling girl. And even then, I shan't touch you until you're ready. I'm not like him, and when we do love one another, it won't be anything like it was with him. But I shall wait until you tell me I can show my love for you. And if you can never face it, then I'll accept that too.'

She wept a little, softly, at his simple, loving generosity.

Then, as Hercules leaped up on the bed and tried to lick her face, she dashed away the tears, cuddled the furry body that was pressed against her and gave her intended a watery smile. 'You're the most wonderful man in the whole world, Jack Staley.'

A tail thumped against the bedcovers.

'And you're the best dog in the world,' she added. But her eyes were still on Jack, rumpled, dirty from the roof still, but hers now. There was no more glorious sight in the whole world.

Epilogue

When Jane saw the letter she cried out in shock then paid the postage and tore it open with shaking fingers. Her mother's handwriting! How had she known where they were?

Aggie came running from the kitchen to find her reading it again, her whole being concentrated on what it said.

'What's up, lassie?'

Jane looked at her and took a deep shuddering breath. 'He's dead! My husband's dead.'

'The Lord be thanked,' Aggie muttered. Then she too stared at the letter. 'How—'

'Your cousin gave my mother your address.'

Aggie stared at her aghast. 'I told her not to tell anyone!'

'It doesn't matter.' Jane looked at her in wonderment. 'Mama kept it from my father. Isn't that amazing? And she won't tell him if I want to stay here. But, oh, Aggie, she begs me to go home and she doesn't care what people say about me.' Jane broke down, sobbing, and when the other woman gathered her in her arms, gave way to a prolonged burst of weeping.

When she had calmed down, she sniffed and said, 'I need to go home as quickly as I can. Will you come with me?'

'Och, lassie, is that wise?'

'Very wise. I promised Marcus once that the only time I'd share a bedroom with him again was when I kept watch over his dead body.' Jane looked at her maid. 'I need to do that, Aggie, to see it all end properly, to *watch* them lay him in the ground and know he can never hurt me again.'

After another pause, she said, 'We'll hire a chaise, the fastest one we can find. I'll go down to the inn and order it now.'

Aggie nodded and went upstairs to start packing.

Samuel Rishmore sent Isaac to tell Eleanor Armistead of her son's death and bring her back for the funeral. He attended the Coroner's inquest in Manchester and stood silently while Jack gave evidence to corroborate what George Duckworth said about the fall down the stairs. He strongly suspected that Duckworth had killed Armistead, or pushed him, or something similar, but did not intend to pursue the matter. His son-in-law would have only been hanged if he had survived and that would have meant raking up a lot of dirt about his past, including Samuel's own daughter's flight from her husband's house.

When a verdict of death by misadventure was recorded, Samuel had a quiet word with George Duckworth, warning him never to return to Northby, then went outside and waited for Makepeace and Jack to join him in the carriage. He sat mostly in silence as they were driven back to Northby. The other two men seemed similarly lost in thought. As they were approaching the town, however, he looked at Jack. 'Still getting married on Sunday?'

'Yes, sir.'

'I wish you both happy.'

'Thank you, sir.' It might take some time, but Jack was determined to make Emmy happy.

When Samuel got home, his wife came rushing out into the hall. 'She's home! Jane's home!' she declared. 'And I won't *let* you send her away.'

He paused. 'I'll not do that. Now we know what Marcus was like, I'll even beg Jane's pardon.'

'Oh, Samuel!'

'Don't start crying all over me.' But he patted her shoulder kindly, then went with her to find his daughter.

He found a thin, elegant woman waiting for him, one who looked much older than Jane should. She stood up, hands clasped tightly at her breast, and waited for him to say something. Instead he moved across the room and folded her in his arms. 'Can you ever forgive me, daughter?' he asked, his voice husky with guilt.

Jane simply laid her head against his shoulder and sighed. 'Oh, yes, Father! No one could have known how bad he was.'

So they stood like that for a while until he pulled away. 'You've heard, then?'

She nodded.

'Shall you attend the funeral?'

'If they'll let me. What I really want, what I *need* to do, is to sit watch on his body. I once promised him I'd do that and somehow I shan't feel free of him till I've kept that promise.'

He frowned. 'Are you sure?'

'I need to. Is his mother here? Will she let me do that, do you think?'

'I'm sure she will.' He'd make sure Eleanor Armistead did allow it. He didn't understand why Jane wanted to do this, but he knew death sometimes affected people strangely. 'Do you want to see your son?'

Jane shook her head. 'No.'

'Charles is a lovely child, not at all like his father.'

Still she shook her head.

The following morning Samuel drove across with her to Moor Grange and went inside first to see Eleanor, who knew some of the details of what her son had been up to. She made no difficulties about Jane's request, though like Samuel she found it hard to understand.

So Jane entered the house she had never thought to see again on the arm of her father, spoke a few platitudes to her mother-in-law, then asked to be taken to the room where Marcus's body was laid.

'The coffin's nailed down,' Eleanor said, concerned at the strange look in Jane's eyes.

'That's all right. I just need to see it, to keep my final promise to Marcus.'

They left her with her husband's body, but when she was still there an hour later, Eleanor looked at Samuel with a determined expression on her face. 'I'm not going to let this continue.'

'She can be very stubborn.'

'So can I.' She went upstairs to the nursery, picked up her grandson and carried him down to the room where his father lay. At the door she stopped. Jane was sitting like a statue, her face devoid of expression. 'Jane!'

The figure by the bed showed no sign of having heard her.

'Jane!' Eleanor said more loudly and walked across to her. 'I've brought you your son.'

Then Jane looked up, refusal on her face.

But Charles was rosy with sleep and gurgled at her, waving his arms. He bore no resemblance whatsoever to his father. His smile was entirely his own and his hair was exactly like hers.

Slowly, still moving like a sleepwalker, Jane stood up and came across the room.

As Charles crowed with delight and reached out to grab the thin gold chain around her neck, Eleanor thrust him into his mother's arms and stepped quickly back.

For a moment they were like a *tableau vivant* of the Virgin and Child, the normally lively little boy staying very still as he stared at the stranger. Then he gurgled again and tugged at the chain. As his soft little hand brushed against Jane's chin, she sobbed and buried her face in his neck, smelling the soapy warm smell of a child, smelling a wholesome future instead of the painful past.

Eleanor guided her sobbing daughter-in-law out of the room into another bedroom, then left her alone with her son.

When she rejoined Samuel downstairs she said quietly, 'I think Jane has taken to the child. He's a most engaging little fellow and needs more attention and affection than I can spare him at my age. Give them a few minutes together then we can go and see how they're getting on.'

'No, let me go,' he said gruffly. He found his daughter standing by the window cradling her son in her arms. Her cheeks were streaked with tears, but that dreadful chilly look had vanished from her eyes, thank goodness.

'How could a man like that father a child as beautiful as this one?' she asked.

'Only the Lord knows. Jane – will you come home again? You and your son?'

She smiled through her tears. 'I'll come and live near you in Northby, Father, but I think I've grown too independent in my ways to live in anyone else's house.'

Thankfully he went to put his arm round her shoulders. It was more than he'd hoped for, more than he deserved.

As she rested her head against him, she sighed, 'I've missed it all, you know. The moors, the northern people.'

'And we've missed you.'

Charles crowed at them and they both smiled involuntarily, then Samuel led them out to the carriage, taking his daughter and grandson home.

On Saturday someone knocked on the front door of the cottage where Emmy was unpacking her things, ready to move here properly after her wedding the following day. She glanced out of the window and recognised Douglas Reynolds, the man she now knew to be her father's brother. 'He's here, Jack. Remember, you promised not to leave me alone with him!'

She didn't know why Mr Reynolds wanted to see her, but she certainly didn't want to see him. Her Uncle Isaac's explanation had made no difference to that. Her father's family had abandoned her mother and therefore Emmy as well. She moved across to the sofa, sitting where Mrs Tibby had always sat, which gave her the courage to hold her head up and face whatever their visitor had to say.

Jack went to open the door.

Douglas Reynolds hesitated on the threshold as his niece gazed at him coolly from the sofa. When she gestured to a chair opposite he sat down, wondering where to start.

Jack sat down next to Emmy and took hold of her hand.

'I'm sorry you've had such a hard time,' the visitor began.

She shrugged. 'It's over now.' She did not want to talk about it to him.

'Did you – um – ever look at those papers I gave you?'

She shook her head.

He looked a bit nonplussed. 'Oh. Do you still have them?'

'Yes. But it makes no difference to me. I want nothing to do with your family. Nothing!'

He flushed and bowed his head for a moment, then said in a low voice, 'After Emerick's death my father gave your mother money and told her never to come to us for help again – and she didn't. We didn't know how bad things were.'

Emmy's voice was level, but her anger showed. 'He'd terrified her. She thought they'd have her put in a House of Correction if she went back to them for help.'

'We assumed – wrongly – that she must have remarried. And then when you turned up again, we thought you'd be safe with your other uncle.'

'Because you still didn't want anything to do with *her* daughter!' Emmy turned to Jack. 'Well, at least I'm not bastard born, love. I won't be bringing that shame on you.'

'I wouldn't have cared.'

'I did.' She looked back at the man opposite them and her expression grew cool again. 'I don't understand why you've bothered to come and see me today. You could have written to tell me this.'

He felt he owed her the truth. 'Your other uncle wanted me to meet you.' And to his surprise he found that Isaac Butterfield was right. This was a decent young woman, albeit one who still bore the marks of her dreadful experience in bruises on her flesh and shadows beneath her eyes, even though it was over a week since her abduction.

'What do you want of me? I'm not going to disappear again just to keep your family's good name unsullied. My mother changed her name to Carter. That should be enough for the Reynolds family, surely?'

'We don't want you to disappear!' he said sharply. 'We want

to make reparation. Give you a dowry, so that you can be comfortable.'

'Money again! Is that your family's answer to everything?' When he didn't answer, Emmy continued scornfully, 'Well, I wouldn't accept a penny from you! If you'd looked after my mother as you ought to have done, none of this would have happened. She might even be alive still. And I'd not have had such a difficult childhood.' Her voice broke on the words, but she blinked back the tears, determined to have her say this once at least. 'If that's all you've come for, you can just go away again. A much kinder woman has given me a dowry and my Jack can earn what we need to live on. I never want to see or hear from the Reynolds family again.'

Jack stood up. 'Shall I show you out now, sir?'

'Think about it. Let us make some reparation, at least.'

She shook her head. She was not going to let them buy absolution from their guilt.

Jack held the door open, his expression grim. When Mr Reynolds had left he closed it with a bang.

Emmy took a deep breath. 'Did you mind – what I said to him, I mean? That I don't want their money.'

He smiled and came to take her in his arms. 'I agreed with you completely. Mrs Tibby's money is truly yours, given with love and earned by love. *Their* money would be tainted.' He couldn't imagine how anyone could abandon a member of their own family as they had. For all his mother's spite and temper, the recriminations she piled on him at the slightest excuse, he still would not dream of leaving her without the means to live in simple comfort.

Emmy leaned forward to kiss his cheek. 'Oh, Jack, you're a lovely fellow.'

'Lovely enough for you to make me a cup of tea?' He saw with relief that his request had diverted her thoughts from the Reynolds family.

'Eh, I've never met anyone who drinks as much tea as you do, Jack Staley.' She led the way into the kitchen, where Hercules greeted her with a hopeful wag, then settled down again in his basket when she didn't produce any food.

Quietly busy, Emmy and Jack put the final touches to their home, both looking forward to starting life here together after their wedding the next day. As always they were at ease together, never short of conversation, enjoying even the silences as long as they were shared. It had always been like that between them and both were convinced it always would be.

The next day the little church was crowded for the normal Sunday service. After the ceremony some members of the congregation left, but many stayed on to watch the wedding of Emmy Carter to the sturdy young fellow who had so bravely rescued her when she'd been abducted.

Among those who stayed were Samuel and Margaret Rishmore, with their daughter Jane who had suddenly turned up again. The sight of her had set the gossips whispering to one another, but no one knew where she'd been or why.

Margaret turned to look towards the rear of the church and said softly to Jane, 'Doesn't she look beautiful?'

Jane nodded. This was nothing like *her* wedding.

The sun sent long rays slanting down through the stained glass window above the altar, painting the lace collar and cuffs of Emmy's blue dress with multicoloured jewels of light as Isaac led his niece down the aisle.

Emmy had thought she would feel shy to be doing this in front of so many people, but with Jack smiling at her from in front of the altar and her uncle beside her, she held her head proudly and walked steadily forward to join the man she loved.

Mrs Bradley beamed at her and Jack's brothers and sister offered shy smiles from where they were sitting next to the Parson's wife, awed to be out here at the front of the church with the gentry.

Only Jack's mother had stayed away, but they had expected that. Emmy was sorry the woman had refused to join them, but was not going to let that spoil her day – or her life. Babs' example gave her courage to face a lot of things, including what had happened to her. She would invite her friend over to stay with them one day soon and tell her how much she had helped

386

her. In the meantime she had written to let Babs and Cook know about her marriage.

The words the Parson spoke caught the two young people up in a kind of magic as they bound Emmy Carter to Jack Staley for as long as they both should live. As she spoke her responses clearly and confidently she had eyes only for him. And if his voice was a little hoarse with emotion and his eyes over-bright, well, no one thought the worse of him for that, for his love shone in his face and everyone knew how he'd risked his life to rescue the woman he loved.

Isaac watched them with tears in his eyes. They could so easily have been facing a tragedy, but instead their love and courage had brought everything to a happy conclusion and they were both moving bravely on from the dreadful events. He only wished his own situation could be equally well resolved, but he was going to commit his wife to a home for the insane and still did not dare bring Lal home, for she was furious at the world and could not speak of her cousin without spitting out hatred. Dinah, though – he smiled – he had some hope for. His younger daughter had started to write to him regularly now.

After the ceremony the young couple were escorted by their friends to the Parsonage where a feast was waiting for them, a meal in which Cook had shown her affection for Emmy in the way she knew best.

When Emmy tried to thank her, Cook said gruffly, 'It's something to celebrate, lass, your wedding is. An' I shall be happy to come round and visit you. Very happy. Thank you.' After which speech, she blew her nose loudly and went to bang the pots and pans around till she had recovered her composure.

In the dining room the guests were standing talking politely. The three Staley children were clustered together in one corner. Eyes gleaming in anticipation, Shad poked Ginny in the ribs. 'I've never seen so much food in my life.'

'Well, make sure you remember your manners.' She put an arm round Joey and gave him a quick hug, for he was so overawed by the company he had not said a word since they entered the house. 'I like Emmy, don't you? I think Mam's wrong about her.'

'Mam's a miserable old sod,' he said.

She gave him a jab with her elbow. 'Shad Staley, mind your language. Think where you are.'

He flushed. 'Sorry.'

A minute later Ginny asked quietly, 'Do you think Jack really will find our Meg?'

'I don't know. If he can't, no one can.'

When Parson brought Samuel Rishmore, his wife and daughter in to join them, everyone fell silent.

Prudence nudged Emmy. 'You and Jack must go and welcome them. This is your celebration, after all.'

Taking a deep breath, Emmy summoned up the image of Babs again and took hold of Jack's arm.

'We won't stay long, but we've come to wish you well,' Samuel said.

Jane just smiled at them.

Always pleased to see a young couple in love, Margaret proffered a parcel and said, 'I hope you'll be very happy together. We thought you might like this.'

Emmy opened it and gasped with pleasure. 'A clock. Oh, it's so pretty! It'll look lovely on the mantelpiece. Thank you very much, Mrs Rishmore.'

'We have something else to tell you.' Samuel hesitated. 'I think it'll please you particularly, Jack. It was your Uncle Isaac who suggested it, Mrs Staley.'

Emmy beamed as she heard him call her that. *Mrs Staley*. It was a name to be proud of, a name that was truly her own.

'I've been wanting to start a shop for my workers – and for the poorer people in the town.' He frowned. 'Grandma Hickley's place is very run down, so I've paid her off and want you to manage the shop for me instead, Jack. With your help I intend to ensure that there is wholesome food available to all at reasonable prices. An army marches on its stomach, you know.'

Jack hesitated but could not be less than honest. 'I'd love to, sir. It's always been a dream of mine to run a shop, but I don't have any experience.'

'No, but you understand accounts now, Isaac tells me, and

that's a start. Anyway, an old friend of your uncle's has agreed to come here for a year or two and show you how to go on. He and his wife are feeling their age and wish for an easier life. The arrangement would suit us all – if you'd agree?'

Jack looked at the man who held so many lives in the palm of his hand, the man who had kept him tied to the mill and was now releasing him. The last of his burdens lifted, for although he'd have toiled in the mill all his life for Emmy and the children he hoped to have, he much preferred another sort of job. 'Sir, I can't thank you enough. It's the thing that attracts me most, shopkeeping is.'

'Isaac says you never did like working in the mill.'

'No, sir. The noise makes my head ache and sometimes I feel as if I can't breathe.'

'And yet you have given satisfaction and done your work to the best of your ability. No one can do more than that. And you've more than proved that you're not a hothead like your father and brother.' Samuel lowered his voice. 'I'm sorry your mother isn't here today.'

Jack shrugged. 'I doubt she'll ever change.' But at least Emmy's money would mean she was no longer a burden to him.

Samuel turned back to his family. 'Well, my dears, it's time we went home and left these young people to celebrate their marriage with their friends.'

'It must have been dreadful to be married to *him*,' Emmy said softly as the door closed behind them. 'I hope Jane Rishmore finds happiness now.'

'You want everyone to be happy,' Jack teased.

'Yes, I do.' She clung to his arm, her eyes glowing with love. 'Though they can't be as blissfully happy as I am because they're not married to you.'

When she raised his hand to her lips and pressed a quick kiss on it, he was suddenly sure that although it might take a while, she would truly be his wife one day. Even after only ten days, she was beginning to touch him, to speak more lovingly. 'Eh, I'll be glad when we can go home and be together quietly. If it's fine tomorrow, we'll go for a walk up on the moors, shall we? I've got a whole week off work.'

She nodded and then pointed, crying, 'Oh, no! Hercules has got into the house again.'

With much hilarity the guests helped them recapture the dog and then raised their glasses to wish the newly-weds long life and happiness.

It was Cass who later let Jack and Emmy out quietly through the kitchen and closed the door on them and the prancing dog with a sentimental sigh. 'Eh, it does your heart good to see how he looks at her, doesn't it?'

And Cook had to blow her nose very vigorously again.

Anna Jacobs is always delighted to hear from readers and can be contacted:

BY MAIL:

PO Box 628
Mandurah
W. Australia 6210

If you'd like a reply, please enclose a self-addressed envelope, stamped (from inside Australia) or with an international reply coupon (from outside Australia).

VIA THE INTERNET:

Anna now has her own web domain, with details of her books and excerpts, and invites you to visit it at:

http://www.annajacobs.com

Anna can also be contacted by e-mail at *jacobses@iinet.net.au*

If you'd like to receive the latest news about Anna and her books by e-mail every month or two, you are cordially invited to join her announcements list. Just e-mail her to be added to it.